PRAISE FOR GRACE HELENA WALZ

"With this Charleston-set debut novel *Southern by Design*, Grace Helena Walz has taken her place among such treasured Southern novelists as Dorothea Benton Frank and Anne Rivers Siddons. Her stories and her voice is one readers are bound to adore."

—Mary Kay Andrews, *New York Times* bestselling author of *Summers at the Saint*

"Fans of interior design, Southern secrets, and good, old-fashioned family drama will flock to Grace Helena Walz's page-turning tale. A story of second chances and long-lost love as atmospheric as the Lowcountry itself, this is a positively charming debut from a stand-out new voice. Add it to your TBR list immediately!"

—Kristy Woodson Harvey, *New York Times* bestselling author of *A Happier Life*

"With bright, snappy dialogue, characters so real they jump off the page, and a Charleston setting to swoon over, *Southern by Design* is a sparkling debut! Walz is going to win fans with this sweet story of big dreams, to-die-for design, and real love."

—Lauren K. Denton, *USA TODAY* bestselling author of *The Hideaway*

"What's not to love about a humid Southern setting, a second-chance romance, and a family full of secrets? This debut novel sets Grace Helena Walz up to become an instant favorite for fans of Karen White, Kristy Woodson Harvey, and Patti Callahan Henry.

Southern by Design is pitch perfect for book clubs, and just the right amount of sweet."

—Kimberly Brock, award-winning author of *The Fabled Earth*

"*Southern by Design* is a refreshing and lighthearted read that beautifully captures the charm of Southern living while delving into the complexities of single motherhood, family dynamics, and second chances. Magnolia 'Mack' Bishop is a relatable and humorous protagonist whose determination to succeed, both professionally and personally, makes her journey one you'll want to follow. The story's blend of witty dialogue, unexpected twists, and heartfelt moments keeps you hooked from start to finish. If you love stories with strong, resilient women and a dash of Southern charm, this debut novel is a must-read!"

—Jennifer Moorman, bestselling author of *The Vanishing of Josephine Reynolds*

"This charming debut has it all—second-chance romance, a balmy Southern setting, and plenty of long-held secrets that kept me turning the pages. As easy to imbibe as a glass of cold sweet tea on a hot summer day, *Southern by Design* is perfect for fans of Kristy Woodson Harvey, Karen White, and Mary Kay Andrews."

—Colleen Oakley, *USA TODAY* bestselling author of *The Mostly True Story of Tanner & Louise*

SOUTHERN
BY
DESIGN

SOUTHERN
BY
DESIGN

A NOVEL

GRACE HELENA WALZ

HARPER MUSE

Southern by Design

Copyright © 2025 Grace Helena Walz

Published by Harper Muse, an imprint of HarperCollins Focus LLC.

This book is a work of fiction. The characters, incidents, and dialogue are drawn from the author's imagination and are not to be construed as real. Any resemblance to actual events or persons, living or dead, is entirely coincidental.

Any internet addresses (websites, blogs, etc.) in this book are offered as a resource. They are not intended in any way to be or imply an endorsement by HarperCollins Focus LLC, nor does HarperCollins Focus LLC vouch for the content of these sites for the life of this book.

Library of Congress Cataloging-in-Publication Data
Names: Walz, Grace Helena, 1987- author.
Title: Southern by design / Grace Helena Walz.
Description: Nashville : Harper Muse, 2025. | Summary: "Sweet Magnolias meets Fixer Upper in this delightfully refreshing debut about a woman bravely chasing her dreams, building a life on her own terms, and maybe even discovering a second chance at love"-- Provided by publisher.
Identifiers: LCCN 2024039610 (print) | LCCN 2024039611 (ebook) | ISBN 9781400345632 (paperback) | ISBN 9781400345656 | ISBN 9781400345649 (epub)
Subjects: LCGFT: Romance fiction. | Novels.
Classification: LCC PS3623.A4555 S67 2025 (print) | LCC PS3623. A4555 (ebook) | DDC 813/.6--dc23/eng/20241023
LC record available at https://lccn.loc.gov/2024039610
LC ebook record available at https://lccn.loc.gov/2024039611

Printed in the United States of America

24 25 26 27 28 LBC 5 4 3 2 1

For Kyle, for believing in this book since the very messy first draft.

PROLOGUE

THE SUFFOLK FAMILY'S HEIRLOOM CHINA plummets to the hardwood floor and shatters. Shards skate across the room. Mama prowls through the mahogany cabinet like an uncaged jungle cat as she methodically removes one priceless item at a time, examines it, and lets it fall.

Delta Suffolk shrinks into the corner of the room, head bowed, and jumps at each porcelain explosion.

"Magnolia, I-I'm—" Delta shuffles her feet. "I didn't—I thought I was doing the right thing."

Mama makes a sound somewhere between a grunt and a growl, then grabs a stack of dishes.

"Quite the armory you've got here," she says.

Smash. Smash.

"*Please*, Magnolia. Stop. That china is generations old," Delta says. "It can't be replaced."

"Exactly like what you took from me!" Mama whirls around and sets her gaze on the woman. "Unless you have a way for us to go back in time and change it."

Never had I imagined my mama and my mother-in-law in such a showdown. They were childhood best friends. *Mags and Dee.*

Delta sat in the front row at my wedding, dabbing happy tears from the corners of her eyes as her son and I made marriage vows we've since broken. Delta swept into my labor-and-delivery room, cooing and doting and oozing delight over my baby girl. Delta patted my hand and reassured me so many times. Delta had a free pass to come and go in my life.

Smash.

But what she took from my mama, she took from me too.

Smash.

What's one more broken thing?

"How dare you!" Mama roars. "I know it was you."

Ned Suffolk bustles into the room and looks between the women. "Dee? Magnolia? What's going on?"

In that flash he looks so much like his son, my ex, and I wonder what would've happened if we'd never met a Suffolk. Now the secret that's lived within this family is being dragged into the light. This man tried for so long to be the father I never had, and the new irony of it slaps me.

"Yes, Dee," Mama chimes in. "Care to explain how you're the one to blame?"

Smash.

I don't even blink this time.

Smash, smash, smash.

Mama is relentless, and for the first time in my life I look at her with pride bubbling in my chest. I've spent all thirtysomething years of my life despising my mother, and now for the first time, I see her for who she really is. She's unimaginably like me, and finally, who she is makes sense.

"All right, all right!" Delta holds her hands up as she presses the words out. "*Fine.*"

There's quiet.

Mama's footsteps crunch over the dinnerware fragments as she crosses the room to where the rest of us stand. She slows, and her hands shake almost unnoticeably. Mama's not a young woman, even if she does harness a youthful rage. My heart squeezes. Now I know what she's lived and what she's lost. She drops into an armchair.

Delta walks over and perches on the love seat across from her. "I'll tell you everything I know. Where do you want me to start?"

"Right at the very beginning. And you'll tell me everything," Mama says firmly.

Delta nods curtly. "Ok."

Magnolia meets her eyes. "You're the only living person with the whole story."

CHAPTER 1

Present Day

Three Months Earlier

I WASN'T ALWAYS CONVINCED THE HOUSE at 29 Smith Street could be salvaged, but as I push through the wisteria-tangled gate this morning, I know it's true: Nothing worth saving is beyond repair. When I first laid eyes on the house, the poor girl was nothing more than a dilapidated shell, her former glory left to fry under the Southern sun.

Naturally we—my team at Bishop Builds and I—couldn't wait to get down to work with the old beauty, peeling back the layers of decay in order to revive her. Those glittery new roof shingles, the crisp white siding, the overflowing flower boxes threatening to burst at the seams, this stone pathway that sounds musical as my footsteps make contact—all of it was hard-won. Those navy shutters aren't one bit of a happy coincidence.

Still, it's impossible not to feel like the lucky ones, tasked with keeping and tending the historic homes of Charleston. It's everything I've ever wanted.

Well, almost.

Fitz throws open the front doors and grins as he strolls across the property. The light catches the new grays in his sandy hair, and his tall, sturdy figure casts a morning shadow across the lawn. He pulls me into a hug. "I just have a feeling about today. This is *it*."

Fitz is my right-hand man at the firm. He is the only other lead designer, one with whom I share a sort of cosmic twinship of taste. We met back at the College of Charleston and bonded quickly over our shared obsession with historic preservation as well as our shared disdain for our given names. It felt almost preordained that Magnus and Magnolia should become best friends.

Fitz pulls back and fluffs my blonde curls. "Hair on point, I see, so you must be ready."

"Assuming the humidity doesn't turn me into a raggedy lion before the judges get here," I say.

An intern calls over from the porch. "Fitz? Can we get your eye on some last-minute art?"

"Duty calls," Fitz says over his shoulder as he takes off toward the house.

A car door slams, and several junior designers banter in muted voices as they hurry toward the house. Michaela points to the tray of breakfast in her hands. "No worries, Boss. This will stay well out of the way."

We all know how important today is. Finally, after months of perfecting our application (over three different rounds, mind you), nitpicking our portfolio, and putting the finishing touches on our showpiece, 29 Smith, it's time for our in-person tour. The board of the Charleston Historic Preservation Society will swan about this home and, hopefully, delight in every painstaking detail as they decide they can't imagine granting any other firm the fellowship position.

The Charleston Historic Preservation Fellowship is a lauded prize as competitive as it is thick in legacy. All the biggest firms in the city have taken their turn to hold the honor, and every time it boosts their standing even further as they lovingly care for the city's best buildings. Charleston is rich in skilled designers and restorers; a city this stunning couldn't maintain the status quo without battalions of talented folks working behind the scenes. And many of these experts and their firms apply. Few are victorious. It is a stamp of accomplishment not even snagging a celebrity client can match.

Movement atop a tall ladder catches my eye.

"Ron, could you pull that shutter just a hair wider?" I call up to my favorite handyman.

"Sure thing, Ms. Magnolia."

"Mack, please." Not even today will I let it go.

Magnolia Bishop is my mother's name, and if anyone were to ask me (an event for which I'm still waiting), I don't want a bit of it. She gifted it to me on my very first day of life, and I'm only surprised it didn't come with surgically attached puppeteering strings for her convenience.

I'm not certain my mother would be too happy with me adopting the name now anyhow—seeing as I'm still carrying around the ten extra pounds she tried for years to diet off me. Frankly, I like my curves. They're a perfect complement to the fuchsia maxi dress I bought for today. And with that loud of a pink, my regular barely-there makeup works. My freckles and sunkissed skin are nature's free glow up.

"Sorry, ma'am!" Ron shouts back. "This better?" He points to the shutter.

"Perfect," I say with a clap. "The same for the rest, please."

I cross the garden to the door. Inside, the house hums as various staff members steam drapes and fluff and chop pillows with five-star precision. I am sure of every design choice—even the loud floral wallpaper in the breakfast nook that admittedly toes the line into over-the-top. Somehow it all works together, my perfect little symphony of color and pattern and texture, whistling and popping just as it should.

I duck back outside and swallow the nerves fluttering up my throat. This gem of a house is irresistible. After all we've poured in, it should be. It's Charleston charm; it's historic integrity; it's *please sign right here on the dotted line.* Right? What I wouldn't give for a booming celestial yes to echo down from the clouds, just for good measure.

The fellowship is a big deal, but it's really just one part of a much bigger picture. There's more at stake here: undeniable proof that I'm a legitimate designer. Proof that the work I've put in has paid off. Proof, perhaps, that my mother and the rest of them were wrong all along, that I really can do it on my own.

The rumble of a vehicle pulling up in front stirs me from my thoughts. A glossy black SUV stops and shuts off. Out of the door steps a Ferragamo loafer, equally as polished, followed by Grady Edgar Suffolk III—my husband. His stringy hair is almost black and reliably slicked back with overpriced hair products.

My soon-to-be ex strides toward me with limbs he still hasn't quite grown into. He moves with a confidence born only from growing up with power and privilege. "Mack, how does it look?"

"So far, so good." I look past him to the car.

His hand meets my back, and I stop myself from pulling away. "Good. I told the crew this was not the day to go halfway."

"Yesss." I draw the word out like a prayer. "Everyone is doing their best, I can assure you."

Grady shrugs and skips up the steps to the wraparound porch, the rising sun highlighting the sharp lines of his face.

I stride toward the vehicle and pull open the back door, and there she is, the only person who could outshine this whole production—my daughter, Hallie. Yes, she should probably be at school, but something about leaving her out of this day didn't feel right.

"Dad! What the heck?" she yells over to Grady on the porch. "You forgot about me?" Hallie huffs, slides over the seat, and hops out. Her auburn curls bounce on her shoulders as her sneaker-clad feet hit the ground with a thud. She looks up at me with her big, round eyes and flashes a smile absent a few teeth that the tooth fairy has long since recovered. I resist the urge to plop my index finger on her delightful button nose.

We stand together and watch Grady slink in through the French doors, muttering something about quality control and being right back.

I wrap an arm around Hallie's shoulders. "You bring your design eyes for today, honey?"

Hallie has impeccable taste for a seven-year-old and could easily outstrip me as a designer before she's thirty. But pursuing design is a choice I'll let Hallie make for herself. I know very well what it's like to have a mother plan your life, cradle to grave.

Hallie bugs out her eyes. "Shined them up just for the occasion."

"Thank goodness. You're much better than Daddy at quality control." We giggle.

We do it like it's a joke, and for Hallie it certainly is. But on my end the sentiment right below the surface is very real.

Grady may technically still be my husband, and officially my partner in this design endeavor, but he is not my ally.

Back when we applied for the fellowship, about ten months ago, Grady was my partner in every sense. We ran the business together. We were married for a decade—happily enough, I thought. We had Hallie. Even my mother doted on him. On paper, it was precisely what he wanted.

But it all came apart one morning a couple of months later when Iris Vance lit up the moms' group text with a single message. At the time I was running Hallie through the carpool line as she choked down a toaster waffle. I let my phone chime in my cup holder like a bell choir of one, and only once I parked in my driveway did I pull it out to indulge in the latest juicy drama.

It was, in fact, juicy. A friend of a friend of a friend had attended a networking event in hopes of finding a new job or a contract gig. She'd exchanged contact information with several people, and not long after received a rather uncouth—and unsolicited—photo of some enthusiastic man's nether region. Out loud I'd call it a *personal picture*; among friends, I'd call it something else. It came with no text, simply the implied proposition via the phallus in still frame. Per the group chat, the woman on the receiving end of the photo *"threw up in her mouth a little at the sight of it."* I'd scrolled back up and braced myself for the image to hit my eyes.

The moms were right; it was nauseating. At least he had good taste in decor—I had the same wallpaper in my own bathroom. When I looked closer, the realization stunned me like a spark from a live wire. My eyes peeled back to double- and triple-check. Mortification ran over me as if it had sprung legs. Because not only was that my wallpaper, but the man with his sorry crotch exposed and photographed into immortality was my very own husband.

This was *Grady*. My high school sweetheart who'd promised me a whole life of our own, that we were on the same page, that marriage would be a perfect second act to our childhood together. The boy who'd been able to convince me to marry him (despite my reservations). And even when, years later, he seemed to lose track of these promises, I still believed, at least a little, that we could make it good.

I'd be lying if I said I hadn't suspected Grady of being unfaithful in the past. The multitude of dinners that ran long, the shocking amount of business that required him to hang out at college bars, the mysterious charges that showed up on our credit card bill— after a while I could no longer justify these *obligations* as work. When I asked, he denied any wrongdoing up and down, and I never had any proof.

Until I saw that photo.

But there wasn't time to swim in the mess he'd made.

We both wanted the fellowship, even—or perhaps *especially*—if our marriage was heading for the dumpster, and we didn't want to spook the buttoned-up board members. So we continued working together, as painful and terrible and uncomfortable as it was, and I pushed aside my hurt and my shame as best I could. I put off digesting the rest of the carcass of the life I'd thought was a good choice. For the sake of my big shot. For the sake of the business.

For the sake of not letting that absurd picture rob me of more than it already had.

"Good morning, Mack." The voice comes from beside me, and I look over to see one of the landscapers on his knees deadheading the begonias in the border.

I squeeze a grateful smile. "Those are exactly the details that really matter today."

"They start looking kind of scruffy once they start to wilt," he says.

My gaze lingers on him. His skin is deeply tanned and weathered from what I'd guess was sixty-plus years in the sun. Still, the rest of him is muscular, and his eyes sparkle with health from behind wire-rimmed glasses. Warmth runs over me.

"I'm sorry, have we met?" I ask.

He rises slowly to his feet and pulls off a gardening glove before extending his hand. "Theo Hartman of Hartman Landscape. When I heard what y'all were up to, I couldn't help but offer our services to the Suffolks for the big day." He removes his hat to reveal short-cropped gray hair.

That's right. Grady's parents' landscapers offered to trek all the way out from Beaufort, our hometown, an hour and a half down the coast. I told Grady we'd be fine with our regulars, that it didn't make a whole lot of sense for Hartman's to make the trip, but Mr. Suffolk, Ned, wouldn't budge. *"Theo is the best in the business. And he insists."*

"I appreciate you going out of the way for us," I tell him as I squeeze and pump his hand. Firm but gentle. "You're sure we haven't met at the Suffolk property?"

He chuckles as he shrugs, then starts his retreat backward. "Maybe in another lifetime, Mack."

I raise a single hand and let myself enjoy this moment. Call it the universe or the heavens, but small things like this gardener's kindness make today feel touched by fate, or destiny, or any of the other woo-woo things in which I'm not a big believer. Maybe it's the pressure that pushes me to admit it, but it's a relief to know other people are looking out for us too.

Maybe between everyone, we really can pull this thing off.

CHAPTER 2

I'M STILL BESIDE THE BEGONIAS when I feel a set of seven-year-old fingers wrap themselves into mine. I look down, and Hallie's staring up, indignant.

"Why was that man ripping off our flowers?" she demands.

"He was pulling off the dead ones, love bug. That's how the plant can focus on growing new ones."

"Oh." Hallie's expression falls to neutral, and she seems instantly satisfied.

That simple explanation was all she needed, and I can't help imagining how my own mother would've gasped and launched into a lecture on *respect* if I'd dared to question an adult at the same age. Respect: something Magnolia has always loved to receive but rarely dishes out.

The squeak of a braking car interrupts the quiet of the street, and Hallie runs to the wrought iron fence to see for herself. She gasps, then sprints back to me, her face lit with excitement. "They're *here.*"

I smile in an effort to appear confident, despite the zero-gravity effect that rushes through my insides at the thought of the committee members right here, in the flesh.

She yanks me into a tight hug. "Go get 'em, Mama."

It hits me like a wave: *I want this.* For me, yes, but also for her, to show her what she can do and what she can build.

"All right, sweetheart," I say. "Let's get you inside."

Hallie skips to her designated post, just like we planned. There, she'll be set up with a stack of coloring pages, snacks to last a lifetime, and a tablet for when she ultimately grows so bored she *"might just shrivel up and die a little."*

Just as she's settled, I hear the gentle pop of doors closing on a car. My stomach twists like a pretzel as the group files through the gate into the courtyard. A woman in a tweed skirt with a neat bob leads the group, a clipboard tucked efficiently under one arm. At her side is a graying man in a seersucker suit, and they mutter to each other as they point at different parts of the landscaping. A woman wearing a neon-green, tailored shift teeters on her razor-thin heels as she struggles to keep up behind them. The last member, a younger man with still-wet hair, darts from the car and joins them, looking suspiciously like he might've just woken up from a nap.

"Hey, there! Welcome." I wave as I walk down the path to greet them.

"Good morning," the lady in tweed says. "You must be Ms. Bishop."

The rest of the group looks up at the house and around the garden. Assessing, surely.

"It's Suffolk, actually. But I guess . . . I guess Bishop's fine as well." I do like the sound of having my own name back. "Do y'all want to start outside?"

I feel the butterflies in my middle grow into seagulls swarming a downed beach snack as I walk them through our gardens, pointing out the restored fountain and the new installation of native plants.

"I can't resist a well-maintained begonia myself." The man in seersucker smiles at the flower border.

I remind myself to send a thank-you gift to Hartman Landscape—well-maintained is no easy feat in the brutal Charleston heat.

"It's gorgeous," the woman in neon says. "Not too stuffy either."

I could swear I see the woman in tweed stifle an eye roll at her counterpart before she speaks. "Timothy"—she turns to the man with the wet hair—"the scoring papers?"

Timothy looks sheepish as he turns back to the car.

"Shall I give y'all a moment out here before we head inside?" I ask. I'd rather eat a roach than stand and watch them whisper opinions until they scratch a number on the clipboard.

The woman in tweed nods gratefully. "That would be best," she says. "We'll meet you up on the porch in a few minutes."

I'm grateful for the pause and turn to head up the wide steps. I could use a sip of water, a wave of air-conditioning, and a glance at Hallie. Before I reach the porch, a low rumble grabs my attention, and I look to the sky for unforecasted rain clouds. There is no hint of gray in the sky, but the sound continues in sharp crunches and one final smash.

I whip around at the gasps of the committee members. The wet-haired man is wide-eyed, finally awake, and the woman in neon has raised her gargantuan sunglasses to the top of her head.

I skip down the steps. "What on—" I stop when I round the corner and see.

A smashed planter box that was just fastened beneath an upper window has crashed to the ground, its perfectly coordinated contents scattered beside the boxwoods.

"We checked the planters three times. This just cannot be possible. Or right. I've never had one fail. Not once." The words run out of me like I've burst a pipe of liquid language.

The woman in tweed gives me an embarrassed smile as she pats her bob. "Well then," she says. "I guess it's time we head inside."

The man in seersucker takes a wide berth as he approaches the house, and the others follow.

"I'm so sorry," I say. "Quite the shock for everyone."

I lead them inside and launch into the history of the reclaimed door we installed. I point out the foyer tile we salvaged from the mucky grip of carpeting glue.

"Carpet glue, huh?" the wet-haired guy says, bending to touch the tile. "I bet you could sell your trade secret for a pretty penny."

I can tell he's making an effort to lighten the mood, and it's a relief. "I wish." I lean in and whisper, "Mostly it was elbow grease and the fact that whoever smeared the glue was a bit lazy."

I get a gentle chuckle from the group and guide them into the formal sitting room. Morning sun streams through the window and highlights the discreet stripe in the cream curtains, and the rich tones of cypress glow in the coffee table. Even the spines of the old books stacked on it are pristine.

The woman in tweed speaks up. "This globular light fixture. It's a bit modern, no?"

I swallow. I was nervous about this piece, even if I do stand by my choice. "It is on the modern side, especially for a house of this age, but one of the things Bishop Builds values is allowing our clients modern elements while maintaining the historic integrity. Real people don't want to live in museums."

"Don't speak for all of us." The man in seersucker forces a chuckle.

The woman in neon swats the air. "Whatever, Hugo. I think it's amaze-balls."

I know without a doubt that elements dubbed *amaze-balls* will not score well with committee members who have pull. I might've overshot this one.

"I appreciate the feedback," I say. "The kitchen next?"

I point the committee out into the foyer, past the grasscloth table stacked with fresh flowers and traditional brass decor and beyond the nineteenth-century art we borrowed for the occasion.

On our way I second-guess the pale celery-green cabinetry. Color is typically bold in Southern interiors, and I adore the pop of color. This one isn't offensive or garish; it's muted. We tested what felt like one hundred swatches to get it just right. Still, most of the older design firms stick to neutrals in the kitchen—creams, whites, tans. It all gets a bit vanilla after a while, and I've always felt it a shame not to dip our toes into the brighter tones Southerners can't seem to resist.

The wet-haired man reaches the kitchen entrance and recoils from the threshold. "Whoa, Nelly!"

My gut drops. He hates the green; he must. Which means *chop-chop*. That's it for us.

The woman in neon screeches to a halt behind him, narrowly avoiding a pileup, and looks past him. "Cleanup on aisle three," she says, her nose turned upward.

I gently squeeze past the pair and halt just as they did. My mouth drops open.

In front of me, blocking my entry, sits a knee-high wall of foamy soap suds that carries on in a sea throughout the kitchen. Two of my interns stand in the center of the kitchen, red-faced and mopping frantically as bubbles continue to erupt from the dishwasher.

"The floors!" the woman in tweed fumes. "These are hundreds of years old, and your staff is throwing a bubble party. I'm only glad Arthur and the others aren't here to see this. Such a travesty, a disgrace! I can't even imagine—"

One of the interns, Cecile, bursts into tears. "I'm so sorry, Mack. This is my fault. I used the wrong soap."

My chest tightens, and I look from the committee members to my interns. There's no question where I stand on this. "It's ok, Cecile. It happens, even to the best of us."

"Well, I'd hope it doesn't happen *often* in your homes." The man in seersucker props his hands on his hips. "I can't imagine hiring you folks in and then getting my irreplaceable hardwoods ruined."

I pull in a breath as my voice threatens to wobble. "This is an innocent mistake. Cecile is a hardworking member of our team, and she's been dedicated to the restoration of this home. We would never be careless with our clients' homes. We treat them as if they were our own."

"You must be a foamy lot then," the woman in tweed says under her breath.

"Can I take you upstairs?" I ask.

My mind is reeling as we make our way up the creaky staircase. I probably forget to explain how a local woodworker helped us salvage some spindles, how seamlessly he incorporated them. We make it upstairs and continue through rooms, me in a mental haze. I point out the repaired stained glass in the bathroom, the newly functional pocket doors in the main bedroom, the linens that were sourced from a historically inspired line.

All of it feels like a last-ditch effort.

"Kinda wishing you'd done a runner here in the hallway," Neon Green says.

"It was a consideration," I say with a smile.

The older committee members breeze into the primary bedroom. The walls are lined in a muted-blue wallpaper with a silvery floral design. The window dressings are traditional—read: flowy, heavy, and hopefully to the liking of the older crowd.

The man in seersucker and the woman in tweed take in the room.

"You opted out of a traditional canopy bed?" the man in seersucker asks.

"The client prefers a lower-profile bed frame," I say. "And if you take a closer look, you'll see it's an early nineteen hundreds frame that fits the history of the home. We even have reason to believe it was crafted here in South Carolina."

He tuts to himself like we tossed a flat-pack bed frame in here. I'm resigned by now. It seems they're decided.

CHAPTER 3

I<small>T'S A TUESDAY MORNING ABOUT</small> a week after our miserable fellowship tour, and Grady is parked on a wooden barstool at my kitchen island. It's right where he used to sit every morning, eating his breakfast and dropping crumbs like he was putting it through a wood chipper.

"What else is there to discuss?" I slump onto the counter and drop my face into my palms. "We didn't get it—which was a fairly obvious outcome to me, the person leading the tour. It's over and done."

"I just can't understand *why*," Grady says. "We shouldn't be dinged for a bimbo intern's mistake. They could've rescheduled, come back and looked when they could actually get inside the kitchen."

"Grady." I stand upright. I open my mouth to tell him the rest of what I think.

"Sorry," he says, rescuing himself. "I shouldn't say *bimbo*, but I stand by the other part. Say we hadn't had soap suds spewing everywhere? It would've been us. You remember how much we sank into that kitchen, right?"

I think of the light fixture, the downed flower box, the lack of a canopy bed upstairs that I tried to gloss over. The soapsuds explosion was certainly the flashiest mishap, but it was not our only issue.

"We just weren't it for them," I say. "You're right: They could've come back another day. They were doing tours all week, but they didn't think it was worth it. They'd made up their minds."

I cross the living room, my wide-leg pants flowing loosely with each stride. I drop onto our—no, my—sofa. It's where I've sat wrapped in a cable-knit blanket, a gallon of mint chocolate chip ice cream in hand, with the TV screen flickering in the dark each night since we lost the fellowship.

The epitome of *doing just fine*.

Even Fitz took off for the French Riviera soon after the loss. Thank goodness he has a trust fund—courtesy of the design dynasty from which he hails, Fitzgerald Interiors—because the man's got expensive taste in self-care.

Grady comes over and sits down, elbows on his knees. "I'm going to say something at the historic preservation office. I've got some sway."

I stretch my arms out and drop them on the sofa with a thump. "Don't. *Please*. For the love of all things good in the world."

"Why not? We were good enough."

I've thought about this a lot in the days since South Broad Interiors was named the city fellowship winner, what it means to be *good enough* and who gets to decide it. I'd thought we were good enough, too, and maybe we were, at some point, in someone's eyes. Maybe if we'd had a better day, it would've been ours—the rumblings had been that we were a front-runner, after all. But even in the moment after the tour of 29 Smith, when I knew it was just a matter of time until I got the disappointing call and the lights went out on this dream, I couldn't point to a single thing I'd do differently if given a second chance. Short of double-bracing the flower box, I don't regret a thing.

"I'm proud of the effort we put in," I say. "But I can't change their minds, and neither can your word."

Grady tilts his head and lowers his voice. "What about my checkbook?" He grins like the devil himself.

"Yes, that's exactly what I want—a fully-paid-for, stolen fellowship award. Then I can walk around town and be proud of what my soon-to-be ex-husband purchased for us."

Grady stands slowly. "Ok, when you say it like that . . ." He pulls his hand up his neck and through his hair and squeezes his face into a grimace. It's how he looks when he's about to unload something undesirable.

"Out with it," I say.

"It's just, seeing as we're not doing the fellowship gig, I think it's time for me to move on." Grady looks away.

"The divorce paperwork's already been filed," I say.

"No, I mean I need to move on from the firm," Grady says. "I think I'm going to join my dad's investment group. I'll work from here and travel occasionally to Beaufort for meetings."

It's been painfully awkward dancing around each other at the studio. I wanted him gone the moment I laid eyes on that photograph of his groin. Which is why the sadness that hits me is surprising. "Whatever you think," I say.

"You've wanted me gone," he says like he's asking for confirmation. "You haven't exactly been coy about it . . . the box of doughnuts labeled *For everyone but Grady*, forgetting to invite me to the staff barbecue, telling the IT guy to freeze my computer every other Tuesday morning."

These things aren't untrue, but they *did* happen immediately after his snapshot was virtually circulated around the neighborhood eight months ago. It was childish of me but also, I would argue, not entirely unwarranted.

"I just can't help but notice that your timing is uncanny," I say. "Were you planning the same move had we gotten the fellowship?" I spring up and gently shuffle him toward the door with my palms. He doesn't answer my question.

Once he's outside on the step, I lay it on him. "Not to mention, you can't quit because you're *fired*." I slam the door shut, the perfect period at the end of a conversation I've finished.

From behind the closed door, Grady barks out a muffled "No, I quit first!"

I wander back through the house, smiling to myself at getting that last shot off before the door closed. It's not my best, most adult behavior, but frankly, I'm tired of giving him my best. Not to mention, the childish tit for tat is a distraction from the feelings that sit beneath it, well below the surface.

Despite the fact that I want the divorce, it's hit me with a surprising sadness. There was love between us. I'm sure there was, even if it came and went. At some point it ran out, despite the trying, and we just ran out of energy to come up with any more. And there were fond memories, but the longer I think about it, those seem mostly from years back. He and I, together, were supposed to make our own path, to step away from our families to be ourselves. Until he changed his mind and decided he liked the feel of being a Suffolk better. And it hurts, knowing he couldn't turn his back on their stuffy social games, on the routine peacocking of wealth, because he knew it meant losing me in the process.

On top of those dashed hopes, I'm now faced with forging the path for Bishop Builds on my own. Grady may not be my favorite person, but he is good with the financials and particularly good at finding jobs that pay real money. He's no designer, but he has been helpful on the business side. Him gone is what I wanted—what I still want—but there's a newness to doing this alone, one I haven't felt in so long. Still, I know I can manage the fresh nerves fluttering in my stomach.

Just as I'm considering opening the fridge to assess whether I'll have to hit the grocery store before dinner tonight, my phone rings. I check it right away as I always do when Hallie's at school.

It's my mother, Magnolia the Dragon.

I hit the green button to accept. "Mother," I say.

"Yes, hi, Magnolia." She clears her throat. "I heard the unfortunate news."

Of course she did. Magnolia sits on the Carolina Historic Society board, and half of her friends are tied up in the Charleston Historic Preservation Society board. It's as incestuous as the fortunes upon which the members' families are built, and not a one of them knows how to keep news of any variety to themselves.

"So you and the girls have been gossiping about me?" I say with a firm yank on the fridge door.

"Heavens, no," Magnolia says. "But Delta Suffolk called me right away when she heard. She knew you'd be heartbroken. Even if you are divorcing her son, she doesn't wish you any misfortune."

"How very kind of her." I dig through the vegetable drawer of mostly squishy, moldy options.

"It's all so sad," Magnolia says.

I sigh, slipping the crisper in place and closing the fridge. "For once we agree. I wish things had turned out differently, too, but I'm not sure the folks on that committee would really get me anyway. The light fixture in the—"

"No, child. I'm talking about the separation."

I imagine her examining her latest manicure, unbothered by the professional loss that's got me in a medium-serious tailspin.

"Well, I'm much more concerned about the fellowship," I say.

"Not to bother," Magnolia says. "I've got something for you that'll fix that all up."

I pause and wait for her to go on.

"But I can't explain now. Victor's got the car pulled around front. I've got to go for auction planning—for the one-legged dogs of South Carolina or something like that."

"The ASPCA?"

"Oh yes, that's right. I'm in charge of the wine, so that's really all I've got covered. Anyway, I'll come to town for lunch tomorrow. I'll send you the details."

"But—"

"Just maybe think about patching things up with Grady in the meantime."

"Mother, I—"

The line goes dead.

I drop the phone on the countertop and resume my task, scouring the pantry. This is nothing new for Magnolia, and quite frankly it's not even close to her worst. Lunch will certainly be more unpleasant than usual because I'll have to, once again, justify why I no longer desire to be married to the man who sent a picture of his penis to another woman—a woman who didn't even want it, mind you. But it's all par for the course in the lives of the Magnolias.

CHAPTER 4

USUALLY WHEN I WAS AT a nightclub, I was bubbly, fun, laughing as I clinked plastic cups with friends, but tonight I'd been cornered by a known numbskull and my drink was just about empty.

An acquaintance, Brad from Business 250, had swept in beside me the moment I arrived at the sticky bar to place my order. We were both juniors at the College of Charleston, or simply "the college" as the locals called it, working through spring semester. Twenty minutes later I'd downed the vodka soda entirely too quickly, and Brad was detailing each maneuver he'd employ to take over his daddy's business one day. I stared at the beer stains across his pastel fishing shirt and considered how I might ditch him without negatively impacting our midterm group project.

"I'll have at least thirty guys—"

"Look, Brad—"

"—reporting to me right off the bat, probably more soon after that. Did I ever tell you about last summer when I worked there? They honestly fired the guy who supervised me because I roasted him so bad."

"*Brad!*" The music was loud with the bass thumping, but I knew he heard me.

"Dad says I was born to take over the business . . ."

Brad kept talking, but I stopped listening.

My best friend, Kendra, tugged on my elbow. "Come on," she said. "Just walk away."

I was stuck between the manners my mother had spent the better part of my life hammering into me and the fact that I actually wanted to enjoy this evening. I didn't want to make things difficult for myself—like I had a tendency to, according to Magnolia—with the class project.

I reluctantly held up my pointer finger to Kendra.

"Suit yourself," Kendra said as one of the other girls yanked her by the arm in the opposite direction.

I turned back to Brad. He was now providing an unrequested verbal tour of his family's fishing boat. He didn't seem to hear my sigh over his monologue.

"I really should go catch up with the girls," I said over the details of the boat's engine.

Brad paused and flashed me a sloppy grin. "Wanna do a shot?"

I chewed on the tiny straw in my cup, wishing my escape was buried inside the sharp plastic edges, then opened my mouth to reply. My eyeballs were burning, so manners be damned.

A wide hand pressed gently at my lower back. I stepped forward to let whoever it was pass behind me, but when I glanced up, my gaze landed on a set of deep brown eyes.

"There you are, sweetheart," the stranger said.

He was tall, standing slightly above the crowd with broad shoulders that weren't bulky. His thick, dark waves fell just below his ears in a shaggy arrangement. A slow smile spread across his face, the stubbly remains of a beard around it.

Brad stopped in his tracks, his eyes darting between the guy and me.

I was momentarily stunned but quickly found my footing. "Sorry." I smiled at the stranger. "Was just catching up with a buddy from business class."

The stranger smiled and offered his hand to Brad. "Lincoln Kelly. Nice to meet you, man."

I leaned into this Lincoln Kelly and placed a tender palm on his chest. My fingers ran across a logo of a band I didn't know, the T-shirt soft, like it had been machine-washed for years. I looked up at him and smiled. "Brad was just telling me how much he enjoys fishing, but I do owe you that dance."

"The dance, yes. The anticipation's just about killing me," Lincoln said, a dimple folding at the corner of his mouth.

Flutters ran through me, and I couldn't help but notice how the space at his side felt precisely my size. "Well, don't keep a girl waiting then."

Brad shuffled a few feet down the bar, and I followed my new friend through the crowd. He took my hand and spun me onto the dance floor.

"So did you sign up for the verbal fishing-guide ramble or does that come free for all the pretty girls?" he asked.

"Hardly," I scoffed, feeling my cheeks turn pink in the darkness.

"So you're the *only* pretty girl he tries to impress with big fish stories?" He twirled me into another spin.

"I meant I wouldn't ever in my right mind sign up for that torture," I said, then dropped into the crook of his arm. "And I'm sure I'm far from the only one."

He dipped me right on cue, as if we'd planned it.

I laughed from my reclined position. "And wouldn't you know, seeing as you patrol this place looking for any damsel in distress to save? Surely you've seen him at this before."

This Lincoln character whipped me upright. "Well, that's where you're wrong. You're my very first damsel—"

"Of the night?"

Lincoln gasped and raised a hand to his chest. "How dare you insinuate this is some sort of party trick."

"Please accept my *deepest* apologies." I patted his arm. "And for what it's worth, you're far better company than Brad."

We stepped off the dance floor to the edge of the room and found a spot to lean against the wall. I glanced over and saw that Brad seemed two winks away from falling asleep face-first onto the bar top.

I winced.

"There's Sleepy himself," Lincoln said. "Don't see his six other friends though."

"What other six?" I asked, scanning the area.

"Grumpy, Happy, Sneezy, Dopey, Frumpy, Lumpy, Bumpy . . ." A grin creeped across his face as the list grew.

I swatted at him, barking a laugh. "Make it stop."

Lincoln raised his hands to acquiesce. "I'm always open to reworking my material. And for what it's worth, I'm not picking on the guy. I'm *definitely* the Frumpy dwarf."

"Really? Because I'm getting strong Dopey vibes about you."

"And I guess you're our Snow White?"

I looked skyward. "*Please*, I'm much more the witch with the poisoned apple than you might guess."

"Now *that* is something I'd like to hear more about," he said. "Maybe next time."

"Next time, huh? We might be getting a little ahead of ourselves here. What did you say your name was—Lincoln Kelly?"

"That's it. But you haven't told me your name yet."

"Mack Bishop," I said. "And in all seriousness, thanks for getting me out of there."

He reached out and gave my forearm a squeeze. "You've already made my night, so I'll count myself the lucky one."

My cheeks flushed with heat. If the lights had been on, he'd see them furiously pink.

The music shifted, and a slow song started.

"One last dance for the road?" he asked.

I had rules about this. Specifically, the one dance rule. Something happened after accepting a second dance. It opened the doors to wistful romance and all kinds of idealism that wouldn't ever fit me. I wouldn't let any young man assume I was his next best thing—whether he was after a single night or a lifetime of Costco runs. Especially when Grady was still in the picture, even if he was firmly on the sideline—right where I wanted him.

"One more. Then I'll let you go on your way to save the next lady in need." I followed him onto the dance floor and hung my arms around his neck.

"I've already told you," he whispered quietly beside my ear, "you're the only damsel."

Despite my knowing better, that it would never work, not for me, I stayed there. Because even if it wouldn't last, even if it wouldn't fit in the light of morning, under the cloud of noise and the fuzziness of the night, maybe I could enjoy the thrill of being with him for a little while.

"Mack!" Kendra called.

My girlfriends stood at the edge of the dance floor, smirking through a gap in the crowd. Alexis crossed her arms and waggled her eyebrows at me when she caught my eye. Hannah held up a single finger as if to say, *Just one?* Kendra pumped her fists.

I shooed them away with the wave of a single hand. They could tease me about it for as long as they wished, and maybe I'd regret it when he suggested a couples nature hike for the morning, but I couldn't pull myself away.

We talked easily and about everything from doughnuts to bad dates, cats versus dogs (apparently he lived firmly in the *chinchilla only* camp as a child), hopes, dreams, and some of the other things it doesn't feel so bad to admit to someone you're not sure you'll ever see again.

When the lights came on, I was still in Lincoln's arms. I looked around and spotted my girls waiting for me at the door.

"I should get going," I said. "My friends are waiting on me."

Lincoln pulled his phone from his pocket. "Can I get your number?"

"Oh," I said, eyeing the phone like it might bite.

His face dropped, and I felt terrible. "It's just . . . It's just I'm not really in the market for a boyfriend or anything like that. Honestly, I'm saving you from all kinds of hurt. Say, for example, we were to date and you fell in love with me, and then you had to meet my mother. She's my only family and a complete train wreck— emotionally, I mean—you wouldn't know it by looking at her."

"Whoa." He grinned. "Who's the one getting ahead of ourselves now? No one said anything about falling in love."

I cringed on the inside. "I just want you to be warned."

"It'll take more than that to scare me off."

"All right, Romeo." I took his phone, typed in my contact information, and hit Save. "No worries if you change your mind."

Lincoln reached out and took the phone. "I'd say the chances of that are slim to none."

With that I jogged over to my girlfriends, who were growing

impatient at the door. We stepped out onto the uneven streets and started for home. Even in the dark, Charleston shone like a gem, the gaslights highlighting every perfect cranny, the rustling leaves of palmetto trees lining the streets.

It'd only been three years since I moved to Charleston after high school, but still it felt more like home than any other place in the world. Back in Beaufort, Mama always had me under her thumb, exactly where she wanted me. *Exactly where she wanted most things.* Moving out had felt like throwing open heavy drapes and letting in the sun.

I'd tried my best to please my mother back home, for the sake of keeping the peace. I'd studied; I'd joined a list of clubs an arm long; and I'd done my best to win over the community with my service projects. Any and all of my efforts to forge my own way (or find my long-lost father) were kept well under wraps. Well, aside from the one time I let Braxton Jackson and his regrettably rhythmic name take me four-wheeling in the mud, and I fell off and sprained my wrist. Even that was barely a transgression, and in the grand scheme of things, Mama had it easy with me as her only child.

Still, Mama barely seemed to notice. She was focused on being a lady of society and inhabiting her spot atop the social ladder—right beside her lifelong best friend, Delta Suffolk. And of all the things in the world, a Suffolk for a spouse was the number one thing Mama wanted for me.

Grady Suffolk was my high school boyfriend, and I'm not sure my mama was ever so proud. He recently became my ex, which quickly recategorized me to persona non grata. Sure, I loved Grady at one point, but now that high school was done, I had to think about the rest of my life. And the country clubs, the buttoned-up philanthropy projects, the overbearing feeling that I was expected to perform like an animatronic doll—it wasn't what I wanted. Just the thought of my fingers grazing the embossed letters of an invitation to the next fancy affair felt like a pair of jeans two sizes too small.

Kendra and I arrived at our apartment, and she unlocked the door. I closed it behind me and turned the lock with a *clunk*. As I walked through the shared living space turning off lights, I chose to leave the pre-party cups sprinkled across the apartment. Back home I'd never get away with that, but this was our place.

I thought about Lincoln Kelly and wondered if he'd call. Probably he wouldn't—I hadn't held back about my situation. But perhaps more of me than I was willing to admit hoped he might. I dropped onto my bed, turned off the lamp, and let my world spin. Reality began to fade in and out as I swirled into sleep, and for a moment I let myself smile—just one more time—remembering the magic on that dance floor.

CHAPTER 5

Present Day

I've been standing in my closet for ten minutes, waffling on an outfit. I've only had a day to prepare since my mother practically demanded the meeting over the phone. It's so hard to know with her if she'll accuse me of overdressing—for attention's sake—or of putting in too little effort. All for a lunch I'd rather not attend.

"Mommy?" Hallie appears in the bedroom behind me. She woke up groggy and complaining of a sore throat, so I decided to keep her home from school. After breakfast she started turning cartwheels in the living room, and I realized we may have called her day off too soon.

I turn, crouch, and take the end of her skirt in my hands. "Look at the sparkle on that thing! How're you feeling?"

"Back to normal." She looks down, then steps back and twirls. "Think Grandmama will like it?"

"There's nothing in the world you could wear that she wouldn't adore."

Truly, as frigid as Magnolia may be, Hallie has been a soft spot for her ever since she was born. If nothing else, it's given me hope that maybe there are more layers to the Dragon.

My own grandparents, Magnolia's folks, weren't really around when I was growing up. Sure, we saw them for holiday formalities and at the church we went to occasionally, but Mother never went out of her way to involve them in our day-to-day. They didn't seem to push for it either. Mother never uttered a word about it—she couldn't abide poor manners—but I don't think she liked them much. I don't remember her crying when they died, back when I was in middle school, but then again, she's never been one for public emotional displays.

Mother had me young, barely out of high school, and I'm sure it caused a kerfuffle—especially back then. My father didn't stick around. Enough fodder to cause a family rift. Likely it explains why Magnolia's folks bought her that gorgeous house; she was in need. And likely it explains just as much why the house was on the other side of town—out of their hair. I'm surprised Magnolia never sold it, and the best reason I've been able to come up with is some misguided sort of gratitude to her folks. I guess they did afford her a life of luxury and comfort.

Hallie ducks into my closet and begins slipping her feet into various sets of high heels. She teeters around like a baby giraffe, and I can already hear the sound of an ankle snapping.

"*Hal*," I say.

She groans. "I know, I know. 'Chunky heels or flats only. I'll snap my ankle and never dance again.'"

Hallie added the "never dance again" part after a friend arrived at school with a cast on her leg and a rather melodramatic story about how her destiny to become a prima ballerina had been cut short.

I kiss the top of her head. "And we certainly can't have any of that."

Hallie laughs and takes off—barefoot—for the playroom.

"We leave in ten," I call behind her in a singsong voice.

It isn't long before Hallie and I arrive at the restaurant and are seated at a table draped with a heavy cream tablecloth. Magnolia's favorite steak house is decked out with enough oak and dim lighting for a gentlemen's smoking room. It also boasts linen napkins, a requirement for Magnolia as she refuses paper napkins at any and all establishments. She's even been known to travel with her own linen napkin and a small laundry bag to contain it post-use.

A black town car pulls up outside the window and Magnolia climbs out slowly onto the sidewalk. Her steely-gray hair is styled into a voluminous bouffant to her shoulders. It doesn't move on account of it being doused in half a can's worth of hair spray. She's dressed in a navy-blue cap-sleeve dress, expensive and new, one she pats flat as she prepares to enter. Despite the full face of makeup, her skin is lined with age.

She looks back at the car behind her and raises a hand in farewell. The vehicle is ridiculous and driven by her chauffeur-slash-errand-runner, Victor, whose canonization should be immediate upon his death. He will circle and find parking, then wait until she's ready to make the hour-and-a-half trip back to Beaufort.

A suited waiter escorts Magnolia to the table. I rise and offer my mother a gentle side hug.

"Afternoon," Magnolia says.

"Will anyone else be joining you?" the waiter asks.

I shake my head. Magnolia has been single for my entire existence and prefers to pretend I was an immaculate conception. She travels alone—besides Victor, of course.

Magnolia slides a miniature lollipop over to Hallie. "Hello, sweetheart."

Hallie is the only good thing I've done, by Magnolia's standards. It doesn't hurt that Hallie's a perfect child by all traditional measures. While we speak, she quietly unpacks her coloring book and baggie of crayons from her backpack; she sits upright, elbows off the table. Mother and I pull out our chairs and settle beside her.

"How are things going with the separation?" Magnolia asks.

The paperwork is proceeding toward a fully official split, despite Magnolia having poured every ounce of her effort into welding Grady and me together. I was prepared that whatever *offer* regarding a design project she'd come with today, nothing would be forthcoming without a last grasp at sticking us back together.

"Well . . ." I'm not sure what the benchmark is for a good versus bad divorce. "It's going ahead as expected, I guess."

"I haven't heard the end of it back home."

From the church ladies, from the tennis ladies, from the club ladies who all have nothing better to do than gossip about the misfortunes of others under the guise of concern.

"Such a shame y'all just throwing in the towel like that." Magnolia's thick gold bangle catches the light, and she keeps her eyes trained on the leather-bound menu. "Any chance you could give it another shot?"

I mash my hands into each other under the table. "Mother, I've told you a dozen times—this was not my doing." I flick my eyes to Hallie. "And now is not the time to rehash it."

Magnolia lays her eyes on Hallie. "Fine."

I adjust myself upward in my seat. "You said on the phone you had a lead for me."

Magnolia nods slowly. "Well, yes, there's that too." She turns to the waiter who's arrived at her side and orders a vodka soda, extra lemon and lime, and a beef tartare appetizer.

"I was really hoping to have the city's work coming my way

with the fellowship," I say after I've ordered drinks for Hallie and me and the waiter has left. "We were so close, and it would've been such a big win for us. We would've been set—"

"Yes, and we all know that ship's sailed—or should I say sunk?" Magnolia runs a finger along the silver handle of the fork to her right. "Maybe what you're missing here, the solution to all your problems, would be to get back with Grady. He's always been very business savvy. I'd imagine especially so for his *wife*."

"Not if my hair was on fire and he had the only bucket of water in town," I say.

"I did try to invite him."

"To lunch?"

The waiter arrives with the appetizer and takes our entrée orders. I'm grateful for the pause it allows for my rising anger to cool. Magnolia spoons the beef tartare delicately onto her small white dish, takes a bite and chews, then dabs at the corners of her mouth.

"Of course, he declined. But I guess what else can we expect, Magnolia?"

"It's Mack, Mother. There wasn't a drop of your name left even on the day you tried to give it to me."

"You might be right." Magnolia swats at the air with a smug smile. "But *Mack*? Gosh, doesn't it sound like the name of some eight-year-old boy who loves to fish and dig worms in the mud?"

I feel my cheeks grow red. She could've said, *"Let me make room inside this name for you too."* She could've said, *"Eight letters is plenty of room for two."* She could've made a shred of a case about me belonging to her.

I stand and take my mother by the arm. I pull her out of her seat as she chirps indignantly. I won't have my Hallie hear the rest of what I have to say to her.

Off to the side I whisper, "Do you think I wanted to end up

divorced? Don't you think I wanted a long, happy marriage too? This isn't easy for me. But after that picture? I still hate going to the grocery store without a hat on. I still feel people looking and whispering when there's an event at Hallie's school. How could you possibly not understand?"

She tuts. "Men just can't help themselves—it's the *urges.*"

I resist my own urge in that moment to knock the old bat upside the head.

"We women just have to learn to let it go," she continues. "You and Grady were born for each other."

My mother, the very woman who prides herself on propriety, turning an efficient blind eye to my husband trashing our marriage via amateur porn. If only I were afforded the same leniency.

"Mother, you don't know the half of how he's let me down," I whisper. She's so emotionally paralyzed she'd never understand anyway. "Not another word about the divorce in front of Hallie."

"And what about your work for the firm?"

I watch the power she feels creep across her face, deepening the valleys of age and twisting her smile. Perhaps that's what built the landscape of her to begin with—spite. "You haven't even said what it is. You called me here under the guise of work, and now all I'm hearing about is Grady. Is there even a real project?"

Magnolia sighs. "Fine. I guess keeping you both working together is my best bet for getting my way, and yes, I do have something for you."

I'm surprised Delta hasn't broken the news about Grady's departure from the firm, but perhaps he and Ned have been keeping it quiet. Delta is firmly in Magnolia's camp, rallying for our reconciliation.

Still, I won't be the one to break the news either. And especially not in this moment.

"Great," I say. "Let's sit."

We arrive back at the table, and before I sit, I lean over and squeeze Hallie, glancing at her coloring. "Wow, look how beautiful the purple is on that one."

Hallie twists out of my grip and holds up the coloring book. "Thanks, Mama." She turns it to Magnolia, who gives her an approving nod.

I settle into my seat, and Hallie flips the page to start a new picture.

"All right, child. Here it is," Magnolia says. "I've been tasked with hiring the team to renovate a gorgeous estate here in downtown, the Daniel House, for the Carolina Historic Society. I'm willing to give you the work, even if we were all mortified about y'all flunking the fellowship tour."

I bite my tongue and wait for her to go on. Anything she gives me comes with a healthy dose of disparagement.

"It'll be best to run through it in person, to show you the work needed, but it's large scale. Every room in the house will need something, and then they'll want it fully furnished and decorated. We might even be able to have it shot for a magazine, but that'd only be if you rise to the occasion and really knock it out. I'll need to be kept in the loop on all the work. I'll visit the site and expect frequent updates. I will by no means be *hands off.*"

"I wouldn't imagine you would be, Mother."

"Precisely. That isn't my style." Magnolia takes a slow sip of her drink. "So, what do you say? I can have our admin set up a walkthrough later this week. Friday, most likely. We don't want to be seen dragging our feet."

It's work, *good* work by the sound of it, but it's also two steps back—right under Magnolia's thumb. That was another thing about the fellowship: It was supposed to be a ticket out of her web.

Now, I'm not sure I have any choice but to take the job, given the bleak outlook before the firm. We don't have fellowship projects, and Grady won't be working his connections.

"Well, it sounds like a fabulous opportunity. I'd love to take it on," I say, forcing a smile.

"Yes, I figured you would." Magnolia doesn't raise her eyes to look at me.

The waiter arrives with our food and we dive into our entrées. Magnolia lets out the occasional sigh, like she's suffering an inconvenience being here. It's her favorite way to act when she does anything for me—like the time she insisted on bringing Hallie's first birthday cake to the party. I tried to talk her out of it three times, but she refused. Predictably, she complained every step of the way, from placing the order, to going to the bakery (where Victor picked up the cake), to carrying it into our home—even Delta had tried to step in and help. But the kicker is that even if, hypothetically, I were to politely decline this offer, she would be flat out on the ground at the offense, calling for smelling salts.

She can't help but be offended and inconvenienced.

Before long, we've picked over our plates, and the waiter asks about boxes.

"Oh, never." Magnolia frowns in disgust. "I don't want my car stinking to high heaven all the way home."

I smile at him warmly. "I'll take two boxes for ours, please." I point to Hallie's three chicken fingers. "Those will make a great dinner with some veggies tossed in."

"And maybe a scoop of mac and cheese too," Hallie suggests.

I run a gentle hand over her curls, the ones she got from me. I love that the auburn is all her own—just as her life will be. "I think we could make that work."

Magnolia takes the check and completes the ticket, and soon

we're out the door, standing beside the town car. Magnolia pops open her car door.

Hallie pokes her head in to chat with Victor, and I give him a quick wave.

"Thanks for lunch," I say.

"You're welcome," Magnolia says. We kiss briefly on the cheeks. "I'm looking forward to designing this Daniel House together."

I smile and call for Hallie. Magnolia slides in after squeezing Hallie in a warm hug, and we wave as the car slowly pulls away.

Magnolia may think she'll have a say in the design of this new project, but that will certainly not be the case under my watch. If my name, the Bishop Builds name, is on a project, it will be to our standards—not Magnolia's. I'll likely have to push down the irritation she'll cause me, play her game a bit, and get sneaky if she really gives me a hard time.

But when we hand over the keys at the end of the renovation, by my word, there will not be even a hint of a suggestion of Magnolia Bishop.

CHAPTER 6

Fifteen Years Earlier

I SLID INTO A PLASTIC AUDITORIUM chair and flipped down the side desk. I had my coffee in hand and a glossy spiral notebook at the ready. Even if it was almost the end of the semester, I'd never lost that first-day enthusiasm. It was Historic Preservation 252, a class that counted for my major and a place I was happy to be after languishing in prerequisites for far too many semesters before.

The volume in the lecture hall grew as students filled the seats and called across the room to buddies. Soon the professor took her position, clicker in hand, and everyone fell quiet. She began telling the story of a prolific Charleston wrought iron designer and craftsman, Philip Simmons, clicking the slides to display a collection of his gate sketches on the screen.

Ten minutes later I was immersed in the story when my phone buzzed loudly on my tabletop. I startled and scrambled to mute the call from Magnolia. Two minutes later the phone erupted again—Magnolia again—and I muted it. The professor shot me a look.

When the phone predictably sprang to life once more, I mouthed *"Sorry"* as I climbed over the other students in my row and left the classroom. I continued through the echoing lobby and out the main entrance.

When the doors closed behind me, I walked over to stand under the cover of the live oaks beside the famous Cistern Yard. Right where no one would hear me. I called my mother.

"Magnolia," my mother said.

"Are you ok, Mama?" I asked. "You called three times in a row. I had to walk out of a class."

"Oh, it's no emergency. Heavens, I wouldn't be calling you for assistance in case of an emergency. You're at least an hour and a half away, not to mention, Victor would be handling my calls if I were indisposed."

I bit back my simmering anger. "Why did you call so many times?"

"Well, yes, I needed to talk to you immediately about the Suffolk party."

I physically covered my mouth to prevent the groan from slipping out. I slapped on a perky voice. "Now is not a great time to discuss it. I have class."

And it wasn't any old class; it was one I enjoyed and hoped to put to good use eventually. Not to mention, I shouldn't have to be on call for my emotionally checked-out mother. As she said, I'd be of little use to her in an emergency—and I suspected for more reasons than simple geography.

"I need a commitment from you, child," Magnolia said. "I'm sitting here with Delta, planning the party. We need a seating chart put together, and you've yet to RSVP."

Ned and Delta Suffolk were having an anniversary party to celebrate thirty years of marriage. I was happy for them, of course— they'd played a big part in my life when I was growing up, but I would rather drink creek water than attend their party. Because their son and my ex-boyfriend, Grady, would be in attendance, and the last thing I wanted was to spend an unnecessary evening with him. Especially when our mothers were still bound and determined to put us back together.

"Oh, tell Delta I say hi," I said.

I really did love Delta. She'd always been like an aunt to me, taking me to prepare the lavish Easter flowers every year at their church, begging Magnolia to let her take me homecoming dress shopping. She seemed to revel in me in ways Magnolia was incapable of doing, as if she truly liked me. She was the hardest part of breaking up with her son.

"Of course, but the nicest thing you could do for her is attend what will be a stunning party in her honor."

The strings of guilt twanged.

Delta twittered in the background, probably saying something reasonable and far more flexible than my mother.

"I need to look at my class schedules. That's close to exams, and if I come home for a weekend, I'll lose a ton of study time."

"Pshaw," Magnolia tutted. "School is fine, but it'll just be a matter of time before you and Grady are back together and you're right here beside me and Delta planning parties and fundraisers and enjoying the pleasures of life."

It wasn't the time or place to have the same argument with her. She didn't want to understand—perhaps *couldn't* understand—why I wanted a career when I could live off family money. I'd tried every way I could think of to explain it to her, but Magnolia was nothing if not convinced that her opinions on life were fact and truth.

I pushed down all the words I wanted to say, pulled in a breath, and said, "Thank you, Mama. I'd love to attend. Please extend my thanks to Delta and my apologies for the late response."

"Wonderful, as I expected," Magnolia said. "Now I'll let you get back to your studies. Even if you won't ever need it."

I ended the call and slumped onto a bench. Little bits fell from the Spanish moss above me, strung up like fairy lights across the oaks.

I couldn't go back in now. I would look like a flaky student, stepping out for a personal call, and in precisely the class that mattered most. Magnolia had ruined it for me, backing me into a corner to accept the invitation to a place I didn't want to go.

Sure, I was grateful for the Suffolks. Ned took me to every father-daughter dance during my elementary school years, sparing me the agony of being left out. Heaven knows Magnolia wouldn't have stepped in, seeing as she would've been the only *lady* in attendance—a mortification unbearable for her to endure. I took my Father's Day crafts to Ned as well, and he even tacked them up on the fridge beside Grady's creations. He filled in as best he could, but at heart, Ned had a clear sense of *how things should be*—particularly when it came to raising his son—and the older I got and the more I made up my own mind, I wasn't sure I agreed.

I think I loved Grady most the younger we were, before he got too molded by the type of life that raised us both. He was an only child, and his parents raised him on a steady diet of sports, business-first mentality, and red meat—"boy" things. For a while it didn't stop Grady from believing he could be whoever he wanted to be, reading books about knights and asking the family's contractor to teach him the basics of woodworking. Grady had promised me in whispers that we'd be our real selves once we got away, once we made a life for ourselves, but the more I watched him walk the Suffolk walk, the more I doubted I could believe him. I knew the force of the pull to stay in step.

Ned and Delta Suffolk had been there for me in ways Magnolia never could have brought herself to be. So I would go to their party, and I would play nice. Like I always did, I would ignore the nagging voice in my head telling me to leave, and I'd get through it.

I looked up at the sound of the auditorium doors popping open, and a swarm of students flooded out and dispersed.

A guy I recognized from class walked up to me and stopped. He had sandy hair, parted neatly on one side, and wore thick, fashionable glasses. His clothes looked expensively tailored and were pressed to perfection. "Let me guess. Family crisis? Lord knows I've lived enough of them—and enough false alarms—to know one unraveling in front of me."

I couldn't help but smile, and I stood and stuck out a hand. "I'm Mack. Magnolia on the class roster online, but don't call me that unless you wish bodily harm upon yourself."

He cracked a laugh. "Magnus, but you can call me Fitz. Similar feelings—bodily harm and such—regarding my given name. Send me an email if you want to copy my notes."

I squeezed a tight smile as I looked him up and down, assessing.

"*Oh*"—Fitz raised his hand and shook it— "this is absolutely *not* me hitting on you." He cackled at the audacity of the thought.

My shoulders dropped in relief. "Sounds like we're on the same page, my friend."

"*Friends*—now that is something I could get behind." Fitz waved goodbye and began to walk away. "Let me know about the notes," he called over his shoulder.

The rush of students from the academic building in front of me was over, so I walked back inside. A few students cluttered the entryway, chatting or setting study dates. I made my way to the front of the auditorium and waited for the professor to see me.

She glanced at me over her tortoiseshell reading glasses. "Mack, is everything ok?"

See? She, too, assumed there must've been an emergency. Maybe I was the normal one after all.

I sighed. "Yes, fortunately. It's my mother. She's a tad . . . melodramatic. And usually about all the wrong things."

This was another perk of being away in Charleston: being able to speak honestly and freely without fear of repercussions due to the Beaufort rumor mill.

My professor smiled warmly. "We all have at least one relative who's off their rocker."

"I'd confidently call myself an expert on melodramatic relatives by now."

She chuckled. "Are you enjoying the class?"

"Yes. I've been wading through general education requirements, and I'm so glad I finally made it here."

"It shows," she said. "You've got a lot of potential. Your past two essays have been top material. I can hear your enthusiasm in the writing."

I grinned.

"Just don't let family nonsense get in the way," she said.

"Thank you. It won't happen again."

The professor nodded. "Make sure to get today's notes from a classmate."

I decided I would email Fitz, my new acquaintance from outside.

I felt like I could fly on the professor's compliment for weeks, and I walked home smiling to myself the whole way. My mother may not appreciate me much, but my professor's assessment was proof that I could certainly make it in this field. Well, perhaps definite success was a bridge too far, but at least she'd given me hope that the thing I picked for myself might work out ok in the end.

CHAPTER 7

Present Day

THE DAY AFTER MY LUNCH with Magnolia, I arrive
at the studio early and park. I dip under the awning,
unlock the double doors, and hustle inside, leaving the
doors open behind me so I can bask in the sounds outside—of the
city awakening, of delivery trucks rumbling and gushing exhaust,
of students ambling to campus. The smell of a bakery wide-awake
a few doors down.

I sit at my desk and paw through the binders of fabric swatches
stacked in wobbly constellations. Before long, Maya breezes in.

Her purse hangs glamorously in the crook of one arm, a cardboard cup holder stacked with coffee cups in the other. The sun
behind her lights the dark, velvety curtain of hair cascading down
her shoulders. She's tall and lean, muscular in a way that looks natural but comes from four days a week of weight training. Even if
Maya looks like a Puerto Rican warrior princess, she's also a former
computer engineer so skilled that she could hack someone's identity
and ruin their credit in less than an hour (though she's yet to be
pressed to use her skills for evil). A true union of brains and brawn.

"Thought someone might have broken in when I walked up
and saw the doors hanging wide open," she says. "You're early."

I waggle my brow. "We have a new project."

"Well, it seems I've come prepared." Maya pulls a cup from the holder and sets it in front of me. "Rocket fuel. Drink."

Maya is an associate designer, our operations manager, and a critical part of our team. She keeps the office running, the clients soothed, and me on my toes. She's also our resident textile expert, thanks to the garage sale sewing machine she snagged as a tween.

I take the coffee gratefully. I was up most of the night, replaying my rapid post–fellowship tour tailspin. How we'd been inches from the city's prestigious prize, but I now find myself in the miserable position of having to lean on my mother for our next big project. She sure loves to save me when it's at my own expense.

Maya looks around. "This place just feels different without Grady."

I nod and squeeze a closed-mouth smile.

"That's all you got?"

"No. I am glad. It's just—I won't ever understand him giving up a place like this. It'd kill me. But you're right. It feels different."

And it feels strange. Grady and I both knew we never had the kind of love to shatter the earth or induce a heaving bosom, but working toward a shared, tangible goal was one thing we actually did well. When we were working, we made sense.

Still, I'm glad I kept this business as mine at heart. Grady had asked, pleaded even, for me to name it *Suffolk Builds*, but his argument didn't have a toe to stand on, let alone a leg: We weren't even officially together at the time. He was still trying to win me back when I inked the paperwork a week before I had my college diploma in hand.

When it all started, I had zero dollars in the bank, zero clients, and zero employees. We weren't an overnight success and instead grew steadily by accepting and excelling at small jobs until we got a shake at the bigger ones. It took time to get Bishop Builds to what it is today—an interior design firm with a reputation for having historic preservation chops. A firm that can afford the rent on this office. Sure, Grady worked here, and he was paid. But this firm? It wasn't ever his.

I turn back to my fabric, pull a few out, and flatten the edges. "Those for Hallie?" Maya asks.

I smile, and Maya extends her hand, then carries them over to Hallie's nook.

Yes, my girl has her own corner of the place. After unearthing her design treasures from the bottom of my washing machine a few too many times, I was glad to give the little magpie a better place to store them than her pockets. She has a desk, a chair, and baskets stacked with secondhand paint chips, fabric swatches, and even small stone samples. She uses them to style and trim the Victorian dollhouse that also sits in her nook. Her one permanent client.

I watch Maya deliver the swatches so tenderly, and I have to say something. "Maya? I want you to know . . . I'm really sorry we lost out on the fellowship. I know we were all optimistic about a win. I hope you're still feeling good about your position here."

One of the worst parts about losing is knowing how disappointed the rest of the team is too. We all busted our behinds to put forward our best work.

"Come on, Boss," she says. "I'm *just* finding my groove here. I can't even imagine going back to a dark computer basement." She scowls.

From what she's told me about her family, interior design isn't held in particularly high regard. Both of her parents are academics, and computer engineering—the career she ran screaming from— was the family plan.

"There's probably a slew of vitamin deficiencies caused by living down there during daylight hours."

"Just call me a health nut," Maya says.

We laugh and settle into a quiet hum of work. The clicking of keyboards, the gentle thump of a coffee mug set down, chatter from the street flowing in through our open doors.

About an hour later I page over to my calendar to check out the rest of my day and decide to get a grasp on the full week. I know what I've got scheduled for tomorrow afternoon—like I could ever forget—but still a groan pops out of me like I don't have a say in it.

"What's got you in a bother over there?" Maya asks.

I spin my chair to face her. "I—*we*, assuming you can make it—have a meeting with my mother tomorrow afternoon. She's got a project with the Carolina Historic Society she's giving us. It should be great work; it's just . . ."

"It's just that it's from your mother," Maya says.

"Precisely."

"Sounds uncharacteristically generous of her," Maya says. "No offense."

"Oh, you're absolutely right. She made it quite clear she'd be as good as joining the design team."

"Do we have a plan for that?" Maya lets out a nervous chuckle.

I nod slowly, like I'm thinking, but it's mostly the same realization settling inside me. "If there's one thing I know how to do, it's work my mother. We'll have to bend to her a little, but in the end I think we can get away with doing the project our way. Whatever we do, we'll never confront her. She hates that, and all it ever does is make her dig her heels in."

"So your mother trained you in psychological warfare, is what you're saying." Maya sips her coffee.

"It's a basic requirement for any debutante, didn't you know?" I laugh, even though it's a true statement all the way through.

Maya crosses the office to the coffeepot and begins to refill her mug. "Speaking of debutantes, a jobsite definitely doesn't sound like Magnolia's scene."

I nod quickly. "That was going to be my second point. I'm not sure she's ever been 'hands-on,' as she described it, with one of these projects before, so I think before long the dust and dirt will scare her off."

Maya shrugs. "Sounds like a problem we can work." She freezes, then pulls in a quick breath. "Also, I have an itty-bitty piece of news about how we might get the firm back on its feet."

Maya grins like she's up to the right kind of trouble as she sits back at her desk, crosses her legs, and looks right at me.

I take off my reading glasses. "Go on."

A crowd of chatty tourists breezes by our open front doors.

Maya lowers her voice. "This is top-secret info. All right, maybe not that top secret, but it feels like it, saying it out loud. I didn't want to mention it until I knew—for certain—it was legitimate, and from what I can tell based on the message I just got, it is."

I feel my shoulders inching toward my earlobes. "Maya, say it!"

"I got a message to our Instagram account from a recruiter with Exquisite Interiors TV," Maya whisper-screams. "They're looking to pitch new shows from the Southeast region, and they love the work we've posted online. I mean, the timing is perfect, right? Like maybe *this* is the reason for all those random acts of chaos on the fellowship tour day."

My shoulders drop, and my hands wander to the throw pillow beside me. "Oh. Well, that's cool."

"Oh, 'that's cool'? What do you mean? This could be us! This could be our new thing, our fresh start."

"It sounds like a one-in-a-million shot, Maya. But I do love the enthusiasm."

A network TV gig is a lovely idea. If I'm honest, I've always wondered what it would be like to be a designer on one of those shows. All the female hosts seem so talented and at the top of their game. Their installs seem to flow so naturally from their minds into the physical space.

"That's not a no, right?" Maya asks. "What harm comes from talking to them?"

Of course I would love to be the next new designer on Exquisite Interiors TV, especially if I'm not trying to force myself into an old-guard-shaped design space. Especially if I can create the designs we're loved for—the reason customers pick us over another group. There's just a tiny snag in my hopefulness, left over from the fellowship flop, that has me feeling gun-shy.

"There's no harm in following up," I say. "You're right. I'll loop in Fitz—maybe it'll spur him to come back home. He and I need to talk about the Magnolia project anyhow. But otherwise, let's just keep this between us for now, ok? I don't want to get anyone's hopes up about this after what happened with the fellowship." Maybe my own hopes most of all.

Maya grins. "I'm hoping they message back soon, but it sounds like they're inviting us to audition. It's invite-only, apparently, because they don't want a deluge of amateur tapes."

It certainly wouldn't be the worst thing. Exquisite Interiors would mean work and publicity, which would mean even more profits for the studio. I wouldn't mind having our jobs adored by the general public either.

"You have my blessing," I say to Maya. I reach over and squeeze her hands briefly. "To keep *discussing*. Keep me updated."

Maya lifts her fists in tiny pumps. "I have a good feeling about this."

I turn back to my desk and smile to myself, and I feel a little seed of hope plant itself inside my heart. I feel it taking root because this would be a way out beyond Magnolia Bishop. If we could get the network TV deal, neither I nor Bishop Builds would ever again have to rely on my mother for handouts.

It really could be the answer to all my prayers.

CHAPTER 8

THE AREA SOUTH OF BROAD Street has an impeccable reputation for a reason: Walking through it is like walking along the uneven sidewalks of heaven. Well, if heaven was built on centuries-old fortunes of questionable origin, that is. It's the following afternoon, and Maya and I are on our way to meet Magnolia to tour the Daniel House.

As we walk the quiet streets, our chatter is interrupted only by the bubbling of the occasional courtyard fountain or friendly hello from a mail carrier.

"Oh, did you see those?" Maya asks, pointing to the stucco facade of a home we pass.

"The brass gas lanterns? You'd need to fire me if I missed something so gorgeous." I wink at her from behind my large sunglasses.

"They're perfection with that salmon stucco."

We flip to walk single file by a towering palmetto tree and the lumpy sidewalk cracked by its growth. Tall stone walls flank the other side, concealing whatever grand property lies beyond.

When we get to the next street corner, Maya stops and turns to me. "I was going to wait to tell you until after the Daniel House, but I feel like I'm going to explode."

I stop at her side. "The *secret project*?" It was just yesterday morning that Maya and I first discussed Exquisite Interiors.

She nods quickly. "She got right back to me—Coco, the recruiter—and she said we were welcome to send a tape and portfolio! She sounded interested."

"*Really?*" I whisper.

"Really," Maya says.

A thrill erupts through me and threatens to disrupt my best efforts at cementing realistic expectations for this endeavor. It feels so Hollywood. I pull out my phone and shoot off a text to Fitz.

"That's so exciting," I say. "I can't wait to talk more. Obviously I'm looping in Fitz, but for now—and probably evermore—lips zipped around the Dragon." I nod in the direction of our destination.

"Secret's safe with me."

We check both ways and keep walking, past the odd drippy fountain, past a quaint deli with a steady stream of patrons. As we round the corner, I catch a glimpse of Magnolia parked outside a tall iron gate looking like she's steps from a Paris runway. I can tell, even from a distance, that her white pantsuit is Chanel. It's a vestige of my upbringing. I shudder in embarrassment when I remember the designer clothing I first wore to worksites.

Now I know jeans and work boots are my best bet.

We take the last few steps up to our new jobsite, and I remove my sunglasses to get a better look at it. It's a wide Georgian mansion with a double porch and a slight lean. Like a once-magnificent specimen, shrunken slightly by the test of time. The paint peels, and even from the street I can tell how much repair work the windows will require. It has shutters but mismatched and only at some windows. I take in the scale of the place through the worn iron fencing along the front of the property.

It's a big job.

"Well," Magnolia says, whirling her gaze to me. "Don't look down your nose at it. This is the *Daniel* House."

I catch a glimpse of a shell-shocked Maya in my peripheral. "Mother, hello. Nice to see you as well. I'm sorry if you thought I was looking unfavorably at the house. I was just taking it in, wondering, really, how much square footage we're looking at."

Magnolia sniffs. "I'm glad you came prepared with questions. I've got the two local property representatives waiting inside, and they've got all the specs. Though they're just interns from the college, so who knows if there might be errors. Really, I don't know why we need them when I'm on board."

She turns, passes through the open gate, and begins her climb up the steps and along the bumpy brick path to the wraparound porch. I count my lucky stars that she's wearing sensible shoes; the last thing I want is her falling on-site and injuring herself. Even if her being bedridden might grant me some reprieve.

I follow behind her with Maya.

The grounds are a full gut. What was once grass is riddled with weeds, and the beds are overgrown and equally plagued by weeds. My mind goes to Hartman Landscape, and I wonder if Theo might be up for another Charleston project.

"Look at the front door," Maya says quietly beside me.

I look up. "Wow. That's a keeper." The wood is thick and solid, perfectly aged.

"Not sure about this door," Magnolia calls over her shoulder. "A bit old and dingy, no? Might need something better."

I pull in a deep breath and shoot Maya a look. "Nothing a good polish can't fix," I call up to Magnolia.

She mutters under her breath the rest of the way up. Before we can reach the door to knock, it springs open and we're met by two youthful faces. At once, their right hands are outstretched.

"Hi, I'm Jade."

"Hi, folks, I'm Douglas."

Maya and I lean in for handshakes and share our names. Magnolia hangs back, hands folded at her waist.

"Yes, we've already met," she says to Jade and Douglas.

"Come on in," Jade says. "We've prepared a quick tour of the property for you and then we have a full list worked up that outlines each component of work line by line."

"Jade and I are the property representatives, as you know. The Carolina Historic Society received the house from the estate of a donor. We're still forming the vision for how the house will be used, but with your design expertise, Ms. Bishop, some of that may naturally work itself out. We do, however, have a budget," Douglas says.

"She's still a Suffolk for now," Magnolia says. "And I'll lead the vision for the property."

"That sounds like a very reasonable setup," I say to Jade and Douglas, ignoring my mother. "I guess you might host board meetings or fundraisers. You could also rent it for bridal showers, engagement parties, small weddings even."

"We're dealing in preserving historic buildings here," Magnolia says. "Not trying to make a buck letting the public spill their boxed wine all over our hardwoods."

Jade smiles tightly. "Well, I'll let the two of you discuss that later. Should we start downstairs, Ms. Suffolk?"

She shows us through the formal sitting rooms at the front of the house and a gorgeous sunroom that, though aged, shines with potential. All of the rooms are empty—no furniture, no art, no suggestion of an identity—and it's just how I like it. I feel a pinch of excitement. Sure, it needs a lot of work. The floors are original but heavily damaged; the walls are peeling in places. Woodwork has been chipped and dinged over time.

"Magnolia," my mother says. "Do you think we can save the floors? Or will we need to rip them out?"

Douglas looks startled. "We were hoping very much to keep anything original that we could, removal being a last resort."

I nod at him. "I think we can manage that. Worst case, we'll have to patch, but before we take anything original out, there will be a discussion with the board."

Jade takes us through to the kitchen, which is dingy and minimal. Kitchens in homes of this age weren't the gathering places that they've become in modern times. They were small, simple, and set out of sight. They were a place for the kitchen staff to work, never a place for a guest to venture.

"Not so much to work off here, Boss," Maya says to me. "Could be a positive?"

"Absolutely," I say. "We can build something that will honor the history of the home while also allowing modern conveniences." I lower my voice. "*Events* even."

"I heard that," Magnolia says. "Events are still a no."

Douglas takes over for the upstairs tour. "Watch your step," he says on the way up.

The staircase is grand and sweeps in a dramatic curve up a double-height foyer. It's a showpiece for this house. But as I near, I notice the stair treads are in awful shape and, much like Douglas suggested, one misstep away from a trip to the ER.

"This will need to be *completely* changed," Magnolia says.

We all ignore her, and Douglas launches into a discussion of the bedrooms and how the layout looks.

"I'm getting all of this," Maya says, jotting into her notebook.

The bedrooms are all similar, aside from slight variations in paint and window size. The claw-foot tub in the upstairs bathroom is gorgeous, and I bend to examine it.

"I love this," I say to Douglas.

He nods. "Same here. Definitely can't buy that these days."

"And just to think this porcelain coating would've been state-of-the-art at the time. We'll have to get it resealed by a specialist."

Magnolia's face is pinched in a sour pout so everyone can be made aware of her opinion on the tub.

We make our way back to the front door.

"We'll send over the specs, the timeline, and the budget," Jade says. "And if you can agree to those terms, we'll complete the preliminary contract and you can start work."

I smile wide. "This really is a stunning home. I know all it'll take is a bit of love and care from our team, and she'll be like new again."

"Let's not promise she'll be new," Magnolia says. "It won't be like new; it'll be more like old."

I turn back to Jade. "I think you know what I mean. The house will be refurbished nicely."

"I understand." Jade gives me an apologetic smile.

"I'll send over the docs," Douglas says.

We share our goodbyes and head back out to the street.

Magnolia brushes some dust from her white pantsuit. "What a filthy house."

I have so many questions about why she's even part of the Carolina Historic Society, considering her issues with anything unclean, but I keep them to myself, pushing them back down and tempering my inner rage like all of us good girls do.

She's the only mother I've got, after all. The only family beyond Hallie I'll have at all once the divorce paperwork is signed.

"Mother, you didn't seem to care much for the house."

"They should've cleaned it before we arrived. A little Pine-Sol on the floors, some dusting, anything." She points to the bottom of her pant legs. "This is Chanel."

I stop myself from asking why she, for even one moment,

thought it was a good choice of outfit. But that wouldn't be proper, according to the Gospel of Magnolia Bishop Senior.

"The team and I are happy to do the work on-site, if you prefer to oversee from afar."

Maya smiles to herself.

She and I both would prefer that.

"Once your cleaners come in, I'm sure I'll be fine," Magnolia says. "It's not quite like I'm going to let you run wild with this place. I'm responsible for it at the end of the day; it's *my* name on the line."

It sure is her name, even if she did try to give it to me. Just like this project that she's supposedly giving to me. Yet she won't loosen even a single pinky finger from her grip on the place. It's as it's always been—me under her reign, no matter how hard I work to escape it.

"The site will be dirty and dusty for most of the project, especially while there's work going on." I tuck my sunglasses back into place. "There's usually little point in cleaning before the construction is done—at least, not to the degree of making it white-pantsuit proof. Maybe we just take it day by day."

Magnolia checks her watch. "Fine. We'll see. I have to be off if I'm going to make it to the club for tonight's famine victims' fundraiser." She pulls her phone from her pocket, taps it a few times, and raises it to her ear. "Yes, Victor, I'm ready." The moment she hangs up, the black car creeps from around the corner.

Victor is an expert in lurking, it seems. Much like his employer is determined to do on this project.

"Ta-ta, ladies," Magnolia says as she turns to the waiting car and pulls open the door.

I sigh as Maya and I turn to walk in the opposite direction.

"Famine victims?" Maya says.

"Don't even ask," I say. "She probably finds a way to make people impacted by famine feel guilty for accepting her donations. She's got a knack for it."

Maya sighs. "Was she like that growing up?"

I shake my head in exasperation. "Somehow worse."

We soon say goodbye and Maya breaks off to head in the direction of her apartment. I make the rest of the walk back to the studio alone. From there I'll grab my car and drive home to the suburbs across the bridge. It's not the glamour of the downtown peninsula, nor the historic builds, but it's home and serves Hallie and me well. She goes to a great school, and she can run around freely in the yard.

It's an easy place to raise kids.

Still, as I walk past the Charleston beauties, I can't promise I would pass up an opportunity to live among them, if it fell in my lap. They have that kind of draw on me.

CHAPTER 9

Fifteen Years Earlier

I PULLED OFF THE MAIN DRAG near Folly Beach and parked my car close to a boardwalk entrance. My golden curls stood up wildly, practically alive from whipping in the wind coursing through the windows as I belted off-key accompaniments to the Top 40 on the radio.

I laughed when I imagined my mother's face if she saw me out here, unkempt in public.

But Folly Beach was a place of freedom, far from my hometown and far from Magnolia's battalion of hair straighteners. It was a place where the core of me was acceptable as is, without the trappings I'd suffocated under as a child. The patent leather shoes that dug blisters into my skin. Even that one foray into childhood pageants that was kept mercifully short due to Magnolia's disapproval of participants she dubbed the *riffraff*.

I grabbed my tote, climbed down the sandy boardwalk, and hobbled across the mounded sand toward the water. I chose a spot and unrolled the towel from my bag, catching whiffs of laundry detergent, and unpacked my water and interior design magazine before stretching out on the cozy fabric and letting the weight of everything go as my skin warmed in the sun.

I had only a couple weeks of papers and exams left, and I was enjoying a little break before my summer internship with a local design firm. The thing paid pennies, but it justified staying in Charleston—well away from my mother. And it was excellent experience to climb the historic preservation ladder toward the future I envisioned for myself as a top Charleston designer.

Not to mention Lincoln Kelly was meeting me here after he finished shooting photos for a newly engaged couple. It wasn't a date, per se, but more of an informal hangout between two interested parties. The morning after the bar, I woke up to a text message on my phone with a gift card link from Lincoln for doughnuts for breakfast—living proof of how lovely and terribly optimistic he was. His only ask? That I let him know my doughnut order.

All it took was *cinnamon sugar* typed on my screen and sent with a whoosh, and the greatest text debate of the century ensued. Regrettably, Lincoln sat firmly in the chocolate cake doughnut camp. It was my responsibility—for the sake of all humanity—to explain how and why that particular doughnut was a travesty to the entire fried dough industry and that the person responsible for it deserved to be imprisoned—or perhaps just fined, with a show of remorse.

My cheeks had ached from grinning.

Still, his no-strings-attached generosity was evidence that he'd gotten the complete wrong idea about me. Maybe he thought I was someone who was just trying on messy for size. He'd probably never guess that only one of my parents had stuck around for me, and the one who did seemed perpetually let down by my existence. Or that the one boyfriend I'd had seemed mostly to like me because I'd been preselected, vetted, and dropped right into his lazy lap. Maybe I was hard to love, or maybe it was just the fallout of the circumstances I was born into, but nothing about me seemed like his type.

Maybe I was just right for a summer fling.

Halfway through my magazine, on the center-spread story about making over shipping containers in the Midwest, I dozed. Sometime later, the sound of a photographer calling directions followed by giggles pulled me from my sleep. I pushed up onto my elbows and watched.

Lincoln was just as he was before: confident, composed, magnetic. But today, standing there in the sunshine, it was as if he were dazzling in ways I didn't first realize. The light lit his limbs, and I remembered how they'd felt around me, firm and solid, like I could fall into them for days and still be standing.

"Great work, guys," he called.

The couple squealed as the waves rolled up and splashed their legs.

When the pair eventually disappeared up the boardwalk, I hopped up, adjusted my bikini, and sauntered toward the water. Lincoln stood in the shallows, tapping buttons on the camera's back. I tiptoed in and flicked small kicks of water in his direction, then stood twirling a curl on my finger in a way I hoped was alluring.

"You seem pretty good at that photography stuff," I said as his eyes hit mine.

A wide smile appeared on his face, and I felt it run across my skin.

"Miss Cinnamon Sugar," he said. "I was looking forward to this all day."

I frowned. "Can we workshop that one? Cinnamon Sugar has a certain adult-entertainment ring to it."

"That's fair. Especially since we're going on dates in the daylight now." He clicked a cover over the lens and waded closer to me.

I shot him my best fake-angry look. "Oh, not so fast. We never said this was an official date."

"I guess you're right," he said. "Maybe it's an unofficial date, but I'm open to official anytime you change your mind. Though you might have to meet me here. I'm working every weekend when the sun's out. Folks—"

"I know, I know. 'Folks can't get enough of beach engagement photos.'" I mimed gagging myself.

"And yes, *I know, I know* your every single love conspiracy theory."

"Oh, that's right." Truthfully, I'd forgotten I'd spilled that much of my guts. "That was right after you tied up the unicorn you rode in on under the rainbow that delivered you to the bar."

He nodded. "Even stopped off at the pot of gold for a few coins to cover the drinks."

"You served me drinks bought with money *stolen* from a good and decent leprechaun? How can I ever look at you straight again?"

His eyes hung on me. "So what you're saying is . . . there's going to be a *next* time?"

I fought the urge to grab him and squeeze him—and perhaps hold on—because he had me: I wasn't planning on this ending right here in the shallows.

I tried to look resigned. "Touché."

We both stood like fixtures in the moving surf, big and small waves flowing in and out and up our legs. He opened his mouth as if to say something, then closed it. He fidgeted with his camera. I stood staring, like a supreme fool, wishing for the return of my booze-induced bravado.

He shifted his feet in the sand and met my eyes. I remembered the first time I'd looked into those pools, and I made up my mind then that this wouldn't be the last time I'd see him. Not if the choice was mine to make.

"I know I said I didn't want something serious, and I meant it," I said. "I'm a bona fide hot mess, even if it is dressed up fancy and expensive and looks not-so-bad. But I also think you're really interesting."

"'Interesting,' huh?" Lincoln chuckled. "That's not always— maybe not often—a compliment."

I bit my lip and said, "In all the best kinds of ways, Lincoln. Maybe we can enjoy each other's company, even if it's only for the summer."

There were no brakes on this thing between us. Even if we did end up burned in the end, I'd rather be scarred than afraid or full of regrets.

"I think I can manage that," Lincoln said.

He linked his arm in mine, and we climbed the beach back to where I'd set up my towel. We settled in the space and let the sand form to the shape of us; all we needed was each other's company, and before long, hours had passed.

"So do you like photography?" I asked. "Or is it just a good side hustle?"

Lincoln pulled himself upright, and his face shifted to something intent. "It's my favorite thing in the world." He took his time, enunciating each word.

"Yeah?" I was surprised at this serious shift in the guy who, so far, was nothing but locked and loaded with witty comebacks.

He nodded and dropped his eyes to the sand. "I've worked at an accountant's office from nine to five since I graduated college last year. It's slowly sucking my soul dry, but this"—he leaned over and tapped the top of his camera—"is what I actually care about most."

"Well, you'll have to show me some of it."

"Stick around for a bit, Mack, and I might even take a good picture or two of you."

Soon the sun started to go down, and we realized we were famished. We decided to pack up and leave in search of food. As I walked back up that boardwalk, the sun setting behind me, I felt freer than I might've ever felt before. And I was certain of one thing.

If this was how a summer with Lincoln Kelly would be, I was fully behind it.

CHAPTER 10

Present Day

I WAKE TO SOMETHING WARM SQUIRMING at my feet. She burrows up from the foot of the bed, tunneling her way to my side. Hallie's skin on mine, the knees and elbows she accidentally jabs into my flesh, feel so familiar they're almost part of me. It's our weekend routine. Once she grows tired of playing in her room and her tummy begins to grumble, she climbs into bed beside me and asks, "Mama, you ready to start a wonderful day together?"

If I were to be honest with her, I might not always say yes. I'm not always up for another day. Not recently. My bed is the place that seems safest in light of all the things that have gone wrong in the real world. But for Hallie, if she exists in this world, then at her request, each and every morning, I will climb out from under the cover of my comforter that begs me to stay. I'll give her my best shot.

I roll over and tuck an arm around her. The crook of my arm touches something satin. "What's that?" I murmur, my voice still thick from sleep.

"My cape." *Obviously* goes unsaid.

Hallie has a flair for fashion that has bled into costumes. And accessories. And costume jewelry. And stealing her mother's makeup. Innocent sharing my own mother would have shut down with a swift iron fist.

"Silly me." I smile as I push my face into her auburn hair and breathe it in.

"Pancakes today?" Hallie asks.

I don't dare to tell her, but nestled here beside me with her angel-soft skin, with her silky hair tickling my nose, with her heart beating so close to mine, there's very little I could refuse her.

"Let's go extra special and add chocolate chips," I say.

With that, Hallie flips upright and ejects herself from the bed. She charges toward the kitchen, not looking back, and it is answer enough to my suggestion.

The familiar clang of pancake-making supplies being pulled from drawers and cabinets downstairs follows, and the sound is the final encouragement I need to put my feet on the ground. Even if I could use some extra sleep after that house tour with Magnolia yesterday.

Soon I'm ladling circles of batter onto a sizzling griddle as Hallie works on finishing the puzzle we started last night. We curl up on the sofa and eat stacks of chocolate-oozing pancakes in silence, and in a flash, they're nothing but crumbs.

Adding chocolate chips, eating on the couch, wearing pajamas past 9:00 a.m.—all are Magnolia unapproved, which is why I so intentionally include them in my own daughter's life.

An hour later, Hallie sits on an accent chair in the front sitting room, peeking through the slats of the shuttered windows, looking for her father's car. He's twenty minutes late and hasn't bothered to call or text. It's another item to add to my Grady Grievances List.

When he finally pulls into the driveway a full thirty minutes late, Hallie hops up, and I follow her outside.

"She ate a great breakfast and is ready for y'all's day," I tell him.
Grady bends and wraps Hallie in a hug.

"What're we doing today, Daddy?" she asks excitedly.

"What do you think about riding around in a golf cart today? Being my extra-special caddy?"

Despite Grady's efforts, Hallie deflates, and her gaze drops.

"Hang on, is she actually playing?" Only once I've said it do I realize I shouldn't have. Grady turns to scowl at me.

"Does it matter?" he snaps. "On my days, I—*as her father*—get to pick what we do." He turns and marches around his car. "Hallie, in the back. Now."

I want to be angry. But as I watch my disappointed little girl slide into the back seat, destined for a day of tagging along as he sips beer, all I feel is helpless. I stand in the driveway and Grady pulls out too fast. Desperate, it seems, to put space between him and his overstepping ex.

The truth of it hurts—that this really is what we've become. I know we weren't always like this, but I didn't see it change. Aren't things supposed to change over the years, as the rest of life does? I thought we were good enough to navigate change and make do.

Make do, how sad.

I turn and start walking back to the house. The rumble of a truck passes behind me, and when I glance back, a moving truck goes by—for the house next door, most likely.

I continue inside but hang near the front windows, hoping for a peek at the new neighbors. The truck stops and a uniformed moving crew spills out. The new neighbor exits the house and approaches the moving truck. He greets the mover with a smile and a handshake, then stops and waits alongside him. Something about him reminds me of something familiar I can't quite pin down.

Still, I don't want to miss the chance for an introduction, and

I do need to check the mail. So I slip on my flip-flops and push out the door.

About halfway down the driveway, I wonder if cornering the neighbors on their moving day is a bit much. Objectively, there are still things being pulled from the truck. But I'm already halfway there, and if they caught sight of me turning and taking off running, I'd most certainly brand myself the crazy neighbor forevermore.

The new neighbor stands facing the street when I arrive at the curb.

I rattle my mailbox as I pull the envelopes from it—perhaps a hair too theatrically—but as I'd hoped, he turns.

I squint as our eyes meet—and time slows.

Or rewinds.

My insides lurch and the mail in my hand cascades to the ground like a paper waterfall as if I've lost control of myself, and all I can do is stand there and watch this train tear off down the rails.

"Mack?" The same dimple folds at the corner of his mouth, right where it's always lived.

"*You?*" My heart quickens into thuds that rattle my chest.

It's no wonder the sight of him, even from a distance, reminded me of before. Lincoln Kelly is before. The distance between us, measurably only a few steps, is a massive gulf and nothing all at once.

"What are—? Do you live right—?" he asks, pointing to my home.

"No," I announce right at him, and I say it about him. About his being here in the middle of my life. He made his choice, and his choice was to leave. Not only is this my territory, but it's been my neighborhood for the last decade. He's an interloper, and there isn't another way around it.

And yet, he just stands there, perfectly blasé about invading my safe bubble, dragging all the sore memories behind him.

"Oh good," he says. "That could've been—"

"Well, actually, I was saying no about—never mind. *Yes.* I do live right there."

I wait for him to tell me more, for him to explain himself. Defend himself, really. To make any good and decent argument as to why he gets to come back here after he walked out with such assurance all those years ago.

This place wasn't what he wanted.

I wasn't what he wanted.

Yet now it seems we share a very similar taste in real estate.

"Well, that's me." Lincoln points to his new home, the one built on a permanent foundation right beside mine.

"No, this can't be right," I say.

He rubs his head. "Uh, looks like it is."

A flash of worry crosses his eyes, and it's the first sign that looks something like an admission. Maybe he's calculating the cost of another immediate move. His front door rattles and swings open, and Lincoln's brow creases as his gaze goes there.

From the door a miniature version of Lincoln calls over, "Dad, I need help over here!"

My eyes go wide.

Lincoln squeezes a tight smile, his gaze back on me. "That's my son. Foster."

His son. He's right there, in an actual human body, more of Lincoln in this world. Foster's hair is dark and thick and dips in unruly waves and curls, and he points to the oversize box of toys he plans to lug into the house with his father's help. I feel the self-righteousness drain from me as I watch his son struggle with the box. It's hard to stay indignant in the face of children.

Especially ones who look right around Hallie's age.

I glance at Lincoln's ring finger. It's empty. My heart double-skips, and my body lights up in a way I thought it had forgotten how to do. I tug at my shirt hem, hoping it'll send the *calm down* message across me.

"Well, welcome, I guess," I say with an awkward chuckle.

A mover descends the back steps of the truck with several large-scale photo frames in hand. Black and white, classic and captivating, everything I once knew of Lincoln's photography, the stuff that turns bodies and places into songs and stories. I'll never tell him, but I've wanted to put his art in so many of my clients' homes over the years. His style is seared on my mind like an ugly scar refusing to budge from my mental list of design choices. And despite my relentless search for alternative art—and perhaps therein proof of the richness of a life without him—I've struggled to find anything else that compares.

"Yours?" I ask.

He nods.

"Still incredible," I say.

"Thanks." He turns and looks at the houses. "And look, I had *no* idea. I thought I was doing a good job of leaving you alone—just like you asked for. I never would've bought the house had I known."

"It'll be all right." I shrug, and it feels desperately inadequate. I'm not sure I believe it myself, not right this moment, but I'm not sure what else I can say.

"I promise I'll stay out of your hair," Lincoln says. "But I should go help Foster with the box before he throws his back out."

He takes off up the driveway. Two movers grasp the ends of a clothing rack, drawing it out of the truck. The hangers on it slide toward the short, balding mover as he leads it backward down the ramp. The sound of the metal hooks slipping is like a blade cutting.

The sight is a cut as well. Because the clothing isn't Lincoln's or Foster's. It is patterned and sequined. Dresses. It's women's clothing, and it belongs to his wife, his partner, his *love*. Their things are mixed together in this truck. Their lives are wound together, the same.

I try to convince myself that this is ok, that the thought of this man with someone else is ok. Maybe this is my nudge from fate that it's *my* time to sell. That I need a real fresh start of my own—perhaps even a true beach cottage now that I'm a single woman.

But still, as I turn and head back up my own driveway, I can't deny the way it stings, the way my freshly puffed-up heart withers. I can't deny that the thought of him with anyone else hurts.

That maybe it always will.

CHAPTER 11

MAYA AND I MEET AT the Daniel House bright and early to get a handle on the work this property will require. It's been a week since we met Jade and Douglas and first saw the place, and now that we're back, we need a plan for the overall layout and the scope of work involved. Big-picture design is the name of the day.

"Did you see this water damage under the sink?" Maya calls from inside a kitchen cabinet.

I'm clicking through my proposed floor plan on my laptop set on a makeshift desk of stacked boxes by the staircase. "Under the sink?" I pull off my reading glasses and head into the kitchen. "I haven't looked through there that closely yet."

I can't help but run a hand over the swoony woodwork on the doorway as I pass through, a wide trim with ornately carved borders. I grab a flashlight from the toolbox and slide onto my knees beside Maya. The damage is obvious as soon as the light hits it.

"Yikes. We'll have to have Sam come out to look and tell us what he can do." I pull myself upright, take out my phone, and shoot Sam a quick text.

Maya pulls off her work gloves. "How's the proposal coming for the board?"

I turn and head back to my makeshift computer stand in the foyer, and Maya follows.

We signed the contract for work two days ago, after agreeing to mutually positive terms, and we're cleared to start the clean-out. In the house's current state, that mostly includes scraping paint off wood molding, pulling down outdated wallpaper, and repairing any wood or siding that's damaged. It's delicate work. Before we start any rehabbing, we'll need to get a design proposal approved by the board. I'm not concerned about the proposal, but it will be a while before this place starts looking pretty.

I grab the computer and turn it so she can see. "I mean, *I* love it, but I'm sure the Dragon will have more than her fair share of comments."

Maya scans the blueprint. The kitchen design maximizes every inch of space—enough to accommodate catering for board meetings or a *dreaded event* of reasonable size. The living areas are mostly open, which will allow for the furniture to dictate the use. Arguably, furniture could be moved in and out, rented for some occasions.

"I see what you've done here," Maya says with a grin.

I shrug. "It makes sense to take care of the basics and let the space be flexible."

"And upstairs?"

I click over. "It's going to stay the same, minus the looks. I'm not changing the original room layout, even though Magnolia asked. I wouldn't be doing my *preservation* job if I did."

"She sure does think she's the queen of the low country, suggesting you blast those walls."

I stretch my palms out beside me, suck in a deep breath, and spring to life with an animatronic smile.

"What on earth was that?" Maya sputters.

"Tried-and-true tactic for dealing with my mother: zipping it all up and acting pretty," I say. "It's just that by now I'm also excellent at using guerrilla warfare behind the scenes to get my way. I told you I know how to work this situation."

Maya grins. "She deserves to be twisted a little herself."

"And the church said amen," I say.

Maya leans toward the computer screen.

"But yes, the designs," I say, regaining my focus. "I don't think we'll have an issue with this blueprint, so once they sign off on it, we can move ahead with construction."

Maya stands upright. "And we should be good on budget, based on this."

Together we head to the front porch. The cover offers a welcome shade, but beyond it the bright sun highlights the desert quality of the front yard—crumbly brown, scorched, like a potted plant left unattended on a windowsill. It's an expansive area that slopes gently up to the house, cut only by the brick path that grades upward in long steps. The lawn and surrounding beds should be grand and lush and draw the eye delightfully to the stunning home. But for now, it's a reminder of how far we have to go.

"Have you heard anything from Fitz?" Maya asks. "We need to get going on our Exquisite Interiors audition materials."

I drop onto the front porch steps, and Maya plops down beside me. The warm, muggy air wraps us, and it's as if I can feel the baby hairs at the nape of my neck curl in real time.

"I got a crazy number of emojis when I told him about the audition, but nothing else. I guess it's time for us to start making the tape?" I ask.

"Yup," Maya says. "We can use our standard portfolio, though we should give it a once-over to make sure it includes all things camera ready."

"What's the deadline?" I ask. "This house is far from finished, and we want them to see how good we can make it."

"Deadline is as soon as possible," Maya says. "Coco said they're really hoping to decide within a month or so, but they'll also hold out for the right people."

"A month is tight," I say.

Not to mention everything else going on in my life: Hallie at home, an ex-husband bound and determined to make things difficult, and a once-summer-love moved in next door.

Maya nods. "I know. They said it doesn't need to be perfect, but they want to see your style, your personality on camera."

I drop my head and examine the tuft of weeds growing up between the bricks in front of me. I think about this endeavor practically—specifically, the fact that I'll be on camera, the real filming required to make a show. Just because I'm a strong designer does not mean I have the cool and charisma of a television personality. In fact, those are qualities I never would've assigned myself.

"I'll need a cohost," I say. "I'm up for this, but I need a friend at my side."

"I think we both know who that'll be," Maya says, her mouth slowly lifting into a smile. "It has to be Fitz. I, on the other hand, am literally *known* among my family for freezing on school picture day. Like, there's an actual montage of me looking like a deer in professional-grade headlights years K through seventh grade."

"Fitz was a theater kid through college, and he might just fire me as a friend if he isn't asked first," I say. "But the montage you mentioned? *That* I need to see."

Maya slides out her phone and begins searching for the photographic evidence, while I sit quietly waiting. The iron gate rattles, and Maya and I look up in unison. A familiar figure huffs to wrench them open, his tousled hair not budging an inch.

Delight runs through me, and I'm on my feet.

"Y'all running a prison out of here or what?" Fitz says, eyeing the latch. "Only other thing you need to keep folks out is razor wire."

"Fitz!" I skip down the steps. "You're *here*."

He nods. "I got over us losing the fellowship sooner than I expected. The French Riviera tends to have that effect on me." He pulls me into a hug. "Not to mention I got jealous when I heard about our potential fifteen minutes of fame and this gem of a project 'I just had to see with my own two eyes,' so I booked the next flight."

"Welcome back, buddy," Maya says, standing and descending the steps as Fitz and I near the porch. "It's never the same without you."

Fitz grins. "So what're we gossiping about?"

"Oh, I don't know," I say. "Maybe the very thing that got your rear in action and on a plane stateside."

Maya looks between us. "Fitz, you ready to dust off your theatrical voice?"

"Depends," Fitz says. "Does it include tap shoes? I wore a hole in many a Fitzgerald floor with those, much to my mother's horror."

The three of us laugh as we climb the porch and stop in the shade. Maya waves us to circle up.

"No chairs?" Fitz says. "We really should have some for meetings of this kind."

I sling an arm around his shoulder. "We're just getting started, not even patching floors yet, my friend. We're a long, long way from rocking chairs on the porch. Not to mention, you know better than to wear dry-clean only to a jobsite."

"I'll bring my own camping chair next time." Fitz waggles his brow.

I swat at him, and Maya clears her throat for our attention.

"Y'all ready to talk work or not?" she asks.

Fitz zips his lips from under my arm and motions for her to continue.

"Well, we were just talking about getting Mack a cohost . . ." Maya's eyes fall on Fitz and stop, looking hopeful.

"All those years of musical theater were for this very moment," I say. "Fitz, you've *literally* been training for this opportunity your entire life."

"You wouldn't consider Hallie? She could be a child star!" Fitz says. "Plus, I can't have her mad at me for swooping up her spot."

"One: I don't think child hosts are Exquisite Interiors' thing," I say. "And two: we've all read the child celebrity bios by now, so we know how that goes."

"Where is the magpie?" Fitz asks, looking around. "Uncle Fitz brought her some fabric swatches from France."

Fitz was one of the first (and strongest) proponents of Hallie's desk at the design studio. He dotes on her exactly like an uncle and is kindling her young talent with such care—mostly by feeding her magpie tendencies with materials.

"School hasn't let out for summer yet. And truancy is a real thing." I shake out my shoulders, mentally resetting. "You're distracting me from the point: You're made for television, more so than any of us."

Fitz shrugs, then wanders over to examine the elaborate knocker on the front door. "I'm sure I won't hear the end of it from the Fitzgerald crew," he says. "But yes, of course I'll do it. I'm just playing hard to get."

"Amazing," I say. "And don't pay the Fitzgerald chatter any mind—you're free to do as you please."

He shoots me a look. "Is that to say Magnolia Senior has given this her stamp of approval?"

I scoff. "Obviously she's in the dark on this. And preferably will remain so until she happens to see us on-screen while at the hairdresser."

Fitz sighs. "I certainly can't see her as one for reality television."

I could fill hours of time dissecting Magnolia's opinions on movies and reality television and celebrities—pop culture in general—all of them rife with contradictions and snobbery. The fact that she tries to pretend that social media and its influencers don't even exist. The fact that she says people shouldn't be so loud about their success when she's not particularly quiet about her own wealth. *"It's all a bit gauche, no?"* I can just hear her saying it now. Because in Magnolia's opinion, any power or money that's not old and storied is *"a tad cheap."*

My phone rings. It's Sam, my hardwood genius who I hope will help us work a miracle on these floors. I hold up a finger and say, "Sorry, guys, it's Sam. I've got to take this."

I wave goodbye and hear mutters about calling it a day, then Fitz offering Maya a ride before I dip inside the house and take the call.

"You're just the person I wanted to talk to," I say after tapping the button to accept, then I launch into an overview of the work.

"I've got a few more days on a project out on Sullivan's Island through next Tuesday. But I could squeeze in my favorite designer tomorrow morning, if you're game?" Sam says.

I don't usually schedule work for the weekends, but since Hallie's started splitting time between Grady and me, I don't mind it so much on the weekends she's with her dad.

"Hallie's with her dad this weekend, so that works great for me."

Sam and I talk through details and set a time to meet. He'll give me a bid, but we both know he's got the job—he's the best around. Still, the steps matter, especially when the budget belongs to someone else.

I end the call and stand in the middle of this grand home in its quiet. It lets out the occasional creak and groan, sounds that have always reminded me of breaths and sighs, the pop of a joint, a much-needed stretch. Like the house is alive all around me.

I know we will make this house over in the best ways we can.

But now I'm also wondering if, maybe, right at the edge of the wild possibilities, there might be a camera crew following us as we do it.

CHAPTER 12

GRADY LIKES TO CALL HIS new place a condo, but it's really a carriage house, a miniature redbrick home catty-corner to a traditional house. Certainly no college rental.

It's first thing Saturday morning, the beginning of Grady's weekend with Hallie, and she and I climb the single wooden step. Hallie raps on the front door. Her purple backpack is slung over her shoulder, the signal of her leaving that throws my body into nauseating aches every time. It's been more than half a year of splitting time, but watching her go won't ever get easier.

After a second knock, Grady unlocks the door. When he pulls it open, he's wearing only a robe. He slips out and closes the door behind him.

"I wasn't expecting y'all." He smiles at Hallie, then his eyes dart back toward the door.

"I'm pretty sure today's your day." I pull out my phone and navigate to the email string between us. I hold it up when I find it. "Here. It says today's you."

Hallie huffs. "I can just stay by myself. My friend Clara said her mom let her—"

"Nice try," I say to Hallie. I turn to Grady and eye the door. "Is there something else you have going on today?" I'm kinder than I care to be, but Hallie's watching.

He rolls his lips, and I know in that moment it's a *someone*, not a *something*, inside. "Sorry," he says.

I lay my hand on Hallie's shoulder and ask, "Feel like playing design intern, Hal? We've got Mr. Sam coming to the Daniel House today."

"Um, yes, Mom. Can I run the sander too?"

"I'm not sure Mr. Sam's insurance covers seven-year-olds operating the machinery, but we will have jobs for you. Go wait in the car, and I'll be right there."

Once she's out of earshot I turn back to Grady. "I know you're going to have your life, Grady, but if you have a weekend scheduled with Hallie, you need to be there. You're her dad. Be ready, and don't stand her up. You know how important that is to me."

I glance back at her, hanging out of the open car door, and I promise myself I won't let him let her down like my own father did to me.

"It won't happen again," Grady says.

I don't believe him. It's sad how different he is from the boy I once loved so dearly, but perhaps it was naive of me to think the two of us could ever work in the first place.

Hallie calls, "Mommy! Let's get to work!"

I turn and walk toward my daughter.

I climb in the car and take off, counting my lucky stars that my daughter is as head over heels for design work as I am (particularly the grubby parts). Our destination is only a handful of slow-driven blocks away, then we pull up in front of the Daniel House. I spot Sam's truck a few cars down, and he's waiting on the porch when we walk up.

"Do we have an extra set of hands today?" Sam asks, bending to meet Hallie's eyes.

"Yes, sir." She pops her hands on her hips and nods deeply. "I'm glad to help with anything that's covered by insurance."

Sam frowns in confusion.

"Yes, no heavy machinery for you today, Hal," I say.

Sam nods. "Well then, while your mama and I talk shop, could you go around and find all the nails sticking out of the floor? Here." He hands her a roll of blue painter's tape. "Stick a piece by each one you find. That way we can get them out before we refinish."

Hallie's eyes go wide as she loops the tape onto her arm like a bracelet and skips off to begin her hunt.

"Thank you, Sam. Do you charge extra for the kid gloves? Because I'm happy to pay for it. Her dad had some *mix-ups* with his schedule."

He chuckles. "Not for you, Ms. Mack. It seems like she'll follow in your footsteps, take over your firm one day, perhaps?"

I make myself smile because I know Sam means well, but there's nothing like the thought of Hallie following the well-trodden path of my life to make my skin crawl. It's exactly what Magnolia wanted for me (minus the absentee father part), and if there's one thing I'm determined to allow Hallie, it's the freedom to make her own choices.

"She sure does love to join in," I say. "But who knows? She changes her mind about most things every other day, so it'll be a while before we know if design will stick."

"It's the same with my nieces," Sam says with a chuckle. "Give me a few minutes to measure and look over the floors, and then we can chat?"

"Sure," I say. "And you know you never have to wait for me to let you in. If I didn't trust you by now, I'm not sure I ever would."

"I guess it's the manners we got drilled into us all those years back," he says.

I give him a look, and he knows I mean it when I say, "You and me both, my friend."

Right as I step away and Sam disappears into the house, I know Magnolia's ears must've been burning—even if she was referenced only very indirectly—because her name lights up on the screen of my ringing phone.

"Mother, hi," I say.

"When were you going to tell me?" Magnolia demands.

My mind goes straight to Exquisite Interiors. But how would she know? Maya and I are still setting up interviews with videographers—a surprisingly sought-after bunch. Fitz wouldn't have mentioned it, not that he talks to my mother.

"I'm sorry?" I ask.

"Grady." She huffs. "He's left the firm."

I let out a breath. This I'd much prefer. *This* I'm prepared for.

"Oh yes. He decided after the big fellowship letdown that he was ready to leave the firm," I say. "I understand his decision, considering the whole his-ex-is-in-charge part."

"And you didn't think to mention it to me? I even said I was hoping the Daniel House would bring you two back together. Did you keep it from me to make sure you got the job?"

"Mother, I—"

"Tell me, did you know before the job?" Magnolia asks.

"I'm sorry," I say. It's muscle memory to snap back into my years-old act. "I should've mentioned it before we took on the work. I didn't mean to break your trust or take advantage."

Maybe it makes me a bad person, but I don't feel sorry. This one single project, though lovely and something I'm grateful for, is also something any mother should be happy to pass on without any strings attached. It's not like she could renovate it herself.

"Very right," Magnolia says. "And it *is* taking advantage to mislead me like that."

But would she have given me the job if she'd known Grady was done with the firm? Would she have punished me for his choice? Would she have twisted this into another familiar quid pro quo to have her way with my life? I want to ask her all of these things, but like her darling little Magnolia Junior, I won't. I know how to play by her rules, and challenging her (or *making a scene* as she calls it) would only cause me personal and professional heartache.

I lean back against the paint-cracked siding. "It wasn't my information to share, Mother. You've always taught me to be discreet. As you say: 'There's nothing worse than being known as a busybody.' I figured Delta would go to you right away with the news anyway."

Magnolia sucks in an outraged breath before continuing. "And that's the other half of it! Grady didn't even share the news with his poor mother until she happened to walk into Ned's office this morning and run into her *very own son*. He told her some story about things not being final yet, them still working things out, but she and I both knew that was hogwash. The day he left the firm, he should've notified her—the work with Ned set or not."

I gasp, hoping I'm selling it well.

"I know," Magnolia says. "Poor Delta, she was completely blindsided. Not to mention, she was furious with Ned."

"Poor Delta." Repeating phrases of my mother's makes her feel like I'm on her side. "And sweet Ned. I'm sure he meant nothing by it. Probably didn't want to get Delta's hopes up that Grady might be around more until they'd come to a real agreement."

"Perhaps. She and I both think Grady knew she'd bust out the waterworks and ask him to stay at your firm. I think for her"—Magnolia lets out a dramatic sigh—"and probably me, too, it feels like the final nail in the coffin on what we've always wanted: y'all two together."

"That *final* nail," I say and throw in a yelp.

"It's ghastly," Magnolia says. "You should've told me. Consider this a directive to do so next time. It's not gossiping when it's family."

I don't mention the fact that very little to do with Grady's life (aside from our precious Hallie) is about to be any of my business.

"Message received," I say. "I guess Grady didn't want to hurt his poor mama." I shudder at the feeling of painting Grady in such a generous light. "Though he does seem to favor Ned. I'm sure that hurts Delta too."

"Precisely." Magnolia's tone has cooled, and I can tell we're through the eye of this thing. "How's everything at the house? I'm glad you didn't add on some garish outdoor wedding pergola to the back of the house. I was half expecting it in the blueprints. Seems I was outvoted on blasting away the upstairs walls, but the blueprints were to the board's liking overall."

Sam approaches the front door, signaling he's done. "I'm glad they were approved," I say. "I kept things in the middle ground as best I could—to account for everyone's taste. But I'm here now with Sam Jacobs looking at the floor. Can I call you back later tonight? He needs to give me the rundown."

"Glad to hear things are progressing," Magnolia says. "To-night we're doing a gala—houseboats for wounded warriors, I believe—so let's talk tomorrow. I'd like to set a date for my next site visit."

"All right, Mother," I say. "Sounds good."

I end the call and make a mental note to remind her to dress appropriately for her visit. Maybe I'll even need to require hard hats. Safety first, right?

I'm still smiling to myself at the idea of Magnolia's blown-out hair being jammed into a dusty plastic helmet when I look up at Sam. "Ready?"

Hallie bounds up behind him. "I've done thirty-four blue-tape dots!"

Sam gives Hallie a high five and turns back to me. "Yes, ready for next steps, but there's also some bad news: I think we've got rot."

CHAPTER 13

Fifteen Years Earlier

I'D NEVER BEEN SO GRATEFUL for a campuswide stomach bug, because it was the only reason I was allowed to take my exam online rather than get a big fat zero. All because my mother strong-armed me into attending the Suffolks' anniversary party.

"*I don't want any of y'all passing around this bug,*" the professor had said. "*And to be completely honest, I've got my daughter's wedding this weekend, so I definitely don't want you passing it to me.*"

I couldn't say I felt the same about the bug; I would've readily endured gastrointestinal symptoms if it excused me from a trip home.

I'd hung my bag neatly on the hooks on my closet door before I settled in to work. I sat crisscross atop my childhood bed with my laptop open. The bed was layered with sheets and linens and duvets and quilts. All were perfectly creaseless, starched and ironed no doubt, and even sitting delicately upon it felt like inadvertently toppling a house of cards.

That was how I felt whenever I came back home to Beaufort, like I was disrupting an ecosystem that no longer supported me. Maybe it was how I'd feel from here on out.

My bed in Charleston had never been made—aside from the days Magnolia had visited, which were unsurprisingly few. It was a nest of mismatched throws and threadbare quilts I'd picked up at an estate sale. I loved it because it felt like me; it was mine.

I was halfway into the multiple-choice section of the exam when my door swung open without a knock.

The Dragon stepped over the threshold. "Are you about done, child? We'll need to start on hair and makeup within the hour. Have you picked a dress?" She marched over to my closet, flung it open, and began flipping through the dry-cleaning-bag-wrapped options. "Nope, nope, nope." She sighed. "You decided not to shop for something new?"

"Mama, I'm taking an exam for class. I told you I'd need at least an hour."

"Yes, but I realized we hadn't gone over your outfit, and you know how I feel about running late."

It was one of her rules for us: Showing up late is tasteless. In principle I agreed that showing up on time was a good practice, but as was the case with all of Magnolia's rigidity, this rule left little room for human error without being slapped with a permanent label. *Tacky, rude, gauche, disrespectful*—her favorites.

"Give me thirty minutes, and then we can talk," I said.

Magnolia looked at her watch. "That won't do. There won't be time for a full blowout. You know I've scheduled Rita and her girls to come out."

She hadn't mentioned it specifically, but the glam squad was on retainer. Scheduling them didn't even require a special event for Magnolia. It could be a regular weekday, as little as a trip to the grocery store, or an annual physical at the doctor. She'd even been known to have them come on a day she was under the weather in an attempt to make her feel better. I'd figured they'd be there today, but then again, they came any day my mother felt like she needed a little pick-me-up.

"Fine," I said, studying the next question. "You pick anything from in there, and I'll wear it."

Magnolia pursed her lips. "You don't want a say?"

"Well, as long as it still fits, I don't mind."

Magnolia came over and plopped down beside me on the bed. "I'm glad you mentioned the . . . *size* . . . thing."

I glanced up and looked her dead in the eye. "Not interested."

In addition to the glam squad, Magnolia had a long-standing arrangement with a nutritionist with a fad-diet fixation. She would menu-plan and food-prep each week. I was doing the Atkins diet as young as ten years old alongside my mother, who was radiating pride. We did Atkins until it didn't work, like every diet didn't work, and we moved on to The Zone. Then the Special K diet, which was so uninspired it shouldn't have been allowed to be a thing.

Magnolia raised her hands. "Fine, I won't say any more, but the—"

"If I want to try the latest diet, I'll let you know," I said. "What is it now? Carnivore diet? Until next week when everyone realizes it doesn't stick and moves on."

Magnolia muttered something under her breath about *health* that I didn't care to hear. "I'll let you finish your work, I guess, but *please*, be quick."

"You've got it," I said.

And finally the door clicked closed behind her.

I walked into the Beaufort Yacht Club at Magnolia's side, and I could feel the tension in my head radiate down my neck to my upper back. I knew deep down my work on the exam wasn't my best. It couldn't be with my mother buzzing in my ear about my hair and my waistline. That was what Beaufort did to me—it bound me up into something tight and anxious and proper. Like the real me was covered—better yet, *smothered*—under its layers of tradition and expectations.

Delta Suffolk swanned over at the sight of us and pulled me into her arms. She smelled like the same sweet perfume she'd worn for years, and her arms were tanned and soft around me. "Oh, Mack, I hope your mama didn't have to bend your arm too hard to get you here. I'm just delighted to see you." When she pulled back, her blue eyes, the same as Grady's, sparkled at me. Her face was framed in the same dark hair as his too.

I smiled. "Of course not. I was itching to come. You and Ned are so important to me."

"She wouldn't miss it, Dee," Magnolia said, taking a turn to hug her friend.

"If you ladies will excuse me," I said and took off in the direction of the bathroom.

My feet already ached in the heels Magnolia chose for the occasion. Once, I could practically run in heels, I was so used to wearing them for galas and auctions for a good cause, but since I'd gotten to Charleston and started walking everywhere in the heat, I'd worn in a pair of flat leather sandals.

I stopped at the sink and ran my hands under the water. In the mirror I looked like the old me: heavily made up into something I was not and never had been. My skin was flawlessly smooth and my red lips elegant and timeless—thanks only to Rita and her team.

In Charleston I was freckled and sun-kissed, my hair wild in its naturally curly state—frizz level chosen by whatever brand of humidity blew in that day.

In Charleston I was me.

A crowd of young debutantes-in-training clip-clopped into the bathroom, giggling about the boys they'd bring as their dates to the ball. I smiled at them in the reflection and moved to dry my hands. They were another reminder of who I once was—but more so of how much I'd changed in so little time.

I pushed out of the bathroom and headed to the bar, weaving between well-dressed adults in suits and cocktail dresses. I reached the counter and picked up a menu. Typically such events served specialty cocktails, and although no one checked IDs, I was now of legal age.

"Shirley Temple?" a familiar voice asked beside me.

I looked up and saw Grady looking well-groomed and dapper in a navy suit. "I was thinking something stronger."

"I'm sorry you got dragged into this. My mom said you weren't sure about coming."

I gave up on the menu and took a glass of white wine from a passing waiter. "It was mostly that Magnolia sounded a five-alarm fire and called me out of class to bully me into a commitment."

"Your sweet old mama?" Grady laughed. *No way.*"

"I know. Typical stunt of hers. She couldn't care less about school."

"The way our parents see it, money can buy most of the things we might want in life."

Grady said it like it was a fact of life, not an absurd advantage offered to the few. I wondered in that moment if he agreed with them. If I had to wager a bet, I'd guess he did. And I was hit with another pang of sadness when I remembered him as a younger boy. *Not him too* was what it felt like.

"Have you seen your dad?" I asked. "I want to wish him a happy anniversary."

Grady smiled. "Where does he usually hang out at these things?"

"Great, I'll find the food," I said.

"Bingo," Grady replied.

Eventually I made my way through the crowd, stopping briefly for a couple hellos, to the buffet that overflowed with fruits and vegetables and meats, alongside the hors d'oeuvres passed around by the waitstaff. I took a plate and used the tiny silver tongs to load it up with grapes and cheese.

"I see you found the real watering hole."

I knew it was Ned Suffolk before I looked up. I set down my plate and reached up to hug his broad shoulders. His face was slightly sunburned from what I'd guess was a long round of golf, and his brown hair was thin on top. I'd wondered on my way into town if things would be different between the Suffolks and me, since their son and I had broken up, but it seemed his parents' affections for me weren't contingent on my being with their son.

Ned squeezed me. "My goodness, is it great to see you back here, sport."

I grabbed my plate and tossed a grape in my mouth. "I didn't know how things would be now with Grady and me split."

"I thought this might be tricky for you," Ned said. "I told Delta we needed to mention the party to you directly before your mama got wind of it. Neither of us wanted you to feel forced into it, considering the whole Grady situation."

I smiled. I did appreciate it, and their warm welcome had put me at ease. "Magnolia is a woman who knows what she wants, and for this occasion, it was her daughter in attendance."

Ned laughed. "Tell me about school. Grady's barely scraping by with Cs at Clemson. I heard you're a dedicated student."

"Would you mind telling my mother that?" I laughed. "She

seems most concerned with making me into a good match with your son."

"I think she and Delta would love to have their children marry and make themselves *officially* family."

A friend of Ned's walked in, and he waved at him. "Sorry to leave you, Mack, but I haven't seen Rick in a decade. Let me go say hi."

"No worries at all," I said.

I took the last few bites off my plate and wandered back out onto the deck, and despite the warmth I felt from the Suffolks themselves, I couldn't completely settle. It was like the chemistry deep within me knew I didn't belong here. Like the parts of me that had blossomed in Charleston, parts I loved most, couldn't breathe this type of air.

I couldn't wait to get back to Charleston.

"Magnolia," my mother called out to me from inside the French doors. "Stop being a wallflower. Mary from the church has a hilarious story to tell you about last week's event."

I pulled in a breath, mentally wound myself into the daughter she wanted me to be, and spun myself around with a glossy smile.

"I sure love a good story," I said.

And my heels pinched with every step I took.

CHAPTER 14

Present Day

W HEN I ARRIVE AT THE bus stop for Hallie's afternoon pickup, my friend and fellow mom Becca is
already waiting. I stop beside her and smile before I
check my phone. It's been several days since Sam came to look at
the floors at the Daniel House, and I'm hoping for a text from him
saying he's ready to start work.

Becca clears her throat, interrupting my staring at a notification-
free screen. "I'm so glad I ran into you!"

She launches into a long-winded explanation about the school's
welcome program for new families. Just as the school bus pulls
up, she asks, "So I was hoping you wouldn't mind being the parent guide for the Kelly family? Just help orient them and answer
all those 'parent questions.' I figured it works since y'all are new
neighbors anyway—I've already sent the email!"

I don't have time to answer before a lively Hallie charges off the
bus and almost plows me down with a hug.

I look back to Becca. "Parent guides, huh?"

"Sorry, Mack. I didn't think you'd mind."

I swat the air. "It's just that I know him from when I was a kid."

"Oh." Becca groans. "Want me to switch? School's almost out

for the summer anyway, so maybe we can just match him to someone in the fall."

"It's fine," I say. "I'll suck it up."

It isn't like I can have her switch it now that she's already sent the email. If there's a last-minute shuffle, Lincoln will know I was behind it, and that's not exactly the tone I want to set with my new neighbor. I will check for another email address—for the *other woman*. She's probably a girlfriend, likely young, toned, and attractive—though perhaps not official enough to be school-email approved. I let myself seethe for a minute at the picture of her in my mind.

"So sorry, girl," Becca replies. "On field day, I'll make sure your name ends up nowhere on the volunteer list."

"Thanks," I say before turning to walk Hallie home. Truthfully, I'd be happy to do three field days to avoid this dance with Lincoln.

Hallie grabs my hand and squeezes it. "Afternoon Glam today, Mama?"

Afternoon Glam is our invitation-only tea party that includes cookies, conversation, and over-the-top fashion. Snacks may rotate, but the dress code is nonnegotiable (one item with sparkle, per attendee). Hallie typically opts for a homemade, bedazzled caftan and an off-center smear of lipstick. I do my best to keep up.

I squeeze back. "Sounds perfect for today."

"You'll need to change when we get home." She eyes me up and down. "Even if you've been having a hard time lately." The honesty of a seven-year-old is refreshing if not humbling—particularly to a freshly divorced thirty-six-year-old.

I smile to myself. "Thanks for taking pity on an old lady."

We round the top of the hill toward our house, and I spot Lincoln and Foster outside in their front yard. Hallie does too. "Mom, there's a kid out there!"

Oh yes, my new *parent buddy*—or whatever Becca called it—and his son.

Hallie gasps. "Oh! That's not just anyone. That's Foster, the new kid in my class. Ms. Jones made me his buddy on his first day and everything. I think we might be best friends." She drops my hand and sprints over across an open yard toward them. "Foster! We're *neighbors*! Can you believe it?"

My daughter's joy is fabulous and wonderful and such a beauty to behold, but sweet baby Jesus does it burn in my veins. This little boy, as delightful as he undoubtedly is, is not my first pick for Hallie's best friend. Reluctantly I follow her toward the Kelly boys, pulling my face into a smile that I hope looks more genuine than it feels.

Lincoln and Foster are busy wrangling what appears to be a tarp, and a water hose sits waiting nearby. "Mommy! Can I do it? Can I do the slip and slide?"

Lincoln flashes an apologetic smile. "She's welcome to, if you're ok with it."

I shrug, then grin at Hallie. "Go put on your swimsuit."

Hallie sprints up to the house and lets herself in.

Lincoln is a slip-and-slide dad, it seems. The kind of father every mother wants for her children, the one who will do the wild and messy activities and probably throw his own body down the watery tarp like a happy projectile. All in the name of fun.

It's new from the version of him I knew that summer. Back then he was fun in the ways everyone is as a twentysomething, but his seriousness—maybe it was his ambition—seems to have softened.

When Foster heads inside for goggles, I take my moment. "So I'm not sure if you saw the email, but it seems I've been assigned as your 'parent buddy.'"

Lincoln laughs at the air quotes I place around the term. "Another item to add to my list of apologies," he says.

I crouch to help unfold a corner of the tarp; it feels better than my hands hanging there idly. "I can give you a rundown on the parents. The relaxed ones. The ones you can't swear in front of. Who to talk to if you really want something done. And never, and I repeat *never*, let Becca talk you into volunteering for the end-of-year field day. I was foolish enough to agree last year, and I'm pretty sure even my eyebrows got sunburned."

"Sounds good," he says.

Our eyes meet, and his hang on me like he wants to say more.

"Mack. You don't have to," he says.

I swat the air. "Being fired as a parent buddy is as good as a scarlet letter around here. Though maybe it'll get me off the hook for volunteering . . ."

"I know this is weird," he says.

I let out a breath and give in. "Yeah. It is. Honestly, it'll probably be good for the three of us to just sit down and set the tone for this whole thing."

Lincoln chews his lip, the same thing he used to do when he was nervous.

"We just need to jump in and start making a new . . . something," I say.

He looks down, then back up, and meets my eyes.

"Just move right on like chugga-chugga-choo-choo," I say.

I'm already pulling the invisible train horn above my shoulder before I fully register what I'm doing, and the only good way for this to end is for the earth to open and swallow me whole. But he's back. With some woman, with his son, and his house. And everything I once dreamed he'd do with me. So it's the occasion, if ever there was one, to dip a toe into insanity.

Lincoln's mouth flickers with a smile. "Uh, yeah. If that's how you put it, how could I say no?"

"Great. When would you two like to come over for coffee? I was thinking an afternoon would be good, and the kids could play while we chat."

Lincoln nods unexcitedly, like he's scheduling a dentist appointment.

"Great. Next week, Thursday?" I ask.

"Sure," he says.

"And your partner? Wife? We haven't met yet." I fold my arms across me to protect myself from the name of the person who ended up with my happy family.

"Wife?" he asks.

"Sorry, I know some folks forgo the official stuff these days." I suddenly feel stodgy, like everything opposite of artist chic. "Your partner. The lady with the dresses."

Lincoln chuckles. "It's just me."

"What do you mean?"

"I'm a single dad. No wife, no girlfriend."

"Oh." It drops out of me as my gut flips upside down.

Lincoln smiles that warm smile that threatens to melt me, then toast me under the Charleston sun. That smile that was once summertime bliss.

"So"—Lincoln shifts, pointing at me—"regarding the three of us—it's just you now?"

I nod my head. "Grady and I separated." I drop my tone as Hallie speeds back outside. "He moved downtown."

"I'm surprised he'd let you—"

"Hang on," I say. "I could've sworn I saw women's clothing come off the truck."

He laughs. "Oh, I have all kinds of stuff for shoots. Those

were just the most popular items I took from the New York studio."

It feels like I'm hit by a breeze from nowhere and billowed with hope. So much so that my feet might lift just a little above the ground. My body prickles and tingles in a way it hasn't in a lifetime, remembering what it felt like to be with him. Remembering the heat of his skin on mine. But I push that memory away, *swiftly*, and squeeze out a polite smile befitting a thirtysomething mom.

"Of course, that makes sense," I say. "I'll set a towel on the steps for Hal. Just send her home whenever y'all are done."

I turn and go, letting Hallie, now decked out in swimwear and goggles, take my place. I carry myself up the driveway. So rigidly I probably look like I'm having a medical emergency. My chest does feel like it might explode, but he can't know any of that.

My heart flips like a fish out of water and makes me imagine kissing him over coffee, pulling him into me as he crosses my threshold like I did as a routine over a decade ago. My lips tingle and pulse in betrayal.

Stop, I tell myself.

No more.

Not another thought.

CHAPTER 15

THE NEXT DAY THE FRENCH doors at the studio open out onto a bright blue sky, birds chirping and the city bustling. It's a perfect backdrop to contrast the miserable luck we're having inside interviewing videographers.

"I don't know, Maya, did you see the guy's face when we mentioned it was for an Exquisite Interiors TV audition?"

She bites a lip. "I know. I'm not sure where he got the idea we were planning a bar mitzvah."

I try to smile, but I know I look like I'm cracking instead. We're both figuring this out as we go.

Maya laughs. "You all right there?"

"I'm just doing anything to stop myself from crying at this point."

We'd lined up five interviews for this morning, and we only have one candidate left. Our first no-showed, and when we called to check in, he sent us right to voicemail. He was struck from the list.

"I mean the second guy *could've* been ok . . . ," Maya says.

"Until the whole part about having severe asthma that would prevent him from being able to safely shoot on-site while we work." I flopped back into the sofa. "Even after the floors are done, he's a no-go on wet paint and would only be available for the finished product."

Maya shrugs. "I did tell him what the gig was when we sched-uled."

"Maybe he's not an Exquisite Interiors kind of guy," I said. "If he'd watched a single program, he would have known off the bat."

I rub my temples before asking, "So the third one?"

"I'm not sure. She said she was running late, so I offered an afternoon time. She promised to call back." Her voice rises in optimism at the end.

I stand and begin pacing. "That was three hours ago. Sure, there might've been some crazy emergency, but otherwise, that's unreliable—and unprofessional."

"Our last guy should be here in ten," Maya says.

"He's the college student?"

Maya pulls up her phone and pecks at it with her pointer finger. "Yeahhh."

"That was a whole lot of sound for very little information," I say.

She puffs out a breath and smooths a hand down her pink button-down. "He says he just uses an iPhone." Maya hands me her phone. "From his socials his videos look amazing. I wouldn't have guessed they were done on a phone."

I have to agree. It looks like a clip from an Apple commercial where they showcase the camera tech. Immediately I feel terribly old not to have the same grasp on my own phone that sits in my pocket all day.

"It's worth a try," I say. "It *does* look really good."

"Plus, Coco said it doesn't have to be professional quality or anything. What they really need is an idea of your personality, your design sense, and the types of jobsites they could showcase."

"I guess it's not like we'd be producing the show ourselves," I say. "But it feels like slacking to turn in something less than perfect."

"Relax," Maya says. "We'll make a great tape."

"It's my competitive side." I say it out of the side of my mouth, but it's far from a secret around here.

Maya laughs. "It'll turn out all right. Plus, if we sit on this and wait for perfection, we might miss out completely."

I decide to believe her for now and check the time. "I wonder how Fitz is doing with the rot inspection at the Daniel House."

"I don't even want to know the extent." Maya shudders, then wanders over to the open door. "If this last interview is in any way decent, we have to give him the job."

"I know," I said. "There's just something about the iPhone deal that feels risky."

"But we have to move quickly on this," Maya says. "If we look good and get in there first, we have a better chance at success."

I'm about to open my mouth to tell her I want to put our best foot forward, how I've grown rather attached to this idea of a show of our own in the last few days, how this tape should be as dang close to excellence as we might possibly be able to get it, when our candidate walks up.

Maya turns to him. "Hi, you must be Collin?" She reaches out a hand.

"Yes, ma'am," he says, shaking her hand.

"Come on in, Collin," I say, standing to greet him and showing him to his chair.

He has shoulder-length dirty-blond hair and is wearing a black suit that's about two sizes too big. His shirt underneath looks new but is wrinkled, likely fresh out of a package. A pocket of fondness forms in my heart for him; he's doing his best. Thanks to my own starched-and-pressed upbringing, I appreciate a few wrinkles here and there.

"So, Collin, we were just looking at your social media accounts, and we're astounded that you film only on a phone," I say. "Tell us more about that."

Collin launches into a detailed analysis of cell phone technology that I suspect neither Maya nor I grasp completely, despite our smiling and nodding along keenly.

"And I mentioned it when we spoke on the phone, but we're looking at putting together an audition reel for Exquisite Interiors TV. Do you think that's something you could manage?" Maya asks.

Collin nods. "Oh, absolutely. I'm a marine biology student at the college, and I shot a sick trailer for the program with all the underwater tech. Here." He pulls out his phone and scrolls to the video.

We watch, impressed. I'm no video expert, but if Collin could make a tape of our work look this professional, it would be something I'd be proud to submit.

"Wow, it's great," I say.

"The professor said a ton of people tried to sign up for the class after that, but it was full in a couple minutes. I've got other departments asking me to do the same for them."

"It's a testament to the changing times," I say. "Collin, I think we've seen what we need to. Can we call you in a bit?"

"Definitely," Collin says.

We stand and walk him to the door, and only once I'm sure he's out of earshot do I turn to Maya. "We have to hire him."

"I'm glad you said it first." Maya squeaks in excitement. "I think he could really knock it out of the park."

"What's his rate?"

"Half that of the bar mitzvah guy," Maya says.

"Like it's meant to be! Feel free to call him and get the ball rolling. I'm all in," I say. "Then, lunch?"

Just as I catch the scent of fried seafood drifting down King Street and into the studio, my phone rattles to life on my desk. It lights up with the photo I have saved for Fitz, the two of us at the taco shack on Folly Beach with his partner, Henry, pulling a face above us.

"Actually," I say, "here's Fitz. Let's find out the damage."

I pick up the phone and click the button to talk.

"Magnolia Junior, can you talk?" Fitz is the only one who gets away with calling me by my given name and only because he never forgets to include the *junior*.

"Talk to me, Magnus," I say. The exception to the rule must go both ways.

"Actually, I'm switching you to FaceTime," Fitz says.

I tap to accept and Fitz hops onto the screen in an emerald-green-and-white gingham shirt rolled up to the elbows.

"You're looking especially dapper today," I say with a grin.

"I always dress up when I'm expecting bad news." The rustle of work happening across the old wood of the Daniel House floats from the phone as Fitz makes his way through. "It softens the blow."

I groan and slip into my desk chair, pushing a stack of papers aside.

"So Sam noticed rot over here in the area back behind where the sink was, but the guys here today say we need to replace some of the floor joists underneath. There's also a second area of rot where the old dishwasher was—surprise, surprise—which Sam didn't catch."

"Right where we had our samples stacked."

"It's no fault of Sam's," Fitz says. "But we might need to consider tiling in here. I'll let you make the final choice—seeing as you're the boss and all." He waggles his brow.

I grin. "Thanks for playing the game, but let's be real: I trust your eyes to be as good as my own. If you're seeing too much area in new wood, we'll start talking tile."

"I think it's for the best, even if it's not the board's first choice." Fitz is cast into sunlight as he steps outside and away from the loud sanding machines.

"Let's have some gorgeous options ready for them to consider when we break the news. Make it a bit more palatable."

"I've already got ideas in mind," Fitz says.

"Send them on over. And hey, I'm thinking about fried seafood for lunch."

"Fleet Landing?" Maya calls over.

"I'll meet y'all there," Fitz says.

The screen goes dark, and I tuck the phone into my bag. I save the edits to the portfolio I'd been tinkering with and shut down my laptop. "Ready whenever you are."

A few minutes later, we step out onto the streets and blend into the crowds of sunburned tourists. We walk toward the sound of seagulls at the edge of the water, along the palmetto tree–lined streets, until the smell of fried shrimp beckons us to our destination.

CHAPTER 16

Fifteen Years Earlier

SINCE OUR DAY AT THE beach, Lincoln and I had texted constantly for a week. By then an actual official date was a foregone conclusion. I'd told him, in detail, about my grand plan to go to college and launch my career, prove to my mama and everyone else back home that I could succeed my own way.

I'd wondered aloud to him if that still left room for a little summer fun.

He'd enthusiastically agreed.

The next Friday evening I stood at the entrance to the harbor, where Lincoln had told me to meet him. I hadn't pinned him for the sailing type—he seemed more of a full-time artist trapped by a boring desk job required to pay the bills.

I walked down the slatted dock, pops of the wood marking my steps toward him. My dress fluttered in the crosswind, and he stood at the edge of the dock facing the water. I cleared my throat, and he turned to me, lighting up.

"Hey, sailor," I said.

He laughed. "Ahoy there!" He saluted me, looking adorably goofy. He was still wearing his work clothes, slacks and a button-up, now loosened at the neck, sleeves rolled up; he looked so different from when I saw him at the beach.

I glanced around the marina, impressed. "How'd you swing this?"

"I have a buddy at the college who let me in." He grinned like he knew it was trouble.

I raised an impressed brow.

Lincoln strode to the sailboat, stepped down into it, and extended a hand back to me. I hopped down beside him. I hadn't been on a sailboat but once before, very long ago, when Magnolia sent me to a wildly unsuccessful sailing camp.

A picnic basket sat stashed on the deck, and a bottle of champagne peeked out from the wicker flap. It seemed like it might easily flip overboard at the rock of a wave, but I was no sailing expert. As I watched Lincoln fumble around the boat in front of me, I wondered if perhaps he was no expert either.

"You know how to drive this thing?" I asked after a solid fifteen minutes of him poking around.

"*Obviously*. Could you just point me to where the keys go?" He grinned, then got back to his rooting around.

I sat, and watched, and waited.

After a little while longer he stopped and slouched against the mast. "Ok, I'll be honest—"

A laugh spilled from me.

"I thought it'd be a little bit more, I don't know . . . straightforward?"

I wiped a tear that slipped from my eye.

"I figured I could work it out on the fly," he said.

"Just like that, huh?" I looked up at him from under my lashes.

Lincoln dropped onto the seat beside me.

"Sailing is serious business," I said. "I should know, seeing as I'm a sailing camp dropout myself."

Lincoln glanced up at the ropes and loops and knots. "I did learn some knots at Boy Scouts . . . before I was kicked out for diverting the nature hike to the convenience store for chips and soda."

"A booted Boy Scout? Seems I've got a real bad boy on my hands." I kicked off my sandals and pulled the picnic basket toward us.

"A toast to a first date flop?" he asked.

"Well, let's not call it quite yet," I said, sliding out the bottle. "The night is young. But I have to ask. Why on earth did you pick sailing, you know, *considering*?"

Lincoln pulled a fifth of whiskey from a side compartment and took a sip. "Isn't that what girls like you like? Sailing, fencing, croquet—cricket, if you were British."

"And what about me, exactly, screams rich-people sporting?"

His eyes searched me. "It's more of an overall feeling. A fancy vibe, I guess."

"Ok, fine." I'd let him have it because, in all honesty, I knew what he meant. I did come from that crowd even if I didn't feel at home among them. "Imagine I lost the fancy vibe. What would you pick?"

His face brightened, like he'd been waiting for a chance to mention this. "Well, if you're asking for classic LK, it would—without reservation—be a traditional Charleston ghost tour. Not a spooky spot left behind."

My stomach dropped. I was handing this guy a lifeline, but haunted and spooky and ghosty were most certainly not my thing. In fact, I'd probably categorize them as a phobia. "You're one of those," I said sorrowfully.

"Those up for thrill and adventure?" He grinned like we'd already agreed to this endeavor. "Interested in the beyond? It gets no better."

"With all due respect, Lincoln—or do I call you 'LK' now?—there's already a lot of very terrifying things about my real life, and it just feels greedy to pile on from the past."

"Oh, come on," he said. "I promise it's mostly all made up."

"Ok, so if it's not even—"

He swatted a hand to wave me off—I suspected because he knew any argument he made wouldn't hold up.

"My family's been doing these for years," he said. "My parents and my sister and I would drive into town from North Charleston and do all kinds of tours. Mom would make us little ghost-protector bracelets and promise us they were made out of love and would scare away the bad ghosts."

"Cute," I said. Something shifted in me at hearing him talk about his family, the example of a complete and loving family so unlike my own.

"I know it's a bit cheesy," he said. "But I don't know, the ghost tours are just a good memory. We didn't have a lot growing up. Actually, my parents really struggled; my dad was a musician and played in bars around town. One of his friends was an actor who worked the tours, and he'd get us free tickets. My mom was a teacher, but then when my grandmother got sick, she had to quit to take care of her." Lincoln's usual playfulness faded as he talked, his eyes dropping to his feet. When he looked back up, his eyes swam with uncertainty. "We ended up living in my grandmother's house with her for quite a while. Nothing like what you grew up with."

I paused. "We may have had money, but it was far from perfect." I knew it sounded hollow, even if it was true.

"Money does give you options," Lincoln said, sipping his drink again. "If it weren't an issue for me, I'd be doing photography full-time, leave the desk job behind."

"In my mother's world, *her* money means she gets to pick *my* life," I said.

"I guess we just make do with what we get handed," Lincoln said. He reached over and squeezed my hand. "So what do you say about that ghost tour?"

He was so eager, like his offer was irresistible. I didn't want to do the ghost tour, that was certain. I'd been sleepless anytime ghost stories were swapped at sleepovers, and Magnolia wasn't exactly the comforting and doting mother I suspected Lincoln's was. But it seemed like a window into him, and I wanted more of that. Honestly, what was the worst that could happen? If I found myself sleepless, I'd pop a bottle of wine and binge-watch something trashy on TV.

"I'm going to need one of those bracelets," I said.

We stood on a narrow side street off Market, in line at a kiosk manned by a person dressed as a ghoul. I was the kind of nervous where it felt like my throat was closing in on itself, and I kept swallowing to clear it.

Lincoln reached down and took my hand. He lifted it and slid a blue rope bracelet onto my wrist. "For protection," he said.

My palm was slick with sweat. "As you can tell, I need it," I said.

He whispered in my ear, "The bad ghosts hate sweaty palms, so count it as extra protection."

My chest released with the injection of relief, and I squeezed a tight smile his way.

Lincoln bought our tickets, and soon we were directed to a horse-drawn carriage. I climbed up into an open row, and Lincoln followed. I sat, and he squeezed in beside me.

He caught my eye and said, "Seeing as I'm your resident ghoul defender, I figured I should make sure to stay close."

"Just a man heeding the call of duty," I said.

He shrugged in mock humility.

With that, the horse took its first steps and the carriage jerked to life. As if by reflex, Lincoln threw an arm around me to brace the jolt. I crept a hand up and set it on top of his. I wiggled back into him, and he bent down to whisper, "You are stunning, by the way."

I turned to look at him, and our faces were barely inches apart. Every bit of my insides fluttered as I held my breath hoping it would happen, that maybe I did deserve something real like him.

And then, like a set of magnets, our lips drew together and landed in a pillowy knot. The rest of the world went dark, like the cord had been cut. And inside me was a supernova, warmed in brilliant light, and I knew I'd never again be the same; he'd introduced me to real magic.

Then the carriage hit a bump.

"Damn carriage," I whispered as we broke apart.

He let out a pained groan. "I could say so many worse things."

He squeezed my hand, and I shot him a look like *to be continued*.

Fortunately, we both turned back to looking straight forward, because I couldn't wipe the dorky smile off my face.

The speaker system clicked on as the tour guide, a scruffy man dressed as a half-dead pirate, began his routine. He wasn't nearly as scary as the devastation-promising Ouija boards of my youth or the fates my so-called friends had promised were bound my way when we'd played.

"Is this guy a zombie or a ghost?" I whispered to Lincoln.

"Unfortunately, he's 100 percent zombie," Lincoln said.

"What happened to these being 'true' stories?"

He squinted. "The tour guides are allowed some artistic license." Lincoln smiled like it was the best part, then pointed to the horse. "But old Pirate Horsey up there seems fed up with the routine."

I nodded intently. "Not a single whinny yet."

I kept waiting to feel the terror I'd planned for, but it never came. Not one part of one story was even partially scary, and I wasn't complaining. Instead, the tour was more like a low-budget parody of a ghost tour. Painfully embarrassing throughout. They must've stayed in business because of those coming for the laughs and the cringe-worthy content rather than any actual frights.

Thanks to the smile I couldn't wipe from my face and the company beside me, I was comfortable and warm for the entire wobbly ride.

Maybe I did like ghost tours after all.

CHAPTER 17

Present Day

WHEN THE BLACK TOWN CAR pulls up outside
the Daniel House two days later, I'm surprised to see
both Magnolia and Delta step out onto the street.
Magnolia is in tennis shoes—Gucci, of course—paired with white
jeans and a Hermès scarf wrapped around her hair. With the dark
sunglasses, her appearance resembles a disguise. Delta is wearing
a much more sensible pair of dark-wash jeans with a cute blouse I
can tell cost upward of $300. Their voices fill the Saturday morning
quiet along the sleepy street.

"Thank you, Victor," Magnolia calls into the car. "I'll call you."

Delta scurries up to me and squeezes my upper arms. "Surprise!"

"Yes, surprise is right," I say as Magnolia walks up. "Mother, you
didn't mention Delta would be coming along today."

Magnolia fiddles with something in her pocketbook. "Well,
Delta is part of the Carolina Historic Society too. Plus, she wanted
to lay eyes on you after Grady moved on to a new job."

I guide them through the iron gate. "Well, the firm is still up
and running like normal. No worries here."

Delta leans over and touches my back. "I don't want you to
get the wrong idea, honey. I know you've got this under control. I

guess . . ." She stops walking, and I turn to face her. "I guess I just feel a little sad and removed with Grady leaving. Do you mind if I see Hal while we're here?"

"We'll have to check with Victor," Magnolia says. "His nephew has a basketball tournament he needs to make it back in time for."

Magnolia has a special soft spot for Victor. She may boss him around until her dying breath, but she shows her appreciation by guarding the small slots of time he does request off. Heaven knows, the man certainly spends more waking hours with Magnolia than with any of his nieces or nephews.

"Of course," Delta says with a hint of disappointment. "Let's see this house!"

Magnolia looks around the grounds. "Doesn't look much improved."

I did prepare Magnolia in great and thorough detail not to expect to see much change on the surface. I even tried to dissuade her from this visit completely, but it seems she'd rather be disappointed than err even an inch too close to losing control over the project.

"Like I told you yesterday, we weren't expecting the rot we found in the frame of the house, so we had to pivot. Sam's crew is getting closer every day on the floors. Whenever we start a project we have to start with the basics, the ugly stuff."

"I don't mind sitting on this board," Magnolia says on her way through the heavy front door, "but I'd rather not have to do all these site visits. They're so grubby."

I follow them inside and click the door closed behind me. "I didn't realize they *required* so much hands-on of y'all. That's quite a lot."

"It's not required necessarily, but seeing as I'm your mother and this is *my* project, I have no choice but to stay in the loop. If I had it my way, I'd do all the designs and plans, and your team would just check the boxes."

"Oh, I don't doubt you would," I say.

"Thanks again for letting me tag along," Delta says. "I can see the potential, even if it needs work. Y'all—I mean, *you*, now—are so skilled."

"Here's what we've been working on." I walk into the kitchen and tap my toe on the new subfloor. "Under here." I turn and point to the sanded hardwoods along the deep entryway. "And you can see that Sam's crew has stripped off all the old stain, and a lot of the wear and tear has come off too. He's amazingly thorough yet careful, and compared to a standard timeline, they're working at light speed."

Magnolia nods and walks over to the area. "It does look better. Takes an awful lot of time, though. Yes, I suspect you were right, Magnolia—you probably could've just sent me the pictures. There's not much to see here."

"It just *smells* like history." Delta hops a little in excitement.

"Smells like it needs a good cleaning to me," Magnolia says.

Delta laughs in a titter. "Oh, Mags, you're such a hoot."

Delta Suffolk must be touched by a special celestial gift to consider my mother a hoot. By any and all standards Magnolia is very little fun and a whole lot of scathing disparagement. She is not funny—at least not intentionally. But by the grace of God, Delta Suffolk is enchanted.

They're a perfect match as much as they are an odd one.

I gesture around the cozy kitchen. "Because of the water damage over time, we're doing tile in here. You ladies want to see the ones Fitz picked out?"

"Do I ever," Delta says.

"Tile?" Magnolia asks. "I wasn't informed about any tile."

"It was sent to your email and to the rest of the board," I say. "The president replied and gave us the green light. I figured you saw it."

"I don't have time for email," Magnolia says.

"Which is why I also followed up with a call to you," I say. "But you were out with the yacht club." *More than a few mimosas in.* "And you told me to just go ahead."

"Hmm." Magnolia pauses like she's remembering it. "Well, I guess I'll just have to accept it, even if I don't particularly like it."

The women follow me into a back pantry area where we're storing supplies as they're delivered. I love the tile, so seeing it again feels like a treat. I pull the squares from the cardboard box and lay a few in the light of the window.

"Fitz and I both adore these, and Douglas and Jade loved them too. Aren't they fabulous?" I run a hand over the textured inky blues and milky whites, then look to the women.

Delta crosses her arms and nods deeply. "Yes, ma'am, those are gorgeous." She bends to touch them. "Might have to have you come put these in my kitchen—just don't tell Ned!" Delta melts into giggles.

"A bit busy for a floor, no?" Magnolia says. "And since when do the interns get a say?"

I could tell Magnolia that the rest of the design is intentionally quiet alongside the tile, about how the cabinets are a creamy taupe and the fixtures will be a muted brass, but I'm not sure she cares to know.

"The interns are on-site reps for the board—in addition to you. Both have strong design eyes. Everyone weighs in," I say, carefully picking up the tiles and slotting them back into their box.

"In that case I'd like to have my say too," Magnolia says. "Please include me in the next design team meeting so I can help and give input."

Maybe my mother does hate my designs or maybe she's just so desperate to keep me caught in her twisted loop, challenging me to live up to her expectations, that she sees criticizing my work as her best option. Still, she knows I want to be the best at historic preservation and design, but I'm not sure she'll ever be willing to admit that I'm even decent.

"All right then, Mother," I say. "Did you want to see the rest of the material samples while we're here? It might save you another in-person visit."

"I guess we might as well now that we've come all this way," Magnolia says.

"Say no more." I grab the large tote with samples from beside the tile. "Let's head to the porch to check them out."

"Don't have to ask me twice. Heavens, is it dusty in here," Magnolia says.

"*Materials* just sounds so professional," Delta says, following us.

We step out onto the wraparound porch and it creaks beneath our feet to greet us. It even smells woody as it bakes in the heat of the sun. I drop the bag onto our trusty folding table and begin unloading and arranging the samples in groups.

I have a discreet woodland-patterned wallpaper for the powder room downstairs and a modern gold light fixture picked out to match it. I set the sample of the kitchen cabinetry beside the creamy swatches we'll narrow down once we're ready. I'll show the plumbing fixtures on my phone.

"We've got the design put together for the downstairs so far," I say. "The team and I are still firming up our decisions for the upstairs. Let me show you the bathroom sink. It's traditional porcelain. Actually, it's not too different from the one in your house."

Magnolia perks up. "Well, I'm glad to have been an inspiration. The ladies on the board do say I have a penchant for a classic look."

I'm fairly certain that's just code for Magnolia having expensive taste, but I know better than to suggest it out loud.

I hold up the phone to show them the sink.

"Oh yes. That one's perfect," Magnolia says. "It seems you're doing a fair job at this. Even if it's ungodly slow-moving."

"Oh, Mags, it's a little better than fair," Delta says. "Let's not be too hard on the girl."

Magnolia shoots her friend a steely look, and Delta snaps her mouth shut.

"I'm glad you think it's all right so far," I say and begin to pack the samples back in. "But especially with historic buildings, we have to be cautious and thoughtful rather than rushing. If something gets ripped out or damaged, it may not ever be the same."

"If you say so," Magnolia says. She pulls her sunglasses down and wanders toward the steps.

Delta leans in and whispers, "It really is beautiful, Mack. No matter how your mama acts about it."

I wink. "Thank you. I've learned by now how to let it go."

More like push it all down and smile nice, but it works the same. Delta is one of the few people who truly knows Magnolia through and through, truly knows how she has raised and treated her daughter. She sees the cold quality, the harsh corners of Magnolia's mothering, and it makes sense why she's always tried to be a loving presence in my life. To cover the gap.

The black car pulls up, and we say our goodbyes. Mags and Dee slip into their ride and it sets off in the direction of home, right down the coast.

Perhaps it's not the worst outcome that Magnolia was un-impressed by the work thus far. Maybe it'll discourage her from going to the effort of visiting again in person. Because Maya said if the Exquisite Interiors network producers like our tape, they'll send a crew to shoot some more footage. And if the stars align and we get a real shot, the worst thing that could happen is Magnolia Bishop crashing the party.

CHAPTER 18

I ARRIVE BACK AT THE DANIEL House first thing Monday morning. Collin should be meeting us here in a few minutes to film some clips.

I speak the words out loud as I type them on my phone. "Do. You. Have. Any. Issues. With. Sawdust? Like. Asthma?" Inside, Sam's crew is busy at work bringing the floors back to life.

"I'm sure it'll be fine," Maya says, lugging the swatch books to the table we set up on the porch. It looks like something that was once used for beer pong, but at least it goes with the bare-bones vibe of the place. "By the way, did you have a chance to review the update for Jade and Douglas? They've got that board meeting on Wednesday, I think, and need to give a progress report and talk next steps."

"Oh, right. I think it's good to go. What would I do without you?"

Maya smirks. "Struggle for sure."

My phone dings with a reply, and I lift it immediately to read. "Oh *good*. Collin doesn't have asthma."

"Are you the boy's medical concierge now? Or did I miss something?" Fitz asks, gliding up the steps, a to-go coffee cup in hand.

"We didn't tell you about that guy we interviewed?" Maya asks.

"Oh, that's right." Fitz chuckles, then adjusts his neon-orange glasses frames. He glances out across the front yard, and he freezes when his eyes land on the gate. "I'm sorry, I know asthma is probably a deal-breaker, but *this* is who we landed on?"

I look to the gate where Collin stands, wrestling with the latch.

I glance over at Fitz. "I *promise* his videos are incredible. Don't judge a book by its cover."

Fitz leans closer. "Or a boy by his wardrobe, I presume?" He giggles.

"Stop!" I playfully swat Fitz's arm and then grab Maya to pull her alongside me as we descend the stairs.

"So is that really a wet suit he's wearing or am I hallucinating?" I whisper out of the corner of my mouth to Maya.

She shrugs as if to say, *We didn't talk dress code.* "I'm afraid so. But he was also the marine biology student, right?"

I don't have a chance to reply before we reach the gate, where Collin has finally found his way in.

"Hey, y'all." Collin shakes out his hair. "Is there a bathroom I can change in? Came straight from ocean lab." His cheeks turn pink.

"I'll show you," Maya says.

"Thanks." Collin slings a bag over his shoulder. "It was a tight turnaround, and I can promise this won't be a typical thing."

Fifteen minutes later, Maya, Fitz, and I stand in the kitchen with Collin. Sam's crew has momentarily stilled the floor sanders, and Collin is getting a slow-motion shot of the "before" floors.

"Sweet," he says. "Now, if you want to go ahead and activate that sander, I'll get an action shot."

Maya hands out masks and safety glasses, and once everyone's set, the crew gets to work. Collin dances gracefully around them holding out his phone, weaving like a well-trained ballerina. From a distance I imagine it looks silly, but the video credits he's already got to his name are not one bit of a joke.

Collin waves us out to the porch, and the sunshine highlights the sawdust on our clothes and nestled in our hair.

"Here, let me give you an idea." Collin taps a few buttons on his phone and twirls it around.

It's only a few seconds long, but the clip is already professional grade.

I smile. This is exactly what I wanted. It looks top-notch. Like something the best in town would have, and if there's anything we need to be picked, it's to be the very best.

"It's incredible," Maya says. "All right, so for the next thing I was thinking we could get some shots of Mack and Fitz looking through design swatches."

Collin nods. "Yeah, sure. Maya, you aren't a cohost?"

"Oh no, no." Maya holds out her hands. "I'm strictly behind the scenes. In fact, I wouldn't have even told them about the auditions had I thought they'd force me in front of a camera."

"I get it." Collin dusts off his iPhone with a special cloth. "I'm a behind-the-lens kind of guy myself."

Fitz loops his arm around my waist, and I point to him with my thumb. "This guy will by my cohost."

"Great. Well, let's get started," Collin says. "Honestly, we won't use all the clips in the end. It'll be edited down. But any time in front of the camera will help you loosen up and feel more natural."

I nod. "All righty."

Fitz starts warming up by singing arpeggios, and Collin quietly starts filming.

We spend the next hour shooting clips in different parts of the property, and just as Collin promised, I become more comfortable with each take. I talk about the colors for the home, neutral shades like white and cream with hints of blues and greens throughout. Fitz pokes fun at my seriousness, and the old stories tumble out:

the historical workout room we painstakingly created, the haunted properties, the time Fitz knocked over a tin of brown paint onto a priceless rug, then proceeded to blame it on the clients' dog having diarrhea. Fitz and I reminisce about our best projects, the stunning Charleston single houses, and our feature in *Southern Living*.

Collin gets a great shot of me pulling a sky-high weed, pretending to be Jack of the fairy-tale beanstalk. Fitz feigns using one of our fabric swatches as a hankie, much to my dismay. We relax, and soon it's as if the camera isn't even there.

I'm sweaty and bleary-eyed when Collin calls it a wrap.

"We've got some awesome stuff," Collin says. "You're both great on camera, especially together."

"We can't thank you enough," Maya says. "I'll be in touch about another filming day."

"Honestly, we might not need it," Collin says. "I watched some Exquisite Interiors audition tapes on YouTube, and if you give me access to your 'after' photos of other projects, I can lay them into the video. From what I saw in the examples, I've got what I need."

"Really? You're sure?" I ask. I'm feeling *anything* but sure. This felt mostly like goofing around with Fitz, and I want our tape to be excellent.

"Coco did say personality and charisma were the key in the video," Maya says. "We'll submit a formal portfolio as well, with our official before and after photos and features of our most impressive projects."

Collin nods. "We can always shoot more, but I have a good feeling you'll like what I can do with this."

I shrug. "That's reasonable. When do you think we can have it finished by?" I ask.

"Not long at all once I get all the photos," Collin says. "A week tops, depending on my schoolwork."

A thrill runs up my spine. It's all closer than I realized.

"Wonderful," I say.

And I mean it. Though talking design and having fun with Fitz on camera isn't specifically what I pictured for my career, at its heart it's everything I've wanted: something that would be mine. Something I earned through hard work that doesn't require me to be anything but my true self.

Maybe there will come a day when I don't have to suffer Magnolia's project management any longer.

CHAPTER 19

Fifteen Years Earlier

MAGNOLIA WAS ON THE PHONE harping at me about coming home for some event she was chairing that sounded like an exact carbon copy of all the other events I'd attended at the Beaufort Yacht Club.

"Sorry, Mama, but we've got workdays for the internship."

"And you can't spare a day to raise money for the designer doggy fundraiser event?"

"Why do designer dogs need help, anyway?" I asked.

"Well, there's this thing with overbreeding. The poor pugs can't breathe because their noses are collapsing. They require a nose job to correct their breathing. It's actually a massive issue."

I wanted to laugh, but it would only enrage my mother.

"Oh, someone's at the door. Got to go!" And I hung up.

I paused briefly to make sure she wouldn't call right back, and thankfully she didn't. It gave me just enough time to slip on a dress, fluff my curls, and spritz myself with a dash of perfume.

Then came the real knock.

I pulled the door open, grinning. "Well, if it isn't my summer lover," I said.

Lincoln rolled his eyes but smiled and took me in a hug. "You make me sound like a hunk of meat. Speaking of which—Chuck's for a burger? I'm starving."

"Let's do it," I said, and together we stepped out onto the street.

I was so comfortable squashed into Lincoln's side as we walked; I wouldn't have minded it taking longer. It had been a couple of weeks by now of us spending time together, and more often than not, he was the highlight of my day.

"How was work?" I asked.

Lincoln groaned. "Mind-numbing misery. Need I go on? The accountant, Marty, is super nice, but staring at numbers and spreadsheets all day drains the life out of me."

We reached the door to the dive bar and pulled it open. The music poured out as we stepped in and squeezed through the crowd to the bar.

I picked up a menu. "Why don't you quit?"

He rolled up his sleeves. "And just decide to live on the street and starve?"

"I mean, find a different job." I gave him a playful nudge in the ribs.

Lincoln leaped back and grabbed his side, laughing. "Hey now. It's not that easy."

We stopped to order burgers and then slipped into a sticky booth. Lincoln reached into his back pocket and pulled out a well-loved stack of Uno cards and brandished them in front of me. My favorite way to spar with him.

I waggled my eyebrows. "Deal 'em. But seriously, though, what's so bad about getting a new job? People do it all the time, and from what I can tell, you'd probably charm the socks off any interviewer." I batted my eyes.

"It's a great job," Lincoln said, cutting the deck and shuffling them together. "I'm making good money. Plus, I have benefits and a decent bonus once a year."

"But you hate it. I'm just saying, there's more than one way to make money."

A server came over and slid two beers in front of us as Lincoln dished out cards on each side of the table. He set the stack of remaining cards in the middle.

"No offense, but you just wouldn't get it," he said, fanning out the cards in his hand. "Not with how you grew up."

"Trust me," I said. "If there's anything my mother is concerned with, it's money."

"True," he said. "But you've also never had to worry about there being enough of it. My parents were *constantly* arguing about bills and rent. I can't count the number of times we moved because we were behind. When you're broke, nothing else in life works."

I knew Lincoln's childhood had been different from mine. Most people's were. But I was only then realizing how much it might've shaped him and the way he moved through the world, as if he was motivated by the fear of repeating his parents' mistakes.

I set down a red two. "I'm sorry. You're right. It's just—when you talked about the ghost tours and all the family fun, it seemed like y'all had it pretty good, like there weren't a ton of worries. You sounded like a family with a lot of love."

"We *did* have a lot of love. We weren't ever short on that," he said, setting down a red card. "But I wish my parents had made different choices—better ones. If my dad had just taken a *real* job, not gone full-time musician, we could've avoided so much of it. Plus, it wasn't only the job choice. He played at bars and clubs, and he drank too much, too often. He said it was part of the gig of being a tortured artist, and he didn't care how it affected the rest of us."

"I guess that makes sense," I said. The life Lincoln had set up for himself was exactly what he thought his father should've done.

The server returned with our burgers, and we set down the cards in exchange for the food.

"Honestly, I blame my dad's selfishness for my parents' divorce." Lincoln chewed. "The stress of not having the money they needed to raise two kids—at least from where I sat—was the reason they couldn't make it work. Me and my sister were elementary schoolers having to deal with the fallout of their messy divorce."

"Otherwise they were pretty good together?" I asked.

Lincoln nodded, and we ate in silence for a few moments. It was easy to ignore the very real fact that, being young and swept up in a fun summer romance, we needed more than just enjoying each other for a couple to make it in the world. Heavens, my own father hadn't even stuck around to see me born.

"And it's not like I'm not hopeful, you know," Lincoln said. He set down his burger and wiped his fingers with his napkin. "One day, I do think I'll make it as a real photographer, but you really have to get a shot out of a big studio in New York or LA. Even if I'd kill for that to be my real job, it doesn't mean I'm going to take the starving artist card when I've got chances like my current job."

"I bet you'll get that chance," I said. "And I think our parents—or lack thereof—have a bigger impact on us than we'd like sometimes. At least in your case, your dad's choices have made you thoughtful and responsible. You won't ever treat a partner or children so casually."

I dropped my gaze.

I'd imagined so often how my life might've been different had my father stuck around. Part of me suspected Magnolia had chased him off so she wouldn't have to split decisions with anyone else. The other part of me wondered if I just wasn't worth sticking around for, but much like Lincoln's situation, the ripples of my father's choices followed me everywhere I went, coloring the choices I made.

I felt the urge to tell Lincoln this, and maybe I would eventually, but the conversation was feeling too heavy. With every part of me that Lincoln accepted without pause, like my ghastly mother and my nonexistent father, it felt like a step too far down a path toward real feelings.

Instead of saying anything else, I picked up my burger and munched on a juicy bite.

Lincoln smiled gently. "Look at me putting a massive damper on things."

I grinned back. "Don't worry, I know it's a tactic—trying to make me let my guard down on the Uno game."

He shook his fist. "Drat!"

"*Drat?*" A laugh spilled out. Thankfully I'd swallowed my food. "What are you, some old-timey cartoon character?"

"I don't know. It was an approved 'diet' curse word we used as kids." Lincoln shrugged as he wiped his mouth with a napkin.

"Now those are some childhood stories I can get behind." I pushed my picked-over plate aside and picked up my cards. "Ready?"

We played in silence, pausing only for sips of beer. The game stayed even for a while, ebbing and flowing in favor of one, then the other. But soon, once my beer was almost drained, I found myself drawing and drawing until I held a good third of the deck in my hand. Lincoln sat with only a few cards.

What I hadn't mentioned yet was that while I adored winning, I was also the world's very worst loser. I usually explained it away as the product of my being an only child, but if I were to speak frankly, it had more to do with my personality—Lord help me.

My face slowly folded itself into a scowl I couldn't help.

"All right over there?" Lincoln sounded surprised.

"Just pulling more. Damn. Cards."

I wanted to be cool about this, to laugh it off, but it was so hard. And the more visibly upset I became (about an Uno card game in a dive bar, no less), the more frustrated I grew.

"Mack, we can stop." Lincoln reached out a hand, looking at me with kind eyes.

I shook my head. We continued to play, and to my delight, I avoided the draw pile for a few hands.

"Can it be?" Lincoln gasped. "Are things looking up for you, Miss Cinnamon Sugar?"

I finally laughed. "Luck of the draw, I guess."

I wondered which cards were in his hand and if he was letting me win. If he was, he didn't let on, and twenty minutes of whittling down my hand later, I won the game.

Lincoln was a gracious loser.

"Good game," he said.

I reached over and shook his hand, and neither of us let go, instead lowering them to the table.

The comfortable feeling of him made me want to stay.

I'd promised myself—and him—that this was just for the summer, but the more time I spent with Lincoln Kelly, the less sure I was that I wanted to set an expiration date.

"I'll walk you home?" Lincoln asked.

I nodded, and we gathered ourselves and left.

We walked the ten blocks toward my apartment, past the odd horse-drawn carriage stacked with high-endurance visitors. I could hear every drip of the courtyard fountains we passed in the silence between us.

We stopped at my apartment door.

"When can I see you again?" Lincoln asked.

I melted inside, and I shifted a hip closer to him. "Is tomorrow too soon?"

His brow crinkled. "Do I have you hooked, Ms. Bishop?"

I giggled. "At least for the summer."

He dipped his head to the tender side of my neck and set a warm kiss on my skin. "Tell me where and when, and I'll be there."

My insides whipped and churned, and I wanted to leap into his arms and stay there. I wanted to let go of the past, a past I didn't like and didn't want. I wanted to say that being with him for a few hours flew by like moments. That he zapped everything into high definition.

"I'm not ready for this to end," I told him.

Then I took his hand and pulled him, dragging him behind me into my apartment.

CHAPTER 20

Present Day

I HATE THAT I CHANGE MY outfit three times before Lincoln Kelly comes over for coffee later that week. It's the opposite of the nonchalant, unbothered look I'm trying for. In front of the mirror, I decide I look casual but put-together in jeans and a flowy pink blouse.

I'm not sure any combination of clothing will feel right for this strange reunion.

Honestly, I never planned to see Lincoln again after that night he announced he was leaving for New York. Even if I couldn't forget about him and that summer we spent together.

As I pad down the stairs, Hallie whips around the corner.

"I see Foster coming up the driveway!" she screeches. One might guess from her enthusiasm that they haven't seen each other in weeks, when in reality, they just spent a full day together at school.

The two of them have played together every day after school since Foster joined her class, and they've already developed a whole mythical world that resides in the grassy area between our homes.

I cross over to the door that Hallie's pulled open and lean on the frame, channeling *nonchalant*. My stomach clenches. When

Lincoln's face comes into view, it's as if the clock turns back a decade, and we're in that little apartment, him ardently promising me I could never understand.

Lincoln strides up and pauses awkwardly on the doorstep. "Thanks again for doing this."

I turn and wave them inside but not before I catch sight of him wiping sweaty palms on his shorts. It's a little bit of reassurance that this isn't easy for him either. "No worries," I say. "I figure with the friendship-on-fire situation between our kids, it's probably for the best anyway."

Hallie steps in front of me and knits her brow. "Foster and I are *not* on fire."

"You're right," I say to her. "Do you want to offer the cookies you picked out after school?"

Hallie darts to the pantry, Foster tagging behind, and after a minute they reappear, each with a cookie hanging from their mouth.

"Can we play outside?" Hallie asks through a mouthful of cookie.

"Hallie, what I meant was for you to offer the cookies to our guests first, maybe with a plate or something." I turn to look at Lincoln and throw my hands up. "But what do I know? Yes, you two have at it."

Hallie and Foster sprint out the back door.

I turn to Lincoln. "Can *I* offer you a cookie?" I grab the box from the pantry. "They're actually supergood. There's a cute little spot ten minutes down the road."

He smiles and takes one. "Thanks. And I don't need a plate—if you're ok with it."

I perch on a barstool. "I am very laid-back on formalities, thanks to being choked with them for the beginning of my life."

Lincoln grins. "Magnolia would faint, I'm sure, at the sight of the kids charging off with food hanging out of their mouths."

"Fortunately for Hallie, she's the apple of Magnolia's eye. Quite unlike her mother."

We chew quietly, sitting side by side in my kitchen, and the moment prickles. Lincoln has grown up; he's different than he was before, but he still knows those parts of me. He knows the scars of my past, and now he's seeing how they've played out down the road.

"I'm sorry," Lincoln says. "I shouldn't have said—"

"No, it's fine," I say.

"It's weird," he says. "I'm not sure if I'm supposed to pretend like you're a stranger when . . ."

He doesn't finish the sentence, but I wish he would. Who am I now, if not a stranger to him? I'm still grappling to answer the same about him for myself. Because back then, when he told me I wouldn't understand and when he told me he wasn't picking me and when he told me it was just supposed to be the summer, he knew every bit of me.

That summer got away from us, and I accidentally got lost in him.

Still, his words are tender, like he doesn't want to hurt me again.

I want out of this memory chamber, so I say, "We were kids back then. We did our best."

He nods, like it's enough acknowledgment to stay in the present. "And to think, what are the chances of us ending up as neighbors?"

"It's absurd." I laugh. "Coffee?"

He shakes his head. "Still can't have caffeine past noon or I'll be up until the wee hours."

"Oh, that's right," I say. "Well, there's sparkling water and sodas in the fridge."

Lincoln takes a water from the fridge and settles back on the barstool.

"So how come you guys moved back anyway?" I ask.

I did follow his career, at least what was shared online in articles and exhibit announcements, and he was right: It had been his chance to make a life out of the thing he loved most.

"It's home here," he says. "It was hard to raise a kid on my own in the city, and I do great work here."

I try to fight the memories of him snapping film of me wrapped in his sheets. *"Curls like a crown for my queen,"* he'd said. Me on the beach. I never liked pictures of myself until Lincoln Kelly took one.

"I get that," I say. "Well, you've found yourself a great school and a great neighborhood." I cross over to my basket of paperwork and grab the packet Becca gave me. "This is the new parent packet. Should we start?"

It feels like a relief to have the small talk over and done with and to move on into the neutral territory of school checklists and volunteer opportunities. But still, as I go over the parent portal and directions on logging in for the first time, I can't help that I'm itching to ask him other things. *How different are you now? Where's Foster's mother? Did you love her?* And when I get to the PTA meeting schedule, all the things I want to tell him keep popping up. *I'm really doing it with my own design firm. Magnolia's still a bear. I really did get what you meant back then.*

Once I'm through the packet, I give it an efficient pat and slide it over in front of him. "Any questions?"

Lincoln laughs. "Well, I guess that depends on what I'm allowed to ask."

I flush red and feel my cheeks and chest burn. "I think it'll take time to get used to this."

I tried for so long to hate Lincoln because he didn't choose me, but it never stuck. Sure, for moments at a time I could harness my inner Magnolia gene and detest his guts, but inevitably the good memories swam to the surface. When I gave up on hating him, I tried to forget him, but he visited me in my dreams and songs on the radio.

I don't think I'll ever be at peace with this man in front of me, but I also don't think I'd have become the same woman if I'd never met him.

"I agree," he says. "But I'll get out of your hair. I'm trying out a new meatloaf recipe tonight." He stands. "Let's hope it's not a disaster."

I follow him to the door. "There's always PB&J to fall back on."

When I open the door, the chatter and giggling between the kids floats over.

"Foster's welcome to stay and play as long as he wants," I say.

"Thanks." Lincoln steps out. "I might need it, considering it's my first try with meatloaf."

We wave goodbye, and Lincoln calls over to Foster to let him know he'll be at their house. I stand in the doorway and watch him go.

When my heart picks up and I feel the flutter in my belly, I remind myself, *He's just a neighbor.* In my mother's voice I tell myself, *Don't be a floozy who makes the same mistake twice.*

CHAPTER 21

THE NEXT MORNING I'M AT the kitchen sink, tap hissing, bubbles foaming, and sponge scrubbing, when my phone rattles on the island. It's Friday, one of our last before school lets out for the summer, so naturally it is also a teacher workday.

Hallie is on her way to the sink with her breakfast plate full of discards.

"Hal, could you grab that and see who it is, please?"

Hallie nods, sets down the plate, and grabs the phone. "It's Dad."

Inside I groan because I can guess what this is about.

"Pick it up for me, honey? I've got wet hands."

As Hallie greets her dad, I shut off the water and dry my hands on a striped dish towel.

"Ok, here she is," Hallie says and hands the phone to me.

"Thanks, Hal. Go brush your teeth and then you can play."

I lean back onto the counter and pull the phone to my ear. "Grady. What's up?"

"Mack, hey," he says. "So I've had a slight change in plans."

Since there's no school and I'm deep in work on the Daniel House, Grady agreed to have Hallie all day. His new employment arrangement with his father is supposed to be flexible.

"Okayyy." I stretch it out.

"I can't keep Hal today. Sorry," he says.

My palm flies up to cover my eyes, and I lower my voice. "Seriously, Grady? We've had this on the calendar for weeks now. I've got meetings scheduled."

"I hate to do it, Mack, but my dad's got some potential investors coming in, and he thinks it'd look good to present a father-son front."

"All right," I say, knowing he won't be talked out of it. I never have and now certainly never will outrank his father.

We hang up, and Hallie comes back into the kitchen, a comic book tucked under her arm.

"What did Dad want?" she asks.

I frown. "I'm sorry, honey, but he's had something come up with work with Grandpa. You'll have to tag along with me to the studio today. Maybe give your house a makeover?"

Hallie sighs and throws her arms out at her sides. "Ugh! I don't want to wait around all day and be *quiet*. We were supposed to go to the park and lunch, and now I'll have a boring mom day."

I count to three in my head and remind myself this isn't about me. She's hurt and feeling let down. Even if it stings a bit to be the boring parent, I'd rather be reliable and boring than fun and flaky.

"I wish you could've done your plans with Dad too," I say. "We'll leave in about fifteen minutes, so pack anything you want to bring."

We walk out of the house right on time, me with a thermos of coffee and my work bag and Hallie with her purple backpack slung over her shoulder. We circle the car to the trunk to load our bags, and a call comes from the driveway next door.

Foster stands there waving. "Can Hallie come over?"

"Have to go to my mom's work today, sorry!" Hallie yells back.

Foster pauses. "What if you stay with us? Let me ask my dad."

Before I can stop him, Foster runs inside, and Hallie and I stand there waiting.

Hallie crosses both sets of fingers, squeezes her eyes shut, and whispers, "Please, please, please." She opens her eyes and catches me smiling at her. "Sorry, Mama. You know I love the studio and being y'all's magpie, but sometimes I just want to do kid stuff."

I pull her into a side hug. "It's ok. I get it. It's also ok if you change your mind about design too. Just because I like something doesn't mean you can't prefer something else. It won't hurt my feelings or change any bit of the way I love you."

As soon as I found out I was pregnant, this was one thing I was determined to do differently than my mother: give Hallie complete freedom to love whatever—and whoever—tickled her fancy.

After a few minutes, Lincoln wanders out, his hair tousled, wearing sweats. It feels entirely like we're imposing on a slow, no-school morning.

"I'm sorry," I say to him. "I didn't mean for Foster to ask you to keep Hallie. The kids were just excited to see each other, and he ran off before I could stop him."

"I'm happy for her to stay with us—if you're ok with it, of course," he says. "Honestly, it'll be easy. These two can play for hours without a single problem. I might even be able to sneak in some editing work."

I agree. I'd thought the same more than once when Hallie got bored and lonely on her own.

"Only if you're sure," I say. "Here, let me give you my number. Call or text if *anything* comes up. Oh, and Hallie is allergic to eggs, so no omelets for lunch."

I walk over to share my number, and the smell of Lincoln sleepy and warm in the morning hits me; it sears unexpectedly.

"Ok, so what about bread, like something it's baked into?" Lincoln asks, suddenly serious. "Or cookies, crackers, that kind of stuff."

"That's all fine. Just no plain eggs—kinda weird, I know."

"I know which foods I can't have!" Hallie calls over. "And where the EpiPen is at home."

"We shouldn't need that," I say, then turn to Lincoln. "Do you have Benadryl? It's ten milliliters if she needs it, and call me."

"We've definitely got some," Lincoln says.

"I guess I should also ask if you're comfortable with that?" I laugh self-consciously.

Lincoln nods intently. "Of course. I would just never forgive myself if I made a mistake with her."

My heart lurches in a fluttery way.

"You're a lifesaver," I say and turn and march back to my car with discreet, slow breaths.

I'll get used to this, I tell myself.

I crank the car and go.

Fitz and Maya are already assembled when I walk into the studio.

"You made it," Maya says. "We got bagels and spreads from the shop down the street."

"Not all heroes wear capes, and Maya, you are that come to life today." I flop onto the sofa—computer bag, sunglasses, phone, and all.

"And to what do we owe these dramatics this morning?" Fitz swivels his computer chair and looks over his lime-green glasses frames. "This is quite the departure from your usual OCD entrance routine."

I remove the sunglasses from my face. "I'll have you know that my neurotic settling of personal items into their correct place is the aftermath of being raised by my mother. And second, what happened this morning has kind of sent me into a small, unreasonable, probably idiotic tizzy."

"Get her a bagel, honey," Fitz says to Maya, getting to his feet and trotting to the sofa. "Next we'll have to try mouth-to-mouth."

I laugh. "Oh stop. I'm just being sassy, and I'm good on the bagel front."

"That's Magnolia speaking," Fitz whispers behind his hand.

"It's my new neighbor. Lincoln Kelly moved in next door, and he's got Hallie today."

Fitz leans down, staring at me. "Did you say Lincoln Kelly as in *the* Lincoln Kelly, and if you did, I might just wring your neck for holding out on me."

I grin. "He's living next door."

Fitz's face turns red, then some odd shade of purple.

"*Breathe*, Fitzy," I say. "I won't be responsible for your untimely death."

He sputters. "What—? Who—? Where—? You'd best fill me in from the word *go*."

I pull in a slow, deep breath and put on my best version of calm. "It shocked me, too, but that house went up for sale, and as luck would have it, he bought it. He's got a son, seven like Hallie, and naturally they're in the same class and have formed a special friendship—"

"Hopefully more platonic than the *special friendship* you had with the child's father."

I shoot Fitz a half-hearted glare.

Fitz wasn't ever friends with Lincoln. They came into my life around the same time—even if only one stuck. Still, I spilled my guts to him back then about Lincoln. My giddy excitement, date play-by-plays, and of course my worries about the pairing. Fitz was a new friend, but I trusted him like I'd known him for years.

"You'll need to catch me up because I'm completely in the dark," Maya says.

I wrangle my composure enough to fill them in on the details of Lincoln's return to town, and to give Maya an overview of the history.

"She's playing it *way* down," Fitz says to Maya. "Girl was *devastated* when he left. She swanned about all summer calling him her *fling*, and then he up and left—like a fling just might do—and she got her heart broken over it."

I wave him off. "Yes, thank you. I don't need my personal mistakes thrown in my face like I'm not already well aware of them. I'm probably scaring Maya."

Maya laughs. "It's ok. Honestly it sounds interesting, like a nice love story maybe."

I smile. "It wasn't nice at the time, but yes, I was in love."

My insides warm, and it feels like a muscle I haven't exercised in a while. I did love Grady, but *this* feeling? It's one I've only ever gotten about Lincoln Kelly.

But all of this is far too real and far too personal to be hashing out at work, especially when I don't know who else might come in today.

"Maya," I say, "want to check in on the audition tape?" I drag myself over to our conference table.

Fitz drops into the seat beside me. "We're coming back to this," he says.

Maya opens her computer and navigates to email. "Yes, I have the video from Collin—I just didn't watch it yet. I figured it'd be fun to watch together." She clicks and adjusts the screen. "The portfolio's ready, and I let Coco at Exquisite Interiors know that we're submitting today."

Fitz claps, and I shiver with excitement.

"Thank you, Maya," I say. "None of this would even be a chance without you."

Maya smiles and clicks Play on the clip.

The screen springs to life, and our smiles fall, our brows creasing. The images are garbled, and the audio jolts, then flows in a robotic frenzy.

"Whoa," Maya says. "Let's try that again."

She closes and reopens the video file, then hits Play again.

It's the same muddy mess.

"Are you connected to the right internet network?" I ask.

Maya looks. "Yup. Everything's good. I'm loading other sites . . . Let me try YouTube." She clicks around. "I'm able to watch videos there."

"What about on a phone?" I ask. "That's how he records it."

"Let me try," Maya says, taking her phone from her bag. After a few seconds she says, "Ugh, it's the same disaster."

"We'll have to call the kid, get him to resend it," Fitz says.

The hair on the back of my neck stands up. "I'm sure it's an easy fix."

I'm lying. All my worries about the college student with a phone who only needs a single day's worth of tape stream back. Did we trust the wrong guy?

"I'm sure you're right," Maya says. "Let me call him. I'm sure this will be simple."

Maya stands and paces as she waits for the phone to ring. It rings and rings. She calls again. No answer.

"Maybe we email him and come back to it Monday?" I ask.

"I will," Maya says. "Maybe a social media DM."

"Yeah, I'd check his accounts," Fitz says.

"I'll do it," I say.

I open Instagram on my phone and type in CC Video. Collin's page pops right up. There's a new post, a small white square with black text:

> Sorry, folks, Collin's phone took a swim at the marine
> lab. Getting a replacement soon. Message me here
> for now. Peace.

I groan. "Collin isn't answering his phone because it's swimming in the ocean somewhere."

"Hmm. Well, it sounds like this is about to get interesting," Fitz says.

CHAPTER 22

Fifteen Years Earlier

I N A FLURRY OF EXAMS, classes had finally wrapped for my junior year, and Magnolia had made the trip to Charleston. Since I wouldn't be packing up and heading home for the summer like I'd done the past two years, Mother decided to come to me for a weekend visit.

Kendra was staying for the summer, too, since she'd landed a waitress job at a restaurant known for big tips from the vacation crowd, so she tagged along with us for the visit. I'd begged and pleaded with her not to leave me alone with the Dragon, and ultimately I convinced her with the promise of a few above-cafeteria-grade meals.

We took the College of Charleston bus over to the Halstead Gallery.

"Am I to expect amateur student art?" Magnolia asked, stepping off the bus and away from the wavy heat rising from it.

"No, it's legit," Kendra said. "They spotlight local artists and have a special partnership with the college."

Lincoln entered his photography routinely and had even been lucky enough to have a few pieces accepted. I guess luck wasn't actually to blame; his work was impressive in its own right.

I grabbed the door and pulled it open, and soon we were inside wrapped in air-conditioned quiet.

A few other families meandered through the exhibitions in order. We started with student work, oils and acrylics mostly, then continued into the local artists' section. Finally, we walked through the photography collection.

Kendra perked up and waved me over, her eyes bulging. "This is Lincoln's," she said in a record-breakingly loud whisper. "His last name is Kelly?"

As I looked it over, I couldn't help the smile that crept across my face. "Little rascal didn't tell me he had anything up right now."

"Modest or what?" Kendra asked. "Your lover is more accomplished than he lets on."

"Can we not use the word *lover*? It gives me the heebie-jeebies." I shuddered.

"You're the one who refuses to call him your boyfriend," Kendra said. "I can't believe he didn't tell you. Maybe he's also secretly a European prince or something and is waiting to drop the news until he knows you're in it for the right reasons."

I thwack her playfully in the belly, and a laugh pops out.

"I didn't tell him we were coming here," I said. "Why would I, because who knew if Magnolia would bite when I suggested it?"

The sound of a familiar throat clearing resounded behind me. "Referring to me as if I'm a fish when I came all this way to visit you is quite crass—no, Magnolia?"

I blushed furiously, from my toes to my scalp. "I'm so sorry, Mama." I spun in place. "I should've chosen better language, you're right. I meant to say that I didn't know if a visit here would be to your taste or not."

Magnolia pushed past me to eye the photo. "Quite right, child.

And you wouldn't be entirely off base in that suggestion. But this one? It's not as bad as the rest."

Kendra smiled and raised her brows, knowing a Magnolia compliment when she heard one. I silently shook my head and tried to signal her to back off with a hand flap.

"So when do I meet him?" Magnolia's eyes settled on me, heavy like she'd gotten lead pupils. "I presume I should be acquainted with a *lover* of yours, Magnolia."

A wave could've run over me, and I'm not sure I would've swum toward the surface for the weight of my mortification. She knew how to bury the best of us with no more than a comment, but especially me.

"Well." I swallowed hard. "I guess that could be arranged."

Later that afternoon I went to the photography lab to meet Lincoln. I knocked on the door, and he was waiting there to open it for me.

"Quite the security clearance required to get in here, huh?" I laughed and pecked him on the cheek.

"The professor turns a blind eye to me using the space as a nonstudent. It's the least I can do to make sure no trouble sneaks in." He pulled me into a hug from my waist and dotted kisses along my neck. "But then again, you've been known to cause quite a stir yourself."

I laughed and extricated myself from his grip. "Not so fast," I said. "I came here on business."

Lincoln cocked his head. "Very professional."

"Eh, nope." I hopped up and sat on the countertop. "This is personal business."

Lincoln leaned back, crossed his arms, and waited for me to go on. He still wore a button-up and slacks from work. He was even still wearing the loafers he usually couldn't wait to rip off every day. The clothes looked so different on him here, surrounded by his art, like a costume layered on top of the real him.

"Tell me, sweetheart," he said.

"Magnolia is in town." I paused because I wasn't certain about the next part. I needed to ask him to do this, and I needed to sound confident.

"I know. I wasn't expecting to see you," he said. "Figured she'd have you tied up every minute."

"She wants to meet you," I said.

Lincoln pulled himself upright, his arms falling to his sides. "No way."

I sighed. "She saw your art at the Halstead Gallery—which I didn't realize would even be there." He sheepishly rubbed his hair. "And it was the only piece she didn't have anything negative to say about."

"I'm supposed to take that as a compliment, right?" Lincoln asked. "Are you sure? I thought I was far from your mother's type."

"I know it wasn't the plan to do the formalities, and it's still our special summer thing, but I think you can still meet my mother and it'll be fine," I said, staring at the countertop as I picked at the remnants of a sticker.

"So it's more of an informal, fly-by thing?" Lincoln said.

"We could call it that," I said. "Plus, I probably exaggerate a bit about how awful she is. Can you do dinner tomorrow? It's her last day in town."

Lincoln strode over and pulled me into his arms. "Have to say I'm surprised, but if you want to, I'm up for it. I guess, what's the worst that could happen?"

I looked up at him, pushed a smile across my face, and nodded. "Yeah, you're right. What's the worst that could happen?"

"So is you bringing guys to meet her a regular thing?" Lincoln grinned.

"Hardly," I scoffed. "She knew my high school boyfriend, Grady, since she's best friends with his mom and we were in diapers together. Delta, his mom, is actually very sweet, but Grady is . . . less sweet."

"Sounds like I'm starting out on solid footing."

I pecked his lips. "Agreed. I have all sorts of war stories in that category, but I'll dish the rest later."

"So are you sticking around here in photo land?" Lincoln asked. "Because if you are, I'm going to put you to work."

I pulled away. "I wish. I've got to change and then meet Magnolia for dinner. I'll call you later with details for tomorrow?"

"Sure thing," Lincoln said. "I'll be here late."

I wandered over to the negatives strung up on my way toward the door. "What are you working on anyway?"

"Marcus Wilson Studio—an application for a big-time New York photography residency."

"That's right. The stuff dreams are made of." I smiled at him.

Lincoln had told me about these apprenticeships a few times now. Mostly, successful photographers in New York or LA would open spots in their studios to up-and-coming photographers. The apprentices would work in the studio, learn from the seasoned professionals, and have an opportunity to break out their own work.

"It's a long shot, but it wouldn't be fair to myself not to try," Lincoln said.

"I'm so proud of my hottie photographer," I said and blew him a kiss on my way out.

These applications were like meditations on the importance of his work to him, but like he assured me, the chances of landing a spot were slim, like drawing a winning lottery ticket. I wouldn't be losing him to the big-city life anytime soon.

"*Summer* hottie," Lincoln said. "Don't you forget."

I laughed and let the door click shut behind me. It was fun, our little shared joke, but with every passing mention, it had begun to grate on me. Because even if I didn't say it out loud, inside I couldn't promise myself my feelings for Lincoln Kelly would fade with the summer sun. I thought that maybe he felt the same, that we could become more.

At least for now we'd enjoy it, but come the end of summer, I wasn't sure he'd be so easy to quit.

CHAPTER 23

Present Day

IT'S ALMOST LUNCHTIME WHEN I arrive at the studio the next Monday. I drop into my chair, my entire body burning and my feet screaming. I kick off my shoes under the desk and feel them slide against the beginnings of blisters on my heels.

"Fitz, please, for the love of all things good in this world, do not let me wear these shoes again." I groan as I massage the soles of my feet.

He chuckles. "It's the price you pay for looking as fabulous as you do."

"Is that Fitz or Magnolia sitting over there?" I open my water bottle and drink generously.

"Fighting words, my friend." Fitz looks over at me. "I am many things, but a dragon I am not."

"Comment retracted."

Before I tore up my feet, I spent most of the morning over on Bull Street, facilitating the fix on Ms. Dorothy Culver's pocket doors. She's an A-list client whose property has already starred in home-and-garden programming half a dozen times. *Enviable* is the only word for it.

Dorothy, as she insists I call her, dresses in elaborate caftans, never answers the door without a swipe of lipstick, and refuses to let a soul leave before they've accepted something to eat or drink (not entirely unlike my Hallie). Dorothy lost her husband several years back, and despite her children's efforts to have her move out of the high-maintenance bungalow, she is adamant that she will be taken out of the home on a stretcher if it's the last thing she does.

I glance over at Hallie's empty perch. "I guess Grady didn't bring Hal by yet?"

Fitz shakes his head. "No magpie landings."

I shoot off a quick text, and Grady's reply comes back immediately. Got caught up. Can have the sitter drop her at your house after dinner?

I frown at the screen, then slap my phone down a little too hard on my desktop. It'd be one thing if Grady himself planned to spend the extra time with Hallie, but by the sounds of it, a sitter is getting paid to do that.

Fitz eyes my mini tantrum and, perhaps in an effort to nudge me past it, asks, "What's the latest from Collin and the tape? Did we hear anything?"

I pull in a deep breath and refocus. "His phone is basically a shipwreck, but like the amazing technology wiz he is, he had everything backed up on the cloud. He's going to send the file today."

Maya walks in and drops her bag on her desk. "Is that Collin you're talking about?" she asks. "I just came from the Daniel House, and the floors are looking amazing. We'll have to stay off them for a while to let them dry, but I've got outside work queued up in the meantime."

Maya's phone rattles, and she lifts it to read a text. "That's Collin. He says to check our inboxes."

Fitz grabs his laptop and carries it to the meeting table. "Let's try this again."

"I hope your computer has better luck," Maya says.

I slide onto the bench seat beside Fitz, while Maya stands behind us. He opens the video file, and this time when he hits Play, the clip rolls.

Collin has added a cute introduction song with Bishop Builds superimposed on an aerial image of Charleston. It fades into a cut of me describing my design career. *"This has always been the thing I wanted most out of my life, to breathe love into these old homes and keep them kicking."* I'd forgotten he asked us these questions right off the bat. The tape cuts to a shot of Fitz and me arranging material selections and then to Sam's crew sanding floors. I'm stunned by how professional he's made us look when it felt like playing pretend.

Fitz's voice comes over a montage of completed projects. *"I'm here to push Mack's designs a pinch bolder—and she reels me in. Oh, and I'm the studio comedian—or jester, according to some."*

I'm close to tears when the camera zooms out on me walking arm in arm with Fitz up the brick path to the Daniel House, then cuts to a whole city view again before fading out.

"It's better than I ever imagined," I say.

"How did he get those aerial shots?" Fitz lets out a whistle. "Better yet, how much did that boy charge?"

"A drone. And not enough for *that*," Maya says. "We're sending a gift—a nice one. But first, I'm getting that to Coco."

I stand up, and I feel like I'm floating. I never imagined feeling so proud of a tape we did with such a quick turnaround. Granted, much of the success was Collin's, clipping the most charming sound bites and selecting the best images, but at the core, it was us and our work.

"I have to tell y'all, I was not convinced about this at the beginning," Fitz says. "Not that I wasn't eager to take a spin in front of the camera. But that really does look like something I would watch on TV."

"Same," I say. "Except I was less convinced of the camera part until I tried it."

Maya's phone emits the swooshing sound of an email sent. "I can't wait to hear back. I'm also texting Coco to let her know she's got it."

We sit there grinning at each other for a while before we get up and head back to our desks. We work quietly, exchanging task-related comments back and forth, and after a while Maya gathers her things and leaves.

I grab a sparkling water and a granola bar from the kitchen, and on my way back, I drop down in an open chair beside Fitz.

"Any good stories lately?" I ask, munching and hoping for a good distraction.

He eyes me. "You're bored."

"I have to finish that quote for the house on Thomas Street before I leave, but I need a brain break," I say. "Plus, I can't stop thinking about the tape."

Fitz reaches over and pats my knee. "I love you, doll, but I'm trying to wrap up so I can dip out early and meet my man to go look at some furniture for his mom's place."

"Eh, you'll be fine," I say. "It's not even noon yet. Anyway, it's been forever since I've seen Henry. How are y'all?"

"Very happy, no complaints." Fitz refocuses on the papers in front of him.

"Mm-hmm," I hum back at him. "And?"

He gives me a look that says *zero fun.* "I'm sorry, are you trying to dish on my love life when your college sweetheart just moved in next door to you? I think that's where the actual gold mine is."

I pout. "I don't know, I was just wondering about a *wedding* or something of the like because I saw this Farm Rio dress that's to die for, but I need somewhere to wear it."

"You can take the girl away from Magnolia, but you can't take the expensive taste out of the girl." Fitz doesn't make eye contact.

He's right. For better or worse, I haven't entirely shaken the fashion love my mother trained up in me.

"Yes or no: Should I buy the dress for a next summer—or spring—wedding?" I know I'm being a pain in the rear, but Fitz does the same to me. Not to mention, he can hold his own.

"It's not that simple," he says.

"Sure thing," I say through a mouthful of granola bar, a thoroughly Magnolia-*un*approved move.

"It's different."

"Ok, tell me how," I say.

Fitz turns, his face serious, a look he rarely wears. "For me and Henry, there's a lot at stake."

I watch him compose his thoughts, and I slow my chewing, realizing I'm probably putting my foot in it in a way *this* Magnolia is not ok with.

"I'll tell you—though this isn't knowledge for public consumption," Fitz says. "My mother and father, as near to the grave as they are, have told me loud and clear that if I were to publicly marry Henry—or any man, for that matter—they would cut me off from the family. No holidays, no inheritance, not so much as a part-time gig cleaning the office at Fitzgerald's."

His usual sparkle is gone. His pizzazz too. They're his armor, which my insistence has ripped aside. I'm tacky as all hell.

"Henry, of course, has said we'd wait until they're gone, as morbid as it sounds. But I've been pushing. I don't want him to think he's my second choice."

"And without the family support?"

"You know the maintenance on historic homes like ours is pricey. We could probably tighten things to keep it, but the rest of our lifestyle would shrink if not completely disappear. And I'd need to figure out a way to curb my trips to Saks. Certainly, they'd need to disavail me of the personal shopper I text on the regular." Fitz looks away. "But I love the man. More than either of my shriveled-up parents."

"I'm so sorry, Fitz." The words aren't enough. I regret all the times I've poked at him about cold feet or reluctance to commit. I really didn't get it.

"How were you to know? I hide it fairly well." He works up a smile. "Now, I don't want your pity. But do remember the privileges you have; the freedom is precious."

I nod, then reach over and squeeze his hand. "I'm sorry, and I'm going to leave you alone now. So you can make it to Henry on time."

I cross the room and sit down at my desk, feeling like a puppy with her tail between her legs.

It's as if Fitz can tell because he looks up and flashes me a smile. "I still love you, Magnolia Junior," he says. "I just might love you a little less if you make me late for my furniture appointment."

CHAPTER 24

IT'S HAPPENING.

Two days after Coco at Exquisite Interiors received our tape, she called to ask if their crew could come shoot some footage, and a week later, here we stand at the Daniel House, cameras at the ready. It's not a deal, but it's certainly a step in the right direction. We arrived first thing this morning, me dressed in a paisley maxi dress and Fitz in a slate-blue blazer. It's now early afternoon, and we're comfortable with the small crew that surrounds us with their cameras and boom mics and a few light reflectors.

"I'd love to get a shot of you opening the front door." Erica is our cameraperson-slash-director for the day. She also has a sound operator, Lucas, who moves about nearly silently, and a few other crew members overseeing lighting.

Fitz and I nod and file into place.

"Action," Erica calls out.

I lean and unlatch the door, allowing it to swing open.

Erica carries the camera in on a perfect glide, then yells, "Cut!"

"The floors are all right to walk on, but if possible we'd like to keep traffic light on them for the next few days," I say. "They're freshly restained. We've been working on the back patio if you'd like us to talk through that."

"That's perfect," Erica says. "Like we discussed, this is truly just to get a sense of your personalities and how you work in front of the camera. Your portfolio knocked it out of the park, so we're already convinced of the actual design acumen. Plus, these historic builds? To die for. Why don't you start introducing the patio work while we walk back?"

We smile and head to the back.

Erica rolls the tape.

"We've actually got some of our crew working back here right now. We're removing the old decking that was thrown on in the late '80s." I pull a face. "Needless to say, it did not complement the historical facade, and we aren't certain it was engineered correctly—even as low to the ground as it is, we don't want any-one stepping through."

As we approach, the hammering and cracking and snapping grow louder, and above the racket, voices call out to one another.

I wave to our lead contractor, Mateo, and he seems relieved to see me.

He eyes the camera. "Is now an ok time?"

"Well, that depends on if you're all right with potentially show-ing up on reality TV," I say.

Mateo chuckles. "Well, my wife loves these shows, so she'd think I'm cool again. For me, I've had enough home construction by the end of my real day. I don't need to watch it."

Erica throws a thumbs-up for us to go on, and Lucas nods like we're hitting our stride.

"Show me what you've got," I say to Mateo.

"Well, let the record show: You asked. Because you're not going to love this news," Mateo says.

He climbs over the rubble and grabs a loose plank of wood from the partially deconstructed deck. He runs his fingers over a section. "Here. You see that?"

I groan. "I see it, and I know what it is."

Fitz speaks up from over my shoulder. "Let me guess. Termites?"

Mateo nods and turns to the camera, pointing to a crawling bug. "So what this—live termites—means is we'll have to tent the house and fumigate to make sure everything is killed off."

I turn to Fitz. "Do we have any tequila, because this is not what I was expecting out of today."

"Honey, we don't even have a cabinet or a single glass here," Fitz says. "Not that that's stopped you before."

I laugh. "Fine, I'll take you making me laugh. Gosh, what'll that do to our timeline?"

"It'll be two days we can't work," Mateo says. "The guys can come tomorrow and tent, if you're ok with it."

"Might not be the worst timing with needing the floors to cure," Fitz says.

"Fair enough," I say. "Consider that a green light on the tent. Will you keep me updated?"

"Sure thing," Mateo says.

"Cut!" Erica yells and lowers the camera. "Ok, did you guys stage that or what?"

We shake our heads in unison.

"Honestly, if I had to make up a problem, termites would be one of my last choices," I say.

"It's quite the expense," Fitz adds.

Erica beams. "It may be bad news for the project, but it's great news for the footage. You guys are naturals, and the comfort and candor between everyone—it's perfection!"

I'm distracted by the sound of footsteps on the porch. No one is inside working because of the floors, and my instincts say I need to stop anyone from crossing inside without shoe covers in place.

"I think someone's here," I say. "Will you excuse me?"

I don't make it to the porch before the footsteps stop, and a familiar figure rounds the corner of the house, teetering on heels toward the backyard. It's Magnolia in a skirt suit, tweed in blue to match Fitz. It's St. John; I can tell even from here.

She's a fashion warhorse.

I stop and wait for her to arrive from across the shabby side yard.

"What are you doing here?" I ask. "You told me you couldn't make it."

Hallie is playing Little Red Riding Hood in her year-end school production. She invited her grandparents, but Magnolia sent her regrets. Delta and Ned accepted immediately.

"Delta swayed me," Magnolia said. "She was right that I could have someone cover for me at the club and that I shouldn't miss my granddaughter's star role. And quite frankly, we've been trying to save the whales since the '80s. I think it's about time they carried a bit of their own weight." She removes her sunglasses slowly and sets a steely look on me. "But it seems if the cat's away . . . You're up to something." Her words stop as her eyes land on the small camera crew.

"I'm here on my worksite," I say, doing my best to calm the flurry of panic inside. "Getting work done."

"Funny. It's sort of my worksite, too, isn't it?" Magnolia wobbles in place on the soft ground. "Since you needed a hand up, some good work, and I was here to help."

Magnolia is still quick. She would've made a good politician if she were more likable and less prone to insults. She knows how to use her position of power to diminish me; we've done this dance a million times before, and I go along with it. She makes me feel small so she can be big, so she can hold on to me.

And I hate that I play into it because of the unsaid thing that follows us around: she's the only family I've got.

Of course, besides Hallie, who I sometimes wonder if I made out of sheer will to extend my family beyond this woman in front of me.

"Yes, you gave us the work, and we're doing it well," I say.

"I'm not here to challenge that—not now that you took a couple of my design suggestions into account."

Or so she thinks.

"But I need a full explanation as to why there are people here filming y'all all dressed up on the property I've been tasked with looking over. The Carolina board hasn't given permission for any of this—"

I step up to her and take her hands in mine. "Please, Mama," I say, feeling like I'm a teenager again. All the years of strength and independence I've drummed up by doing things my way begin to falter. "I can explain, but let's not blow this up."

Her face purses as she looks at me, considering. "Fine, but this isn't the end of it."

My phone rattles in my pocket, and it's a number I don't recognize. Still, Hallie's not with me, so I answer.

The voice on the other end is young and perky and decidedly panicked. "Ms. Suffolk, oh my god, I'm so glad you picked up! Grady's not answering."

"I'm sorry, who is this?"

"I'm Lacey, Hallie's babysitter. We were having dinner, and she asked to try some of my fried rice, and I let her, and she didn't see the eggs, and I didn't know she was allergic, and I have no idea what to do."

"How much did she have?"

"Only a tiny bite, but I saw her scratching, and now she's got a nasty rash all over her back."

I could kill Grady. The very first thing we tell sitters is about Hallie's egg allergy. Fortunately, if it was really only a bite, it's manageable.

"Do you know where he keeps the medication? She needs Benadryl."

"No, ma'am, but I'll look." Her voice shifts. "Hallie, do you know where your dad keeps the medicine?" There are footsteps, then shuffling and rattles.

"I'm coming," I say. "I keep Benadryl in my car for occasions like this. Give me fifteen."

CHAPTER 25

I'M SPEEDING AS RESPONSIBLY AS possible to Grady's place, and Magnolia is sitting in the passenger seat. In my distraction, I give her the rundown about Exquisite Interiors.

"But why on earth would you want to be on reality television? It's a bit tacky, no? That's daytime talk shows, and by God, I would rather shrivel up than embarrass myself like that."

I blow through a barely-still-yellow light. "That's not what Exquisite Interiors is."

Magnolia sighs. "So what is it? You know I don't watch the crap."

"They follow the work and produce a show that's interesting to viewers—showing the design process and the build, the challenges, us addressing issues, a gorgeous outcome."

"So they want to make y'all look like idiots for not getting it right the first time?" she asks.

I sigh. "Maybe just watch an episode, and you'll get it. But I'm doing this. I want something of my own."

"And the whole studio isn't your own?" Magnolia asks. "I just simply can't see how showing all your mistakes on television is the way to achieve any sort of success at all. Heavens, it's all *a bit much*."

If I wasn't so panicked I would laugh, because my mother is not, and will not ever, not in my lifetime or any alternate universe, be in a position to call anything *a bit much*. She is *a bit much* come to life.

"It doesn't feel like my own when we're relying on work funneled from your committee," I say. I pull out of a slow lane and make it a few cars farther.

"What's the point of being from a wealthy family if you can't benefit from a little nepotism here and there?" Magnolia mutters.

"I want to earn it, not inherit it," I say.

"You don't want *me* involved," Magnolia says. "Which is quite obvious, considering the measures you're now willing to go to."

"*No*, that's not it." I turn onto Grady's street. "You and Hallie are the only family I've got." I say it even though I hate the reminder. "I want to make something of my own, not cut you off."

I pull into the driveway and see Grady's taillights up ahead.

"But a show is so far from the quiet prestige of the city fellowship we almost had," Magnolia says.

Her casual use of *we* jabs me like a bee sting, but I let it go.

"Maybe it seems desperate and loud to your crowd, Mother, but not to me." I hop out of the car and slam the door behind me as Magnolia follows suit. "And if it is desperate and loud, then maybe I am too."

Magnolia gasps.

I take off to the carriage house just as Grady jumps out of his car. We jockey to the door as if it's the last leg in a race around the world.

"I've got this," he tells me.

"Fat chance." I elbow past him, flashing the children's Benadryl at eye level.

We tumble into the apartment and right to Hallie, Magnolia lagging behind. Hallie looks fine, save a few red pocks on her face, sitting there watching home renovation shows.

Lacey, on the other hand, is in tears.

"I'm so sorry," she says. "I feel terrible."

I reach out and squeeze her hand. "It's not your fault. Grady should've told you about the egg allergy and also what to do if she gets some accidentally."

I rip the medication bottle from the packaging and pour a pre-memorized dose. I glide over to Hallie and hand off the medication cup. "Your drink, madam."

She grins at me and downs the dose in a single shot.

I run a gentle hand over her forehead. "How're you feeling, birdie?"

Magnolia rushes up behind the sofa. "My sweet grandbaby, you appear to be breathing."

"Just a little itchy." Hallie looks up, the beginning of tears in her eyes. "I can still do the play tonight, right? I've practiced so long for it."

Grady stands off to the side looking sheepish and pays Lacey for her babysitting hours. I drop down beside Hallie and bundle her into my arms, squeezing her tight. Yes, she's fine, and yes, this really should be a small deal, but it also didn't have to happen, and it could've been much worse—if the sitter hadn't been so attentive, if neither of us had picked up, if Grady had let her wander into a worse kind of danger.

"If you're feeling up to it," I say. "The medicine usually works fast."

Magnolia drops down on Hallie's other side and gently squeezes her knee. "I'm not sure anyone needs to be eating fried rice at two in the afternoon, but I guess that's a college student for you."

I lean farther into my Hallie and run my fingers through her hair just like she loved when she was a toddler.

"Jeez, Mom." Hallie wriggles free of my grip.

"It just feels like I haven't seen you in weeks," I say.

She grins, and I notice one more gap.

"Another?"

Hallie nods proudly. "Yup. And the tooth fairy in Dad's neighborhood brings *twenty whole dollars* per tooth! Can you believe it?"

I shake my head. "Wow. No. I *cannot* believe it." Not one damn bit. "Five more minutes, and then we're heading home for a rest before call time."

"It's fine," Hallie says, getting up and shuffling toward her room. "I've seen this one. They turn the barn into an event place, and then the designer gets proposed to. If you ask me, she didn't seem too surprised."

I look over my shoulder at a shamefaced Grady.

"I can't believe him," I mutter to Magnolia, only because she's here and not because I expect her to take my side.

She purses her lips. "Between you and me, child, his intelligence was never top-notch. Which is a great shame considering the stock he comes from."

Magnolia stands and marches over to Grady, who waits, prickling, at his kitchen counter. "You'd best keep your sitters informed."

Grady nods. "It was an innocent mistake."

"There's not a thing innocent about putting our Hallie in harm's way," Magnolia says. "I trust you'll tell your mother about this because I'd rather not have to relive it at our post-theater dinner."

Hallie's voice floats out from her room. "Almost done, Mom!"

I pull myself up from the sofa and it feels like a treat not having to tell Grady off. Usually, my mother would take his side—particularly regarding things to do with the breakdown of our marriage—but Hallie reconfigures this alliance.

"I'll be waiting in the car." Magnolia exits with a tired sigh.

Grady levels his gaze at me. "What? I mess up *once*, and you think you're winning?"

I raise my hands. "What on earth about this situation makes you think I'm *winning*?"

"Somehow you always end up looking like the good parent."

Whenever this came up in the past (which wasn't infrequently), I always soothed him, made promises about his strengths as a parent. I promised him we were a team who picked up each other's slack. But now? That's no longer my job. He can have himself a pity party and clean up after it as well.

"I'm sorry you feel that way."

Grady rolls his eyes. "*So* high and mighty."

"Says the guy paying twenty bucks a tooth."

Hallie emerges from her room, backpack in tow, and goes to her father for a hug. I afford her just enough time for a quick goodbye with the terrible man, then carry her off to the car.

CHAPTER 26

Fifteen Years Earlier

I PULLED LINCOLN'S TIE TAUT AND straight, then patted him on the chest. "Mama won't know what hit her," I said.

After Lincoln agreed to the dinner Magnolia requested, she made a reservation for this evening.

Lincoln turned back to the mirror. "I hope she likes me. I'm still surprised she wanted to meet me to begin with, but I feel good about impressing her."

I combed through my purse, checking for the essential items. "Anyone with more than a fleeting involvement in my life is a cause for Magnolia's interest. How else is she supposed to keep tabs on me?"

"I'm surprised she hasn't hired an on-the-ground spy," Lincoln said.

"I wouldn't be surprised if she had by now." I crossed the room to him. "But look at you. Who could resist?" I pecked him on the lips.

"We should get going," Lincoln said, grabbing his wallet and keys. "Showing up late doesn't sound like your mother's style."

Lincoln and I began the walk to the restaurant, arm in arm, as the sun descended on the city. We rounded the corner by the waterfront as the sky turned pink and purple, and soon we were at the entrance of Mama's favorite steak house. The host asked for the reservation name, directed us to a table for three, and there we waited for my mother.

We sipped from sweaty glasses of ice water, and the nerves kicked in a little as I watched Lincoln. I noticed his rigid shoulders, the way he sat ramrod straight, like a country boy on his first visit to a city, and the way his eyes skated over the silverware as if it were a puzzle. He wasn't his usual self.

"You good?" I asked.

Lincoln nodded. "Just some jitters."

It struck me then how different this restaurant was from the casual places we usually spent our time in. That probably should've been obvious, if not for the fact that I grew up in fancy restaurants, and fine dining was so much a part of my life that I hadn't considered that it wasn't muscle memory for everyone. I'd assumed this would be routine for him, too, when I should've stopped for more than a fleeting moment to consider it.

The sight of Magnolia approaching pulled me back to reality. I was on my feet at once. "Oh hi, Mama, you're here."

"Well, I was the one to make the reservation, wasn't I?" She took me loosely in her arms and air-kissed me. She then leveled an iron look at Lincoln. "Good evening, young man."

Lincoln stood, caught himself on the bulky chair, and narrowly avoided falling into Magnolia. "Oops. Sorry. That chair came out of nowhere."

Magnolia's face pulled into a shape that fell somewhere between a smile and a grimace. She pulled her chair out, removed her pearl-colored jacket, and sat. "Have you seen the waiter? I'm suddenly dying for a vodka soda."

I tried to catch Lincoln's eye so I could shoot him a smile, but he was looking at my mother.

"It's nice to meet you, Ms. Bishop. I'm Lincoln Kelly." Lincoln held out his hand across the table.

Magnolia made a show of removing the tabletop items in the way before reaching an unsure hand out. "Yes, I've heard you're Mack's summer boyfriend. How nice."

Lincoln's neck turned pink, and the color slowly rose to his cheeks. "She's a special young lady."

"Mm-hmm," Magnolia said. "I'm not sure I believe you if you're only interested for a summer."

The waiter arrived, and we each ordered an alcoholic beverage. I would've gone ahead and put in an order for a pitcher if it wouldn't have given my mother palpitations to have her daughter behave in such a way in one of her favorite establishments.

My foot tapped restlessly under the table. I should've been kicking myself for not realizing how awkward this would be. Magnolia wasn't interested in a casual meeting; she was there to scare this guy off.

I wished she hadn't called him my summer boyfriend. Even though I still said that, he and I both knew things had changed. We didn't have to say it out loud to know we'd moved beyond that.

"I hear you're quite the philanthropist, Ms. Bishop," Lincoln said.

He had guts to keep trying.

"Yes," Magnolia said, eyeing the menu like she didn't order the same thing every time. "Each week there's a new need, so my ladies and I see to it."

"I used to volunteer at the local shelter with my mom—back when I lived at home."

Magnolia raised a brow over the menu.

"We'd play with the kids, do laundry, serve meals, clean," Lincoln said.

The waiter arrived and distributed our drinks, and I gulped greedily.

"I'm not the hands-on type so much. That's all a little much for me, but I'll direct funds," Magnolia said. "So, tell me about your family, your pedigree—so to speak."

Lincoln swallowed. "Well, I come from a local family—different from yours. My mom was a teacher. She retired early to care for her aging mom, and my father is a musician. I have a sister who is killing it in nursing school right now."

"His dad was really popular in the area," I said, nodding eagerly at Magnolia. "Probably could've gotten a record deal if someone had given him a real shot."

Lincoln looked over at me, his brow creased in confusion.

"He really wasn't," Lincoln said. "He loved it, but he usually drank too much and had to end early."

I was trying to throw Lincoln a life preserver, a little morsel to assuage the Dragon. But alas, he was determined to flounder.

Magnolia eyed me. "So which was it? Successful and knocking down Hollywood's door or a barfly?"

I shrugged, dropping my gaze. "For whatever reason I got the impression he did pretty well with it."

Lincoln gritted his jaw so tight, I could see it across the table. He looked right past me to my mother. "I'm not sure how she got confused, Ms. Bishop, because he's certainly square in the *barfly* category."

Magnolia bit her lip as she pretended to stare into the depths of the menu; she was fighting a smile, seeing she'd just placed a barb between us.

She was far more palatable for the rest of the dinner, asking about my studies that I knew for a fact she was barely interested in. She even asked about Lincoln's work.

"I'm working at an accounting firm right now, a full-time junior role, but eventually I'd like to be a photographer for a living," Lincoln said. "If I can figure it out."

Magnolia let out a grunt. "Weddings and such?"

"Actually, I'd like to do fine art photography, like the one of mine you saw at the Halstead Gallery. I've been applying to photography studios with apprenticeship programs. It's highly competitive and unlikely I'll get a spot, but I'm determined to throw my hat in the ring."

"Lincoln is definitely a top candidate. He just submitted his portfolio to Marcus Wilson in New York." I look over, but he still won't make eye contact. "We're both keeping our fingers crossed, even if the odds are a stretch."

"My artwork is what I care about most in the world," Lincoln said.

I turned back to my mother. "Shall we skip dessert? I don't know about you, but I'm stuffed."

Lincoln waited to take off until we'd said goodbye to my mother, but once she was gone, he shrugged me off.

I raced to catch up as he strode down the street.

"Lincoln, stop," I said. "Look, I'm sorry it tanked."

"*Tanked?*" He stopped dead in his tracks. "You tried to pretend I was something I wasn't. Did I miss a memo somewhere or something?"

I sighed. "It wasn't what I meant. I was trying to give you a leg up on her."

"By lying about my family and trying to make it out like my dad was some famous musician he definitely was not? And then alluding to the fact that I'm a front runner for the studio positions we both know are as rare as a winning lottery ticket?"

"I didn't want her to make you feel like crap," I said.

"I knew she wasn't going to be impressed by my pedigree, but I thought at least you didn't care either." He turned and kept walking.

"I *didn't*. I *don't*," I said. "I wanted her to be impressed."

Lincoln stops again. "Which would require making things up, right? Because she'd never be impressed by who I actually am."

"I was trying to protect you," I said.

"You were trying to protect *yourself*, Mack. You know who I am, and I thought you liked me for me. But I guess when it comes down to it, your mother's opinions and standards trump all."

I stood there, still; I couldn't argue. He was right that my mother, Magnolia the Dragon, had a hold over me, and even if I disagreed with her, it was a compulsion to conform and please.

She was still my mother.

"I'm sorry," I said.

"Me too," Lincoln said, turning one last time. "I'm sorry for ever agreeing to this in the first place. You should sleep at your own apartment tonight. I need some space."

After that I didn't chase him. I'd never seen him so angry before, and I knew it wasn't because of my cruel mother. It was because of me.

CHAPTER 27

Present Day

THE DAY AFTER MAGNOLIA CRASHED the Exquisite Interiors shoot is a slog. I am running on sheer willpower as Hallie—who is now fully recovered—and I watch the termite tent be erected around the Daniel House.

The yellow-and-red-striped monstrosity looks like a deranged circus tent, and I can't help but feel like I belong inside it. I'm going to have to walk the rest of the Exquisite Interiors audition process like a tightrope act with my aspirations on one side and my mother and her opinions on the other, heckling me as my toes wrap the high wire.

Magnolia is so good at ruining things she doesn't like, deconstructing them bit by bit over time. Remarkably persistent. All I wanted was to see the audition through without her interference. Then at least the outcome would be based solely on our work.

Still, I can't dwell on the difficulties of having her in the loop; I will manage it, as I always do.

Hallie stunned the crowd last night as Little Red Riding Hood—even if she did look like she'd gotten a dose of lip fillers beforehand due to her continued reaction to the eggs. The trouper didn't complain a bit, and we all cheered wildly as the curtain fell on the duck-lipped leading lady.

We, her family, haven't always been well-behaved or on the same page about much, but our collective pride in Hallie is something we can rely on. Around her is one of the few places every one of us can gather.

"You know a lot of kids get to have a beach day or a water balloon fight for the first day of summer break," Hallie says, crossing her arms and eyeing the fumigation tent.

"And how many of those kids will know the ins and outs of termite remediation before second grade?" I ask.

Hallie scoffs. "How much longer?"

I check my phone. "Maya said she's on her way to take over. Then we can go."

The termite guys were an hour late, and what I expected to be a short endeavor has engulfed most of the day.

"Can we at least order pizza for dinner?" Hallie asks.

"Sounds great."

Hallie settles herself on the porch steps and pulls out a graphic novel about cartoon cats. Before long she's smiling to herself, and my guilt begins to recede.

My phone rings, and I pull it from my back pocket. It's my mother, so I let it go to voicemail. I don't have the energy for her right now.

Once the call rings out, a text pings.

> Good morning, Magnolia. I just left the Breakfast Benefit for Bruxism, and Dee told me all about Exquisite Interiors Television. She is a fan herself, and it seems several other ladies in attendance at our table enjoy it

as well. I guess it's not complete trash after all. Please
call me.

My chest lifts slightly, and I pick up the phone and call.

"You got my message?" Magnolia asks.

"I sure did," I say. "I'm glad Delta was better able to explain the
show to you than I was."

"Yes," Magnolia says. "I misunderstood the variety of television,
but I still have my doubts. I'll need to supervise, as a representative
of the board."

It's probably as good as I'm going to get.

"I understand," I say. "I follow the lead of the crew; they know
what they're doing."

Magnolia huffs. "We'll work it out as we go."

I hurry off the phone before my mother tries to give me more
grief on this issue, and it isn't long before Maya shows up. I give
her a brief handoff on the project and ask that she request an
invoice from the company. Hallie tugs at my arm as we discuss
some nuts and bolts regarding shooting with the network early
next week.

By the time Hallie and I drive across the towering white bridge
over the water to our home, I wouldn't mind falling right into bed.

"I'm starving," Hallie says as she climbs out of the back seat.
"When will the pizza be here?"

"Putting in the order now," I say.

I hear the rushing sound of a child on wheels and whirl around
to see Foster on his scooter whip up right behind us.

"Hey," he says, skidding to a stop.

"Hey," Hallie says. "Guess what? Yesterday my babysitter gave
me eggs, and I almost blew up like a puffer fish."

"Puffer fish are awesome," Foster says. "Did you know they don't have scales?"

"That's so cool," Hallie says. "Want to come play? We're having pizza for dinner."

"Oh, can I have some?" Foster asks. "I think my dad is making chicken from a recipe again, and he's not very good at recipes." He pulls a face.

Hallie turns to me. "Yeah, Mom, can Foster join us?"

I know the battle very well of trying to find new and interesting dinner ideas with a decent amount of nutritional value. I feel for Lincoln. "We'd love to have you, Foster," I say.

"Maybe my dad can come too? He's been a bit lonely recently," Foster says.

I turn all the way around at the comment.

In theory it makes sense—newish city, single parent, new work most likely. But the man who left this sleepy beachside town for the bright lights and promise of Big City Art, the one who found the success we both knew he was capable of, even if it meant leaving me behind in the process, wasn't one I'd expected to be lonely.

"Yes, of course. I'll text him and see what he thinks," I say.

I head inside and the kids follow. Foster closes the door behind him, removes his shoes, and sets them neatly beside the door, while my daughter gallops like a wild mustang into the living room, muddy sneakers and all.

Lincoln replies immediately to my text, graciously and politely accepting my invitation.

"Hal?" I call into the living room. "I'm going to take a quick shower. You kids all good?"

"Yup," she says. "We're reading animal fact books, but can we have TV in a bit?"

"Sure thing, but only the approved shows."

I wonder what Lincoln's position is on screen time. There's so much about him I don't know anymore. Well, aside from his sweeping professional success that I pretended for years I didn't follow. It was so hard to hate him. I tried, and considering that I am a woman who comes from a gene pool laced with stubbornness, my failure was surprising.

I remember one of his first write-ups and the casual shot of him perched on the arm of a chair. He looked like the same boy from North Charleston—humble, hopeful, and whip-smart with a camera.

I was jealous for a while. How could I not be? He'd set out on his own and earned his success. He'd proven himself. Meanwhile, here I was in my midthirties still crawling back to my mother for a project.

I crank on the shower, and once the water runs hot, I step in and let it wash away the grime of the day. Termites always give me the ick.

An hour later, the four of us sit around my kitchen table, two pizza boxes lying open between us.

"You saved us tonight," Lincoln says. "I realized just before you texted that I was missing several ingredients for our chicken piccata."

Foster presses his hands together and looks skyward in thanks for the reprieve.

Hallie giggles.

"Well, we had quite the exciting day ourselves, so I was certainly not cooking."

Thank goodness the kids are here. They're such a delightful buffer against difficult topics and digging up the past. Plus, who doesn't love to bat around fun animal facts?

"All right." Hallie drops her crust onto her plate. "You almost done, Foster? I want to go outside before it gets too dark."

Foster attacks his slice, gnawing it like a beaver. He swallows in a way that looks painful. "Yup. I'm done."

The kids drop their plates by the sink and dash outside barefoot.

I drop my napkin onto my plate and fold my arms, smiling after them. I look over and catch Lincoln watching them the same way. I take the last sip of my wine.

"I never in my wildest dreams expected you to be the one to move in next door," I say. "But I was certainly hoping whoever did would have a kid like Foster."

Lincoln nods. "He calls Hallie his best friend. She's made the transition almost seamless for him. She's been so welcoming and kind—not once has he sat alone at school or felt left out during recess."

Mom-pride swells inside me. "I'm so glad. But to be fair, I don't think a drop of it is charitable—she and Foster are just on the same level. She digs the kid."

Lincoln smiles, and as the dimple folds beside his mouth, I can't help but remember how much I used to dig him too.

Lincoln stands and takes my plate. At the sink, he starts the water.

"Oh, you don't have to do that," I say.

"It's easy," he says. "And far fewer dishes than I was looking at with my home chef attempt."

I wander over to the island. "Thanks."

Lincoln begins rinsing the dishes.

"So how're you liking it back here so far? It's a big change from New York," I say.

"No kidding," he says, slotting a plate into the dishwasher rack. "It's different, but good. The house, for one, is massive. I was looking for something in this school district, and none of the homes were small."

"Yeah, when Grady and I bought this, I always thought we'd have more than one kid." I realize once I've said it that I don't necessarily want to dissect my missing out on the children I wanted—and especially so with Lincoln.

"I've found that little in life seems to work out the way we think it will," Lincoln says.

"Aside from your big, flashy career," I say.

Lincoln grins. "Yes, that's the one thing that went to plan."

What I really want to know about are the other things that went wrong for him. Yes, because in some way it'll make me feel better to know he's not as perfect as he looks right now. But also because something inside me tugs at me, keen to know the parts of his life that've happened since he left.

"So will Foster's mother be visiting much?" I ask. "Hopefully you have a better situation with your ex than I do."

Lincoln shuts off the water and closes the dishwasher.

"She and I were a flash in the pan—not really an ex situation like you've got on your hands. Foster was a most unexpected gift, and enough to justify our paths crossing—or crashing together, more like—for a while." Lincoln folds his arms. "I don't expect her to visit, even if it would be nice for Foster."

My heart squeezes for the boy. I know intimately how it feels to be without a parent. "For what it's worth, I'd do it over again with Grady for the sake of having Hallie."

"I'm sorry you ended up with him," Lincoln says.

The way his eyes linger on me, it's almost as if he's asking if he's responsible. If it's a mess he made. And even though I did try to blame it on him for years, I now know better.

"It was my own mistake. Following the Magnolia Plan like I

couldn't help but do," I say. "I knew deep down he was her choice, so I made it into mine."

I pull myself up from leaning on the counter and head to the window—to lay eyes on the kids, but also to put distance between myself and this conversation. It's starting to get dark.

Lincoln joins me, eyeing the yard. "Don't be too hard on your younger self, Mack. You had it rough with the Dragon."

I smile, but I keep looking out the window. I know if I look at him, certainly if he meets my eye, all bets are off. Maybe I'll gush about the past, about regrets, about him, and he doesn't want to hear it. He is being kind, a good neighbor, Hallie's friend's dad.

He doesn't regret leaving; he got precisely what he wanted in New York.

I pull in a breath. "I'm going to call them in. It's almost dark, and Hallie is a beast in the morning if she doesn't get enough sleep."

"Good call," Lincoln says. "And thank you—for dinner, but also for welcoming us, despite the way things ended."

Woof. It was spoken.

All I can do is nod tightly and dash toward the front door. I yank it open and call out into the dusk, "Kids! It's time to come in!"

CHAPTER 28

EARLY THE NEXT WEEK, FITZ and I stand toe-to-toe in the upstairs bathroom at the Daniel House, and thank goodness the camera crew is here because we're having it out over our one greatest sticking point.

"Look," I say. "*Look.*" I drop and crouch below the pedestal sink some dummy installed in the '90s. "It's already damaged so much we can barely patch it."

"Hardwoods," Fitz says. "They should stay."

"They're a no in a bathroom," I respond. "I know, I know, *historically* they should stay, but this room is going to get used. How will it look if two months after the reno, they're calling us saying the floor's messed up?" I hook my thumbs in the loops of my work overalls and rock on the heels of my work boots. The floor creaks below me almost as if in agreement. "Plus, now while the tub's out getting refinished is the time."

Fitz reaches out a hand to lean on the wall but pulls back as he takes in the yellowing of the paint. "I think if your mother has her way, she and her ladies who lunch will be the only ones powdering their noses in here." He looks to the cameraperson.

"Fortunately, this building is owned by the entire Carolina Historic Society, and I vote they need *tile* in a bathroom for it to be used for a gathering of any reasonable size."

Fitz sighs. "So it's less museum, more event space?"

I shrug. "There's no sense in letting it sit and rot. People should enjoy it."

Fitz turns to the cameraperson. "She doesn't want that broadcast if she knows what's good for her."

"*There* we can agree," I say. "We're keeping the use of the space unspecified for now."

Fitz throws me a wink. "For such a tiny room, I guess I'll give in and let you tile it."

I throw my hands up. "Victory!"

"And cut!" Erica yells. She sets the camera down gently and stretches. "This comes so easy."

"It helps to be friends," I say.

"*Best* friends," Fitz says. "Even if we never got around to the matching necklaces."

"Do you guys have time to shoot at the studio today too?" Erica raises a brow. "We have some meetings with senior producers next week, and if I can get some variety in takes, I might be able to convince them to come check you out."

"Producers?" I ask.

It makes sense that they exist, and of course this would have to go up a flagpole before we'd move on to anything official. It's just that the term *senior producers* makes me think of someone in a boardroom, not someone on a jobsite.

"The ones who make the choices, presumably?" Fitz says, crossing his arms. "Give us an hour to freshen up, and we can shoot at the studio on King."

I double-check my phone. "Grady's dropping Hallie there in an hour." I frown.

Fitz lights up. "Well, it's my lucky day. It's been too long since I've hugged the magpie."

Erica follows the comments back and forth, her hand itching to raise the camera.

"Magpie, *not* child television star," I say. I turn to Erica. "I'm sorry, but I'm just not comfortable having my daughter on camera."

Erica nods. "That's fair. If she happens into any of the shots, we can cut it so her face doesn't show."

It sounds reasonable. And again, I remind myself that this is essentially an extended audition reel and not yet something that would be televised. For those cuts I'll also have to remember to keep the comments about my mother under control.

Fitz turns to Erica. "I'll work on her. I know Hallie would translate to the screen like a *star*."

I fling my arm around Fitz and pull him out of the bathroom by the shoulders. "He won't be working on me, Erica, but we'll see you at the studio in a bit. I'll let Maya know you're on the way."

Erica laughs as the pair of us tumble down the steps, bickering about the matter, and out onto the street.

An hour later, I'm approaching our studio dressed in wide-leg dark jeans, a signature white button-down, and large gold jewelry. I'd never admit it to my mother, but I consider this a modernization of her go-to style. It's probably unconscious, from all the grooming she did of me as a child, squeezing me into designer labels one Zone bar at a time, but even I can admit the woman has an eye for a classic look.

Fitz rounds the corner ahead wearing a delightful linen jacket in flamingo pink, paired with khakis and a blue pinstripe shirt.

He catches sight of me, eyes me up and down, and tosses a chef's kiss my way. I raise my sunglasses as I near him and dramatically fan myself. "The heat coming off that jacket."

Fitz grins. "I was saving it for something special like this." He squeezes my arm. "We're so close."

"Mama!" Hallie's voice comes from across the street where she waves wide, her other hand held in Grady's. He looks both ways and they cross over.

Behind Fitz, Erica is drawing near with one of the sound guys. Fitz turns and waves.

Suddenly Hallie's arms are around my waist. "I missed you," she says.

"Not to mention I missed *you*," Fitz says.

Hallie leaps over to him and gives him a matching hug.

"Erica, hi!" I call over. "This is my daughter, Hallie."

Erica sets her camera down and wipes sweat from her brow. "Great to meet you, Hallie! I've heard all kinds of good stuff about you."

I feel a tap on my shoulder, and I know it's Grady pecking from behind me. I turn slowly.

"Y'all get a local news segment or something?" he asks.

The sun reflects off his overly gelled hair, and I fight the urge to rub it with my palm and mess it all up.

"Actually, this is Erica. She's our cameraperson shooting our audition for a slot on Exquisite Interiors TV," I say. "Nothing official yet, but we're having fun with it."

"You and Fitz are easy to film," Erica says.

Grady turns pink, then red, and I can imagine the steam building inside his head. Fitz must observe the same because he puts his hand on Hallie's shoulder and says, "Erica, can the magpie and I show you around the studio? Get some still shots of the space, maybe, before Mack and I pick up?"

"Perfect," Erica says, grabbing her camera and following them inside. She waves the sound guys in behind her.

"What the hell, Mack?" Grady throws out his hands. "When were you going to tell me about this?"

I look at him deadpan. "I have about two minutes, Grady. So you can choose if you'd like to hand off information about Hallie's stay with you or interrogate me about how I'm running my business."

"*Your* business? I mean, we *both* built this, and you didn't think to loop me in on a shot at a network television deal?" Grady steps closer.

"You resigned. You left. I would've let you stay had you asked— very much against my better judgment." I check my watch. "I've now got one minute."

Grady huffs. "You'll be hearing from me about this."

"Fine," I say and spin on my heels. "I've got to go."

Grady continues to rant out on the street, something about *getting his airtime* and him being *the obvious cohost.*

I skip inside and see Fitz charming Erica, showing off our luxe interior. Hallie sits at her desk adjusting her fabrics that sit along-side her cup of colored pencils and her dollhouse.

I turn and latch the front doors behind me. "Just going to close these up." I giggle to myself as Grady continues his tirade out on the street. "The mosquitos are such pests this year."

"Thanks, doll," Fitz calls over. "There was an especially angry one with a terrible comb-over that just flitted by."

Erica doesn't falter, likely assuming these are just odd Charlestonisms, but I chuckle. Before long Fitz and I are bantering up a storm over a swatch book of fabrics to die for just as the golden hour hits. The sun cuts through the slats in the front door, and by the grace of God, not a single dust mote mars the air. Eventually we pop open the doors to the patio and shoot some takes out in front of the jasmine.

I'm proud of this place, of our work, and I wonder for the first time if maybe losing out on that fellowship was exactly what we needed to get us where we're going.

CHAPTER 29

Fifteen Years Earlier

IT HAD BEEN THREE DAYS since our explosive dinner with Magnolia, and Lincoln and I had exchanged precisely five bare-bones texts. Even my best girlfriends told me I was wrong—that I, the one who knew Magnolia, should've done everything necessary to avoid that encounter.

"Having him lie about his family to your mom is as good as telling him he's not good enough."

"Did you even warn him in the least?"

"I'm not surprised he wants space—and maybe for a while, Mack."

These were things my best friends had said, the ones who were usually rife with *forget that guy* or *he wishes*.

Probably because everyone loved Lincoln. He had no pretense; what you saw was what you got, and my eyes couldn't find an insincere or ugly part to him—even if he was a bit overly obsessed with financial planning for a twentysomething.

Lincoln wasn't taking my calls, so I'd apologized via text. He'd said it was ok, but again, it was over text and unconvincing. Plus, I was faced with the reality of his absence, a test run of what my life would be like without him. I didn't want our summer to end; I loved having him around. Maybe somewhere deep inside I loved him too.

Which made my appalling display at dinner even more regrettable.

So there I was at his door, knocking with an offering of the chocolate cake doughnuts he loved and I hated, hoping I could get us back on track.

He didn't exactly look thrilled to see me when the door swung open. He wore khaki shorts and an old concert T-shirt. It reminded me of the night we met. "Hey."

I held out the doughnuts. "A peace offering."

Lincoln stepped back and lifted a hand. "Come on in."

I dropped the doughnuts on his countertop, cluttered with mail and cups and take-out containers. He might've been a good guy, but his cleanliness was on par with the rest of his gender.

"I know I said it over text, but I want to say it in person: I'm sorry. I thought I was protecting you from being stomped all over by the Dragon. I know how much that hurts, and I didn't want that for you. But instead, I just hurt you." I looked right into his eyes. "I should've thought the whole thing through, at least discussed it more, but it just felt like it should be easy breezy like everything else with us. That's the thing about us—it just comes so naturally."

He dropped his hands at his sides. "Look, I don't blame you, Mack. I believe that you didn't mean for things to go the way they did, but it's just that you have to understand that they went that way for a reason."

"Yes, because I shouldn't have jumped in," I said. "I should've let you do your thing, and it would've been fine."

"Maybe. Maybe not." Lincoln shrugged. "Honestly, it went that way because we come from two very different places. Magnolia is a big part of your life, and we both know she's not going to let you branch out from that. From her and her ways."

"You're right. She's got way too much sway over me," I said. "It's something I want to change."

"It's probably not something that'll resolve itself before the end of the summer," Lincoln said.

"No, stop. I'm doing better at keeping her at bay every day—especially now that I'm here, and she's an hour and a half away." I took his hands. "And there's another thing I've been thinking about. Maybe if I could find my dad, it would remove some of her hold on me. If I had a real-life second parent, I'd have more family than just her."

Lincoln's face twisted in confusion. "I don't know, Mack. I think this thing is between the two of you Magnolias."

"But it's worth a try," I said. "I've always wanted to know him, and it could make over my entire family tree. What if I have half siblings? What if there were more people I could call my own?"

Lincoln leaned on his counter, looking at the floor. "I think that's a *you* thing, Mack."

I crossed my arms, a flash of anger in my chest. "So this is it? You're done?"

He looked up and over at me. "I don't want it to be." His voice was tender, and he turned and walked closer. "But this whole thing with your dad . . . It's sort of a big deal, and I just don't think it's right to tie it to anything to do with us—or me. I wouldn't feel right about you doing it on my account."

My hopes swelled at the sight of him moving in my direction and the gentle rumble of his voice. "No, of course," I said. "It wouldn't be for you. It would be for me because I want to. I think it would help me, as a person in general—especially if I want to be in a lasting relationship at any point in my life."

I kept it general so I didn't let on that he was the one who came to mind right away. The facts of him and me together might not add up, but everything about my feelings for him did. Still, I'd already come close to scaring him off, thanks to my mother. Coming back too hot and heavy was a risk I wasn't willing to take. I might feel desperate to keep him, but I certainly didn't want to look it.

Lincoln reached out and set his hands on my waist. "We've already got the summer clock ticking down, so why not enjoy what time we have left?"

I dropped into him, wrapping my arms around him, and the feeling of his arms around me was pure relief. I hadn't lost him.

"Well, yes and no on the timing." I pulled back to look at him. "I mean, I wouldn't mind us going past summer. What do you think?"

Lincoln grinned. "Definitely no more dinners with your mother, but we can see how things go."

I shuddered. "Definitely not." I let out a deep sigh. "I hate that she's all I've got."

Lincoln released me from his grip and guided me over to the sofa. He sat, and when he tapped my leg to lift my feet into his lap, I really believed he'd forgiven me. "So when you say she's all you've got, what *is* the deal with your dad?"

I hated talking about it, but I trusted Lincoln. And that seemed as good a time as any to spill, considering my latest thoughts on the matter.

"I don't have much information," I said. "Ok, *any* information, not even his name. Magnolia says he's a bad guy, *dark and twisted*, et cetera, et cetera, and maybe she's right."

"But do you really think your mother would be with someone that bad?" Lincoln pulled a face. "As far as I can tell, she's picky about most things. Hard to believe her being flexible on picking a lover."

"Skipping right past the concept of Magnolia having sex." I shook myself out in a full-body wiggle to dislodge the thought. "I totally agree. She's always surrounded herself with the 'right type of people.' Honestly, I wouldn't be surprised if he's a great guy she just froze out. He probably wouldn't agree to get the car she wanted or buy the house she wanted, and keeping me from him was her payback. I mean, it's at least halfway plausible."

Lincoln stared off, like he was thinking, and in the quiet my mind went to the next place it always did.

"And yes, Magnolia could've misjudged someone," I said. "You and I both know from our very recent experience how wrong she can be about people. But I think I've lived not knowing for too long."

"You're sure this isn't about the dinner, right?" Lincoln asked. "This sounds serious."

I sat upright and folded my hands in my lap. "I'm sure," I said. "And I *am* serious about this. I realized over the last few days that Magnolia may very well never approve of the life I want to choose for myself. Whether it be a partner, a job, a home, whatever it might be, she's got a very specific idea of what I should be doing."

"And maybe your dad could be someone else to support you in being who you want to be?" Lincoln asked.

"Exactly," I said. "And I've wondered for too long now how my life might've been different with him."

Lincoln reached out and squeezed my arm. "It's up to you, Mack. Always will be."

I smiled tentatively and dropped into his side. Lincoln wound his arm around me, and I stayed there. Before long we found our typical rhythm, turning on the TV, eventually poking fun and laughing out loud. I meant it when I said being with him was easy breezy. Maybe after we'd survived the Magnolia challenge, the greatest of all from where I sat, the bond between us had grown stronger.

It felt impossible that he wouldn't see the same thing. He had to feel it too. It was like a physical being by now, the love between us. He just *had* to feel the same way.

CHAPTER 30

Present Day

I T'S JUST OVER A WEEK after our last shoot, and as Erica had hoped, she was able to schedule the senior producers for a visit to the Daniel House. I arrive on-site in the morning, and it's the first day that feels like the house is actually coming along. The termite tent is nothing more than a bad memory, and cabinetry is being delivered for the kitchen and bathrooms. Maya's already here meeting with the stained glass expert for the window upstairs.

I open the door and Mateo's crew is already at work placing the kitchen cabinets as they are carried in from the truck.

I let out a squeak of joy. "Mateo, these look amazing."

"You designed it. We're just following marching orders. We'll start installing once we have it all set out and are certain on fit. You'll be around to sign off?"

"As if I'd dip out on kitchen cabinetry," I say. "That's one of my favorite days."

"Just wanted to confirm," he says. "And the floors—they turned out great."

I stop at his side and drop my gaze. "I never doubt Sam—or you, for that matter."

"Y'all are filming today?" Mateo eyes my crisp linen pants and round-neck tee.

I laugh. "How could you tell? My lack of actual work boots?"

"That's right," he says.

I give him a wink and turn to go back through the house. The light floods in in golden beams now that the ground floor windows have been repaired—and given a preliminary wipe-down. I don't even mind the dust it highlights; it's proof that work is happening and proof that the house has history.

Outside on the porch I drop into a rocking chair. It's the first time we've installed patio furniture before the construction is complete, but today the Exquisite Interiors producers will be touring the home, evaluating our work, and eyeing our aptitude for on-screen charisma.

Maya pops her head out the door. "There you are." She perches on the edge of the chair next to me. "I've got good news. Theo Hartman said he'd love to sign on for the landscaping."

"Amazing," I say.

Together we eye the dusty mud wasteland stretching between us and the street.

"I'll set the meeting as soon as possible." Maya chuckles.

"You're a mind reader," I reply.

Work continues throughout the morning, the house buzzing like a hive, until things slow around lunchtime. Maya and I grab a bite from a deli around the corner and order two strong coffees to sip on the way back to the house.

I'm on the porch tipping back the last gulp of my coffee when beyond the gate, a silver Toyota Corolla pulls up and stops. The back door pops open, and Magnolia hauls herself out, cash in hand.

I wasn't able to dissuade her from attending today's meeting, despite my very best begging and pleading. Not now that there's another arm to this project in which she was adamant to be included.

Magnolia stomps up the brick path, muttering under her breath, and when she reaches the porch, she stops and props a hand on her hip. "I cannot believe I let Dee convince me to use Uber." She pronounces it like *yoo-ber*. "She said it was easy and convenient, but she didn't mention the vehicle would smell like three-day-old hamburgers. I have a right mind never to let Victor take a vacation again."

I stop myself from laughing. "It can be luck of the draw sometimes," I say. "But how young and hip of Delta Suffolk to use Uber."

Magnolia rolls her eyes. "I think she's going through a three-quarters-life-crisis or something like it, but I'd much rather she buy a boat or a flashy car than act like she's some college student getting into a car with God-knows-who."

"Good news is that you made it," I lie. I'm nervous enough to navigate the next level of network scrutiny even without the captain of my constructive-criticism team in attendance.

"Is the powder room in order?" Magnolia asks. "I should freshen up."

"Downstairs is functional, but not pretty," I warn.

Magnolia turns up her nose and takes a seat in a rocker. "I'll just have to be tacky and check my lipstick out here in front of the general public."

Before long Fitz arrives, and not far behind him is Erica with a couple new sound techs and three professionally dressed new faces.

I dreamed about who these senior leaders would be last night, and the people before me in the light of day are certainly more down-to-earth. Not one of them resembles a zombie, not even in the slightest.

The first woman extends her hand. "I'm Shante. I'm the executive producer for the Southeast region. Nice to meet you." She wears a flowy maxi dress in shades of brown with a pop of bright pink.

"Jonathan," the man in the blue jacket says. "I hold the same role as Shante." He nods to his other colleague. "And Beatrix."

Beatrix has curly gray hair, shoulder length, and wears a gorgeous linen skirt set paired with large-scale wooden jewelry. She smiles from behind red glasses frames. "Yes, same for me." She laughs. "We're excited to be here."

"Trust me," Erica chimes in. "They're going to knock your socks off."

"Well, we sure hope so," I say. "So without further ado, welcome to the Daniel House. It was built in 1890, and the Carolina Historic Society recently received the property from the late owner's estate—"

Magnolia clears her throat.

I close my eyes slowly and beg the universe to let this be nothing more than a passing tic. I pull in a breath to continue, but Magnolia beats me to it.

"Yes, hi." Magnolia squeezes between Fitz and me. "I'm Magnolia Bishop of the Carolina Historic Society. I'm Magnolia's mother—or Mack as you know her—and I'm involved on-site too."

Erica's eyes dart between Fitz and me.

"I'm glad you mentioned it," I say, gently placing an arm around my mother. "We're so grateful to have received the commission from the board. They are very supportive and *quite* hands-on compared to other organizations in the Lowcountry."

Magnolia beams with pride. "I take good care of my projects—I need to protect my reputation."

"And we're here to protect the building," I say. "Can we show you inside?"

Erica surreptitiously begins shooting footage as I lead the group up the steps to the porch.

I'm not surprised by Magnolia making herself known to the crew. She isn't one to sit quietly in the background. But the way her chest puffs up, oh so slightly, and the way the tips of her cheeks turn barely a shade pinker than her blush, I'm starting to wonder if she's dreaming, at least a little, about having her own moment on-screen.

I could also be imagining it.

Magnolia was clear about her taste being far too highbrow for reality television, and it's entirely in keeping with her personal brand for her life thus far. (Though she'd deny she has a personal brand at all. Again, *far* too pedestrian and commercial.)

I push open the front door. "You'll notice first underfoot, these floors," I say. "We have an incredible team, with Sam Jacobs at the helm, who stripped, patched, and restained the original flooring to something gorgeous."

"Wow." Shante nods.

"You're right about that," Jonathan says.

Magnolia shuffles to the front. "They turned out stunning," she says.

Out of her sight, Fitz throws me a look, and I shrug. The compliment is likely for herself—seeing as she's now taking credit for being hands-on. I wouldn't be surprised if she's soon claiming to have laid the tile herself.

"Mack," Magnolia calls over. "Show them the sink I inspired you to choose."

I give her the eye and cross into the kitchen. "Yes, thank you, I've got this under control," I say. "Fitz, do you want to discuss the tile in the kitchen and how we got there?"

Fitz takes off, charming the socks off all three producers as he tells the story of the beyond-repair boards, the water damage, and the tile we selected, the tile my mother was so clear to state she didn't care for. I keep my eyes trained on her in case she feels the need to take a dig at our design choices. Fortunately, she remains quiet.

I show the producers the progress in the powder room, and Erica films an interview clip of me discussing the wallpaper. Fitz stands beside me.

"When we pick a wallpaper in a home like this, we do our best to choose a pattern that might've been around during the time. William Morris was taking off in England at the time, and we still love those patterns—and new ones inspired by his design aesthetic—for a home of this age. It's not perfect, but it's about being thoughtful."

"Not to mention," Fitz says, "if original wallpaper were around these days, it would probably be a flaky mess that'd dissolve with a single sink use."

I laugh. "No kidding, especially with the way my daughter flings soapy water around every time she washes her hands."

"She's a saint, that child, so y'all will need to cut that comment," Fitz says directly into the camera.

"So yes, getting away from my angel baby and back to wall-paper," I sing. "We needed something practical that also honors the age of the home."

"Cut!" Erica yells.

The producers stay quiet for the most part, observing while we film. It seems most of their outstanding shows deal with newer builds, so when we talk about saving original components and doing repair work, their attention piques. It gives me and Fitz opportunities to highlight the unique aspects of working in historic homes. We even get to share some stories of past project mishaps and garner a few encouraging laughs.

Erica checks her watch. "I think that's it for today. It's after five, and I know you started early."

"It was a pleasure to meet you all and see your work. I love what you've got going on," Shante says.

The others say their goodbyes, and Erica walks them out to the street. "I'll call you soon, Mack," she says. "Have a good evening."

Once the network folks are out of sight, I enjoy a deep breath in the quiet. I'm happy with how things went—equal parts optimistic about what's to come and proud of the design work we've completed thus far. I'm not sure I could've planned a better tour of this house, and even Magnolia was on marginally improved behavior.

"We knocked it out," Fitz says, squeezing me in a hug. "Margaritas tonight?"

"Absolutely," I say. "Grady's got Hal, so I'm free."

"Magnolia," my mother says. I'd partially forgotten she was still around, inserting herself in my excitement. "A word before you go off to drink those ghastly beverages? I'm staying the night at Charleston Place Hotel, and Victor will come pick me up once he's back on shift in the morning."

I turn around. "How about I drive you to the hotel and save you the misery of a rideshare?"

"That'll work," Magnolia says.

"Usual spot at six?" Fitz asks me.

"I'll see you there."

Fitz leaves, and six can't come soon enough. *Chats* with my mother rarely go well, and especially because I'm currently feeling good about this whole thing, I have no doubt she's going to have something to say about it.

But she's the only mother I've got, so I'll stuff down my discomfort and grit my teeth through it.

Like I usually do.

CHAPTER 31

OMENTS LATER, MAGNOLIA SITS IN my passenger seat as we wait behind a horse and carriage tour moving painfully slowly.

"I think we need to showcase the Historic Society, if y'all get the show," Magnolia says.

"Didn't you hear me mention it?" I ask. "I'm going to name-drop you plenty."

"No, I mean a real feature," Magnolia says.

My regret doubles at offering to be her driver. We started with her being disgusted over the idea of giving Exquisite Interiors a shot at all, and now she wants her group to be front and center. Whatever she must do to control my life, I guess.

"It wasn't long ago you called the show crap. Remember that?" I ask.

She swats the air. "You knew what I meant. I hadn't watched it; I didn't realize people actually got things like homeware lines, cookbook deals, and sponsorships. I thought it was more like something only played on loop in a dentist's office, not viewed regularly in millions of households across the country. People actually get famous from this, Magnolia."

So that was what this was about.

"Mother, are you wanting your own fifteen minutes of fame?"

"Oh heavens, no."

I turn to look at her, and she's not a single bit convincing. She looks hopeful and wanting, and for the first time I realize I might just have a little bit of an upper hand here.

"Really?" I ask. "Because every time I've brought you through the house, you've only nitpicked the work we've done. And today you were *all* compliments."

"I only want the best for you, Magnolia. To make sure you're living a good life like you deserve. Why wouldn't I talk up your work in front of the camera, to the very people handing out contracts?"

I turn on my blinker and cut around the campus. "In theory I appreciate that, but I know what I'm doing. I would love your support, but I'm not sure what I can promise the Historic Society."

Magnolia folds her hands in her lap.

She looks out the window, and we sit quietly for the rest of the drive. I know there's something brewing as we fly past the palmetto trees, past the market thick with visitors. She didn't get her way, even if I didn't say no, and Magnolia never gives up on a fight.

I pull into the round driveway of the Charleston Place Hotel, and as we wait for the position by the door to clear, she turns to me.

"I understand I was mistaken about the show. I should've done my research before I took a stance. But I'll have you know that if you get the show, and my board and I aren't in some way included, I can't say you'll see another job handed down from us," she says, then she puts her sunglasses back in place and exits the car.

I wish I could speed out, gravel flying behind me, but I'm blocked in until the unloading car in front moves. It's nothing I'm unused to, being trapped under my mother's threats of any and all varieties.

She talks about wanting me to have this good life, have success, but it only goes so far. It only counts if it's in her approved ways with her blessing, nothing of my own creation. It has to be something she has a hand in—benefits from, in the best cases.

Maybe her realizing that the show could actually be a good opportunity has her in new territory. Finally there's something that's mine that she doesn't necessarily have a say in. I'm not sure her threat holds much water; if we get the show, we'll have more interest, more work coming; we wouldn't need her society's referrals.

But I'm certain she'd make my life difficult in other ways. And then there's the impulse inside me to please her, to put my own wants and feelings aside and make her happy.

It's not as strong as it was before, when I was younger, but I don't think I'll ever outrun it completely.

Finally the traffic clears and I'm back on the road, my muscles slowly unclenching as I put physical space between me and my mother. Only the promise of margaritas and chips and salsa is keeping me going.

La Cocina is its usually flurry of bright colors, thumping pop music, and sizzling smells. It's exactly what I need. I push into the door, and I'm met by a gentle hum of chatter and laughter. A plate of steaming, smoky veggies floats by me.

Fitz waves from a table for two tucked alongside the large wall of windows. I duck past the colorful paper flags strung up for a birthday celebration. He's already ordered us drinks and my favorite queso dip.

"Fitz, if there wasn't already a spot waiting for you in heaven, you've secured it this evening."

He chuckles from inside his glass. "I won't be banking on it too soon, considering how hard I hit the casino a few weekends ago in Vegas."

"Eh." I take a sip and savor the tang on my lips. "I like to imagine God has a bit of a sense of humor."

Fitz grabs a chip and swirls it in the queso. "Well, anyways, I figured I'd get us going here because I wouldn't wish whatever car conversation you and your mama had on my worst enemy."

I unroll my napkin and set the silverware on the table. "I'm not sure you'd believe me if I told you."

"Try me," Fitz says. "Or better yet, let me guess: Magnolia wants to sub in as cohost."

I laugh, choking down a gulp. "I mean, it's not *verbatim* what she said, but you've got the gist of it."

Our waiter arrives, and Fitz and I place our tried-and-true orders.

"I could see it all over her face," Fitz says.

I drop my head into my palm. "But why? It wasn't days ago she told me it wasn't worth a moment of my time."

Fitz clears his throat and sets his hands on the table, like he's about to call school into session. "Let's start at the top. What is the one thing in the entire world Magnolia cares about most?"

"Her status, and most specifically it being seen as paramount and generally admired."

"Now step back, and there we were at the shoot. Those producers looked sharp, like *people in charge*, and each of them had a specific air of confidence that only comes with power."

I sigh. "Plus, it sounds like she actually watched the show. Delta Suffolk, an avid fan herself, sold her on it."

"And what's the other thing your mother cares about most?"

"Making her mini-Magnolia suffer?"

"Hmm." Fitz squints. "Close. Maybe I could give half credit for that. I was looking for *keeping her mini-Magnolia from straying too far.*"

"But haven't I done that with the studio? Stepped out on my own?"

Our entrées arrive, and I'm grateful for the pause. I shovel an oversize bite of shrimp taco into my mouth.

"You certainly have," Fitz says. "The studio is your crowning achievement, and when you applied for the fellowship gig that so many of her friends are wound up in, I think she probably felt like she got a foot in."

I swallow. "She was definitely *encouraging* about the whole thing. Probably more so than with anything else I've done professionally. I'm sure it swayed me a little, even if I didn't realize it was happening at the time."

"Right." Fitz wipes his mouth with his napkin. "And I bet that felt good for Magnolia to be part of it with you."

I shrugged. He was right. She called far more often and actually wanted to know about my work. She even complimented Grady and me as a working duo when typically what she cared about most was that we were married.

"I just don't want her fingerprints all over this," I say.

"And why should you let her?" Fitz says. "She'll throw a fit if you don't let her in, and then—"

"The *and then* is what I'm worried about," I say. "She's my mother. I don't particularly like her, but I do love her—even if it's all a bit twisted."

"I know what you mean," Fitz says. "Mine are almost as bad as her."

It hits me that I haven't followed up after Fitz admitted his struggles with his family and Henry. We were so wrapped up in the show, it never came up.

"So no progress with them on the Henry front?"

Fitz shakes his head. "And I finally hit the wall," he says. "Henry still says he's fine to wait, but I *know* the man. I can just tell he's antsy. And honestly, I'm done putting him out because of my awful family."

"The wedding?" I've always looked forward to celebrating their wedding, but now it sounds so resigned, overlaid by the family hate.

He nods. "He wants it. I want it. The only thing standing in our way is my parents—the mighty Fitzgeralds—and the family fortune. I talked to them again, hoping for the best, but it was the same old, same old. And now I have to choose: marriage or money."

"And your house?"

"We're keeping it, but I might need to call in some Bishop Builds favors over time, if you know what I mean. For now, all the extras are on hold—indefinitely."

"But Exquisite Interiors—"

Fitz sets down his fork and sighs. "I was thinking that too. If it works out, that'd be a massive help because I'd have my salary at the studio plus whatever they're willing to give us. We could actually save for retirement and have a vacation—something my spoiled behind hasn't had to worry about before."

"We have to get it," I say. Knowing Fitz needs it like this lights a fresh fire under me. "We have to."

"It would definitely help. Even if it's just an ego boost." He waggles his brow.

I let out a laugh. "Yes, because *confidence* is something you're lacking."

The rest of the meal melts into easy conversation about non-threatening things, but the thought never leaves my mind: Whatever we can do to make Exquisite Interiors work, it will feel like fighting for Fitz too.

And if there's anyone beyond Hallie I would go to the ends of the earth for, it's him.

CHAPTER 32

Fifteen Years Earlier

I LEANED BACK AGAINST MY LITTLE car, packed to the brim with laundry and books and heaps of unnecessaries I wouldn't need for a weekend. I always overpacked, but with Lincoln in the picture I'd committed even less time to whittling down my selections. He held me in a hug, sandwiching me between him and the car.

"You sure you have to go?" he asked.

"Mama would have my head if I missed the boat festival. It's an annual summertime tradition." I squeezed him, then pulled back. "So yes, I'm sure I can't stay."

He dragged his fingertips lazily across my shoulder, then paused at the base of my neck, flashing me a grin.

I grabbed his hand. "Don't you start that or I'll be hours late."

Lincoln sighed and stepped back to pull my car door open. I climbed in and blew him a kiss, then I took off. I needed to make good time if I wanted to stop at the local library and check its records and old newspapers. It was the first step in searching for my father, and I had a plan: look at one year before my birth and fan out from there. The man might not be local, and he may not have stuck around, but Magnolia was a lifetime Beaufort resident.

So keeping the science of conception in mind, he had to have been in town nine months before my birth, if nothing else.

It was a long shot. The search would take time—especially if the library hadn't yet made its archives digital—and it would be a piecemeal start. I could almost guarantee it would be painful. But this was all I had to go on.

Three hours later, I was a picture of disappointment. The only reason I wasn't in a puddle on the floor was thanks to the kind librarian Rhonda. She'd helped me pull the microfilm from storage rooms and sat with me, but the stuff was bulky and unbelievably time-consuming to navigate. I spent my only hour and a half here figuring out the machinery and reading one article about a local knitting group that was making blankets for the children's hospital.

"And you're sure you couldn't get a name?" the librarian asked.

I shook my head.

"It's not even on the birth certificate?" she asked.

"Blank by design," I said.

"That's too bad. If you had a name, we could do a records search on our database. Not that I could guarantee anything, but it wouldn't be hours of combing through newspaper articles. We'd just have more options overall."

I nodded. "Thanks for your help anyway; I'm going to see what I can do to find out the name."

She patted me on the back, and I could tell she felt for me. If I were more familiar, I bet she'd have given me a squeeze. "I'm here Monday through Friday if you ever need me. Even if it's just for a good cry."

The drive over to the house was short, and as I crept up the driveway the double-deep wraparound porch appeared. Magnolia sat out there sipping a drink. Vodka soda with lemon and lime, if I were a betting woman.

"Drive was ok?" Magnolia asked. She wore a pressed white button-down that had been starched to heaven and back. Her oversize gold studs caught the sun as she drank from her glass.

"Yup," I said, then yawned. "I'm tired, though. Had to cram in a couple papers early to skip out for this weekend."

Magnolia patted the corner of her mouth, checking her red lips. "Well, school's important for now, but it'll just be a matter of time before you're more concerned with society life here. Before long you'll be engaged, eventually married . . ."

"I'm not so sure," I said.

"Nonsense. You and Grady are prized by this community."

I walked to the porch railing, leaning over. "That's lovely and all, but we broke up. I'm with Lincoln now, remember?"

"It's nothing but a silly bump in the road. I know Grady will forgive you."

"And what if I don't want to be forgiven?" *Or* need *to be.*

"You're really that willing to give up a catch like a Suffolk?"

I knew before I spoke that I was making trouble, but on the heels of my library letdown, I didn't care. "You didn't end up snagging anyone, and you're doing ok. You've actually done quite well without my father, right?"

Magnolia prickled. "Every mother wants better for her child than what she had."

I huffed, and my limbs went loose. "Won't you tell me more about him? Just a name? *Please*, a name is all I need."

Magnolia dropped her hands into her lap and sighed. "I guess we're doing this again then."

"One little name won't hurt," I said.

"One little name that will open the floodgates to the past." Magnolia lifted herself out of the chair. "You don't know what you're doing. I've protected you and loved you and given you everything you could want all these years, and that's not enough?"

"I can handle it, Mama. A name is all I'm asking for."

"It's a whole lot more than that." She shook her head. "And you'll be sorry if you keep up with this; you'll only have yourself to blame."

"I'm done not knowing. I'll manage it fine. The *not knowing* is what I can't handle."

"This is real trouble, real people, real hurt beyond anything you've ever known. It's not a little treasure hunt."

I swallowed the fear that boiled up. The little voice that said maybe she was right. She knew him, after all. I held up my hands. "I'm sorry." I sighed. "I don't want to ruin the weekend." It was true, but also I didn't have any more ammunition to battle her. I would never be more convincing with my hypotheticals and my feelings.

Magnolia pulled in a deep breath. "You're right. We should be getting dressed for the event."

I followed her inside, and for the rest of the evening I played along. I fought the angry tide that rode in like waves as I pushed it away with my insistence that anger wouldn't do any good. I smiled and I joined in the brainless chitchat. I sipped and nibbled and didn't chew my nails.

I was the perfect daughter.

I was her perfect Magnolia.

Even if my insides felt volcanic.

CHAPTER 33

Present Day

MAYA, FITZ, AND I SIT outside on the back patio at the studio. It's a warm summer morning, and we have shade for our meeting until the scorching sun peeks over the rooftop around eleven thirty. The courtyard around us is bricked with wisteria climbing across and over the walls, its fragrance a permanent perfume during the blooming months. It's a dreamy spot to review the good work completed in the week since the producers visited, as well as our outstanding to-dos.

On the low table between us are the coffee and pastries I grabbed from a bakery on my way in this morning. Each time I buy something like a butter-loaded croissant, it feels like payback for all those nights in high school when Magnolia refused to allow me to eat anything but Special K—per the latest diet.

"How are things with Ms. Dorothy?" Maya asks me. "I know she only wants you as her point of contact, so generally I leave her alone."

I smile. "She's as sweet as the tea she plies me with every time I go over, but I don't think she's got anything for us right now."

"Which is probably all well and good considering that we need to start planning the furnishings at the Daniel House," Fitz says.

In the days that've passed since the producers visited, real progress has been made. We've done drywall repairs and mended woodwork. Mateo was even able to work his magic on the dining room medallion enough that we could keep it. The kitchen has cabinets and fixtures, and the downstairs hall bath is complete— aside from wall art and decor. The railings on the staircase, our centerpiece, are each being patched and shined one by one.

"This might've been the better week to have the producers come on-site. When things are really moving along," I say.

"I don't know that it makes a difference," Maya says. "Plus, we haven't done paint or furniture yet, so there are plenty of *reveals* upcoming, if they want a flashy moment."

"True," I say. "But don't you think we should've heard from them by now?"

"I'm not so sure," Fitz says. "It's only been a week, and we'd be hearing if they're green-lighting a pilot. It's no small decision— I'm sure there are multiple rounds of red tape to get through."

I sighed. "You're probably right. It's just that I can't help but wonder about the worst."

"Let's not plan our own funeral while we're still in the game, Boss," Maya says.

I smile at her, something about her enthusiasm reminding me of Hallie. I glance at my watch. "Hallie should be here by now," I say, pawing around for my phone.

I text Grady: Here at the studio. Weren't you dropping Hallie by this morning? I thought we said around 9:30.

A few minutes later, my phone pings.

Just pulled up to your house. We said your place, not the studio.

"Grady freakin' Suffolk is going to be the death of me," I say.

"And probably many more of the unfortunate souls who come into his orbit," Fitz says. "What's new today?"

"He took Hallie to the house instead of bringing her here." I scroll through my phone and find the exchange. "I knew I was right. It's almost as if he's trying to make it hard."

If it's not him missing our preplanned handoffs, it's babysitter snags and last-minute work requirements.

"You want me to go grab her?" Fitz asks.

"No, of course not," I say, gathering my things. "Y'all eat the rest of those pastries or take them with you. Guess I'll be working from home the rest of the day."

"Ok," Maya says. "And don't forget, you have a meeting with Theo Hartman tomorrow morning at ten to discuss landscaping at the Daniel House."

"Thanks, Maya. I'd lose my head without you."

I cross inside and begin packing up my laptop and gathering any samples I'll need for next design steps. Fitz and Maya grab the food and follow me in, muttering about the patio already feeling too hot. I can't ignore the heat sitting heavy in my chest over Grady's nonsense. I should ask him to bring her here himself, but after he pitched a fit over the Exquisite Interiors shoot, I'm trying to keep him at arm's distance. I sling my bag over my shoulder and grab my keys when my phone buzzes in my pocket. I almost ignore it, sure it'll be Grady checking in on my ETA.

Instead it's Lincoln. Calling.

I pick up slowly. "Hello?"

"Hey," he says. "Hope I'm not interrupting, but I've got Hallie here. Her dad saw her run over to Foster and asked if she could hang until you got here."

"I'm sorry, Lincoln. He shouldn't have," I said. "I'll be there as soon as possible."

"It's ok. I offered to take Foster downtown to visit the market candy shops, so we could drop her off—or bring her with us."

I hear Foster's pleading voice in the background.

"Scratch that," Lincoln says. "It's now a request: Can Hallie come to the candy shop with Foster *before* we drop her off? He wants me to say *please, please, please.*"

I smile and slip onto my desk chair, bag dropping to my side. Lincoln is so great with Foster, and Hallie too. So good that he's hard to reconcile with the young man I once fought with before he hopped a flight and never came back. He always was easy to like, but is especially so now. Easy to be with. Easy to rely on.

Easy to love—for any individual lucky enough to get there.

But I shouldn't let myself get too tangled up with my new neighbor. It's the responsible, *adult* thing to do, after all, but it's moments like this when I can't help but wonder: What if things had worked out differently between us?

I smile. "If you're sure you're ok with it," I say. "Otherwise, I can be home in fifteen minutes, ten if I speed."

Lincoln laughs. "I'm completely free today, and I wouldn't hear the end of it if Foster had to endure this trip without his best pal."

"Thanks," I say, and we hang up.

Fitz is at my side, grinning like a Cheshire cat. "And who was *that?*"

"I bet you could guess," I say.

"You're holding out on me." Fitz pulls up a chair, props up an arm, and stares at me.

"He's great with the kids," I say. "They came over for pizza the other night, and things were . . . *good.*"

"Excuse me while I pick my jaw up off the floor," Fitz says. "So did that *good* include any butterflies or googly eyes?"

I roll my eyes in a way that I'm sure totally gives me away. "We're neighbors, and on the way to being friends."

"Ok, Bambi with the fluttery eyes over there," Fitz says. "You know I've been reading you like a book for years now."

I drop the act and let my hands flop onto the desk. I lower my voice to a whisper. "Ugh, it's so awful because he's still superhot, and I kinda wanna kiss the guy, but then I remember he ran away to a different state to get away from me. Like, yuck. It makes me sound so shriveled up and desperate."

"He *did* run away to a new state," Fitz says. "But he was running toward Marcus Wilson, not away from you. So maybe your beef should be with Marcus—he's an attractive guy, from what I've seen in pictures."

"Trust me," I say, "you and I both know I had—*have?*—beef with Marcus Wilson."

Fitz sighs. "He'll officially be our scapegoat from here on out. A paint color doesn't turn out? Marcus Wilson. A windowpane cracked? Marcus Wilson. We get hit by the flu? *Again*, Marcus Wilson."

"Poor Marcus," I say. "He didn't know what he was stirring up for himself."

Despite what I say, I can't really blame Marcus for what fell apart between Lincoln and me. Not if I'm honest. Yes, Lincoln left, but I wasn't innocent in the situation. I played my part, soaked in Magnolia's influence, so probably Lincoln and I are both to blame.

Just as I'm about to dig back into my work, I see Erica's name light up my phone screen.

"It's Exquisite Interiors," I announce, and Maya and Fitz are at my sides, crowded around the phone.

CHAPTER 34

I SQUEEZE MY EYES SHUT TIGHT and tap the green button, then put the phone on speaker.

I clear my throat, but still my voice wobbles. "Hey, Erica. I've got you on speaker with Fitz and Maya."

Fitz places a hand solidly on my shoulder, and it's just the thing I need to ground me.

"Mack, I'm so glad I caught you," Erica says, "because I have news."

I hear background noise like she's driving. The tone of her voice is flat and neutral, and it makes me assume the worst. She's seemed so on our side thus far that it *must* be her own disappointment bleeding through.

"How free are you next week?" Erica asks.

My stomach drops. *Another* audition? Or an interview now? What more can we show them at this point?

Fitz speaks up. "For the network, of course we're available." He gives me a gentle nudge.

"So, are we—? Was there any feed—?"

"Sorry," Erica cuts me off. "I'm driving back from shooting in the North Carolina mountains, and it's torrentially downpouring. Let me be clear—the producers love you guys and they want to shoot a pilot."

The three of us chirp in yelps of excitement as well as several silent screams complete with hands flung out.

"Erica, that's incredible news! We're thrilled," I say, doing my best to sound professional.

She chuckles. "I wanted to catch you before the weekend so we can get going on a contract. That'll need to be signed before we start shooting the pilot, so I'm hoping we can get it finished next week, then get back to shooting the following week. It's a bit tight, but everyone's excited to get this pilot done and out to our audience. *Holy City Flip* is the name we've got going for it so far."

"Ok. I'll be watching my inbox," I say. "We're happy to move quickly. Thanks for everything you've done to get us this far."

"Like I've always said, you're easy to film. But I'll let you go. The roads are getting twisty."

"Sure thing," I say. "Talk soon."

My phone hits the tabletop with a clunk, and I drop my head into my hands and let out a whole-body breath. *A pilot.* This means at least one episode of our very own show, *Holy City Flip*, set right here in the most beautiful city on earth with my very own team, will exist. It's not a contract for a full season—that would only come after a good response to the first episode—but we're one step closer.

Fitz screams. "Amazing. Yes!"

Maya grins and hops in place. "Everyone I talked to on the organization side said they thought we had a good chance. I didn't say anything in case I got everyone's hopes up and then the tide changed, but still, I've got that good feeling in my stomach."

"We need to celebrate! Champagne? Dinner out?" Fitz says.

I laugh. "I've got the magpie coming soon, so whatever we do, it needs to be tame."

Fitz huffs. "Hal wouldn't begrudge us a little fun."

I smile and let myself feel the moment. It's only now that I allow myself to honestly try on the dream, to let myself envision our show, because before, it was all too uncertain. Before, it was so much like the fellowship dream I'd tried on so often that I'd practically worn holes in the knees of it. And my excitement is not even about the potential for stardom that a successful series could bring; it's the fact that even the smallest steps beyond the grip of my mother's influence are like letting the light sweep in. It's freedom and success of my own I want, not fame.

I look around this studio, at the papers we scribble on, the books of samples, our shelves of books by designers we admire. The seats so well-worn from our dedicated rituals of doing the work. This moment of recognition makes it feel real, like we haven't just been pretending all along.

"Thank you, guys," I say, looking between Fitz and Maya. "This place wouldn't be the same without either of you."

"Thanks for trusting us," Fitz says. "Even at my family's firm, they wouldn't let me pick a finish before twelve others approved it."

"I'm excited to keep learning," Maya says. "I'm lucky to have fallen into this industry."

Fitz tuts. "Computers really are quite a bore—even if we are all reliant on the little ones in our pockets."

I turn to Maya. "I will be learning until the day I die. But you've earned your place here, Maya. You're not a rookie anymore, so don't be afraid to act like it."

"Mm-hmm," Fitz says. "A pinch more swagger, please."

It takes the three of us a while to settle, and I don't begrudge us the enjoyment. But eventually we resume our work talk—even if it is punctuated by pilot-related comments—and formulate our calendar for the following week. Eventually we each grab some food brought from home and bakery leftovers and make lunch for ourselves.

Soon after, the front doors click open, and a gust of warm air follows a backlit Hallie and Foster inside. Each carries a crinkled paper bag, the tops tight in their fists, and they charge like an over-caffeinated pair of donkeys. They screech to a halt in front of my desk with pink-and-blue candy stains and even a few smudges of chocolate around their mouths.

"Mom," Hallie says. "Mr. Lincoln is the *best* babysitter I have ever had."

Fitz creeps closer to us.

Foster nods in a sugary hurry. "Hallie is welcome anytime! Really. I don't have any brothers or sisters, but she lives next door and we're best friends now so she's basically like a superfriend and maybe we could get walkie-talkies?"

I stand. "Well, I'm glad y'all had a good time. You're both lucky to have such a good friend."

Lincoln appears in the doorway looking out of breath. "Those two are *fast*," he says. "I'm going to need to train for the next time."

Next time. As the words soak in, they sizzle beneath my skin. Not that either of us would stand in the way of the kids' friendship at this point, but naming, out loud, that we expect these encounters to be routine in some way, in any way at all, feels like flipping the world upside down. Like dropping into another world where he never left, a world where I was enough to make him want to stay.

"You might stand a better chance of keeping up if you ate half your body weight in sugar," I say.

He grins and shakes his head as his chest rises and falls. "I'm strongly against doping."

I laugh and it feels like my exterior is cracking like eggshells, like the sensible cover of adulthood might not matter in the company of a man who once made me feel so alive. "Touché."

Fitz glides over. "Hello, Lincoln Kelly." He pulls himself up to sit on my desktop and crosses his legs. "I'm sure you could surmise, but I'm Fitz."

Lincoln nods. "Yes, nice to meet you."

"Tell me, how'd you get back here?"

The protective edge to Fitz's words is palpable, but just below the surface is a hopeless romantic who would cry buckets over a one-who-got-away scenario made right.

"It's a long story," Lincoln says.

Fitz checks for the kids and finds them outside in the courtyard, bouncing off the walls. "I think we deserve more of an explanation than that, yes? Especially after you left our girl here heartbroken and devastated for months."

"Fitz." I step forward, waving him off. "No, no, no. We're not doing that. It was a very long time—"

Maya joins me, standing at my side and hovering like she's ready to jump in to help.

"And quite frankly, you've never truly been the same since," Fitz says, crossing his arms defiantly as we lock eyes.

I shoot him a look that says, *I could kill you right now.*

Lincoln's face flashes with something like surprise. It must be in response to Fitz's forwardness, because even if Fitz is laying it on, the basic facts of what he said aren't untrue. There's no surprise there.

"Well," Lincoln says, "after my father died last year, I wanted Foster and me to be closer to my mom and sister here in North Charleston. And since we're all being *honest*, I guess I found some of what I was looking for in New York—"

"Yes, your illustrious photography career," Fitz says.

Lincoln sighs like Fitz is testing his patience. I get it because he's testing mine too.

"I did find success, and I'm grateful for it. But with time comes wisdom, and I've realized that not everything is about career and success. That there are other things in life that are"—Lincoln glances at me—"important too."

Fitz bugs out his eyes and whips his head to look between us while my gaze stays locked on Lincoln. Fitz then catches Maya's eye, and she gives him a knowing smile.

My mouth falls open a hair, and a flush runs over my face. Did Lincoln really mean to look at me when he said those words? Is he admitting fault? Or even *regret*? For a moment it feels so good to imagine that him showing up here really could undo the hurt of years ago. That in some way, I might find relief from the guilt of taking my mother's side.

"Anyway," Lincoln says and clears his throat. "Foster and I should be going. It was nice to see you all."

Lincoln strides through the office and calls Foster in from the patio. The moment is gone, and I'm sure now I was just making up that look. Of course, he wasn't wrong: He got the career he wanted. He got to quit the day job crunching numbers, so it was the right choice. Surely he wouldn't change a thing.

Lincoln wrangles Foster inside and through the office.

"Thank you," I say before they tumble onto the street. "Hallie had an awesome time with you guys. I owe you one, Lincoln."

He glances back. "You don't owe me a thing, Mack. See you around."

I turn on my heel and work hard to hold myself still as I walk back to my desk. I already know Fitz will be circling, so I preemptively hold up a single finger to him when he approaches.

"No. We're not talking about this. Not today when I want to celebrate our pilot."

Fitz sighs. "I guess that's fair."

"Where to for dinner tonight?" I ask, solely to move the conversation on.

Fitz and Maya begin batting ideas back and forth, discussing reservations versus something more casual. I sit there pretending to listen, but I can't stop thinking about Lincoln, just here, right now. I loved him. I loved him with the most real parts of myself, parts he's one of a very few to know even to this day. I loved him then, and just because he left and I was too proud to go after him doesn't mean I stopped loving him.

It really does create a bit of a complication for me, seeing as he's living next door. A *quagmire*, as Mother would say.

CHAPTER 35

Fifteen Years Earlier

LINCOLN'S BED FRAME WAS JUST like him: straight-forward, sturdy, and timeless. I ran my hand over the side of it, the rest of me inside the thick down comforter. Lincoln was at his 1980-something gas stove cracking eggs in a pan with toast popping and seasoning the cozy home with its scent. We'd been together for months by then, spending each and every free moment together.

So much for a summer thing.

"Order up," Lincoln said, arms filled with plates.

I stretched and rolled myself from the bed and padded over to the wobbly bistro set. He put down the plates and joined me.

I dug into the fluffy eggs. "My compliments to the chef," I said through a bite.

"Can't have my girl leave hungry."

I laughed and blew on my hot coffee. "My fangs come out when my blood sugar drops. It's a medical condition."

Lincoln smiled gently, and we ate in comfortable silence until the plates were bare.

"You cooked. I'll clean," I said, gathering the dishes from the table.

My arms were elbow-deep in soap suds when Lincoln arrived at my side.

"Look, there's something we—"

"I told you," I said with a grin. "I can't take you up on the offer for bowling unless you sign a waiver. You're great, and I've been known to throw things when I lose."

The fact that Lincoln was bowling on an actual team with a group of three seniors over on James Island was information I'd unearthed a few weeks ago. They weren't allowing spectators at the moment, which I found awfully suspicious, but he'd already provided dates for the matches I'd be allowed to observe. I was already working on a "bowling girlfriend" T-shirt for the special occasion.

Lincoln looked back at me seriously.

"I got some news," he said.

My hands stopped in the water. I whipped them out and grabbed a dish towel as I spun to face him. "Is everything ok?"

He stood still in a way I'd never seen him do before. "Yeah, it is."

I let out a deep breath and went back to drying my hands. "Good, so what is it?"

"Well, remember all those long-shot applications I sent to photography studios?"

"Yeah, of course. You said you'd never get one. Probably never even hear back from the stuck-up idiots."

Lincoln bit his lip. "Well, turns out I did. Hear back, that is."

I felt the blood rush out of my stomach, down to my toes, and what felt like outside my body entirely. "Oh."

Lincoln tried on an unsure smile. "I actually got offered a spot at the Marcus Wilson Studio in New York. Can you believe it?"

This was probably the moment I was supposed to screech in celebration for him, maybe rush to him and cover him in kisses, maybe cry in pride if I wanted to really do it up big. But all I felt was gutted, cut open along the middle like a prize fish caught and forgotten.

"In New York?" I said. "Like, you'd move there?"

Lincoln nodded slowly. "Yeah, that's the deal."

I swallowed hard as tears crept up my throat and spilled out of my eyes. "You weren't supposed to get it. You deserve it, of course—but you said this wouldn't happen."

Lincoln frowned. "What do you mean?"

"How could you do this?" I heard the words come out of my mouth, and I knew I didn't have a right to say them, but I did anyway. Because I felt them. To my core. "You're leaving?"

"So you're not happy for me?" Lincoln turned and began to pace the small apartment. "Wow, I knew you were an only child, but . . ."

"Congratulations," I said, flat-faced. "I'm sorry—it's an honor to be chosen, and you should be very proud."

Lincoln slowed. "Thanks for the formalities, Mack," he said. "But why don't you tell me what you *really* mean. What's your deal?"

"My deal?" I crossed my arms. I looked down so I could put my thoughts together, but as I contemplated the why he was asking for, my arms slowly slipped apart and fell to my sides. I looked up and met his eyes. "I love you, Lincoln. This thing between us is different for me—it's made me notice different parts of me. I don't want you to move."

Lincoln's face softened. "Look, I've been fighting off those same feelings—"

Fury hit me, and the words flew out. "*Fighting off*?" I demanded. "You've been fighting off feelings for me? Wow, how nice."

Lincoln threw out his hands. "You called this a summer fling. What was I supposed to do? Literally, to this very damn day, you've called me your summer lover or some other cutesy version of it. I met your mother, and it was the ultimate train wreck. She made it very clear I couldn't be a guy that would work out in the long run."

I couldn't argue with him because he was right, and it would sound unbearably lame to make my case that what I said wasn't what I meant.

Lincoln pulled in a breath. "Look, I'm sorry I raised my voice, but Mack, you have to understand. This is my chance to make it as a real photographer. It's my chance to break free of the accountant's office."

"It's all you've ever wanted," I told him.

That was the moment I sat on the very edge of all my hopes. My insides swelled as they waited to see if he would tell me I was wrong. I wanted more than anything for him, even if he left me, to tell me I was a fool to say that. I wanted him to say that photos and a career big enough to carry a life weren't all he might need. He could say it, even indirectly, even without an ounce of gusto, but I begged the heavens and the earth that he'd say he wanted me too. Just a few simple words . . .

Lincoln held my gaze for an excruciating beat, and he didn't open his mouth. He nodded firmly.

"And I'll be fine," I said, knowing the shake in my voice gave me away.

And then for the very first time in my life, I channeled my mother, the original Magnolia, the source of all things cold and unfeeling. She'd never let Lincoln hurt her, and she'd tell me he wasn't worth my tears.

I dabbed my tears on my T-shirt and sucked in a breath. "I think I should get going," I said. "Can you handle the dishes?"

I didn't wait for an answer before I calmly hung the dish towel back in its place and walked to the bedroom. There, I pulled on my jeans and systematically loaded my things into my tote bag.

Lincoln followed me. "Can we talk about it? Mack, I love you too."

He stood in the doorway with a face full of hope, like I'd have something to say about it. Like it wasn't all a little too late. I turned back to my packing.

"Can we stay in touch?" Lincoln asked. He crossed the room and touched my arm gently.

I looked at him with a steely glare executed perfectly from years of receiving it from my mother, and I hoped it hurt him like it had me for all those years. "I'm not really a long-distance-relationship kind of girl," I said.

With that I slung the bag over my shoulder and marched out of the apartment, shoulders back, head high. It was the first time I was grateful for Magnolia's raising, because these things were muscle memory enough for me to pull them off. On the inside I was a swirl of hurt and shame—never enough, not even close. He didn't want me, and I couldn't imagine tomorrow without him.

I trudged home, down impossibly quaint streets, past happy tourists toting ice cream cones, an insult to my inner unraveling. The farther I got from his apartment, the more my facade fell away. My shoulders slumped, my chest heaved, and eventually I dropped to a bench so I could hang my head.

It wasn't supposed to go this way.

I pulled out my phone and I blocked his number. I set a filter on my email to delete his messages.

I wouldn't be burned by him again.

Because he was getting what he wanted, what he'd earned. He was getting his dream in arm's reach, one he very much deserved, despite the way it stung me.

They were so very lucky to have him.

CHAPTER 36

Present Day

IN THE END, WE EAT our celebratory dinner at the studio,
takeout from the best Thai place in town. I don't want anything fancy—probably because it'd just remind me of Magnolia, the very person this accomplishment sets me apart from.
Plus, Hallie crashes dramatically once the sugar wears off, and
even a jaunt to the restaurant threatens to undo her entirely.

I manage to forget about Lincoln for a while, but as Hallie and
I drive across the bridge toward home, across the water speckled
in gold from the setting sun, I can't help but remember. I glance
in the rearview and see that Hallie's asleep in her booster seat.

I pull into our neighborhood and through the winding streets
to our house. It really wasn't fair of Fitz to put Lincoln on the
spot like that, demanding answers for why he broke up with me
a decade and a half ago. It's especially grating considering how
generous Lincoln has been, letting Hallie tag along with her new
buddy, saving me from a couple of sticky spots.

Once I get Hallie tucked in and know she's good and asleep, I
slip into my flip-flops at the front door. I skip across my driveway
and over the green space to the house next door. I knock.

There's no answer.

I wait and knock gently again. I hear rustling from the yard and walk around to the side of the house, following a path of solar lights. The grass is still warm as it reaches up and over the base of my flip-flops, and soon I'm at the waist-high picket fence.

Lincoln stands in the backyard, leaning to pull and tinker with plants, some sort of light contraption attached to his head.

I knock on the fence, looking right at him. I prepare to smile and wave when he looks up. But when he does, he nearly blinds me with the light.

"Sorry!" He fumbles to shut the light off and ambles over to the gate. He smiles and pops it open. "You've caught me doing my night gardening."

My heart squeezes. "Night gardening? Tell me more."

He chuckles. "It's a necessity for this climate. All you need is a headlamp, and weeding works just as well in the dark. Not to mention, the water won't disappear under the sun." He waves me through the gate.

"I won't keep you from your duties," I say. "Plus, I've got Hal asleep at home." I glance back at the house.

Lincoln points. "You can still see your house from our back patio, if you want to sit."

I don't think twice before I follow him there. The nighttime bugs chirp enthusiastically in the warm air, our Southern symphony. I'll only be a few minutes, and it'll be nice to relax for a moment after this long day. I settle into an old wrought iron patio chair. It grates against the concrete as I shift it. I cringe.

"He'd sleep through a hurricane," Lincoln says, apparently reading my thoughts.

"Thank goodness." I plant myself. "Hallie can hear a pin fall clear across the water."

Lincoln flips on the string lights and at once we're in our own fairy garden, flanked by potted plants, a well-loved grill, and a healthy stash of kids' yard toys.

"I wanted to come apologize for earlier," I say. "I didn't realize you lost your dad recently, and so I wanted to say I'm sorry about that too."

Lincoln shrugs. "You know things weren't great between us. He took off for the West Coast not long after I went to New York, and we sort of lost touch. I tell myself it was for the best; he didn't seem to want to be a dad. But it showed me how important the rest of my family is—my mom and sister."

I nod. "Happily-ever-afters in the dad category aren't always on offer."

He squeezes a brief smile in understanding.

I pull in a quick breath. "Also, Fitz shouldn't have cornered you like that today, and I hope you know I didn't put him up to it."

Lincoln laughs. "From first impressions, Fitz doesn't seem like one to be *put up to things* by anyone."

"Quite the valid point," I say.

"And it wasn't a big deal," Lincoln says. "Honestly, it's not like we can ignore what happened forever, what with us living next door and the kids being friends."

I feel a tingle run through me, but I can't quite decide if it's excitement or fear.

"I guess you're right," I say.

We both stop and let the singing bugs fill the silence. There's a longing for Lincoln that has never quite left me, and looking at him here, in the most darling garden this side of the bridge, makes me feel years younger. Careless and swept up in how easy it is to delight in him.

Still, he might have quite opposite feelings, harboring resentment over the cold way I cut him off. Maybe he's nothing but relieved to have avoided getting caught up in my family politics. Maybe he's even seeing someone else. I feel jealousy prickle at the mere thought of it. There are so many reasons my relentless fondness is a recipe for hurt, but I'd be a liar if I said a little part of me didn't hope he wished things had turned out differently too.

"I didn't think I'd ever see you again," Lincoln says eventually.

I glance down. "I blocked your number." I sigh regretfully. "If it helps, I did it to protect myself more than to hurt you."

"I probably deserved it," he says. "Back then I thought I knew everything."

I smile. "That was me too. All-knowing expert on life. I mean, I led you right into the lion's den to a dinner with Magnolia Senior and didn't even stop to wonder if that was a terrible, awful idea. *Easy breezy*, if I remember right." I flop my palm across my face.

We laugh.

I feel myself loosen with relief, my shoulders dropping, as I admit my part in things. I wasn't as blameless as I told myself I was back then. But still, the catch in my chest happens, the one that's reflex by now when I remember how he left. That moment when all I wanted was for him to admit that I was important to him too. I wanted him to want me at the same time.

But he didn't.

I've never been able to shake that.

I shrug. "But it seems to have worked out all right. I mean it when I say it this time: I'm happy for you. Your work is incredible, and you made it. You got what you wanted."

He reaches out a hand that lands on my arm. His eyes meet mine and don't make any move to leave, and I wonder if he agrees. I think about all the magazine articles, the exhibitions I saw online, the artsy parties at which I'm sure he was fawned over. He didn't just *make it work*; he *made it big*. There isn't a way he could have that and carry any regrets.

But then I think about that comment earlier at the studio. Maybe I'm making something out of nothing.

Maybe not.

All I want is for him to tell me what he meant.

"I did want the career, but I also wasn't looking at the whole picture," Lincoln says. "I'm sorry about how I hurt you. I didn't handle it well. Not only was I blinded by the need for financial security, but I thought I was the only one with real feelings. I thought I'd be an idiot if I made a big deal of me leaving after you told me you didn't want more than a summer thing. I imagined you pouting for a second, then giving me a peck and telling me to give you a call when I was next in town. Until you said it, I had no idea you had real feelings. I felt the same, Mack. I loved you too."

My chest lights up like a star exploding in space, and it feels like it could shatter me. Like it's been waiting for this. I look at him, and I believe him. We were young and dumb, both of us; I made my fair share of mistakes too. Maybe that's why I never could make him out to be the big bad guy I thought he should've been for leaving. Why no matter how hard I tried, I couldn't hate him because he didn't deserve it, and even if he'd done worse, I simply wasn't built to hate him.

I was built to hold quite opposite feelings for him.

And now, years later, and even if his words don't match the exact script I wanted all those years ago, what he said sounds an awful lot like, *I wanted you too.*

"I should've quit calling it a summer thing," I say. "It was far more, and I was just too proud to say it first."

Lincoln catches my eyes in a way I haven't seen—no, *felt*—in a decade and a half, and it turns my limbs to butterflies, my brain to pulp. I don't look away. I don't because I don't want to. I didn't then, and I don't now. And I've been chasing this feeling for all these years in between.

His hand on my arm squeezes gently, and I can feel the electricity running between us, not a day aged in fifteen years. My skin shivers, despite the muggy night air. I should be sensible; I should be an *adult*, but my attempts are shoddy at best. I let myself feel every memory of him, and I let myself revel in it.

I float toward him.

Lincoln meets me, knowing just where, like a preplanned spot. We came to this place so many times. And when we're together, the space around the edge of it is so narrow, it's almost impossible not to fall in and down into the depths.

Lincoln's hand creeps up and wraps around my neck. He pulls me in gently and all at once, and our lips meet. It's like unlocking a part of myself that's been sleeping all these years. He stands and lifts me with him, and I wrap my arms up and around him like he might escape me again. He's the same, but firmer and wider, and as I run my fingers over the folds of his skin, envy burns at the way they remind me he's lived years without me.

I pull back for breath.

"Years later and *still* . . . ," he says.

"No matter how hard I tried to forget," I say.

He pulls my face back to his, and my mouth parts to meet his once more. I squeeze my body against his. I wasn't wrong about him when I fell for him all those years ago; I wasn't only young and naive. I wasn't wrong when I thought Lincoln was good and lovable and every drop of magic I remember.

"Finally." The word escapes his lips.

I pull in a breath to reply but stop as the lid of a trash can slams at the fence.

We freeze.

Whip our heads to look.

I hang on his neck, and we stare silently at Mrs. Andrews's side of the fence, checking for the shadow of a figure spying over the shrubs. I look back to him, and the laughter spills from us.

"Damn it, Mrs. Andrews," Lincoln whispers.

I release myself from his front, surely red-faced and disheveled. "You think she saw us?"

Lincoln rubs at his chin, framing his grin, the same way he always has. "Who knows. She's harmless anyhow."

I nod, looking at him. My racing heart echoes in my chest. "But I definitely should get going. Before we find ourselves too far down memory lane."

Lincoln chuckles, letting his hands drop from around me. "If you must."

I sneak back over to my house, tiptoeing across the grass as if Magnolia Senior will be standing and waiting, tapping her watch as I, once again, return after curfew.

I swing my door shut gingerly behind me and slide down it, giggling. Maybe I can still be alluring, even after all the mom stuff I've been through. I've never felt more like the twenty-year-old version of myself since the first time around, and it's a rush that's still hammering in my chest.

Lincoln, *Lincoln Kelly*, is back.

And maybe some lost little bits of me too.

CHAPTER 37

I T'S A GORGEOUS MORNING ON the Charleston peninsula the following morning. Blue skies, chirping birds, and sunshine front and center. All right, and maybe I'm still up in the clouds a little over my kiss with Lincoln last night. I haven't told anyone about it, and I'm not sure I will quite yet. It's nice to keep it all to myself.

Not to mention if I told Fitz, he'd rake me over any coal he could find, talking about the *implications* of it.

I pull up to the Daniel House and park. I walk slowly up the brick path to the house that's come so far. Paint is about to go up inside, and Marco's crew is already at work repairing and patching siding. Soon enough, she'll have a fresh new coat of white paint on the outside, her iron railings shiny black, and the ceiling of her wraparound porch haint blue.

My phone rattles in my bag, and I dig through to find it. I recognize Jade's phone number.

"Hey, Jade," I say. "What's new?"

She clears her throat. "Hi! Good morning. I just wanted to call because I've been trying to reach your mother, Ms. Bishop, for a few days about progress on the house. The board has been emailing her and hasn't gotten what they need, so they asked me to check in with you directly."

I stifle an eye roll. "Ah, I see. I'm sorry. Magnolia is notorious for not checking email and deleting anything she doesn't feel like dealing with."

Jade lets out a breath. "I don't want to step on anyone's toes, but could we take some photos this afternoon? Nothing formal, just Douglas and me with our phones?"

"Of course. The crew usually wraps up around five, sometimes a little before if it's been a hot one. I'll let them know you're coming."

"Thank you." Relief soaks Jade's words.

"Anytime. You can always come to me if Magnolia is MIA."

I hang up the phone, and just as I'm dropping it back in my bag, the front gate jangles behind me, and I turn.

"Hey, Theo," I say. "Thanks for meeting me here."

Maya said he'd jumped at the chance to work on our reality show project. I mean, who in their right mind wouldn't? Especially now that the local rumor mill had found this tidbit of gossip regarding our likely debut as reality television stars. Already we've seen an uptick in followers on social media. "I'm happy to." Theo props his hands on his hips and looks around. "Seems we've got quite the blank canvas here. The perfect starting place, in my opinion."

I join him in examining our barely-hanging-on grass that might actually just be weeds and the scorched-out beds.

"Yup," I say. "We don't need to save a thing. Not that there's much to save."

"I drew up some general designs based on the pictures Maya sent me, so we could go over those first, if you'd like," Theo says.

"That's great." I turn and start walking to the door. "Why don't we set our things down inside first. Plus you can get a sneak peek of the inside."

"An offer I couldn't refuse." Theo follows me inside. "And just know—the designs I've put together are only a starting point. If you've got certain plants you'd like to include or others you can't stand, just shout and we can move things around."

My shoes clop on the shiny floors as I deviate off the paper-covered section to the kitchen that now has cabinets. This room may not have been the center of the house when it was built so long ago, but it's still the spot that feels like a command center to me.

"Ok," I say. "I have a few favorite plants, but between you and me, I don't have much of a green thumb."

Theo chuckles. "Oh, I bet you'd get the hang of it pretty quick if you gave it a try." He stops in front of the kitchen and looks around, eyes wide. "I mean, if you can do this? You could remember to water a plant or two."

"Easier said than done," I say.

Theo joins me at the newly installed breakfast table, one we pulled from storage until the final furniture pieces are placed. "I'll talk you through what I've done, the general feel, and the budget, and then once we're sure we're on the same page, we can go outside and talk specifics."

I nod. "Music to my ears."

Theo launches into his pitch, and all of his ideas are spot-on for what I have in mind for this property—traditional but fun, bright, and lively. Again, it's probably the post-Lincoln effect, but this is running more smoothly than I imagined with Theo being an out-of-town contractor, even if I was impressed by him on the day of the fellowship tour.

"Now, lay it on me, Theo," I say. "How much is this going to cost?"

He grins. "Well, it's right in the budget you set for me. I'm not the type to overspend someone else's money."

"Wonderful," I say. "Let's head outside and you can show me where it all goes."

Theo and I dip outside, and he begins his guided tour of our gardens-to-be.

"I think if we line the entry path in boxwoods, it'll really give the house that grand entrance it deserves. We'll keep them pruned short—or your regular crew will—but they'll have a great effect and set off the richness of the brick really nicely."

I nod and follow him all the way down to the front.

"Now along this front iron fence, I'm thinking we want privacy," he says.

"Definitely," I say. "It's not a super-busy street, but in case of private events it could be nice."

"I think so too," Theo says. "We'd plant tall, slim evergreens along here, and they'll grow just slightly above that high fence line. They'll be easy to maintain and won't grow out of control every spring."

I know landscaping is important, and I've seen firsthand its impact, but something about the Daniel House is in such dire need. The house itself is finally showing off all the work we've put into it, and in contrast, the scruffy gardens stick out like a neon safety vest. We can't have Theo's plans in place soon enough.

"We'll do more lawn than a typical historic home downtown," Theo says, walking up the gentle slope to the house. His eyes land on the path. "And I've got the perfect guy to repair the bumps in the brick. It won't be perfect, but we'll save it."

"That's fabulous. The last thing I want is people tripping on their way in. And I'm on board with more lawn. Filling all of this with plants or breaking it up with hardscape would be a nightmare for maintenance. Not to mention visually busy."

"And here I was preparing to have to argue with you on that one," Theo says with a wink.

We reach the top of the slope and stand in front of the porch. "I may have grown up as a debutante, but there's a deep-seated practical part to me as well," I say.

Theo laughs but quickly returns to his presentation, the consummate professional. He walks us around toward the back and points out where the beds will flow, and we discuss the back half of the property.

"I know it's a large space back here, and it'll need to function to host an event, but I really want the feel of it to be like that of a family home," I say. "Now that I'm hearing myself say it, it sounds like an oxymoron."

"We don't want it to look like a massive blank slate when there's not event furniture set up," Theo says. "I think we can avoid that by adding a bit of variation to the landscape, even if it must be on a larger scale."

"Exactly."

"What about a gravel area with a nice fountain in the middle? Again, we'd use a boxwood divider around the border but also to create pockets around the fountain in the center. It's really up to you, but it could be left open as a walking area for tours and such, or for event tables and chairs to be set up. If for whatever reason in the future a single owner took over, they could easily re-landscape the area without tearing out pavers or concrete. Especially with the termite damage y'all had and that terrible deck, we want to go easy on the grounds for a while."

I laugh. "Maya kept you updated on all that? And yes, I love the vision."

Theo shrugs. "What can I say? I was excited about this project from the get-go. You had me hooked since the first one. I went to Charleston Southern for college, so I have a special place in my heart for the gardens of this city. I called more than once to *check in*."

"Well, at least you can say you were all-in before the reality TV bonus got thrown in," I say.

We smile and walk to the back end of the property where we problem-solve creating a screen for the property line. Theo and I agree on some fast-growing evergreens in front of a high wooden privacy fence painted a dark emerald to camouflage.

"We can run a trellis up in the same color, and we'll have vines growing over it before you know it. It's so far back from the house that it'll blend in, and eventually those evergreens will fill in any gaps."

We make our way back to the house, and I thank Theo for his work. Before I send him on his way, I ask him the same thing I need to start asking all of our contractors.

"I have to get forms for everyone eventually, but if Exquisite Interiors happens to be filming on your workday, are you comfortable being on camera?"

Theo pulls his keys from his pocket. "Oh, I'm not sure I'm the best to be on camera, but if they catch me in the background, it won't be an issue. I've actually got a few guys I'm sure would jump at the chance to shoot a clip."

"Works for me," I say.

We shake hands and Theo takes off. The plan he leaves behind has me even more excited for this home to come together.

CHAPTER 38

Fifteen Years Earlier

I WAS HOME FOR THE ANNUAL end-of-summer bonanza on the Beaufort Green, a well-manicured lawn surrounded by live oak trees draped in Spanish moss. Round wooden tables were set up across the area, and a stage, quiet for now, would come to life with a band later this evening. It had been less than two weeks since Lincoln and I broke up, and the event was a welcome distraction.

Magnolia and I approached the crowd, both dressed in A-line summer dresses and large brimmed hats to save our skin from sun damage.

"The Suffolks are right over there at our table," she said.

Every year Mama sponsored a table together with Delta Suffolk.

We reached them, and I pulled a wooden folding chair out for myself and sat. "Hi, Delta, you look lovely."

Ned came around the table and dropped a kiss on top of my head. "Good to see you, sport," he said, then took off in the direction of the stage where equipment was being carried up.

Magnolia began to settle beside Delta when a friend from the flower guild jogged up.

"Magnolia Bishop, if you don't look like salvation come to life," her friend announced. "We've hit a snag with a couple of auction items. Would you mind taking a look?"

Magnolia smiled wide, just like I knew she would at being referenced as *salvation itself*. "I'd be happy to lend my expertise," she said. "Dee, Magnolia, I'll be back in a few moments."

I paused in the quiet she left behind, and as I looked around, it was easy to appreciate the beauty of the place I called home. It helped that I was actually glad, for once, to be away from Charleston. There, I'd been spending the majority of my time moping around my apartment, mostly after Lincoln, but partially for my own naivety. Really, what had I been thinking? A summer fling rarely ended well for anyone, and it was also the *last* thing appropriate for the offspring of Magnolia Bishop. I should've kept things buttoned up, like Magnolia had always taught me, and getting upset over things like this would only bring me further heartache—and probably embarrassment.

If I wanted to be my best self, I had to stifle the ugly emotions before they tarnished my shiny appearance. Apparently, that was the way to a good life, at least according to Magnolia.

"When do classes start for the fall, honey?" Delta asked me over the rim of an icy cocktail. "Can't be long."

"Two weeks," I said. "Although it kind of feels like they never actually ended for me, since I've been staying busy with my internship."

Delta beamed. "You really are quite the go-getter, Mack. I know your mother is so proud."

I shrugged. This was what Delta was supposed to say about her friend, but I suspected she and I both knew it was a mixed bag when it came to Magnolia's opinions of my studies. "We both know her primary concern is that I marry well." I laughed through a smile to soften the comment.

Delta grinned. "Well, I can't fault her there, because she and I share the same hopes in that department."

The chair beside me slid out, and I looked up to see Grady making himself comfortable in the spot.

"Speaking of which," Delta said. "Let me give y'all a moment."

I stifled a groan. I might've made my peace with Grady being part of the evening, but that didn't mean I wanted painfully orchestrated *moments alone.*

Grady slung his arm over the back of my chair. "Hey, pretty lady."

I smiled back, wondering if there was any hint of me baring my teeth like the cornered animal I felt like. "Hey back."

"I tell you what, Clemson's great and all, but I can't wait to get back here to Beaufort," Grady said, looking out across the party. "The Clemson football scene is a blast, but otherwise, it's all a bit . . . agricultural . . . for my tastes."

"Huh," I said. "Family traditions, I guess."

All of the Suffolk men had attended Clemson, so Grady didn't have much choice. Still, he never seemed bothered about college, as long as he was guaranteed some good times. On the other hand, my college choice was the one place I felt like I had elbow room, since Magnolia never went herself and held no dying allegiance to any institution.

"How about you? I miss you, Mack." Grady put on that smile I used to love. He really could be charming when he tried.

I shuffled the auction booklet in the place setting in front of me. "Charleston is amazing. I'm excited about my major, and I've made a couple friends. So it's not too bad—and certainly no farm vibes."

Grady laughed, and I smiled at him reflexively. In that small flash of a moment, I remembered how I fell in love with him.

"I know it made sense to break up when we left for school," Grady said. "But I need you to know that I really will be waiting for you. Honestly, I'm ready to start winning you back now."

He'd always bought into the Bishop-Suffolk plan dreamed up by our mothers. Then again, he never seemed stifled and clipped by the Suffolk ways like I was by my mother. That was one very big way in which he and I were different.

"That's sweet," I said. "But I really am focused on school right now. I want to get a good start on my career, and honestly, I can't see myself leaving Charleston after graduation. It's where the work I want to do lives."

"So it's not a *no thanks*."

I scoffed. "Nice try, Casanova. How about we start by getting a drink before you put the moves on."

Grady stood and pulled my chair out in the precise way he'd learned in cotillion class. I took the elbow he held out for me, and arm in arm we strode to the bar. We reached the small crowd, and many faces were familiar. We broke off and greeted neighbors and business owners who lunched and brunched and golfed with our parents. More than one lady mentioned their delight at seeing the two of us together. Maybe Magnolia wasn't entirely off base when she mentioned how much the community loved us as a duo.

Finally we got to the front of the line, all hands shaken and necks hugged, and took our cold glasses beyond the tree-lined green to the waterfront.

"We're not bad as a team, huh?" Grady said, leaning on the thick metal rails over the sloshing water.

"Can't argue with you there," I said.

Because in these settings Grady and I worked. We were both from this place and had been groomed in the social niceties, the small talk, the common references. But beyond this place, I was a different person. In Charleston I spent my time in art and design, thinking about creating. Physically I looked like someone else. Here, it all felt like a bit of a show. Here, I felt like it was my job to be perceived, to play the friendly face of the next generation, to wait in line to take the place of the Magnolia Bishops and the Delta Suffolks, and that didn't feel like me.

It was a nice life, but it never did have space for all the parts of me.

"Honestly, I have a whole lot of other stuff on my mind," I said. I stood upright and turned to face him.

"Yeah? Don't tell me it's boy trouble."

He laughed like it was an impossibility, and inside I cringed at how close to the target he'd come. Yes, Lincoln was a sore spot, but it was his leaving that highlighted my greatest need.

"Can I ask you a favor?" I said.

Lincoln's leaving wounded my heart and my pride, but the part that hit me hardest was that he wasn't the first man to walk out on me. His departure felt like confirmation that I was impossible to stick around for.

Grady smiled. "Anything I can do to earn some brownie points."

"Great," I said. "I need you to talk to your mother for me."

"All riiight." He drew out the last word.

"I need you to ask her about my dad. I need his name."

Grady's eyebrows jumped. "What? You know she'd cut off a limb before she broke your mama's trust." He let out a breath. "It's a long shot."

"But your mother is my last lifeline. She and Magnolia have been best friends since before they could walk. There's no way she doesn't know who he was. There's no way she wasn't around when Magnolia was pregnant, when she had me, when I was a baby. But in my history, it's all a shadow. Delta knows, Grady. And she's right there, chatting with those women."

Grady cracked his knuckles as he eyed the crowd. "I'll try, but not tonight. She's certainly not about to spill anything here in front of all these people. Plus, she'll be annoyed no matter the time I ask."

I grabbed his forearms and squeezed. "*Thank you*, Grady. I can't tell you how much this means."

He wiggled me toward him and pulled me into a hug. "I'm happy to help. Especially if you might consider a date in exchange."

My face was pressed to his chest, thank God, when I rolled my eyes at the comment. This would be no quid pro quo situation, but I was more than happy to let him think there was a chance if I might get my information. "You're a crafty one." I playfully punched his chest and spun off him. "I'm going to go to the ladies' room."

"Whatever a guy has to do." Grady laughed. "I'll meet you back at the table."

The hope was fuel enough to get me through the small talk of the evening. I knew Grady would try, and I thought he was most likely to talk his mother into revealing something. Maybe this would take me one step closer to unmasking my father.

A girl could hope.

CHAPTER 39

Present Day

A LITTLE MORE THAN A WEEK after Theo and I walked the grounds of the Daniel House, the Exquisite Interiors crew takes over the property to begin shooting. We spend most of the morning getting folks oriented, and eventually a small tent is erected for the cameras and sound equipment and the crew and support staff. I'd known it would be more than Erica and a few others, but the scale of the production is overwhelming. I can't imagine how it would work if we didn't have twelve-foot ceilings.

We film the exterior before the heat of the day sets in, to show the siding repairs and a swatch for the new paint color. We also introduce the landscaping concepts, and just as Theo promised, he has more than one enthusiastic participant on his crew.

Fitz and I step inside the cool interior of the house pretending like we're cucumber-cool Hollywood types. Soon the hair and makeup crew pounce to fix what melted off our faces in the humid air.

"Erica, I didn't realize you had so many friends," Fitz says as a makeup artist dusts his face with an unknown powder. He turns to me. "Does the color match me ok? Last thing I want is to be looking like a mime with a chalky white complexion."

"Trust me," I say, "no one will ever, not once, not even for the briefest second, mistake you for a mime."

Fitz throws me some side-eye. "You're saying I run my mouth?"

I shrug with a silent look of wonder.

"If the shoe fits, Fitz," Erica calls over.

Fitz melts into laughter. "You've been hanging around us far too long, honey. We're ruining you," he calls back.

Erica approaches, lugging the camera onto her shoulder. "Anything for high-quality hosts," she says. "Now, let's focus. I need y'all to welcome us into the house and point out the details that are original, the work you've done, and how that work happens. Let's start from the threshold of the front door." Erica passes us to round up the rest of her support folks before she calls out, "Action!"

I pull in a breath. "Hey, y'all," I say into the camera. "I'm Mack Bishop."

"And you can call me Fitz," my cohost says.

"And this is *Holy City Flip*," we announce together.

"Cut!" Erica calls. She peers out from behind the camera. "Excellent. Now, let's start on the details."

"What if we went up and did it on the second-story porch?" I ask. "It might be a different camera angle, but the shot would open up into the large bedroom, which is currently being wallpapered."

"Love it," Erica says. "It's not like we're shooting this in the order it'll end up."

She and the crew follow us as we mount the stairs. The runner rug hasn't been installed yet, but the railing is buffed and shiny, stripped of the stray paint marks we discovered upon closer inspection.

"Freeze," Erica calls. "Guys, let's shoot them going up the stairs. Mack, can you lead on project discussion?"

I throw her a thumbs-up.

"Action," Erica calls.

I turn to Fitz as we slowly climb the wooden stairs. "How are things looking on the runner?"

"It's been ordered—that rich-red chintz look that'll go right from the bottom to the top landing where we'll transition back to hardwoods."

"Do you think that's the best bet? Leaving the upstairs hallway as hardwoods?"

Fitz pauses and leans on the railing elegantly. "Ya know, I wouldn't mind continuing the runner through the hallway. With the angle there, it'd work well."

"Not to mention protect these original floors a bit from wear and tear," I say, turning to finish our ascent.

"I love it," Fitz says, stepping on the landing behind me.

"Cut," Erica calls.

The crew shuffles upstairs behind her and we make our way down the newly taupe hallway to the primary bedroom. I take the heavy brass knob and turn it, and as the door swings open, it bumps into a ladder.

"Oops. Anyone up there on that ladder?" I ask through the crack.

Katie, our wallpaper expert and installer for the day, squeezes her red-cheeked face in the gap. "Hey, Boss, yeah, we've got a guy up there. Do y'all need in? Because there's buckets of glue and a cutting table and rolls everywhere."

"Ah, I see. No, we'll change plans. I don't want shooting to delay your work—or worse, create issues."

Katie nods and clicks the door shut.

"Why don't we take a short break?" Erica says. "We've got a ton of tape from the day already, so you've earned it by all standards."

"Working hard or hardly working, as my daddy used to say," Fitz says as we make our way down the wide staircase, through the entry hall, and out onto the porch.

Fitz and I drop into two rocking chairs along the front-facing side. I close my eyes and let the hot air run over me. Any sweat will be dabbed right up by hair and makeup before the camera clicks on.

"I hate to be the bearer of bad news," Fitz says, "but it seems your dastardly mother is here."

I pop open my eyes and shoot upright to see for myself.

Magnolia and I discussed this in detail. More than once. She wanted to come for the pilot shoot to manage things and to make sure I mentioned the board enough times and likely to take credit for the whole operation. And she's even more likely to offer her assistance as a host now that she's decided it might actually lend her some cachet in her circles.

I scan the yard and my gaze lands on her, marching up the newly smooth brick path like she runs the show. I leap up and meet her halfway.

"Mother, *what* are you doing here?" I say in an angry whisper. "We *agreed*. I would give you updates on what was happening with the show, and you would let me handle it."

She sighs. "Yes, but I wasn't willing to miss it."

"There will be more than one shoot," I say.

She lifts her sunglasses. "So why does it matter if I'm here? This is my project to oversee for the board."

"You can stay on one condition: You don't say a word to the crew, and you stay out of the way," I say, glancing left and right to make sure no one important from the network is watching this mortifying exchange.

"Fine." Magnolia steps past me and up the porch. "Oh, Dee

and Ned are stopping by too." And then she continues on into the house.

I turn at the sound of a celebratory scream at the gate, and there, as promised, are Delta and Ned Suffolk. I smile and wave. On the inside, I'm fuming; if we wanted a live audience, we would've sent out the invitations ourselves. Delta and Ned arrive in front of me, and Delta pulls me into a hug.

"We're just so proud of you, honey," she says. "And I promise we'll stay well out of the way—even if we have to camp out behind the bushes."

Her I believe, at least, when she makes this commitment.

Ned pulls me into a hug. "You've earned it," he says. "We can't wait to watch y'all on TV. You know Delta adores anything home-and-garden-related."

"Thank you, guys," I say. "We don't have anything guaranteed but a pilot, so maybe it's a good thing you're here to soak it all in."

"Oh, and why on earth haven't they signed the full season yet?" Delta's face crumples into worry.

"It's the process." I put a reassuring hand on her shoulder. "Pilots have to test well, and then they green-light a season of a show. Of course, it's what we hope for, but it's not a promise."

Delta lets out a breath. "Well then, it sounds like it'll just be a matter of time."

Ned takes Delta's arm. "Let's let Mack get back to it, huh? Or there won't be a show to put on the screen."

"Oh, quite right," she says and turns to follow her husband. The pair disappear around the grounds to where the crew has set up their tent out back.

Fitz appears at my side. "Do you need an emotional support mocha latte? I'm ordering myself something for delivery."

"You're a saint," I say. "*Please*, and a brownie too."

Fitz giggles. "You know I'm far too fun for sainthood." He clicks around his phone. "And, scale of one to ten, how worried are we about your mother today? And why are Grady's folks here? Didn't they get the memo that Lincoln's back?"

"*Hush*," I tell him. "Are you trying to start drama by mentioning him?"

"I guess an all-out family brawl is the wrong type of reality television in this case," Fitz says.

"And as for your first question—you know full well Magnolia never dips below a level eight for potential destruction, even on the best of days."

Fitz and I make our way back up to the porch. We've just dropped back into the chairs for a moment of peaceful rocking when Erica pops her head out.

"Sorry," she says. "I know we're on break, but we've got a situation in here."

I'm already on my feet. "Let me guess. My mother?"

Erica nods sheepishly. "She's asking to be in a scene."

I groan. "Over my dead body."

Fitz and I follow Erica into the house. I push away my anger, stuffing it down into the place inside me where it knows to live. I push away the frustration that grates on me. Because the last thing I want is a loud argument in front of this crew. I need to be professional, which means I need to treat my mother like the escaped zoo creature she's committed to behaving like.

I approach her slowly with a smile and promises to come back to her. Promises to work her in. Promises that her turn will come.

Promises I have no intention of keeping.

CHAPTER 40

FTER THE DAY OF SHOOTING the pilot, I've granted myself a short reprieve. More specifically, I will be *working*—I use that term loosely—from home today in my pajamas. I just dropped off Hallie at her day camp—also in my pajamas—and I'm back at home, heading across the kitchen for the coffee maker.

Yesterday, my mother was not a silent observer on set, which came as a surprise to not a single person in attendance who had more than ten minutes of experience with her. Fortunately, Erica has a *unique* mother herself, so she came well-equipped with de-escalation tactics.

I grab the coffeepot and fill my mug to the top, then lift it. Before I get a sip, my phone rattles on the counter with a call. I glance at it, and when I see that it's my mother, I silence it and watch until it rings through to voicemail. I pull in a deep breath and prepare to enjoy my first sip of the steaming brew when the thing jolts to life again.

Seriously? I mean, yes, of course, this is not only happening but should be predictable.

I give in and answer. "Mother. Good morning."

There's a pause before she speaks. "Hi, yes, good morning, Mack."

I feel a ripple of serotonin release at her using my actual name.

"I felt I needed to call after yesterday," Magnolia says.

I take my coffee and drop onto my favorite spot on the sofa.

"I didn't behave appropriately on the set," Magnolia says—just as my chin hits the floor.

When I'm certain it must be an auditory hallucination, she says, "I think I got excited about the prospect of the show, and it sent me wild. I've been on with the psychiatrist and asked if I need to be sent to a rehab. Perhaps this is a manic episode, I'm wondering, at least according to my early searches online. I was so unlike myself."

"I'm sorry—a psychiatrist, Mama?" I'm not certain what my mother's mental health history is or isn't, but I *am* certain it's out of character for her to share something this personal with me so casually.

Magnolia sighs. "They don't recommend I be admitted to the rehab. In fact, they said it was highly unlikely it was a manic episode given I'm fifty-plus years old and have no history of bipolar disorder. They said given the situation, it was probably a normal response. Can you believe it? *A normal response*—as if I don't have a fifty-plus-year track record of utmost propriety and stoicism. I'll need a second opinion—naturally."

I have to smile to myself. "Mama," I say slowly. "We're all really excited about the show. It's all right for you to be excited too. Playing it cool doesn't make you any more proper or appropriate than the next guy."

"I'm certainly not convinced," Magnolia says. "I think I'm losing it with age, going soft or loopy or earthy. Oh my goodness, Mack, if I start wearing bohemian clothes, *please*, I beg of you, send me somewhere. I would rather be confined overseas than show up in harem pants to the club."

"I can manage that," I say. "But I'd guess the chances are slim."
There's a pause between us.

Magnolia's voice is quiet when she speaks again. "Did I ruin the day for you?"

An actual chill runs up my spine and over and out through my limbs. I sputter and rush to clear my throat. "Oh no, not at all," I say.

It's not the truth, but it's the only response I can form at this rare, impossible show of tenderness from my mother, the Dragon, for my benefit.

"Good," she announces, her brisk tone restored. "I would never want to stand in the way of your success—only support it in my own work. I'll let you get back to your work."

"Thanks, Mama," I say, wondering if the version of her that visited a moment ago can hear me. "I appreciate the call. More than you know."

Magnolia clears her throat. "Yes," she says tightly. "Oh, and I'd be remiss not to mention: Don't wear white on shoot days again. It drains your complexion completely, which is not how anyone wants to look on television."

There she is.

"Thanks for the feedback," I say. "Talk to you soon."

We hang up, and I drop the phone into the couch pillows.

I let myself sit and finally enjoy my coffee. Well, try to enjoy it. Magnolia's moment of humanness has me actually worrying there's something wrong with her. I've always wondered what was behind her brick-wall persona, and I'm not naive enough to think she's a cookie-baking grandmother type. But if nothing else, that call is proof that there's more to her.

Eventually I get to work picking out the last bits of decor for the Daniel House. By next week, we should be able to start installing furniture and decor. I scroll through my favorite sites and add a bunch of things to a few different carts—some ceramics, a small side table that'll go beautifully in the front entryway. I'll need to head to my go-to antique store to source a few older pieces too.

I'm about to head for the kitchen to fix myself a sandwich when there's a knock at the door.

I pull myself upright and peek around the corner, hoping it's not the door-to-door salesman who was around last week. Through the glass in the front door, I spot Lincoln. At the sight of him, I blush and jerk back behind the wall. We've exchanged a couple of friendly texts since our kiss, but neither of us has mentioned it.

I haven't seen him until now either.

I lean over and check my reflection in the mirror above the console, wishing I'd actually showered, or at the very minimum refreshed my curls with a misting spray. I resign myself to my au naturel appearance and head to the door.

"Hey," Lincoln says when I pull the door open.

"Hi."

We both grin as our eyes lock. I feel my face turn warm, and I can see it in him too.

"Come in," I say.

Lincoln follows me inside, and I say, with my back to him, "Sorry, Hal's not here today."

Lincoln clears his throat. "That's no problem," he says. "I'm here for you."

The butterflies erupt in my stomach, and I want to hate the way it feels like a decade and a half ago. I should be immune to this by now or at least not feeling so wobbly in the knees.

I turn at the kitchen island. "Well, lucky me."

I say it without thinking, and it comes out far flirtier than I like.

Lincoln grins. He opens his mouth to speak but stops after he pulls in a breath. He takes off his ball cap and runs a hand through his hair. "This seemed much more straightforward in my head."

Anticipation rises in my chest, because if he's feeling nervous, this has to be about the kiss.

"About the other night," he says.

I pull in a breath. "We don't have to ... You don't ..."

I'm not sure what I'm trying to say, but certainly I'm trying to protect myself from any option besides him coming here to tell me how much he'd love to do it again.

Lincoln lets out a tight laugh. "What's that?"

"Sorry, you go." I cover my mouth with a hand, lean back on the island, and wave him on.

"Look, I'm in no position to ask you this because of how I messed up in the past, but Mack, being back here, getting to know you again, the other night ... Would you want to go out some-time?" Lincoln has his hat in his hands and he's kneading the bill into something very cylindrical. "Again, it sounded way more cool and charming in my head."

A smile creeps across my face, and I nod. "I'd love that. And it did sound charming—at least to me."

Lincoln strides toward me and puts his cap back on his head backward. He wraps his arms around my waist and draws me into a hug.

"Sorry, is this too much?" he asks.

I giggle into his shoulder, my arms wrapped around him. "It's nothing compared to the other night."

I feel the tension in his shoulders release, and he pulls back a little. "You can just tell me, you know. As we figure this out."

I look up at him. "It might take a while to get the weird wrinkles out of this whole thing. It's not often a girl starts re-dating a guy she used to love."

Lincoln's brow flickers. "You really did feel that way back then?"

I nod.

Lincoln sighs. "I guess I thought you could've—*probably did* change your mind after it all fell apart."

"Oh, I tried." I laugh. "But apparently I didn't get much say in it."

Lincoln leans back, and I break the hug, our arms falling slack.

"So when's our second first date?" I ask.

"I hadn't actually thought that far," Lincoln says. "I was too nervous about asking. I do, however, have seven different plans for how to manage your surefire rejection."

"Well." I look around. "You got lunch plans? I'm starving, and the fridge is bare bones."

Lincoln grins. "I've got my keys. You ready?"

I look down at my sweats and remember the frightful bags under my eyes that I spotted earlier in the mirror. "Like this?"

"What's wrong with that?" Lincoln asks. He turns and takes my cheek in his hand, drawing closer.

"I look like I live without running water and definitely without a mirror."

"Then mirrorless, unwashed women must be my type." He is so close his lips are almost to mine. Then he grins and closes the gap.

The heat of the kiss covers me, the closeness to him a thrill and a comfort at once.

I pull back before it overcomes me. "I'm sold. Say no more." I break out of his arms to grab my wallet and phone.

"And I didn't even have to make my second point."

I start toward the door and look over my shoulder. "Which was?"

He follows. "That I've seen you after the worst hangover of your life—or at least by that point in your life—and let me tell you, that was one for the books."

I laugh and reach for the door handle. "It's still the worst. I like to think I learned my lesson."

Lincoln shudders. "Captain Morgan was a bad choice."

I open the door and we step outside. "Couldn't agree more."

I follow Lincoln across the lawn to his truck, and it strikes me that I can't remember the last time I felt this way. I was married to Grady for years—technically still am—and I can't remember. I can't remember Grady ever making me feel special or chosen in such a basic way. Sure, he bought expensive gifts and took me to expensive restaurants and highbrow events, but he never took me to lunch looking like a creature from the depths of the ocean.

Lincoln stops at the passenger door and pops it open. "Your chariot, my lady."

I climb in, and he looks at me before he closes the door, and it's pride and admiration on his face.

He thinks he's the lucky one, getting this date, but I know better: It's me who's the lucky one.

CHAPTER 41

Fifteen Years Earlier

I T WAS THE FALL SEMESTER of my senior year, and I sat in a trendy new Charleston restaurant—a renovated garage with floor-to-ceiling windows, chrome fixtures, and icy-white modern art. Every sound bounced off and around the hard surfaces, a noisy cloud that covered the place. Design wise, it was uninspiring, but the reputation of the food and cocktails had spread. I sat beside Grady and across the table from Magnolia and Delta.

"Go easy on the bread basket there, honey," Magnolia said to me, followed by a coy wink to Grady.

I reached for another pat of butter and swiped it on my bread generously. "Oh, I'm doing the butter diet, Mama. Surely you've heard of it."

"Oh, you ladies settle down," Grady said from inside his bourbon glass. "Y'all both have as much bread as you'd like."

In the two months since school had started, he'd called and checked in, even once sent just-because flowers. He'd even arranged this dinner as an opportunity to see me—and probably to use family pressure to hammer home how well it fit for me to take him back.

I glanced up from my plate of grilled snapper and mashed potatoes, and my heart stopped when the blur of a familiar figure passed the window. A perfect replica of Lincoln's height, his frame, his walk. Could it be him? Or just my mind playing tricks? And if it was him, had he seen me? Did he see me here with Grady?

Part of me hoped he did; I wanted him to see me out with another guy, looking like I'd moved on.

But then I remembered that Lincoln was gone. He'd left me just like the very first man in my life.

"How's the fish?" Grady asked.

He still hadn't gotten up the guts to ask his mother. But I had been back to the Beaufort library several times, and during each visit the librarian, Rhonda, sat and worked alongside me. She was patient and always prepared with a tip, but neither her expertise nor my persistence took me anywhere close to uncovering the identity of my father. Not without a name.

"Good. It's really good." I glanced over the table. "Delta, how's the steak? Sure looks incredible."

She finished her bite. "It's to die for, honey."

I watched her surreptitiously as we fell into the quiet of polite eating. Delta Suffolk sat right here across from me with the information Magnolia refused to share. I had a right to know, and if Grady wouldn't ask her, I would. There wasn't a chance she'd give in over the phone, so it had to be tonight, in person.

By the time the plates and glasses were cleared and the bill was delivered, I was beginning to panic about missing out on cornering Delta. Then she excused herself to the ladies' room, and I took my chance.

"You know what, I'll head there too," I said.

Magnolia tutted as she reached for the bill. "Delta doesn't need an escort."

I ignored my mother and followed Delta into the bathroom. I stood waiting by the sinks when she emerged from the stall.

"Oh," she said. "Mack, I didn't realize you were right behind me." She smiled and started the water.

I slid in beside her at the sink and followed suit. "Well, between you and me, I was hoping for a moment with you."

Delta's eyes glinted as she caught my gaze in the mirror. "Is this a little something to do with my son?"

I smiled regretfully. "Not this time. But who knows, maybe in the future, we'll have more to discuss," I lied.

"All right, sweetie. Well, ask away." Delta snatched a few paper towels from the dispenser and turned to face me as she dried her hands.

I steadied myself and looked her in the eyes. "I need to ask you about my father. I've searched public records, the library archives, the internet—all of it—and I've come up empty-handed. Magnolia won't even tell me a name. I know you knew my mama back when she had me, even from before that, so you have to know." I stepped closer and took her dry hands in my desperate soapy ones. "*Please*, Mrs. Delta, tell me what you know."

Her face slowly fell, every drip of excitement over the possibility of a tidbit of romantic gossip draining. She was still and white. "I'm sorry, Mack." She gently pulled her hands from mine. "You know I can't betray Magnolia's trust."

"I wouldn't tell her it was you," I said. "I promise. She'd never know."

Delta shook her head and turned away. She reached for another paper towel. "What I *can* tell you . . . is that you're better off knowing nothing. Your mama is a wise woman, and I would've made the same choice in her position."

Delta pulled a tight smile before tucking her chin and ducking out of the bathroom. Tears threatened at the back of my throat, so I dipped into a stall and slammed the door behind me, latching it. I dropped onto the toilet and let my tears run.

First, I'd been certain I'd figure it out like some amateur true crime podcaster on a lucky streak. Next, I'd hoped Grady's attempts with his mother would give me somewhere to start. And then I'd thought she'd tell me, like I had a better pulse on her than her son. All of it seemed embarrassingly optimistic looking back.

I was never going to find him. Not without a starting point.

Not when all the rest of them were in on it together.

The rest of them who thought they knew better than me. My mother especially, keeping and withholding this information, just like she'd done of herself for so long. Thinking she knew better.

And now Delta Suffolk and her audacity to think she, too, knew what was best for me.

Grady would probably take their side too; he always toed the family party line. He would tell me to cut it out, knock it off, enjoy the lavish life I had. Because what good comes from prodding and prying? It's nothing but uncouth for the women in our circles.

I pulled out my phone and texted the only person I knew would understand completely because of his own family issues: my friend Fitz. As if he'd been waiting for the text, his reply came immediately. I'm getting in the car. Be there in 10, 15 tops.

It felt like the only thing holding me up was his care.

I pushed out of the bathroom stall and did my best to wipe the streaked mascara from my cheeks. I walked out into the restaurant and stopped at the table where the three of them waited quietly.

"Thanks, everyone," I announced. "I've got a ride on the way, so I'll wait at the curb." I waved my phone to suggest I'd called a rideshare. "See y'all soon."

I walked away before they could protest—away from them and

the life they'd love to see me trapped inside. I walked away feeling wound up and torn up and completely misunderstood. No feeling was quite as jarring as not belonging among the people who were supposed to be like family.

When Fitz pulled up and I slipped into his passenger seat, I felt rescued. I was safe, and there in the safety of his car I let myself cry.

CHAPTER 42

Present Day

I STRETCH AND REACH TO WRAP my fingers around the brass spaniel dog on a high wooden shelf. Fitz and I are shopping at Devereaux Park Antiques, my favorite Friday afternoon activity. It's a century-old spot a tad off the beaten path, slightly dark and musty, but the finds are out of this world—and never overpriced like they are at the shops downtown. Devereaux has a furniture section, a decor section, and an architectural salvage yard in the lot adjacent.

It's a haven for local designers.

I hold the brass statue out to Fitz. "Isn't he a doll? I'm getting him for the Daniel House."

Fitz glances over from a stack of ceramics he's gently peering through. "He is, but I'm more interested in hearing about the other darling man in your life."

It's been about a week since my lunch date with Lincoln, and I haven't been able to stop thinking about him.

"Oh, so you're done giving him a hard time?" I ask.

Fitz scoffs. "I wasn't about to let him waltz back in here without a bit of ribbing. Remember, I was the one helping you through the aftermath of him, and I didn't hear the end of it about how awful he was to leave you right after you'd fallen for him. We could barely enjoy a cocktail together without you needing to rehash the whole thing."

"That's fair." I join him at his side. "You took the brunt of it. And Fitz, he's even better than I remember."

I don't look up from the china because I feel like the old me. I feel like that twentysomething willing to take a risk—for herself and maybe for love. It's wonderful and freeing, but also keenly unnerving when I remember how it hurts when it doesn't go to plan.

Fitz wraps an arm around me. "You deserve something good, honey, so I'll keep my monkey business far away from it."

When I look up, Fitz is serious—a rare occasion—and I know it's for my sake.

"Thank you," I tell him. "But don't get the idea that I don't want you around. I think it'd be fun for y'all to get to know each other—just separately from whatever this is between him and me."

"*Whatever this is?*" Fitz says. "Sure sounded like love on pause to me."

I wander over to an old record player and begin inspecting the woodwork on the sides. "He hasn't committed to that, so we'll have to see."

"Whatever you say," Fitz replies.

We continue looking quietly, bringing items to the front counter as we find them, eventually in stacks and piles. They know us well, and we can be here for hours, treasure hunting. Eventually we find a gorgeous blue-and-white tobacco jar, a set of oyster plates, a clock, and a high-back accent chair. We head outside into the heat to check out the architectural materials before we go.

"You've got most of the big items for this house, so we can call this whirl *browsing only*," Fitz says.

"The day we skip this section is the day we miss the holy grail,"

I say. "There are always more jobs, plus I wouldn't mind an antique door for the butler's pantry."

"Fair enough," Fitz says.

We walk the yard and little tickles our fancy. They have many of the old, heavy doors this home already has, and we've restored the ones in place in the Daniel House.

"Look at that," I say to Fitz, pointing out a gorgeous claw-foot tub.

"It's nice," Fitz says. "I'm just not sure about—"

We're interrupted by the ringing of my phone. We both pause, and I know he's thinking the same as me: Exquisite Interiors. We shot three days of that first week and once earlier this week. It didn't take long for it to feel second nature to have cameras following us around. The crew signed off on Monday, claiming they had enough material, and the production team has been working up an early version of the pilot. For the past few days, we've been waiting for word on how it's coming together.

An unknown number scrolls across the screen and I flash it at Fitz.

He shrugs. "Could be someone we want to hear from."

"Could also be one of a million scam calls," I say as I answer. "Mack Bishop," I say into the phone.

"Hi, Mack," the caller says. "It's Shante Robertson from Exquisite Interiors. How are you?"

"Oh *hi*, it's great to hear from you." I gesture at the phone to tip Fitz off. "We're just out here at our antiques spot sourcing some items for the Daniel House, actually. We're so close to being done on the construction that we're itching to put all the pretty parts in it."

"How fun," Shante says. "That's my favorite stage."

"Mine too," I say. "It's when it really starts to feel like home."

Shante laughs. "I wish I'd gotten you on camera saying that, but I guess we can call it a practice run."

"Erica's made us great at retaking a scene," I say, laughing along.

"That's wonderful," she notes, "because we've tested the pilot in-house, and the response has been amazing. You and Fitz are a hit, and the historic twist on construction is setting this show apart."

"That's wonderful news!"

"Yes. We'd love to offer you guys a contract for a full season."

I do a silent scream and shake the phone. "That's incredible! Thank you. This is the stuff of dreams."

I can hear the smile in Shante's voice. "I'm glad. We'll set up a meeting to talk through contract details and go over everything that's involved. A full season is a real commitment, and it's the type of job that it's critical to stay on time for. We like to be up-front about that before anyone signs on the dotted line."

"Of course," I say. "We're ready for the challenge."

"Perfect," Shante says. "My assistant will email to set things up. Talk soon."

"Thanks," I say.

I end the call, and Fitz's arms are already wrapped around me. There, between the old bed frames and hopeful sinks, we hop in a circle holding each other.

We did it. We're really getting a chance.

All these years I've felt under my mother's thumb, indebted to her in some way that makes me bend to her, but *this*. This is all mine—and Fitz's. She might've tried to insert herself and take over, but she won't. Because she can't.

And *this* for Fitz is a lease on life away from his family too.

"We did it, Magnolia Junior," Fitz says. "We did it."

"Me and you, kid," I say.

Fitz wipes at a happy tear. "I'm going to need a new wardrobe."

I laugh. "Let's wait for instructions from the wardrobe team before we get ahead of ourselves."

We turn to head back to the store.

"Contract or not, there isn't a soul alive who can tell me what to wear," Fitz says.

I don't argue. He's right, and to be frank, I just want to enjoy this moment. Anyone who wants to buy himself a new wardrobe won't hear a word from me because I'm getting to shoot a full season of *Holy City Flip*.

CHAPTER 43

WE'VE HAD TO START LOCKING the studio doors. It hasn't even been two weeks since we got the call about the show, but the Charleston rumor mill is as mighty as that of any small town. By now, everyone and their auntie knows that Bishop Builds is going to be featured on Exquisite Interiors, and far too many come by our storefront to rubberneck.

Maya pushes the doors shut, flips the locks, and looks out the window, up and down the street.

"Maya, would you like me to order you a security officer uniform?" Fitz asks. "I could even get some Mace and handcuffs for you, if you'd like."

The seriousness melts from Maya's face. "Only if they have it in anything but navy. That's not my color." She floats back over to our desks.

"Of course. We'll get it tailor-made in whatever color you like," Fitz says.

We've had a deluge of well-wishers descend upon the studio. Most of them are our people—clients, current and old, business owners we're friendly with—but a few have caused problems. Internet sleuths trying to *get the tea*, as they call it, on us before we start production. More than a few new faces are also interested in securing employment before the cameras start rolling.

So we're keeping our office locked and screening visitors. It's such a silly and unexpected necessity, though I admit I need the focus. Maya has been helping us go through the contract line by line while our lawyer reviews it separately. Shante was great during our meeting—explaining very clearly their expectations, typical schedules, and what we can expect for a day-in-the-life. It's the perfectionist in me that simply *must* review the contract for myself.

Plus, if anything were to go wrong, I'd hate to have to admit I didn't read the thing.

"Here it says that the network would put out a casting call for properties to be considered on the show," Maya says. "Are we at all worried that their vision might not be the same as ours?"

"That's a great point," I say. "I'll write it down to discuss with Shante on our next call. I don't want to have to accept a project that doesn't fit the bill for us."

"Quite right," Fitz says from across the room.

He's working on closing out the work from the Daniel House— the paperwork of it, specifically. It's a key part of the process with a historic board to demonstrate the work order has been completed. Then we'll do a final walk-through before we hand the keys back over to the Carolina Historic Society. Or, most likely, its representative, Magnolia.

"Did Magnolia email you back with answers to those questions we had?" I ask. "When I called to tell her about the full season, I only had a second to chat."

Fitz pulls down his new orange glasses frames. "What do *you* think?"

I groan. "I'll call her. Honestly, I could use a break from this anyway. Take five, Maya?"

Maya nods and drops onto the sofa. "Agree, 100 percent."

I unlatch the French doors to our garden patio and settle on the bench across the way. The smell of the jasmine vines is sharply sweet, and the iron of the bench is warm below me. I thumb through my phone and tap to call my mother.

She answers after a single ring. "I've been waiting to hear from you," she says.

"Hi, Mother. I know, Fitz sent you an email. You could've called—"

"No, not that," Magnolia says. "Exquisite Interiors. We need to discuss."

I did call my mother and fill her in on the fact that we'd been awarded a contract for a full season. I *also* did it at a time I knew Hallie would need my help in a few minutes, and I'd have to hang up.

I didn't want her to ruin it for me.

"Oh," I say. "What is there to discuss?"

"I assume you'll be featuring the Daniel House?" Magnolia asks.

"It'll be part of the pilot. There's a chance the producers will pivot to another home if the board has an issue with us showing it, though."

It's an intentional move because I knew this was coming. She won't derail my show by trying to wield power over what she will or won't allow to be shot, so I got out ahead of it. I suggested to Shante that the Carolina Historic Society might have sticking points with the Daniel House, and she said it wouldn't be a problem to scrap parts as needed.

She *didn't* say we'd nix the house entirely, but I'd also rather have that than my mother bossing around the production crew. How would that affect our chances at making this into a long-running thing?

"Oh." The word pops out of Magnolia, and in the silence I can hear the fight draining.

"We've got another project coming up in the same area—a neighbor loved the work and asked to peek," I say.

"Well, I guess . . ." Magnolia trails off.

The feeling of holding any amount of power in the face of my mother is something so new and mighty that it almost reverberates inside me. This is where I've wanted to go, and only now have I found my way here, thanks to the full-season deal.

"I'd love to show the Daniel House, of course," I say. "I'm proud of our work there—we really did our best for you. Not to mention a shout-out to the board could bring new properties or donors your way."

Magnolia sniffs. "Whatever you think," she says.

I have imagined this moment for so long—the moment when Magnolia can't hold something over me. For so long, I imagined all the clever quips I'd throw back at her. Every different way to say, *And who's getting the last laugh now?* How easy it would be to gloat having won, having beat her at her own game.

But not a one of those phrases feels good. Or right.

God help me, but I do love my mother. I may not like her very much, or very often, or even very noticeably, but I do. In some strange little way that probably only exists between Magnolias. I don't want to hurt her—I'm not sure I ever did. I only want her to quit hurting me.

"I think the Daniel House would be a stunner on TV, and with your blessing, we'd love to have it as our showcase home on the pilot."

"Why, yes, I think you're quite right," Magnolia says right away. "It's a beautiful home, and it deserves to shine."

"I agree," I say. "I'll see if we can do a quick blurb on the board, but the producers will have the last say on that. Hosts can suggest but not dictate."

Magnolia hums. "I understand."

"All right, Mother, well, we're snowed in with paperwork here, so I'll let you go—but only if you promise you'll get back to Fitz. Today."

"All right, Mack. Good luck with your work," Magnolia says. "And remember to double-check Fitz's paperwork for the board. My child won't be the one causing backlogs in the office. I won't hear the end of it."

I smile to myself. "Oh, never. Bye for now."

I pass back inside and pull the French doors shut behind me. I look up from my phone screen and stop in place.

"What are you doing here?" I ask.

Grady Suffolk III stands in the middle of my studio, arms crossed, foot tapping. "Mack, you're done on the phone. Good."

I continue to my desk and slide into the seat. "Again: Why are you here?"

Grady drops into the chair across from my desk and props his foot on his knee. "So I'm unwelcome here now?"

"Cut the crap. What do you want?"

I stare at him until he sighs reluctantly. "Well, I wasn't going to come right out with it," he says.

"Of course you weren't," I mumble under my breath.

"I heard about your good luck with the television network," he says.

"It wasn't good luck. We worked our tails off, worked on the application, shot tape. It wasn't a lottery situation."

"Fine," he says. "Yes, you're right. I wanted to see if you could use my assistance."

Naturally. I figured this was what he was sniffing around for when I saw him. He hasn't called to check in on the firm even once since he resigned. Sure, he and I talk at Hallie's pickups and drop-offs, but he hasn't mentioned his former workplace to me once. And he used to be well-known around here. Vendors knew him— some even liked him, regrettably. Clients spoke to him routinely. But only now, after network television interest, does he remember the little place he came from.

"Ah, well. Not particularly, no." I stand and start walking to the door. "Thanks for asking, but we're doing quite well."

Grady stands slowly, like he must adjust a single limb at a time. His friendly demeanor shifts. "You're sure?"

"Deathly sure," I say, squeezing my eyes shut then open for effect.

I flip the door unlocked, then pull it open.

He lingers, looking close to pouting. "Well, let me know if you change your mind."

Grady steps out and down onto the street.

"I won't," I say, and then I close the door and flip the lock.

I walk back into the middle of the room and prop my hands on my hips. "What did we say about keeping out the riffraff? From here on out, Grady is on the no-fly list unless he's dropping off the magpie."

The staff giggles and carries on. I may feel a slight tenderness to burning my mother, but Grady I'm less concerned with. Like he told me on his last day, he's a big boy and can handle himself. He doesn't need me.

And I certainly don't need him.

CHAPTER 44

THE NEXT MORNING, HALLIE AND I stand at Grady's carriage house downtown knocking. After I drop her off, I'm heading to coordinate the furniture delivery at the Daniel House.

Hallie peers in a window, fogging the pane. "Don't see anything."

I hope I mask my irritation when I say, "I'll call him and see what's up."

The phone rings, and when Grady answers, I can tell it's on the speakerphone in his car. "Hey, Mack. I'm sorry."

It's all I need to hear to know Hallie will be my design sidekick for the day. I look over at her standing patiently, waiting on her father. It digs at me, again, in that familiar father-free spot inside me. I never wanted this for her. In fact, Magnolia promised me marrying Grady would be a ticket to happiness. Now everyone can see how wrong that went.

"Where are you?" I ask, trying to keep my tone even. "Hallie and I are at your place for drop-off."

I can't help but wonder if this is some twisted "payback" for my swiftness in dismissing him from the studio yesterday.

I hear the white-noise sound of the road. "There's been an accident at my parents' property, and I had to split right away. Mom's in a complete state about it, and Dad was dealing with getting the first responders some space."

"Oh," I say. "All right, then."

It's a valid excuse if ever there was one, and I know once he references his folks he's not lying. I'll make the most of an extra day with my darling girl.

"Well, I hope everyone's ok," I say. "I'll call your folks to check in later."

"I know they'll appreciate that," he says. "But I need to go. I'm pulling up and it's all flashing lights and sirens."

I hang up the phone and smile at Hallie. "Would you like to help arrange furniture today, my love? You know I can always use your eye."

Hallie sighs. "Did he forget about me?"

I move to her and take her in my arms. "No, honey. He was really disappointed, but there's been some sort of emergency in Beaufort."

"I could've gone too," Hallie says. "I'm a great helper, and I don't interfere."

I run a hand across her forehead and cup her chin. "*That* you absolutely are, but there are certain situations that are just for adults to manage."

Hallie pouts and balls her hands into fists.

"I can call Lincoln and see what he and Foster are up to."

A jaunt back across the bridge would eat into my work time, but it'd be worth it to smooth this over.

"Can't," Hallie says. "Foster's got reptile camp, remember?"

"Ah," I say.

I do remember now, and I should've had it at the forefront of my mind, considering I had to call to see if Hallie could get in as well. The best I got was a spot on the waitlist.

"The camp should've just let me in. I'm *one* extra kid. And a good listener."

Hallie looks right at me, as if I'm the one controlling the camp roster. As if I even knew this camp existed before Foster moved in and signed up for it.

"I'm sorry it's not working out. And you're right, you're a great listener and a great kid. It wasn't personal," I say. "Maybe I can see if Maya is going to be at the studio?"

Hallie shakes her head. "If I'm just going to be pawned off, I might as well go somewhere I'm actually useful—like the Daniel House."

I hide the smile that threatens. "Couldn't agree more. And I'll be grateful to have your help."

I text Fitz on the way to the Daniel House, and once he confirms he's coming for furniture installation, I ask him if he'll stop for Hallie's favorite pizza for lunch. I promise him he'll be her most favorite and save her day. Fitz agrees and promises to throw in one of the cookies they sell at the counter.

An hour later, we're at the Daniel House watching as a gingham-print armchair, a pair of mahogany side tables, and a wood spindle floor lamp wrapped in plastic are unloaded from trucks. I'm focused mostly on getting the right pieces in the right rooms, and from there, our team can easily adjust the layout. Already I've realized one of the benches for the upstairs hallway is too small and will need to be swapped out, and a cabinet arrived damaged on one corner. No shipment is perfect, I know as much by now, and I have items in storage that can sub in until the final options arrive.

Fitz appears at the gate with pizza boxes in hand.

I meet him halfway and take them from him. "I seriously owe you for this. Grady had a legitimate excuse this time—for once—but it's starting to wear on Hal."

"I'd bring pizza every day for my magpie if she needed it," Fitz says. "How's the furniture?"

I smile. "It's fabulous. Seriously, we knocked it out on this one. And we don't even have accessories or art in yet."

"So I'll be swooning is what you mean," Fitz says.

I turn to head back in, but Fitz's hand on my arm stops me.

"Before you go in," Fitz says. "I have news."

"Oh no. Bad?" I ask.

He shakes his head. "Mostly good, a little bit bad."

I stand there, and the steam rolling off the pizza boxes warms my skin. "Tell me, Fitzy."

"Get the Farm Rio dress, Magnolia Junior," Fitz says with a layer of sadness.

"We're having the wedding." I say it quietly because I know the "we" doesn't include everyone it should. "I will be there, and Hallie will be there with all the bells and whistles our money can buy."

Fitz cracks a smile. "Speaking of, and because I know it's been a rough day for her—can I ask her to be the flower girl?"

"Well, of course." I set down the boxes on the path and pull my friend into a hug. "But shouldn't you propose to the other groom first?"

Fitz laughs and I can feel the joy rumble across our embrace. "*Details.* I'm fairly certain he'll accept, and Hallie can be trusted to keep a secret."

"Christmas two years ago," I say, leaning back.

"Didn't crack once, even when you offered ice cream to dish what she and I picked out for your gift," Fitz says.

I pull out of Fitz's arms and squeeze his hands. "Whatever you need, wherever we can fill in the gaps, we're here."

"Good," Fitz says. "Because I've already got a laundry list of tasks lined up for us this weekend."

I laugh and recover the pizza. "I never doubted you. And I'm all yours."

"So no big dates with that handsome photographer?"

I grin. "That's Thursday. We're going to meet his old mentor, Marcus Wilson, at Spoleto."

"Very swoony." Fitz wraps an arm around my shoulders, and we climb up to the house. "Sounds like Sunday will be a perfect day for wedding prep and gossip."

"I can promise at least half that equation," I say.

We work our way through the maze of newly delivered furniture and eventually find Hallie. She's thrilled to see her uncle Fitz and even more so when she discovers what he brought for lunch. And as Fitz describes her duties as flower girl in the upcoming wedding (fiancé pending), Hallie looks on with the utmost of serious looks, nodding, bound and determined to be the best flower girl the city has ever seen.

She reminds me of myself.

CHAPTER 45

Twelve Years Earlier

I STOOD IN THE WHITE STALL, dressed like a bride, and all I could think of was how much it looked like a costume. Like pretend. I wasn't actually doing this, was I? The white lace dress draped over my curves like it was part of me, my golden curls filling the open back like they'd planned it. Magnolia sat in the other room, comfortable in the viewing area, alongside my best friend, Kendra, and of course, Magnolia's best friend, Delta Suffolk. The three of them were patched together on the blush sofa like the three parts of Neapolitan ice cream.

Today was my sixth official wedding dress shopping trip—not accounting for the surreptitious window-shopping and boutique drop-ins I'd done on my own. After a stretch of striking out, I'd wondered if maybe I was just destined to find it alone. I hadn't. And by then, even Magnolia was to the point of lying about how much she liked the dresses I tried on in order to speed up the process.

I could tell by the imperceptible twitches of her face what her true feelings were.

The boutique associate slipped the lace dress back onto a hanger and stepped out to replace it on the rack. I stood in front of the mirror in my undergarments, alone. I looked at myself, a bride-to-be. Also, a stranger. But before I could think on that more, the associate was back with the next pick.

"Ok." She shuffled in behind the wide cupcake dress. "This one is a beauty, but I'll need to help slip you into it."

I stepped into place, an obedient mannequin, and stood while I was zipped up and clipped in.

The associate stood back and clasped her hands. "Ready for the big mirrors?"

I knew the dance by now, the parading, the oohs and aahs. I hit every step, and this time there were tears.

"Oh, honey!" Delta was already on her feet. "It's beautiful. This is what you'll wear to become my daughter."

"In-law," Magnolia added. Delta always wanted a daughter but had gotten a boy instead. "Yes, it's very nice, indeed."

Kendra lit up. "Gorgeous, Mack."

I smiled, the same way I had in a handful of other dresses. It was beautiful, but just like the others, its magnificence didn't push it anywhere close to feeling like *the one*. I ran my fingers over the elaborate beaded bodice. "You think?"

My audience beamed back, nods and excited claps abounding.

"I guess maybe it's the one?" I myself was sick and tired of the searching and the fitting rooms and the parading around like a show pony. I waved Kendra in to join me in the fitting room, and my friend squeezed in beside me, the tulle underlay popping out and tickling our ankles.

"Is this it?" Kendra asked.

I cocked my head to the side, and my face crumpled into a mess. "I don't know. Maybe I'm just over all of this, ready to have it done."

"Well, don't rush it," Kendra said. "You only get married once."

Her words sent a shiver through me. I hoped it was excitement, but a part of me wondered if it was dread.

I pulled Kendra closer and whispered frantically, "*What if this is a sign?* All of this dress shopping and nothing to show for it. What if it's a bigger sign?"

Kendra whisper-yelled back, "Girl, you can't overthink this! Do you know how long it takes some brides to find a dress?"

"I don't feel bridal in any of them. A lot are super nice, but it's like they don't match me. They don't want me. They won't accept me because they know good and well I shouldn't be getting married."

To him—the words I left unspoken.

Kendra glanced down and then up again. "Look. You probably need a break from all this wedding stuff."

A break or an escape—either would be tempting.

"I won't argue that, but I don't think that's what's going on here."

"What do you want to do?" Kendra's words hung between us. "Whatever you choose, you need to have your wits about you when you do."

She was right. I didn't want to impulsively call off this wedding and send Mama and Delta into a fit that would have them packed into the back of an ambulance and off to a conjoined hospital room. Not unless I had no other choice.

Kendra helped me out of the dress in silence, and we sat side by side on the small plastic bench beside the mirrored wall. Kendra had pulled her phone from her back pocket and showed me the screen. Grady had posted a countdown to the wedding on his Facebook, tagging me in one of our engagement photos.

"That change anything for you?" Kendra asked.

I pasted on a smile. "It's reassurance."

Hand-on-the-Good-Book-honest, I was lying to my friend and to myself. My worries hadn't ever been about Grady's commitment to the wedding; he'd shown full well he was all in. I believed Grady loved me—in some way of his—though the social circles that supported our union were also a means for him to have the life he wanted.

Those were things I knew and things I understood. And though I'd promised myself I would never speak his name again, not since he walked out on me almost three years ago without a backward glance, I couldn't shake the feeling that even if Lincoln was just about as scummy as he'd acted, our love had been real.

And something about the love between Grady and me seemed lesser in comparison. Maybe it was just less excitement—less chaos, most likely. But it shouldn't be too much to ask for a girl to feel butterflies in her wedding dress.

Or when she thought about her husband-to-be.

"Let's call this one a strong maybe," I said to Kendra and the dress. I lifted the hanger and pulled the mass of fabric from the room, landing it delicately in the hands of the sales associate.

CHAPTER 46

Present Day

LINCOLN AND I HAVE BEEN texting every day since our impromptu lunch date, and we've had a couple of pseudo-dates in between: meeting for coffee on my deck and making a joint run to Costco. All of it is fun and sweet and, most of all, light-years away from everything I thought I wanted from Lincoln when I first met him.

It's a little scary how easily he's slotted right into my life—*our* lives, if I include Hallie in the count.

Today Lincoln invited me to join him at the Spoleto Festival downtown, and I jumped at the chance. Not only is it a major annual art event for the city, but his old boss, the big bad villain who once stole him away from me, Marcus Wilson, has a feature.

Lincoln and I weave through the crowd hand in hand, making our way to the gallery. He looks back to check on me, adorable in his sunglasses and casual shorts and tee. I'm wearing a flowy dress, perfect for the thick summer heat.

"Want to stop for a drink?" Lincoln asks.

I nod, and we dip into a nearby café. The blast of cool air-conditioning is like a balm. "We could also just stay here." I fan myself.

Lincoln laughs. "There's no pressure, Mack. I can meet you back here afterward, but Marcus would kill me if I no-showed his exhibition."

I shake my head. "I was just playing. Plus, I've got to meet the man responsible for my heartache all those years ago."

"Ah, there it is." Lincoln slides up to the counter and orders something iced.

He turns to me, and I order an iced tea with a shot of lemonade, a drink made for a day like today. We grab the cold cups and head back to the street. Within minutes sweat beads along my lower back.

"Here," Lincoln says. "The Winship Gallery, this is it."

I follow Lincoln into the small entryway and up the narrow creaky steps to the second level. We pass into a large open space, painted bright white from the wood plank floors to the tall ceilings. Photographs are displayed in small groupings, but Lincoln sees what he's looking for right off the bat.

He strides up to a man wearing black jeans and a black shirt with curly gray hair cut short. He lights up and reaches out a hand to Lincoln. They shake and pull into a hug.

"I think I see a few more grays since I last saw you," Lincoln says.

Marcus laughs. "Probably from everything you put me through over the years."

Lincoln smiles and turns to me. "This is Mack Bishop, my guest for today."

I smile to myself at how delicately he introduces me. There are so many land mines surrounding *who I am* to him, but still, he gracefully finds his way. I reach out a hand. "Nice to meet you, Marcus. I've heard wonderful things."

Lincoln turns back to Marcus. "Remember that girl I mentioned the first year?"

Marcus groans. "*No*. No more Mack." He stops and his eyes fall on me as he registers. "This is *the* Mack?"

I raise my hands. "Guilty."

Marcus whistles and rubs at his beard. "Lordy was this boy torn up about you. Almost talked himself out of staying a few times."

"Which, if I remember correctly, you were mostly ok with at the time," Lincoln says.

"Eh," Marcus says. "I wasn't too happy about accepting you under the circumstances we did—not that I'd ever mention it when you were an apprentice—but I got over it with how good your work became."

My brow knits and I look at Lincoln, whose expression matches mine.

"What circumstances?" I ask.

Lincoln looks at me. "I swear I don't know. What do you mean, Marcus?"

"Oh." The word is heavy like an admission. "You didn't know. Looks like I've put my foot in it . . ."

Lincoln reaches out and takes Marcus's arm as he starts to back away. "What is it?"

Marcus lets out a breath. "There was a sizable donation from a family friend of yours. They asked that we review your portfolio for immediate admission to the program, and the president and top fundraiser went over my head. Your work was good, but if you hadn't been shuffled up—"

"Family friend?" Lincoln asks. "No, there must've been a mistake. My family never had a friend with money to donate to art programs, let alone sums enough to sway an admissions council."

"That's all I know," Marcus says. "I didn't have much of a say in it."

"Who was it? What was the name?" Lincoln demands.

The realization hits me first, and it's like watching an accident happen, knowing this is the last moment he'll be without the scar of knowing.

"I just don't see how . . ." Lincoln's voice drifts into silence as he stands unmoving, thinking.

I clear my throat. "Marcus, was it a woman who donated?"

He nods. "I believe so, if memory serves."

Lincoln's head whips in my direction, and I see the understanding hit him. "Magnolia Bishop."

Marcus nods slowly. "I wouldn't have remembered on my own, but now that you say it, it rings a bell."

I look at Lincoln regretfully, knowing I'll see only feelings I'd never wish upon him shape his expression. "I'm so sorry. I had no idea. Not now, not before."

Lincoln's eyes are wild, and he bops around like he's shaken. He stops and looks at Marcus. "You're here tomorrow?"

Marcus nods.

"Mind if I come back then?" Lincoln asks.

"Of course," Marcus says kindly. "I'm really sorry, man. I had no idea you didn't know or I would've kept my mouth shut."

I step in. "I'm glad you told us. Magnolia is my mother, and it seems she was in the business of arranging marriages back then. We'll see you tomorrow, Marcus."

I take Lincoln's hand and lead him, shell-shocked, down the stairs and back out onto the street. I walk us toward the studio, and with each step the fury toward my mother grows. I've always known how she plays me, how so often she's toyed with my life like it's her own personal dollhouse, like I'm her property. Even the small steps forward we've taken recently now look like something to be suspicious of in my mind's eye.

By the time I reach the studio doors, my hands shake as I struggle with the keys in the lock. Finally I pop it open and enter, flipping on the lights.

I go straight to the coffee maker, and even though it's far too hot for hot coffee, I fill the reservoir and dump in the grinds because it's the only way I know how to take care of Lincoln. My mother shouldn't mess with my life, but I'd take it ten thousand times over before letting her have a single touch on his.

Lincoln slumps onto the sofa, and once I'm sure the door is locked, I bring him a water from the fridge. I unscrew the cap and hand it to him.

"I'm so sorry, Linc. She had no right to meddle."

He looks at me. "Am I a fraud?"

I fight the tears sitting at the back of my throat. Even though I know, rationally, that I'm not, I feel responsible for this. For bringing her into his life.

I shake my head. "You just got a taste of the rich-kid life."

Lincoln lets out a sigh. "I hadn't thought of that."

"It's what all the wealthy families do—buy their kids' spots. Which just makes it tougher for good, regular kids, just like you were, to get in."

"I've always prided myself on the fact that I made this career happen, that it was hard work and dedication that got me here," he says.

I reach out and take his arm. "And it did. Magnolia's check gave you a shot to play the game. It didn't give you your skills or your work ethic or your amazing eye or your charisma that charmed so many reporters into covering you."

Lincoln pulls a smile that fades at once. Like he's trying too hard.

"I'm sorry I brought this on you," I say. "It's bad enough how she interferes in my life—even to this day—but you?" I look at him and every feeling I've ever had of fondness, of longing, of admiration, of love—it floods me. He's better than Magnolia. Probably better than me too. "You're all the good parts, Lincoln, and she could never spoil you."

I rest my hand on his knee and let it sit.

Eventually he lets out a loud breath. "And now I'm thinking about everything else that set in motion." Lincoln wraps a hand over mine. "She broke us up, didn't she?"

My insides curl at the words laid out in front of me because I've been fighting considering that part. It's the only real reason she'd throw money at the situation: It was a problem to be fixed. We, he and I together, had to be undone, and that was the clean way to do it. All she had to do was write a check and make her wishes known. The rest took care of itself.

"My mother . . ." I swallow the tears. But they sting, and they burn, and they cut at my insides in a way I haven't felt before. "This is probably the worst thing she's ever done to me."

I let my tears run in this quiet, still half-dark studio, the place where I've made my dreams come true, and outside on the street, the party rages on. I hear the happy chatter and the too-loud laughter of people who haven't just suffered a deep betrayal.

Magnolia has always thought she's known best for me; all the withholding and the stepping in was done in the name of *what's best for me.* Until now, I couldn't know, not for certain, whether she got it right or wrong.

I pull myself up straight. "I would've gone with you," I say. "If you'd asked, I would've gone."

Lincoln's arms are around me as he rubs gentle circles on my back. "I should've stayed."

"No." I wipe my tears. "If anything about Magnolia's meddling works, it's the part where you got your shot. But whatever she thought about keeping us apart, she was dead wrong. I mean, look at us."

Lincoln's hand is on my cheek. He cups my face and says, "I'm sticking around this time. For as long as you'll let me."

I manage a wet smile. "You're sure, considering I still can't divorce my mother?"

"I hate to tempt fate, but I think we've seen the worst of her," he says, then lays a gentle kiss on my forehead.

We stay here, recovering in the studio, for a while. Eventually I go get the coffeepot, and by then it's actually cool enough to enjoy. I am calm by the time we push out of the doors and lock them behind us. Well, at least on the outside.

I still have fury like a fireball ready to unleash on Magnolia, my mother dearest. I'm an expert by now at keeping my true feelings for her in check; it's just that now, I know I'm ready for that to change.

In the quiet I have counted every wonderful part to this man at my side—including his willingness to forgive, his patience—and I've come to one clear conclusion: I'm done with Magnolia's rules. I will not stuff down my anger. I will not smile and pretend like my mother's transgression against him, her betrayal of me, too, is any version of all right. I will no longer be in the business of saving face for the Bishop women.

I've got an overdue temper and an axe to grind; I have no reservations about letting this get messy.

I'm hitting the road in the morning.

To go give my mother a piece of my mind.

CHAPTER 47

IT'S FIRST THING IN THE morning when Hallie and I park on the sleepy street where Fitz and Henry live. It's a quiet, elegant corner of the city, and their historic single house sparkles in the row of similar structures. The homes aren't ostentatious in this neighborhood, but they're certainly major characters in the architectural history of the city. All are well-kept on the exterior, gardens neatly tended, not a peeling spot of paint in sight. They're quietly luxurious.

Hallie bounds out of the car while I pull myself out slowly, checking my pockets for all the necessities. The only sound is the cork of her sandals slapping the stone sidewalk and then bopping along the wooden decking of the porch that spans the full side of the home.

I click the car locked with a bleep and follow her. Fitz stands in the doorway in his pajamas, his tabby cat in the crook of his arm.

I shoot him a grateful look. "Thanks for taking her."

I'm heading to Beaufort this morning to talk to my mother, and I needed a stopgap until Grady picks her up midmorning as we'd planned.

Fitz ruffles the hair on Hallie's head. "Nothing like an early bird landing," he says. "Henry's just finished baking some cinnamon rolls, Hal. And there's fruit to munch on too."

My stomach rumbles.

"I heard that," Fitz says. "Come on. Inside with you. There's no harm in a quick bite before you hit the road. Lord knows your mama isn't going to change in the meantime."

I follow him inside the house and am met by the spicy-sweet aroma of the promised treats. "Though she might go on the run if she knew what I was about to level at her."

Fitz laughs, sets the cat gently on the sofa, and rounds back to the kitchen.

Henry greets me with a hug and a kiss on the cheek, then goes with Hallie to show her where they moved their puzzles.

Fitz drops steaming coffee and a cinnamon roll in front of me, and as I bring the mug to my lips, I groan. "I didn't realize how much I needed this."

Fitz smiles and busies himself with unloading the dishwasher. Even the contents of his dishwasher are stylish—beautiful ceramics, heavy-duty cookware. Not a cartoon character or plastic doohickey in sight.

"Am I an idiot for even trying to confront her?" I ask.

I called Fitz once I got home last night and filled him in on all the gory details. He was just as shocked as I was to hear the extreme lengths Magnolia had gone to back then, simply to keep Lincoln and me apart. Sure, our long-ago dinner wasn't great. Fine, it was an absolute disaster.

I guess if there's anything Magnolia's willing to go above and beyond for, it is control over my life. Always has been.

Fitz shrugs, grabbing the silverware caddy. "I guess that depends on what you're hoping to get out of it."

I stare into the brown swirl inside my mug. I'm not sure I know. "It's a great question. I . . . Well . . ."

My eyes land on the cinnamon roll in front of me, and I decide

to pull off a large bite. I point to my mouth as I chew exaggerat-
edly, an excuse for my silence.

Or lack of answers.

Fitz shoots me a look like he knows I'm holding back. He props
a hand on the counter and waits.

Finally I swallow the bite. "I don't expect her to understand. And
she's not one to change her mind. It's not like she'll apologize."

Every statement sounds like an excuse, a reason to ignore her and
keep on with my own life. When I told Lincoln about my plans, he
didn't seem to feel strongly. *"It's up to you, Mack. Really. I'm no longer
in the business of trying to win your mother over—just you."*

"Probably she won't, honey," Fitz says. "But she might admit to
something. You might work something out."

The morning fog starts to lift from my head, and I feel myself
inching closer to honesty. "I want her to hurt a little, frankly. It's
her time to pay," I say. "She's hurt me so much and so often and
for so long, and all I've done is allow it."

"And why's that?" he asks.

"Because she's all I've ever had!" The words erupt like a projectile,
and I feel better having gotten them out. "Aside from Hal, she's it.
And maybe that was a little bit by her design, turning my father
into the big bad wolf and all. I hate the fact that it's true, that it
gives her so much control."

Fitz sets down his mug and comes to my side, wrapping me in
his arms. "You're doing the right thing," he says.

"I hope so. It's time for it to stop. I'm not willing to risk her
messing things up between Lincoln and me again."

Fitz pulls back so he can grin and bat his eyes at me. "Now
we're cooking."

I swat him playfully on the arm. "Stop. I shouldn't have admitted that."

"Y'all planning a wedding yet?" Fitz asks.

Obviously the answer to this is no. But there's also something different about re-dating someone you once loved, as real adults with two serious lives. No, I'm not planning a wedding, not right now, but I'd also be lying if I said I couldn't picture a real future with the guy, not too far beyond the horizon.

"You'd already know if that was the case," I say. "But I need to get going."

I choke down the remainder of the cinnamon roll, then call into the back of the house for Hallie. She comes skipping, puzzle pieces in hand, and burrows into my chest for a hug. I kiss her head and remind her to use her manners with her uncles.

I follow Fitz down the pristine entryway runner rug, his art hung without a tilt, no mystery crunches underfoot. This must be what it's like to have a home where children don't live. Fortunately, I've made my peace with the glittery nail polish stains on my living room rug, courtesy of Afternoon Glam.

I stop at the door and square my shoulders to Fitz, releasing a deep breath. "I've got this. I'm strong and fierce, and I can do it."

Fitz grins. "You took the words right out of my mouth. And when all else fails, remember this: For all the ways you're different from the old bat, you're just as stubborn and well-equipped for a showdown with her."

I pull him in for a quick hug and thank him again for helping.

"Go. Hold her feet to the fire." Fitz waves me out the door.

And I go. Down the porch, to the street, and into my car.

And soon, to my mother's doorstep.

CHAPTER 48

I'M IN BEAUFORT AT MAGNOLIA'S doorstep, hammering on her front door. I'll keep at it for as long as I need to, like a persistent woodpecker. I'll *rap-rap-rap* as long as it takes. Even the neighbors are beginning to poke their heads out of doors (to my delight).

"Mother, open up!" I shout.

Magnolia wrenches open the door, holding her robe closed, and pulls me inside. "What on earth do you think you're playing at?"

"I could say the same for you." I walk through the house and into the kitchen.

"And why are you here?" she asks.

"I thought about calling, but I need to do this in person."

Magnolia glides to the other side of the kitchen, putting the island between us. "Really, you just expect me to drop everything because you've decided you need a chat?" She picks at her manicure.

"You paid to have Lincoln moved out of the city." It feels like dropping a match in a roadside fireworks tent.

Magnolia startles, her eyes popping wide.

"Yes, I found out about your convenient little *donation*," I say.

"How?" she asks before she realizes it. "Not that I mind. I figured you'd find out eventually. By now, it's all water under the bridge. You're glad you didn't end up with a washout like him."

I look her straight in the eye. "He's back in town, and actually, we've been dating, if you can believe it. His old friend and colleague Marcus Wilson was at Spoleto, and he let it slip, not realizing it had ever been a secret in the first place."

Magnolia's face tightens, like she's resisting a frown. "I just don't think we need to get all hot and bothered over a little something that happened decades ago. And what's this about him being back?"

"Not quite decades, Mother. And how *could* you? You think you have the right to mastermind my life by moving chess pieces around behind my back?"

She flaps a hand like there might be some kind of an in-between. "I wouldn't describe it that way exactly—it was the boy's choice in the end. Yes, I made the donation with a small ask, but I was glad to support the studio even if he declined."

"Sure, he made the choice, but that doesn't grant you any kind of immunity. You paid tens of thousands of dollars to take my boyfriend away from me," I say.

Magnolia sighs as if realizing she won't get off easy. "You're right. I did interfere with your life, and I'm sorry it hurt y'all. But I was doing it for your own good, Magnolia."

I land a palm on the counter. "Mack. Especially for *this* conversation, it's Mack."

"Mack." She says it like a polite admission.

"How in your mind are you making this into 'the best' thing for me? I know you didn't have great luck with guys, but Mother, you *saw* how I felt about Lincoln. It was obvious."

"That was exactly why—I didn't want you to risk everything you could have, throw it all away."

"Love is always a risk."

"Not every kind." Magnolia's chest puffs slightly. "The Suffolks? They're reliable, people who don't do divorce—"

"Except for me and Grady."

Magnolia looks resigned as she lets out a breath. "Right. Not until the two of you."

I almost feel for her as I watch her fiddling with the stack of mail in front of her, because I know what it's like being a mother. Countless times I've made decisions for Hallie, choosing things I believe are the best for her. I haven't always been right, but the point here is that Hallie is still a child. I was an adult at the time.

She looks up. "I didn't want to hurt you; I needed you to see that Grady was a better choice."

"And what do you know about good choices? Because you had a child with a man who is apparently so awful that you won't even tell me his name. *That*, especially, removes any right for you to pick someone for me. I was desperate for your love. You were my only parent because you never let me know the other one. Yet you have all these *good reasons* to take my choices, to take Lincoln."

"You will never understand the situation between your father and me. *Never*. And it'd do you good to leave it alone," Magnolia says, her jaw setting.

I feel like my toes are hanging over the edge into an abyss of some kind, like if I keep pushing, I could break the bond between us permanently. But it doesn't scare me. Maybe it's what I was looking for all along.

"And maybe I won't," I say. "Probably you'll withhold it from me, but I won't ever value these *important decisions* you've made on my behalf if you're not even willing to explain."

Magnolia springs toward me, finger pointed, eyes glittering with anger. "It would do you good to respect your elders, which is something you know nothing about. My folks protected me from your awful father, and I repaid them with obedience."

"*Please.*" She won't get me that easily. "Fighting for the life and for the man I love isn't disrespectful."

"Pushing yourself into other people's business is disrespectful."

"And how exactly is this *not* my business?" I ask. "You chose to have me. You carried me and birthed me and raised me, and at every step you made it my business. He was the man who gave me to you."

"He never gave me a damn thing!" Magnolia yells. "And don't you ever say that again. *I* did everything for you, and all he gave you was a bit of DNA and not a thing more."

"If he's such a nothing, you wouldn't have kept him from me." I know I'm daring her, hosing gasoline on a spark.

She shakes in place. "Want to know how bad your father is?"

I freeze, like if I move, she might take it back.

"That man is *just* like Lincoln. Say the word and I'll tell you the rest." Her eyes stick to me, unblinking.

Her face shows that she's mad enough to tell me every nasty thing about him even if it's only to prove herself right. I've waited my entire life for this moment, a moment I wanted to be a mile marker, cherished in some way. But that isn't the type of woman I was born to, and this might be the only chance I ever get.

"Tell me," I say.

"He's here, Mack." She pulls in a breath, and in the pause her body settles. When she meets my eyes again, she is terrifyingly calm. "He lives right here in Beaufort and has all along, the man you insist on calling a *father*. He knew you were here and lived in the same town as you grew up. He never contacted me. He never stopped by. He never tried to know you once. He didn't care enough to make a ten-minute drive. And I loved him for that summer we had, really and truly I did, just like you did Lincoln, but no amount of love can change a man like that. Theo Hartman never gave a damn about me or you, and he gladly lived a separate life only miles away. Happy?"

Goose bumps shoot over me and my skin prickles again and again like I'm misfiring. I taste acid in my mouth and rock under the nausea of my insides turning inside out. I rush to the sink, feeling like I'm about to heave. Hot tears sting as I hover above the drain. Theo Hartman.

That can't be right. I try to work it out, to figure out how the rest of it goes together, but I'm deafened by the ringing in my ears.

Magnolia's hand meets my back tentatively, and her voice is softer. "I'm sorry. I am. I didn't want you to know any of this. I didn't want to tell you, but it's the only way to get you to understand. Why I *had* to do what I did."

I lean there, grounded on the cool ledge of the sink.

"I couldn't let you feel that same pain. Not the years of what it felt like knowing he was right there and never came."

I straighten and face her. I open my mouth, and I have so much to say. There are so many details that don't make sense, but it's all too much and again my ears are ringing so loudly that I grab them and squeeze. "Wait," I say.

I step past her and head for the guest room. Inside, I close the door and lock it, and I dive onto my former childhood bed. I bury my face.

My father planned the gardens at the Daniel House. *I really liked him.* Theo Hartman was there. He felt familiar because he makes up half of me. But did he know who I was, more than just another Suffolk? Had he known his daughter was leading the charge? And why did he come? After all that time.

I pull out my phone and search for Hartman Landscape. In a single click, the website is before me, his local office address listed at the bottom.

Still, the man I met that day is impossible to reconcile with Magnolia's version. Theo was careful and kind and attentive; he never came across as one to abandon a pregnant girlfriend or his child. Could there be more than one Theo Hartman in town? Of course not.

But if he was so callous to live his life of success and plenty right alongside me and Magnolia, he must be just like she says he is. Maybe Theo's just a good actor when he's in work mode. For the first time, I understand how my mother would want to shelter me from this, because his being here all along is especially cruel. The fatherly basics would've been so easy. I think of him treating me, an apparent stranger at the worksite, with such generosity, all the while ignoring me as his child.

But how? I think about Hallie and about how it would kill me slowly to live without her. The fibers of my body would pucker and split if I never knew her, if she lived a whole life a few minutes away.

Magnolia, finally, I see.

I scroll down the Hartman website and tap their phone number to dial. I raise the phone to my ear, but all I hear is ringing and ringing and ringing.

This was never how I expected to feel when I finally got the name of my father, and if I'd been asked a decade ago, I would've called finding him in the same town a best-case scenario. How convenient that I could run right over and introduce myself. But now, this present-day me is the one to face him. I have no peace, only new questions.

Damn it. I hate it, but maybe Magnolia was right about this.

I raise my head and pull in a breath big enough to propel the violent scream I release into the pillow below me. I sit in the reverberations of it and feel the sting on the inside of my throat. Slowly I stand, straighten myself, and march out of the guest room.

CHAPTER 49

I FIND HER IN THE KITCHEN, waiting right where I left her. Magnolia's eyes are red-rimmed, and she looks up hopefully.

"I finally get it," I say. "It doesn't excuse what you did, but I see why you're the way you are."

Magnolia nods slightly. "I never wanted it this way, I promise. It wasn't supposed to go this way—*any* of these ways. I . . . I wanted Theo to stay too."

It rocks me, watching my mother sit in the same pain I did after Lincoln left. How many times I've said the same thing, with Lincoln's name instead. Somehow, in her attempts to save me from suffering, she landed me right in it.

I begin to gather my purse and pat around the counter for my sunglasses. "We'll have plenty of time to talk it through. Right now, I'm going to find him."

"At his home?" Magnolia asks.

"At his business," I say.

No one answered my call to the office, so I'll go in person. I'm not in the mood for emailing and desperately hovering over my inbox until someone—who likely won't be Theo—replies.

Magnolia rushes to me and pulls me into a deep squeeze. "Are you sure?"

I'm not sure at all. Honestly, this could just make it worse. "What other option is there?"

She looks at me with a tenderness I've never seen from her before. She understands that this has already lived underground too long. She knows there's no sense in keeping it buried.

"Do you want company?" she asks.

I shake my head. "I think I need to do this on my own."

"Very well," she says. "But *please*, be careful."

I nod once and turn to go. I'm not sure there's any amount of care possible to shield me from whatever is about to happen, but I appreciate her sincerity. *Theo Hartman, though—really?* Hours ago, I would've said he was a sweet old-man gardener, the owner of a landscaping company who was humble enough to come touch up my border flowers on a big day. But now, it's all muddled.

On my phone I search again for the address for Hartman Landscape and paste it into my maps app. Twelve minutes, it says. *Twelve minutes* away for all those years. Twelve minutes from every first, every spelling test, every T-ball game, every prom.

I crank the engine and roll back down the driveway. I go through the twists and turns of the quaint business district to a more industrial section of town. When I arrive at the address, I pull into a large parking lot with a fleet of trucks lined up. There is a one-story office with the logo I remember on the sign above.

I park and walk up to the entrance. Only then do I notice it's dark inside and there is a sign on the door: *Closed Until Further Notice.*

I pull a face and see it reflected back at me in the dark window. Companies like these don't just close on a Friday. It isn't a holiday. I see movement inside, and I raise a hand to peer through the glass. I see a woman cleaning with a cart of supplies. I knock on the window, and she sees me. I wave and point to the locked door.

Slowly, she comes over, flips the lock, and cracks the door.

"Yes, ma'am?" the cleaner says.

"Sorry to disturb you," I say. "I wasn't expecting the office to be closed. Online it says these are open hours."

The cleaner's face drops. "You didn't hear."

I shake my head slowly. "I don't think so."

She pulls in a breath. "I'm sorry to be the bearer of bad news, but the owner recently died in an accident."

The owner. My mind rushes to protect me as it wonders if someone other than Theo could qualify as an owner.

"Are you talking about Theo Hartman?"

She nods. "There was an accident at the home of one of our longtime customers. An incident with a flatbed truck."

My gut flip-flops. "You can't be talking about the Suffolk property?"

"You know them? Mr. Theo was on the mower that day," she says. "He and Mr. Suffolk have a close relationship, so he agreed to fill in when one of the crew called in sick. He was always like that, happy to get back on the truck when help was needed. The flatbed was backing up after being given the all clear, and Mr. Theo saw one of his guys step in the way with a loud leaf blower going. The guy couldn't hear over the noise, so Mr. Theo ran over to warn the guy, to get him out of there . . . and he ended up putting *himself* in harm's way instead."

My vision blurs as tears pool in my eyes, but I have to make sure there's no room for misunderstanding. "Theo's really . . . ?"

The cleaner shuffles her feet, her head dropping for a moment, like she's reluctant to restate the ugly truth.

"Yes." She meets my eyes briefly, then looks away. "He's no longer with us. I'm so sorry. It was a horrible accident. There was nothing anyone could have done."

The lovely cleaner says some other things in a gentle voice, but I hear nothing as I turn and walk away to the curb where I can catch my breath.

"I've got you, Mack." It's my mother's voice, and her arm loops around me and supports me. "I followed at a distance, in case you needed me."

I barely hear her as my ears start ringing, but the cleaner perks up, looking between us. "*You're* Mack?"

I keep moving to the curb, and Magnolia helps me there. It doesn't matter who I am right now.

"I've got something in here that I think is for her," the cleaner says gently.

Magnolia waves her away, distracted. "*Please*, can't you see? Another time."

The door closes behind us with a *click*, and the cleaner is gone.

I drop onto the curb. Traffic rumbles by on the road, life impossibly unchanged for everyone else.

"What happened, doll?" Magnolia asks.

I look up at her, and she looks as different as she sounds. And thank God for it. "He's gone, Mama. Theo's dead."

Magnolia goes white. "No," she says. "When? How?" She springs back and begins to pace.

I recount the story to Magnolia, of the accident at the Suffolks'. I watch my mother to see how she'll react. Because yes, this is a lost opportunity for me to meet my father. Miserable timing and a tragic event. But if Theo was Magnolia's Lincoln, it will hit her differently.

"Hang on now." Magnolia freezes and turns to me. "The Suffolks have been using Hartman?" She goes to the door and raps on it.

The cleaner opens it, wide-eyed. "Did you want the—?"

"Tell me," Magnolia demands. "How long have the Suffolks been using Hartman?"

"For a while now, ma'am," the cleaner replies. "It started when we were crowned 'top landscapers' by the local newspaper, and Mr. Suffolk called wanting to employ the 'premiere' service. We were swamped with new calls at the time, but he offered to pay a premium—like all those rich people do to make sure they get the best and nothing less."

Only then does Magnolia seem to crack. She wraps her arms around herself. "I never wished any ill will on Theo, despite what happened between us, but this? This with the Suffolks is a whole other thing."

The cleaner retreats tentatively into the office, bracing the door until it closes without a sound.

Magnolia resumes pacing in front of the small storefront, muttering to herself. She stops and peers inside, then pulls away, still distressed. She looks wild and unleashed, and surely, I can see now, she never stopped loving Theo.

I've been—*I am*—that person too.

I come to her side. "Mama?"

She stops at my voice, and when she looks at me, there's a fresh glassiness over her eyes. Rage.

"Mama." I say it firmer.

"It's Delta," she says in a whisper I barely hear.

Magnolia raises her head and opens her mouth and lets out a devastating cry into the sky. *Wounded* is what it sounds like.

"Here." I go to her side and gently take her arm. "Let's figure this out."

"Oh, I'll be figuring this out." Magnolia whips away from me and marches to her car.

"Mother, stop!" I call behind her. "You can't drive. You'll wreck in this state."

She tosses me the keys. "Fine, you drive."

We hop into the vehicle with the efficiency of departing bank robbers.

"On one condition," I say as we buckle our seat belts.

She glances over.

"Tell me what the hell is going on."

CHAPTER 50

THE SUFFOLKS LIVE FARTHER OUT of town, out where the lots are large enough for estates, and the drive gives us time we need.

"Delta knows Theo Hartman," Magnolia says.

"But she would've told you if she knew Ned hired him," I say. "Y'all have been best friends since forever. Maybe she didn't recognize him? Maybe they didn't cross paths?"

"Have you seen the trucks? There's no missing the branding. There's no missing the name." Magnolia stares straight out the window.

"After what Theo did to you—to *us*—she wouldn't have wanted him on the property," I say. "There's no way she knew, Mama. It just doesn't add up."

"Mm-hmm."

"She wouldn't intentionally keep it from you."

"It's because she's got something to hide," Magnolia says. "Otherwise, she would have called me up the very moment she saw that man in her yard or a truck with his name on it on her street. She never liked Theo, always tried to talk me into ditching him."

"You can't possibly think she had something to do with the accident?" I sputter.

"Of course not. Delta might be a snake in the grass, a liar, and a cheat, but she's not a killer."

"Ok, I still don't get it."

"Theo left for Charleston Southern soon after he left me—*us*. My folks were adamant that I not go looking for him or speak a single word to him if I wanted them to keep helping me. I couldn't have survived without their financial help, and I was mad enough at Theo to agree. Plus, my responsibility was to you. So by the time he came back, and presumably took over his daddy's business, I was even less interested in seeing him. We'd already made a life, you and me. We'd figured it out. The last thing I wanted was him and his frigid little heart coming back around and messing things up again. Delta agreed she'd keep watch, to make sure it never came out who he was to us."

I scoff. "Some watchdog."

A few moments of silence sit between us, and I'm surprised by my sadness at Theo's death. I've lost the opportunity to get his side of the story. Lost the opportunity to ask him to start fresh. Lost the opportunity, at the very least, to know why he didn't want me. But mostly, my insides are screaming that the whole thing doesn't add up. Theo was warm with me; he gave more than necessary, and even in his death, he was being a good guy, filling in on the grunt work.

Maybe he was different all those years ago. Maybe all of this loveliness was a second act, his penance for what he did back then. Maybe he couldn't figure a way back to the Magnolias, couldn't reconcile trying after he messed up so bad.

But still, he was made up, at least partially, of good.

"You know, Mama, I met Theo. He did the grounds on the Daniel House. He came for the fellowship tour and helped us get through the last days leading up to it. And it was Ned who recommended him to Grady."

Magnolia lets out a slow sigh, her eyes trained on the horizon beyond the window. "Ned wouldn't have known who he was to you. And I guess even if Theo was a no-good father, at least he did you right on the landscape."

I look over at my mother in the passenger seat, and she looks resigned. She also looks tender, hurt in a way I've never seen before. It's then I'm sure what I saw in Theo were the same things she saw in him. She and I are more alike than I've ever known, and just as I believe my impressions, I believe hers too.

What if, just like me, she was overwhelmed by the chorus of people around her when all along, she was the one who was right?

"What if you were right about Theo? What if he really was that man you fell in love with?"

After a pause, she looks at me. Tears run down her face in silent streams.

"I think I've made a right mess of this."

CHAPTER 51

DELTA SUFFOLK BEAMS AS SHE swings open her front door. "What a surprise! But I'm always glad to see you ladies." She dips to check her planter. "I knew I'd regret this black-eyed Susan with this heat. It's already crisp."

Magnolia shoves past her. "This isn't a friendly visit."

Delta and I follow her into the spacious entryway, and Magnolia makes a sharp left into the formal dining room that has a small sitting area adjacent. That's where she stops.

Delta scurries in behind me, looking both perplexed and concerned. "Unfriendly? What on earth, Mags? Is everything ok?"

Magnolia stands tall but frozen in this formal room. She is formidable, and for the first time, it's a comfort, a reassurance, knowing we're in this together. Her strength has for so long felt automatically adversarial, and this is the one good thing to have come from the muck that's fallen out around us. She is strong—just like me. And seeing her here, fearless like this, is assurance that I'll be all right as well.

"Theo Hartman has been working on your property for months."

Delta's eyes flutter to me before she shoots Magnolia a specific look.

"She knows," Magnolia says. "I told her."

Delta mashes her hands together as she studies the hardwoods.

"I'm sorry, Mags. I should've told you. I tried to get Ned to fire them, but he loved their work. He simply refused."

"And is that all?" Magnolia demands.

"It was a horrible accident, Mags. If I could've prevented it, I would've. You're mad at me because he was here working and this is where it happened. If we'd never hired him, he wouldn't have died—"

"Oh, don't flatter yourself, Delta," Magnolia says. "You're far too weak-spirited to be responsible for anyone's death. You don't have the guts for it. But lying and sneaking around? Manipulating and fixing behind the scenes? That's less of a problem for you."

"What did you want me to do—*tell Ned who he was?*" Delta flails her hands. "I'm sorry, but I was caught in a tough spot."

"A tough spot of whose creation?" Magnolia reaches out and takes the back of a chair. Her knuckles are white where she grips it. "Tell me the rest of what you've done—what you did *back then*. I'm not bullshitting around this any longer."

Delta stands silently. Her eyes are trained on Magnolia, and her mouth wobbles and her limbs shake. Still, it's as if she thinks looking away is some final admission of guilt.

Instead, Magnolia turns. She crosses the room to the china cabinet in three swift strides. She pulls on the door of the hutch, giving it an extra tug to pop it open. "Your mama's?" she asks Delta.

"Suffolk stuff," Delta says. "Of five generations."

Magnolia pulls out a small dessert plate and examines it closely, running her fingers over the intricate lattice detailing on the rim. "It's gorgeous." She holds it between a single finger and thumb and lets it hang. "Probably irreplaceable."

And she lets it slip, drop, and shatter on the floor.

Delta and I jump in unison at the sound.

"Oopsie," Magnolia says. When she turns, her eyes are so piercing that I can almost see them strain. "You were saying?"

Delta clears her throat as she sheepishly edges toward the broken china. "I don't have a clue what you're getting at, Magnolia. Is this about Theo's death?"

Magnolia answers from within the cabinet. "Not specifically, but thanks for letting me know about that, by the way. I probably won't plan to make it to the service, but I might send an arrangement." She spins to face Delta. "Funny, you didn't think to mention it to me."

Delta is tight and still, as if she's hoping to be overlooked. "It's just—"

"Frankly, in a town this size, the fact that you thought I wouldn't eventually find out that Theo Hartman died on your property is absurd. But perhaps it speaks to your intellect more than anything else." Magnolia swipes two teacups into each hand. "Aren't these just darling?"

Smash.

They hit the floor together.

Then a dinner plate.

Smash.

"Magnolia, I-I'm—" Delta shuffles her feet. "I didn't—I thought I was doing the right thing."

Mama makes a sound somewhere between a grunt and a growl, then grabs a stack of dishes.

"Quite the armory you've got here," she says.

Smash. Smash.

"*Please*, Magnolia. Stop. That china is generations old," Delta says. "It can't be replaced."

"Exactly like what you took from me!" Mama whirls around

and sets her gaze on the woman. "Unless you have a way for us to go back in time and change it."

Smash.

Delta lets out a peep.

Smash.

"How dare you!" Mama roars. "I know it was you."

Ned Suffolk bustles into the room and looks between the women. "Dee? Magnolia? What's going on?"

"Yes, Dee," Mama chimes in. "Care to explain how you're the one to blame?"

Smash.

I don't even blink this time.

Smash, smash, smash.

"All right, all right!" Delta holds her hands up as she presses the words out. "*Fine.*"

Mama's footsteps crunch over the dinnerware fragments as she crosses the room to where the rest of us stand. She slows, and her hands shake almost unnoticeably. Mama's not a young woman, even if she does harness a youthful rage. My heart squeezes. Now I know what she's lived and what she's lost. She drops into an armchair.

Delta walks over and perches on the love seat across from her. "I'll tell you everything I know. Where do you want me to start?"

"Right at the very beginning. And you'll tell me everything," Mama says firmly.

Delta nods curtly. "Ok."

Magnolia meets her eyes. "You're the only living person with the whole story."

CHAPTER 52

IMPOSSIBLY, THE SUFFOLK HOUSEKEEPER ARRIVES with a tray of afternoon tea and sandwiches and slides it onto the small coffee table between us. Ned and Delta nod awkwardly in appreciation and inside I cringe. Usually we'd all sit in the sunroom on a nice day like this, and surely the housekeeper thinks she's beating them to the punch with her delivery.

"Thank you, Marcy," Delta says. "Why don't you take off early today?"

With the housekeeper on her way, Magnolia turns an icy but tired gaze at her friend.

"So you figured it out, huh?" Delta says to Magnolia. Her eyes have doubled in size and are misty.

"I have a good idea, but I need to hear you tell me."

"It was me," Delta says. "I was the one who told your parents about Theo and the baby. I thought I was doing the right thing. You were so much better than him, Mags, so much better than a shotgun wedding and all those broken dreams."

"I knew it," Magnolia says. "He never went to my parents. It was my own mother and father who masterminded keeping us apart."

"I guess so." Delta stares into her lap.

"You were jealous of us, weren't you?" Magnolia asks.

Delta sighs. "Sure, maybe a bit, but that's not why I told them. You had so much potential. You could've married so much better." She fans her hands out to gesture at her surroundings. "I wanted something like this for you, and I just knew you'd want the same once you got back to your right mind. I knew—*thought*, I guess— you'd thank me eventually."

"I've always had my own money," Magnolia says.

"You really think your folks would've kept you in the will if you chose Theo? Come on, Mags, you know they wouldn't have accepted him. And can I be brutally honest?"

"I'm not sure there's a better day for it." Magnolia lifts her hands and lets them drop back on the arms of her chair.

Delta leans in and lowers her voice. "I honestly didn't think you'd keep the pregnancy."

She shoots me a pinched smile that looks like *sorry*, and I look away.

Delta keeps going. "I thought your folks would take you to the clinic before school went back so we could go to the University of South Carolina together and do everything else we planned."

Ned darts his eyes between the two women and me like he's playing catch-up. "Delta, honey, you really shouldn't . . . Mack's sitting right—"

"Ned," Magnolia cuts in. "Just so you're up to speed—Theo Hartman? He's Mack's father. It seems Delta told on us to my parents, who then turned around and chased him off and barred me from contact. They told me he'd changed his mind and taken off. Maybe he did change his mind—both could be true. Or maybe they convinced him to change his mind. All three of them are dead now."

Delta lets out a quiet sob. "I was too stupid to see what might happen. I thought they'd ground you and get you an appointment, and then life would go on. But then it went so differently. Your folks made things worse when I thought they'd help."

Ned offers a crisp handkerchief to his wife, then says, "Theo and I were something of pals there by the end, and he was never anything but an upstanding guy. What did your folks tell you about Theo, Magnolia?" His eyes pinch with sadness.

Magnolia's mouth begins to shake, but she pulls in a determined breath. "My parents said Theo had approached them and told them everything—about the relationship, the pregnancy, our plan to keep the baby together—and that he wanted out. They said he wanted nothing to do with me or the child—*Mack*—that it was all too much for a kid like him, without a way to support us." She turns to me, takes my hand, and squeezes. "That Theo wanted a career and to better his circumstances, and he couldn't be a father at the time. They said he didn't want to tell me himself in case I tried to change his mind."

Delta's voice is shaky. "And once I started it in motion, I couldn't see a way out. If I told you the truth, and you ran off to Theo, your parents would've disowned you. You would have been homeless and broke, and they wouldn't have cared to save you unless you cut Theo off. Somehow it seemed like the best way to keep you from getting hurt again. Not to mention, I couldn't be sure he wasn't after your money, considering your status," Delta says. "I didn't trust him with you, Mags."

"*You* didn't want to play the roommate shuffle everyone else does for college—or stick around here and go to junior college," Magnolia barks back. "So instead of letting your best friend do things her own way and have a father for her child, you took him away from me."

"You were my only friend, Magnolia. And when you and Theo started running around, I was all alone. I knew I shouldn't have done it, but I was too young and dumb to realize how ugly it would get." Delta covers her eyes with the handkerchief. "I don't deserve your forgiveness, but I am sorry. I never imagined it would get this bad."

"I had time to think on the way over," Magnolia says. "And honestly, we all made questionable decisions back then, early on—hell, even now—but there's one thing I can't get over. I cannot understand how every day that we lived here in parallel you had a chance to make it right. Of course, I'd have been mad, but if you had come clean, maybe we could've gotten past it. You had so many chances, Delta. You had all those years to fess up, and then for months he was here on your property, and I was a phone call away, and you never spoke up. Not until you were found out. Not until it was too late."

Finally I find my own voice. "And because of you, I won't know my father." Delta's gaze jumps to me like she's forgotten I'm even here. "And Hallie won't know her grandfather. Did that ever click? You and Theo share a grandchild."

"I thought about it a lot," Delta tells me. "It was the worst part, knowing you wouldn't meet your father, but I guess I always hoped our family could make it up to you. That once you and Grady married, you'd be a part of all this. Ned and I would be extra parents to cover the gap. You'd never want for anything. I guess that was why I was always so hung up on y'all being together—my own guilt."

Ned pats at the corners of his eyes. "He was such a good man. Goodness, this is a wreck."

"And I lost out on that," I say. "And more so, Magnolia did. Delta, I don't know how you live with yourself."

Delta nods intently. "I take responsibility, but Magnolia, Theo never came to find you either. *That's* why I never decided to tell you in the years that've passed. You wrote him off because of what your folks said, but even if he thought you hated him, he should've come to find his child. At the end of the day, whatever they offered him or threatened him with won out over his child."

A sadness shadows Magnolia's face, and it looks like she's thought the same before.

Even I've thought it.

Finally the shakiness that has gripped each of them in this conversation rolls over me. *His child* is what Delta said, what she called me. I pull in a breath.

"Theo didn't choose me, that's not news. It's something I've known my whole entire life, and it has always stung. Even more so now that I find out he was just down the street all along. But my mother did." My voice cracks. "She chose me, and she gave me her name too. I'm proud to be a Magnolia."

Ned cautiously extends a hand to touch mine, and he looks so meek that I let him. "I'm sorry, Mack. I can't imagine how hard it must be to hear all this. For what it's worth, my life wouldn't be the same without you. Even if things have changed between you and Grady, your Hallie is the best thing to come along since we had our boy. And regarding your father—I didn't know Theo was anyone but just him, but I do remember something that you might want to hear."

"Of course," I say. "I want to know all of it."

Ned shuffles to the edge of his seat. "Now that I'm hearing the story, I remember. I mentioned y'all having the chance to go for the Charleston fellowship and how excited we all were. I told him to look you up, Bishop Builds, mainly because I was proud as heck and wanted to brag a little. Well, Theo found your site, and he bustled in the next day insisting he take the crew out to prep your grounds for the big day.

"At the time I poked fun at him for being hungry for his fifteen minutes of fame, hoping to land a fancy house project. That man hated to drive more than ten miles to a job. Even that was a stretch. He loved keeping our business because we had a ton for him to do in a few square miles. It struck me as odd—both him wanting to go and such a low-key guy being interested in notoriety or prizes—but now I'm wondering if he saw your picture and something clicked. At the time I just chalked it up to the fact that he always spoke fondly of Charleston and the college years he spent there."

"You've always been the spitting image of your mother," Delta says but doesn't make eye contact.

"We'll never know what my folks told him to keep him away," Magnolia says. "Not now that he's gone."

Delta sobs. "I'm so sorry. I'm terrible. This is all my fault. No one was supposed to die."

None of us rush to comfort her.

She's right.

And now there's so much lost.

Magnolia sits back in the chair, her head tipped back, eyes closed. She is weathered and betrayed. Her best friend, her parents, her lover—all lost to her in one swoop. None of these things were her choosing, and she didn't ask for any of these people to interfere.

It makes me think of Lincoln, and in the face of the painful secrets that have been kept from my mother, our past looks like no more than an anthill to step over.

The secrets and the withholdings have slowly killed off branches of my mother's life all these years, and only now with the truth brought to light does it seem so obvious that this is what should've been done all along: Delta should have told the truth. Only now that Theo is dead does it seem so obvious how simple the solutions were. To come forward, to repair the breaks, to say sorry.

Lincoln and I are so mendable. If nothing else comes from to-day, from the searing pain of seeing my mother betrayed twofold and losing my father once and for all, it will be that I won't keep secrets. I won't recede and assume and let them guess.

Magnolia begins to shift in her chair and pulls herself to stand. "I think I've heard enough."

I stand, and together we walk out without pleasantries. When we're halfway down the front steps, Delta opens the door behind us. She says, "I'm so sorry, again. Give Hallie a squeeze for me."

Her mentioning Hallie feels like a reminder that we're still attached, that she won't ever be severed completely. Heavens, if she isn't strangely consumed with Magnolia.

But we don't turn back.

We get in the car and leave.

CHAPTER 53

THE RIDE BACK TO HARTMAN'S is mostly silent. Magnolia and I exchange a few mumbles about meeting back at her house before I exit her vehicle and head to my own. I think we've both run out of words and are in some degree of shock.

I'm grateful it's only a short drive back to her house, and she waits in the driveway for me.

"I'm takin' to bed," Magnolia announces as soon as we cross the threshold.

I know that means she'll disappear for the rest of the day and possibly even for tomorrow.

"Fair enough," I tell her.

This leaves me alone in my mother's house, restless but not yet ready to go home. Despite the bombshells and despite the immovable facts, I'm struck by the feeling that this is not done. That whatever whim of the universe planted me here on this day to see truth rained down isn't finished.

The day replays in my mind on a loop, and it's then I remember: The cleaner mentioned something. She recognized my name. She said there might be something for me.

Perhaps it's the final piece.

Before I leave, I call Grady. He picks up right away.

"You get Hal ok and everything?" I ask.

"Yup, all good here." Grady sounds upbeat, so I know his mother hasn't gotten to him yet.

"Great," I say. "Just so you know, I'm in Beaufort—in case anything comes up. I have a whole bunch to fill you in on, but the headline is that our families are on the outs. The *grown-ups* are, at least."

"Yikes, that sounds like a conversation I'll need a drink for," he says.

"A double. I'll keep you posted."

I hang up and hop in the car. I feel more grounded after hearing Grady's voice; it's a reminder that I have my own life outside this Beaufort circus I stumbled into today. It makes me think of Hallie and my house with the softest waffle blankets and of Lincoln next door. It reminds me of my little studio still tucked back on my favorite Charleston street. It reminds me of Fitz and Henry, their mighty friendship that's wrapped and covered me in every storm.

It reminds me that Exquisite Interiors likes us enough to let us shoot a full season.

From here, my life in Charleston looks so wide and deep and like every one of the dreams I made up as a little girl in this waterside town.

I roll down the windows and let the salty coastal air rush in. It feels like company in this moment. I weave around the streets I learned to drive on and through my favorite downtown strip. I can't help but let some of the memories of my childhood creep in, and to my surprise, there are good ones too. I remember Magnolia taking me to the Christmas tree lighting and letting me get both popcorn and ice cream, even though it froze my fingers off. I remember Magnolia quizzing me for my social studies tests—the ones I struggled with most. I remember her driving me to a horse-riding camp forty-five minutes away for two weeks in the summer.

Eventually I pull into Hartman Landscape, park, and climb out of the car.

Of all this heartache, I think the worst part is missing out on knowing Theo. With everything that's happened, I'm certain Magnolia's parents were wrong about him. That the things they said about him weren't true, that my mother knew best.

I scan the parking lot as I walk toward the building, and a small sedan is still parked here. When I turn back to the office, I see the cleaner inside through the window. She spots me, too, and hurries over to push open the door.

"You're back," she says.

"You're still here," I say.

"Home isn't a great place for me." She averts her eyes. "I'm working this job to pay for my college classes so I can get my own place. Mr. Theo always let me hang out in the break room after my shift to do homework." She gulps. "I kinda figured he wouldn't mind if I kept it up."

I manage a small smile. "From what I've seen and heard, it sounds like he'd be glad."

"Was there something you needed?" she asks kindly. Her eyes stop on me, a question lingering in them. "Do you want to come in? I'm Karina, by the way."

"Yes, Karina, thank you. I'm Mack—but maybe you already know that? I'm Theo's daughter."

She nods, and I follow her into the building, through the short hallway, to the entrance of an office. There we stop. The office is basic. There's a large wooden desk with a cracked leather desk chair. A small bookshelf sits alongside the singular window, and the spines upon it are predictable—landscaping, soil science, accounting, an Excel handbook. I search for framed photos, evidence of a wife, kids, or grandkids, but I find none.

"Was this Theo's office?" I ask.

Karina's eyes turn watery. "It was. I didn't know what to do—whether to clean it or leave it. Part of me didn't feel right cleaning it, like it'd be removing the last signs of him. But eventually I decided to go in and at least tidy up. Someone's going to have to deal with the bills and payroll at some point."

"I get it," I say.

"It's the last impressions he left on the world," Karina says.

I nod, but all I can think about is that the final impression he made on me would wipe out any discarded coffee cup or scratched-out paperwork in a tidal wave. "May I?"

Karina motions me in. "I found some letters on his desk, a few of them. I didn't really read them once I realized they seemed super personal—and important. But it wasn't until I heard your name that I realized I could actually get them in the hands of the person they were meant for."

My heart speeds up. *Letters for me? From him?* All I can manage is a frantic nod.

"I know today's been a lot already. If now is too much, I can hold on to them for as long as you need." Karina walks slowly to the desk and picks up a few neatly stacked sheets of paper. She looks back at me with a tight, optimistic smile. "They're yours."

I'm at her side in a flash, still nodding frantically. "Yes, I want them."

She hands the stack to me. "I'll be in the break room. Take as long as you want."

My hands shake slightly as I hold the words of my father, and I drop into his desk chair. The arms are marked with snaking cracks, but underneath me it feels soft, the cushioning still comfortable. It feels good, though slightly intrusive, to sit where he sat. A yearning kicks in deep inside to know him, to talk to him.

I look down, and my pulse stutters at the two words handwritten neatly at the top: *Dear Mack.*

CHAPTER 54

Dear Mack,

MY NAME IS SCRAWLED ATOP the paper. I start to read but stop and flip through the stack. Each page starts the same: *Dear Mack.*

Dear Mack,

Boy, do I have an awful lot to tell you! Your mama and I know each other. I was her boyfriend, but it all . . .

It ends.
I turn to the next.

Dear Mack,

I sure hope I'm not about to mess up the beautiful life you have for yourself, but there's some things I need to tell you. I used to be in love with your mother. Honestly, I loved her for a very long time, but I was kept from her. Her parents said she didn't love me, and it made me

The next.

Dear Mack,

I just needed to tell you what an impressive young woman you are. The way you've built a business you love and how you're just so fit to lead and create, I can't get over it. I just wish I'd known about it all for longer. I wish I could've been there for the whole thing. Also, funny thing

Finally, the last.

Dear Mack,

I've tried to figure out the best way to write this letter, and I've only convinced myself of one thing. There is no good way to write this letter, no good way to tell you this story. But I must tell you, and so I'll start right at the beginning.

I met your mother one summer when my daddy was working on her parents' yard. He started this company as a mowing business—just his beat-up truck and a crappy mower—when I was a kid, and we were struggling to make ends meet. Magnolia and I took a liking to each other and eventually we shared a romantic relationship. We were young and head over heels, and eventually Magnolia became pregnant. With you.

We were terrified as any two kids with a baby on the way would be, but we wanted to stay together. We decided to work things out to make a life together and raise you. But just as quick, her parents were at my door, banging it down to warn me to stay away from Magnolia. She had turned eighteen a few months prior, graduated high school a couple weeks ago, and

*they said if I didn't cut things off, they'd toss her out—seeing
as she was an adult in the eyes of the law. She was supposed to
attend the University of South Carolina in the fall.*

*They said Magnolia would be on her own, and I would be
responsible for ruining her good life and good reputation. I
didn't want to lose her—I loved her—but I also had nothing
material to give her, nothing but my love. In the face of their
money and power, I shrank like the kid I was. I was powerless.
I didn't come from a family with means. They convinced me I
couldn't take care of her, let alone a child. I never felt like I had
a choice. I begged them to let me see her for one final goodbye,
but they refused.*

*When I asked about the baby, they said Magnolia had
decided to "have an appointment." That it was already a done
deal. I wasn't sure if I could believe them. Most of me didn't,
but the other part of me wondered. Still, digging around would
only land Magnolia in trouble with them—the only people who
could give her what she needed, what she wanted, as they said.*

*I thought it was the right thing to do in the situation, but
I've since come to regret not chasing down my suspicions sooner.*

Here is where I failed you, Mack.

*I was mad when I went to Charleston Southern, so I
kept my head down and studied landscape architecture, only
returning to Beaufort years later, after I'd graduated and my
father needed me to take over the business. I avoided Magnolia
like the plague and anyplace I knew she might go. Seeing her
would only be salt in the wound. It would only be a reminder
of her parents ripping her from me—and worse, taking our
child.*

*But then Ned Suffolk told me about Bishop Builds and his
son and the city fellowship. I knew the name, your mother's*

*maiden name, and I was curious. Seeing your picture online
knocked the wind out of me, honey. You are the spitting image
of your mother, and I knew you were mine. Your age, the
timeline, there wasn't any way you weren't mine.*

I was overjoyed and gutted in one swoop.

*But now you've lived your whole life without me. You
probably thought I was dead or in prison or worse, just never
cared enough to come around. You already seem to have it all,
an amazing life. Do you even want a father to step out of the
shadows? I am terrified to hurt you, Mack. But I think the
right thing is to come forward, to tell you my story, and let you
decide.*

*So, here it is: I'm here and I want to know you. I already
love you. But just say the word, and I'll get lost. I want this
to be your call, but what I cannot live with is you thinking I
didn't love you.*

*I made mistakes, I admit that. I was young and scared
and didn't have a dime to my name. I faltered in the face
of Magnolia's parents' power. I should've fought harder. I
should've come back around sooner.*

*But if I'd had the choice—probably if I'd been better—it
would've been you and only you. All the rest be damned, I
would have crossed the surface of a thousand suns to be with my
baby girl.*

I'm just so very sorry it's come around this way.

With love and admiration,
Theo

I'm on my feet. I manage to call a quick thanks into the back,
and I run out into the humid evening.

Magnolia needs to know. Theo wanted me. He wanted to be with us all along. He wanted her too. He never changed his mind. Hurt on lies on wounds on hurt, and all buried in the red clay for decades.

What a waste.

I speed through the night and for the first time today, I smile.

It's a swirl of agony and joy, but I smile because he loved me all along. I wasn't left in disgust. Theo isn't coming back, and I won't have a father, but now I can rest in the knowledge that I've always had a father's love. The grounds at the Daniel House—that was his big act of hidden love.

Heavens, what a gift these words are and will always be. Theo Hartman was exactly who I met. He was the young man my mama fell for, and he was always a man who would've stood by his family.

Despite the lies that have twisted this family, I am loved.

And my mama too.

Both of us.

CHAPTER 55

I BURST INTO MAGNOLIA'S BEDROOM, AND the door collides with the wall with a bang.

She shoots upright with a yelp.

"Mama!"

She raises her eye mask off a single eye and squints at me. "What in good gravy . . ."

I drop onto the bed, inches in front of her, and gently pull the mask off her head. I take her face tenderly in my hands, and as if I'm declaring it by proxy, I say, "He loved you."

I feel her throat constrict in my hands as she swallows. "He left, honey. I'm as sorry for you as I am for me."

I shake my head and drop my hands to the letter in my lap. "I found this. He thought . . . He was told lies just like you. They intimidated him and threatened you. Here, read."

Magnolia takes the letter and holds it up and out, squinting, so I grab her glasses from the nightstand. She mutters a thank-you and I sit quietly to let her read. I watch her face go slack and tighten at the memories and new revelations. She gasps and covers her mouth at the very part I knew she would, the part about the pregnancy ending. Her eyes well and overflow.

I reach out a hand and set it on her knee. After a few moments, she sets down the letter and looks back up at me.

"It's a sort of peace, yes?" she says.

I nod, and I know she has the same odd feeling in the pit of her stomach. "He wasn't perfect, but he cared," I say. "Kind of like you and me."

Magnolia squeezes her lips, and she looks young with her hair loose across her nightgown.

"I'm so sorry, Mack. I'm sorry that this is the family I brought you into, and I'm sorry I haven't done a thing to undo all the nastiness from before. Hell, I didn't even realize most of it until today." She reaches over and pulls me into her. "It was my job to protect you, and I thought that was what I was doing. Stupid is what I was, just like them. I thought I was protecting you from the same heartbreak I had with your daddy, but instead I was just landing you in the middle of the exact same thing, throwing around my money to keep the two of you apart."

"It's funny," I say. "The same day you see that is the same day I understand why you'd think it was ever for the best."

"It's not fixed." Magnolia tells me this like it's permission.

And she's right. There's still a lifetime's worth of hurts and struggle between us; it's not something possible to remedy in twenty-four hours, even if that long ago feels like another lifetime. I'm still angry with her. Also, I feel for her; I see how she was wronged and hurt, and I see how inside her mind many of the things she did looked like love. I've never loved her more.

"We have plenty of time," I tell her. "We'll make a way."

Magnolia takes me by the upper arms firmly. "Starting now. No more meddling, no more lies. From here on out, we're honest—even if the truth isn't pretty. Now, go get your man."

I sputter a dry laugh. "Huh?" It's the last thing I expected to hear from her.

"I'm dead serious," she says, and she's up on her feet and shooing me off the bed. "Where are your keys? Your purse? I'm casting you out, child—and for a good reason this time."

I stand and suddenly a small thrill erupts inside me. "Really?"

"Is this not the most enthusiasm you've seen from me in your entire life?" She prods me out of the bedroom and toward the front door and hands me my keys. "You can do it, honey. You're a Magnolia."

I smile. "I like the sound of that." I turn to go, but something stops me. "I have to tell you something, but you might not like it."

"Lay it on me."

"I'm not sure that once I leave this place I'll be able to come back," I say.

This town has twisted and throttled and let me down one too many times. Unlike all the people I still want to find a way to love, I can cast this place aside and move on. It never felt like home for me, and now I have reasons to back up my gut sensation.

"I've never minded the drive to Charleston," Magnolia says.

"You can leave it behind too," I say. "If you want."

I know now that this place has hurt her in all the same ways it has me. And perhaps in even more ways than I'm aware of.

Magnolia pats my hands. "Don't you worry about me. Now, *go on.*"

I skip down the porch steps before she changes her mind and yank open the car door. I hop into my seat and tap the address into my maps app.

ETA: 8:16 p.m. at Lincoln's doorstep.

CHAPTER 56

I TURN ONTO MY STREET AN hour and a half later, and it's a wonderful feeling being back in my cozy neighborhood. I can't stop thinking about Theo, but the way he exists to me, he can come with me wherever I go. He's portable in the most delightful way, one that could only come as a by-product of my past suffering without him. I smile at the revelation.

I feel so ready to talk to Lincoln because I've never before known how powerful it can be to set the truth free. I am outrageously (embarrassingly so, by the standards of some) in love with him. I've known it for a while now, and frankly it's lived inside my bones for years, though I was unwilling to admit it. My feelings are far too big, and far too bulky, and inescapably *loud*, to keep them in. And even if I could, I don't want to play it cool because I am not cool. Not at all. I am all in and ready to get down in the mud for us.

When I approach the driveway, the first thing I notice is that the blinds in my front sitting room are still open, and I can see into the lit-up house. As I get closer, I see what looks like a downed tree in my front yard and a figure moving around it.

I park, climb out, and jog over.

On closer inspection it's not a full tree but a large limb lying across the lawn, and it's Lincoln, chain saw in hand, moving around it in the near dark. He quiets the whirring saw when he spots me.

"You know, I think this is what a modern-day knight looks like," I say.

He sets down the chain saw. "A summer storm ran through with some big gusts. Took down this limb. I figured you were having a hard enough time as it was, and I could just take care of this for you."

I look at him, and the feelings vibrate inside me. "I'm so lucky. And honestly, the day, it . . . It was . . . It was not as awful as I expected." I let out a puff. "It was bad at times, and still is in parts, but it was also really, really great in a lot of other ways."

Lincoln reaches out and places his hands gently on my shoulders.

"I just booked it home from Beaufort—*at Magnolia's request*—to make a big romantic gesture. Or something like it, my best shot at it. Definitely to make it clear how much I love you."

His face leaps. "Now *this* is going to be a story."

"Yes, that's what I'm saying. And so much more. So much more. Lincoln, *she told me about my dad.*"

His brows shoot even higher.

I nod. "Yeah, and I found out a lot about what happened between them. There was a whole mess with Delta Suffolk keeping stuff from Magnolia, and I'll fill you all the way in, but"—I step closer and take his hands—"I need to talk about us first. *You* are my priority."

Lincoln runs his hands from my shoulders down my arms and takes my hands in his. His touch steadies me and quiets the world around us.

I look into his eyes. "I'm sorry it took me so long to figure this out. That for so many years I let her waltz around my life, and that she ended up hurting you as a result."

"You're kidding, right?" He chuckles quietly. "The person who was most hurt by her was you, Mack. I got over her dinner insults *years* ago."

"This Marcus Wilson thing is new. Well, kind of."

"I don't blame you for it, Mack. That was your mother."

"I just want us to . . ." I roll my lips for a pause. To make sure I get this out right; it's important. "I want us to have a real shot at a future. Missing out on you is probably my biggest regret. I know there aren't any guarantees, and maybe we won't work out in the long run, but this time, I can't let my family chaos be the reason for it. I would walk over hot coals to make the goodbye from our history disappear. And no amount of money in the world can buy a talent like yours, Lincoln. Nothing close. Even with a Polaroid camera you make actual magic. You wouldn't have made it past week two in the studio if you weren't cut out for it. And if I have to spend every day of the rest of our lives together proving to you that you are worthy of everything you've built and more, then so be it. I love you, Lincoln Kelly. Then and now."

Lincoln releases my hands and wraps his arms around me, pulling me in. He lowers his mouth to my ear. "I can't bear the thought of your adorable little toes on hot coals," he says, then leans back to look me in the eyes. "I'm all in, Mack. All the way. I love you more than I could ever explain."

"I promise she won't be a problem. Truly. You'll need the rest of the story before it makes sense, but she's sorry for it. She realizes how bad she messed up, and she won't be an issue going forward."

"I like the sound of that." Lincoln runs his thumb tenderly along my jaw.

My insides sizzle, and I raise myself onto my tiptoes to put my mouth on his. Lincoln runs his hand through my hair as he presses in to deepen the kiss. We stay there as long as we can before we catch the attention of the neighbors, and eventually we come apart.

"I guess I have some things to tell you as well," he says, and I lean back to look at him. "I started on my own repairs while you were gone. Figuring out a way to make good on the freebie Magnolia gave me so it doesn't eat up my soul. I tracked down the three people I cut in line—so I could make amends."

"The photographers who applied to the studio?"

He nods. "One of them is a top surgeon in the city. When I emailed him, he replied right away. He actually thanked me, said missing out on that spot opened the path for him to go to medical school.

"Another is a fine arts professor at Columbia. She agreed to forgive me if I guest-lecture a class and critique photos for her students."

"And the third?"

"The third will be interviewing with Marcus next week—for a spot in the gallery."

I wrap my arms around him and hang myself on his neck. "You're the best man I know."

"There is one thing I was hoping you'd help me with," he says. "I'm opening a studio here, and I'll need a designer to help me find a place and put it together." He nuzzles into me. "If you know anyone, that is."

"You betcha."

"I had a good feeling." He lifts me into a basket of his arms.

"You know, I can't help but wonder if maybe we are a little bit meant-to-be, Lincoln Kelly. Considering we've failed miserably, the world just keeps helping us put ourselves back together."

"But I will fight for you and chase after you every time," he promises.

"We are all things magic that I never believed in until I met you," I say.

"You're saying it's unicorns and rainbows?" His delight covers his words. "After all these years?"

"I'm saying there might be a dash of it."

And I mean every word.

Despite myself, I'll admit that it feels like fate is on our side. Like she's kept nudging us toward each other and back to our senses.

Perhaps I owe a bit of gratitude to that unicorn Lincoln tied up under the rainbow when he stepped into my life and saved me that night in the bar. And to the leprechaun willing to part with the gold coins that bought those very first drinks.

A salty breeze rushes in from behind Lincoln, covering me in the smell of him, and I am grateful to have a love as deep and as real as the one Lincoln Kelly brought into my life. I know now that the fierce flames we sparked a decade and a half ago have always been real. That when I fell in love with the ease of switching on a light, I wasn't wrong. I wasn't only young and naive. Now, years and a lifetime later, I see it and feel it so deep in my bones that I forget how I ever could have questioned it at all.

EPILOGUE

One Month Later

THE HOUSE IS ALREADY BUZZING when I pull open the iron gate and pause to enjoy the view from the long pathway. The brick is bright after a gentle power wash once Mateo and his crew signed off on the job as complete, taking their dusty boots and wheelbarrows with them. The Daniel House towers above me, still, but it has been made new.

The peeling paint is only a faint memory, and the crisp creaminess of the siding now glows in the sun. The wrought iron is like a black gem, and *the grounds*. The grounds are bursting and blooming so wildly that more than one crew member has ventured to touch plants and flowers to prove they aren't artificial.

Yes, the Exquisite Interiors crew is here to film the final reveal of the Daniel House. I hear them flitting around in back, by the tent they've set up out of sight. Fitz and Maya are already inside.

I'll make it there, too, but I'm determined first to enjoy this moment before it descends into a busy whirlwind of excitement. I glance along the beds, and my heart squeezes. This landscaping is the last thing Theo did for me, giving me this flowery explosion at the height of bloom right as the people with cameras pull up. I won't have the rest of my life with him, but I've gained more than

I ever thought I would. I was loved all along, unknown to us both at first, and then in secret. Finally, that missing piece of me is at rest; the hole slowly disappearing.

I pull in a breath and smile to myself as I approach the porch. The railing is shiny and smooth to the touch, and the haint blue Maya chose for the ceiling is precisely what I wanted. The porch is fitted with beautiful rattan seating in pockets, side beverage tables and potted plants scattered between. The wood door has been buffed to a shine, the original hardware stripped of years of buildup.

I pop open the door, and the noise hits me.

"Finally, the lady of the hour graces us with her presence." Fitz double-kisses my cheeks and ferries me along the deep entryway to the stairs. The walls are rich in color and decor, and every feature adds depth.

I am overflowing with pride for this place.

Maya waits by the stairs. "Again, I'm here for *prompts*, no camera time."

Light streams in from the windows along the staircase, and it lights up with another layer of grandeur.

Erica waves down from the landing above. "We're getting a ton of amazing shots up here of the staging. Incredible. The art is just spot-on—historical enough, but not stodgy." She throws us a chef's kiss and turns back to her work.

Fitz nudges me with an elbow. "See? I told you the house could hold a modern piece or two."

I roll my eyes in jest. "Rebelling against traditions even to this day. What would the rest of the Fitzgeralds say?"

"Eh." Fitz shrugs. "Not so sure *that's* what they'd be talking about." He holds out his left hand and waggles the fingers. The light catches the gold band.

I gasp and grab his hand, pulling it close for inspection. "*You got married?*" I whisper. "*Without me?!*"

Fitz laughs, pulling his hand back. "Hardly. You think I'd forgo an occasion like a wedding? *Please.* We're engaged."

I practically jump on top of my friend, I'm so eager to hug him. "Amazing. Excellent. Incredible. I'mjustsohappyforyou!" I stand back and smile at him in admiration.

Fitz winks. "The check from the network helped us feel a bit more comfortable stepping out of the Fitzgerald safety net."

I grab his arm and squeeze it, then shake it, then squeal because I can't hold it in. "Drinks to celebrate tonight? When's the engagement party? Can I help? What—"

"Magnolia Junior," Fitz says. "You're making me wish I'd pocketed the ring." He points to the crew. "We're *working*, girl."

I nod and mime zipping my lips. "Business mode. But you can't say you're surprised. How else would I react?"

A familiar figure floats in from the kitchen and stops at the bottom of the stairs.

"Mama," I say. "You feeling ready?"

Magnolia is here as the representative of the Carolina Historic Society. I pitched the idea to the producer of touring her through the home as our client, and they went for it. I'm not even particularly nervous, considering how changed my mother is since she first stepped foot in this house all those weeks ago.

Nowadays Magnolia's shoulders sit a permanent two inches below where they used to, and it's a rare—and typically warranted—situation to see her pucker in disgust. I might even dare to say she's finding herself a second lease.

"As ready as I'll ever be," she says. "I'm not sure I realized what I was getting myself into. The makeup girl's got me feeling like I'm wearing a mask. Y'all think it looks ok?"

Maya comes to her side. "It's totally normal. Mack always says the same thing."

"Me three," Fitz says. "And I don't even get the lashes."

Unofficially, the team and I are helping Magnolia decorate the new house she purchased out on Sullivan's Island. It's small and so different from the family home she raised me in. It turns out, Magnolia wasn't too keen on sticking around in Beaufort after the fallout either. She's done with Delta Suffolk; after everything that happened, she just couldn't find a way forward for their friendship. Still, they'll be cordial during shared Hallie-related events.

"All right. Well, I guess I'm ready," Magnolia says.

Before long Erica and her crew are calling action on a scene with me showing Magnolia the exterior.

"As you can see, this area in the back is gorgeous and has a particularly flexible space," I say.

"Oh, it's wonderful," Magnolia replies. "I think I like the fountain best."

I smile as we walk slowly toward it. "Yes, it was the design of the late Theo Hartman, our landscaper extraordinaire."

I catch a quick shimmer in Magnolia's eyes, but only because I'm looking for it. To a stranger, there'd be nothing to see.

"Sounds like he was a great man," she says.

I pause for a moment, but Magnolia springs back into action.

"Please, tell me how we can accommodate groups here," she says.

She's still Magnolia—and most certainly not one to blubber on camera.

She's also come around to allowing the space to be rented by groups—much to the delight of the board. Properties like this, even once deeded to the historic society, require costly maintenance.

"Oh absolutely." I reach for a preplanned folder that holds several hand-sketched designs for seating arrangements, depending on the type of event. I describe each one and point out how the architectural features of the home complement it.

"Wow, y'all thought of everything," Magnolia says as we head around the side of the house.

"Yes, and to think, all that used to be here was a termite-infested deck."

She and I laugh, and Erica yells, "Cut!"

"All right, Ms. Magnolia," Erica says. "Let's have you do some still interview headshots with Tristan." A second cameraperson waves. "And Mack, I'm going to get you and Fitz out front next."

"Meet you there," I say and begin to slowly make my way to the front.

As I round the corner, I hear the familiar high-pitched chirping of my darling magpie and her best friend, Foster. They sit on the porch, Lincoln laughing along with them. He skips down the steps to me when he sees me.

"Sorry, are we too early?" he asks. "The kids were so excited they kept nagging me to leave."

I smile and shake my head gently. "You three are always welcome on the jobsite—within reason."

Lincoln laughs. "This is really amazing. Seriously, stunning."

"Thanks," I say. "That means a lot coming from Charleston's newest premiere photographer."

Lincoln shies away, laughing and shaking his head.

His new studio is already getting its footing—a space rented, one enthusiastic "coming soon" news article, and internship requests left and right. Lincoln has decided to start an apprenticeship program—much like Marcus's was for him—though no spots will be available for purchase. There isn't a day that passes that I don't look at this man and feel an unnerving amount of delight in knowing he's mine.

Hallie is on my toes. "I can't believe I get to do it this time!"

"I said one shot of you running through the house or the gardens, but no face time on camera," I tell my daughter. It's a sticky place between wanting to include her and protect her at the same time.

Hallie pats the bow she carefully clipped atop her ponytail earlier. "I'm mature for my age. I can handle it."

I drop a kiss on her head, careful not to mess up her hair.

Hallie turns back to us. "Do I *have* to go to Dad's tonight?"

"Yes, ma'am," I say. "Your dad loves you, Hal. Plus, he said he's taking you out for pizza and the arcade."

Things between Grady and me have settled. Finally. After the fallout with his mother, he was shocked in a way I haven't seen him before. The fact that Delta kept the truth buried for all those years was something he couldn't understand. Maybe it's out of guilt for his mother's betrayal, but he's been more reasonable. He wasn't even pushy to be included in today's shoot.

For a moment I considered inviting him to join us, but it was a moment that passed quickly.

Fitz pops out the front door. "Well, hello, baby designers," he says to the children. "Which one of you is shooting this scene for me? I'm beat."

Fitz comes down the steps and greets Lincoln with a handshake.

Magnolia flows out the front door a few steps behind him. "They're not quite ready to shoot my interview, but *look here*, everyone's arrived." She smiles at the kids and greets Lincoln politely.

Magnolia apologized to Lincoln as soon as she was upright again after that day at the Suffolks'. It was genuine, and Lincoln was gracious. When she sent me out to chase after him that night, it wasn't a fluke; her words have stuck.

And it makes living the life I want—*always wanted*—so much easier with her on our side.

Erica joins us from inside. "Great, you're here," she says. "You two ready to shoot the closeout? I like the lighting for it right here."

Fitz grins. "We've been practicing."

The kids scurry down from the patio, and Fitz and I climb up to it. Erica arranges us in the grand opening and calls for a crew member to prop the front door and clear the hallway so her shot can see right through to the wide spiral staircase.

"You remember how ugly this all started, kid?" Fitz says to me.

I nod, feeling the bubbles of pride in my belly. "We really did our best."

"And action!" Erica yells.

"I'm Mack Bishop," I announce.

"And you can call me Fitz."

We look at each other and smile with all of our hearts. "And this has been the Daniel House."

"Join us next time," I say, "for the latest episode of *Holy City Flip*."

ACKNOWLEDGMENTS

There are so many people who helped in the creation of this book, and I am abundantly grateful for each of you. It is a privilege to know you and to work alongside you. From early reads to revision upon revision (heavens, this story has seen *revisions*), to pitching and all of the unseen heavy lifting required to get this book from manuscript to published book, it was truly a team effort.

To my editor, Laura Wheeler, thank you for believing in this story enough to try three times. From that first Twitter pitch years ago, it seemed too good to be true how our tastes aligned. Your insights have elevated this story to a whole new level, and I can undoubtedly say that without your keen eye, it wouldn't have the same shine and sizzle. The final version of the story, the one we made together, is my favorite. Beyond your editorial prowess, your warmth and contagious enthusiasm make the daily work so enjoyable. I couldn't ask for a better partner. Also, please note my restraint in including zero exclamation marks in this passage. Despite their absence, it's *thick* in exclamation vibes.

Thank you to everyone at Harper Muse for working tirelessly to develop and promote this book: Amanda Bostic, our publisher leading the charge, as well as Becky Monds and Caitlin Halstead; Savannah Breedlove, production editor; and Natalie Underwood, managing editor. Margaret Kercher and Taylor Ward in publicity; Nekasha Pratt, Kerri Potts, and Colleen Lacey, the marketing team. Jere Warren and Patrick Aprea for digital marketing. To Halie Cotton for the gorgeous cover.

To Jodi Hughes for an immaculate line edit. Thank you for helping me tighten every sentence and for checking every detail. Fear not, I will keep better track of my timeline henceforth.

To my agent Margaret Danko, for fighting for this book with such zest. You have been a true advocate every step along the way. From answering my endless questions to bearing with my follow-ups during submissions, you are constantly calming and reliable. Thank you for your meticulousness, for asking all of the questions I wouldn't know to ask myself, and for always having a top-notch sense of humor. Your organization and efficiency are the stuff of Type A dreams—much to my delight.

To my agent Kim Perel, for seeing the promise in this story among your slush pile and for taking a chance on me (and my revision skills). I will never forget your email saying that you loved the manuscript or the call where I could barely hear you over the hammering of my heart in my ears. Thank you for opening doors for me and for every bit of support you've layered on to make this book the best it can be.

Margaret and Kim, you are the dream team. I'm so here for it.

To everyone at High Line Literary Collective, I'm so proud to call this agency my literary home. Thank you for all you do.

To Sarah Berke, my writing partner and my dear, dear friend. You are the first person I text with my publishing news, and you are also the first person I texted when we got lice. You are an impeccable human, and I'm so lucky to call you my friend. You have walked every step of this writing journey beside me (practically in real time), and I wouldn't be the writer I am today without you. The part of me that writes is not a part of me that everyone in my life knows, and you, my friend, are the one who knows that part best. Thank you for the emotional support and the pep talks. Also, the endless practical support: the reads, the comments, texting about hypothetical nonsense I'm prepared to throw at my characters. You're the real deal.

To Kyle, my husband and the one to whom this book is dedicated. Thank you for never telling me I was crazy to keep going. Thank you for letting me start conversations about my writing with "I'm not looking for feedback on this, but . . ." Thank you for telling me I was wrong when I said maybe I should get a Real Job. Perhaps most importantly, thank you for being an equal partner and parent. For the meal planning, the grocery trips, the school runs, and the laundry. For tagging in and out of these unglamorous yet critically important tasks that keep our family moving. And finally, thank you for always commenting fire emojis on my Instagram posts. I will never feel alone with you by my side.

To my children, for blowing kisses through the glass office doors while I work. I'm sorry the book doesn't have any pictures.

To my parents, Rose and Shane O'Toole, thank you for nurturing my intensity since the very beginning. For sitting beside me in the storms of my life until they passed. For showing me, in action, that it's never too late to try something new, that we can be many things at once. Let it be known that my mother was in no way, shape, or form inspiration for the matriarch in this story—well, unless you count her nice parts. I am so lucky to have you both.

To my siblings, Alice and Leo, for your enthusiasm and support. I would've turned out awfully as an only child.

To Brett Mason, my oldest friend and the very, very first reader of this story. Thank you for being that person I trusted enough to take the leap of faith and *actually show it to people*. Your support and encouragement—especially before I was truly confident—have been invaluable.

To my mom-squad friends, Megan Drummond and Sarah Schneider, who balance me out and assure me that motherhood really is, in fact, this hard. I love your children like my own, and our friendship circle that's grown from three babies to nine children over the years has been a complete gift.

To the teachers and staff who work with my children at school: You are angels on earth. Because of you we have a place to send our children, a place they love to go, where they are nurtured as capable, competent people. A place where they learn to read—the ultimate gift. Without you, I simply wouldn't have had the hours required to write this book and to endlessly revise. You have a permanent place in my heart.

And to everyone who has touched this book behind the scenes, I am so grateful.

It belongs to all of us.

DISCUSSION QUESTIONS

1. Mack and Fitz are both close friends and colleagues. Have you ever worked with a friend? Was it for better or worse?

2. If this story were made into a movie, who would you cast in each role?

3. This book is written from Mack's perspective. Which character do you think would have the most interesting retelling from their own perspective?

4. Mack lives in the suburbs across the bridge from downtown Charleston, but the historic homes in town are where we see her work focused. Would you rather live in the suburbs or the city? Do you prefer a more modern home or something vintage or historic?

5. After Mack leaves Beaufort for Charleston, she feels stifled and uncomfortable when she returns home. What kind of relationship do you have with the place where you grew up?

6. Mack had very strong feelings about Lincoln leaving for the opportunity at Marcus Wilson's studio in New York. Do you think she overreacted? How do you imagine yourself reacting in the same situation?

7. Mack is very intentional about raising Hallie differently from

the way she was raised by Magnolia. Are there specific decisions you make for your life (and/or your children's lives) that are opposite to the way you were raised? If so, why?

8. Mack has always been determined to design a life of her own making—free of her mother's interference. Still, so much of Mack's upbringing and her mother's pull seems impossible to escape. How much impact do you believe our upbringing has on us as adults? How much control do you believe we have to build a life beyond the one we grew up in?

9. What messages about family did you take away from the story? How do you think Mack's concept of family changes from the beginning to the end of the book?

10. At the end of the story, Magnolia and Delta aren't close, but Magnolia never says she wouldn't rekindle their friendship. Let's take a poll: Who thinks Magnolia should forgive Delta given their shared history and friendship? Who thinks Magnolia is better off without someone who would betray her the way Delta did?

11. Mack grew up without a father involved in her life, and by the end of the book she learns the full story of everything that transpired between him and her mother. How do you think Mack's own experiences without a father in her life will impact the way she deals with Grady in their co-parenting of Hallie? How might her own experiences impact the co-parenting in both positive and negative ways?

ABOUT THE AUTHOR

Photo by Lisa Liberati Photography

GRACE HELENA WALZ received a master's degree in social work from the University of Houston and has worked with children in foster care, as a medical social worker, and in a mental health capacity. She currently resides outside of Atlanta, Georgia, with her husband and two young children. She writes women's fiction in the moments between sticking Band-Aids on scraped knees and coordinating pint-size social engagements.

Connect with her online at gracehelenawalz.com
Facebook: @gracewalzauthor
Instagram: @gracehelenabooks
X: @gracehelenawalz
Pinterest: @gracewalzauthor